MIDNIGHT SEDUCTRESS

"Get out of here," he said curtly, fury making his voice a husky rasp.

Rhianna didn't move, didn't attempt to hold the blouse over her breasts, but stood staring at him with wide, unreadable eyes.

Then she cleared her throat and said softly, "I intend to keep my bargain, sir. Here. Now."

He watched in disbelief as she shrugged out of the blouse and let it fall to the floor in a glide like the silent fall of snow. It puddled at her feet. Mesmerized, he watched as she removed boots, stockings, and breeches.

It wasn't until she stood in front of him wearing only the silk mask and hood over her head and face that he could speak. His voice came out in a hoarse croak.

"Take off the mask."

The
Moon Rider

Virginia Lynn

BANTAM BOOKS
New York • Toronto • London • Sydney • Auckland

THE MOON RIDER

A Bantam Fanfare Book / June 1994

ISBN 0-553-29693-0

Published simultaneously in the United States and Canada

PRINTED IN THE UNITED STATES OF AMERICA

RAD   0 9 8 7 6 5 4 3 2 1

To Lisa Higdon, Linda Kichline, and Lisa Turner, who have been behind me in a very difficult time of my life. Without all of you, I would never have come so far. . . .
And to Jane Harrison, who took time from her busy writing schedule to support, encourage, and listen.
Thanks!

The

Moon Rider

Book One

England, 1790

Chapter 1

Rain swept in heavy sheets across the moors, pelting the few remaining mourners in the Lancaster family cemetery. Most mourners had already fled to the sheltered warmth and comfort of their carriages, but one lone figure remained inside the marble crypt.

Slight shoulders vibrated with intensity, and a blunt, shaking finger traced family names carved into the stone. The finger paused over the blank spaces that would soon bear two more names; a strangled sound escaped into the dank gloom of the crypt.

"Damn them!" came the boy's hoarse whisper, sounding as if torn from his very soul.

Fenster Goodbody winced at the anguished sound.

"Here, here, my son." The vicar stepped inside, brushing fat, glistening raindrops from his greatcoat. He cleared his throat, focusing on the taut form standing so straight and stiff in front of the new entombment. "Lord Chance . . . I mean, my lord . . . I know how you must feel upon losing both your parents so suddenly, and—"

Shivering, not with chill but with suppressed fury and grief, the youth whirled around, sending the clergyman back a startled step. Hot, angry eyes, so brown they were almost as black as his shock of unruly hair, fixed on the vicar with a smoldering gaze.

"No, you don't know how I feel. Neither you nor anyone else has the least idea how I feel, so don't presume to offer unwanted condolences. . . ." Chance paused, breathing harshly through his clenched teeth as he glared at the vicar.

"Well . . . I . . . I . . . never meant," Goodbody began in a nervous stutter. The youth looked like a feral panther poised to spring, his muscles taut.

Chance flung back his head and took a step forward. "Go back to your little church and write a sermon for next Sunday," he grated, his voice wavering between adolescent baritone and alto. "And make certain you abolish the theory that God has any mercy, Reverend Goodbody."

Any rebuttal that Fenster Goodbody might have tendered remained unspoken as Chance brushed past him and stormed from the crypt into the driving rain. The vicar stepped to the door and watched as Edward John Chance Lancaster, only recently the Viscount Wolcott and now the new earl of Wolverton, stalked across the cemetery like an avenging fury. He threaded his way through the bleached, time-weathered markers jutting up from the drenched earth, shoulders hunched against the weather and any attempt at consolation from well-meaning friends or neighbors. Goodbody's helpless sigh slid into the damp air. Chance—such an odd Christian name for a boy of good birth, yet so fitting in this case.

"Chance," his mother had said at the boy's christening, "is a prophetic name, and much better suited to such a beautiful child than John or Edward." Her doting husband had agreed, willing to give his lovely young wife anything she asked of him. His devotion had lasted until their deaths just three days before.

"It's a shame," Reverend Goodbody's wife had stated

earlier in the day, "that such a young lad should be or-phaned, but at least he inherits a title and estates."

And what good, the vicar wondered wearily, would that title and the estates do a sixteen-year-old boy? He needed his mother and father, not the title of earl nor the vast lands connected with Whiteash Manor. Ah, it was a pity that the earl and his beautiful wife had not survived the fever that had swept through the manor house, claim-ing the lives of some servants and lifelong family retain-ers as well.

"Fenster?"

The vicar started, his head jerking up to see his wife darting in from the rain. He hadn't seen her approach the crypt, but was suddenly glad she was there. He managed a smile.

"Yes, Lavinia? I was just . . . just . . ." His voice trailed into silence as Mrs. Goodbody shook rain from her cape and threw back the hood. Drops glistened in her hair. She stepped forward with an anxious frown.

"What happened, Fenster? You're upset."

"No, no, I'm quite all right, dear, really I am."

Lavinia gave a disbelieving snort. "You're not. It was Lord Chance who upset you, wasn't it? The wretched, cursed boy. He has behaved like a wild animal since the day he was out of leading strings, and now I'm afraid he will be worse than ever. . . ."

"Lavinia. Have you no sympathy for the youth? Mercy's sake, his father died in his arms three days ago. He has undergone a great shock, losing both his parents to a fever and his older brother in that dreadful massacre in Paris, and all within six weeks' time. I cannot imagine why the earl allowed Anthony to go to Paris when the entire country is in an uproar over there, what with the revolution going on, but I suppose the boy was as deter-mined as the rest of the Lancasters seem to be. It's just that he was the heir—so foolish of them. Well, now it falls upon Lord Chance's unwilling shoulders."

"That's no reason for that wretched boy to behave as if he hates every living soul, Fenster, you must admit." Lavinia pursed her lips into a righteous pout. "God gives us all trials, and we must endure."

"But God is not to blame for his troubles," he said gently. "Any blame should be put upon the French rabble for murdering innocent English citizens or perhaps even on that slovenly serving wench from Hampstead who gave Wolverton's head groom the fever that he brought back to Whiteash Manor. I'm not certain God deserves all the blame we sometimes lay on His doorstep."

"There are times, Fenster, when you stray too far into the vicinity of blasphemy. Consider your position."

"My position is to offer succor to suffering souls, Lavinia, not heap blame upon our Lord."

"Excuse me," an unfamiliar voice interrupted, and Reverend Goodbody turned. A dark shape shadowed the doorway of the crypt, blocking the gray light and leaving the interior almost black.

"Excuse me, but are you the vicar?" the cloaked shape inquired. "I am Oliver Trentham, the barrister down from London. I was told that I should meet with you to make arrangements until the new earl's guardian arrives."

Goodbody felt a wave of relief. He hadn't known quite what to do about leaving a young man alone in that great, rambling manor house without proper guidance.

"Yes, I'm Reverend Goodbody. Due to the fact that no family members are in residence, I suppose I'm the logical choice." He hesitated, uncertain what he was supposed to say. A gust of wet wind spit rain down his open collar, and an idea occurred to him. "Shall we discuss this over tea, sir?"

"Indeed. Hot tea would be just the thing in this dreadful weather."

Goodbody felt ill at ease in the huge Whiteash Manor parlor with its lavish furnishings and thick Persian and Aubusson rugs. Lavinia had been put out that she was not invited up to the house for tea, and he knew she would pepper him with questions about the furnishings. It was amazing to him how females seemed to set store by the very things they often reviled the loudest, and Lavinia was no exception. Yes, she would demand a detailed description of the house and then talk about how wicked it was to have so much worldly affluence when there was so little for others. Reverend Goodbody sighed, and studied the room more closely.

Wind rattled the mullioned windows that stretched across one paneled wall. Dark, heavy draperies were drawn back to allow in gray light, and he could see trees waving skeletal branches in the driving rain. It was a gloomy day befitting such grim proceedings.

Hobson, the retainer who had been with the family for years, silently poured tea from a heavy silver pot. Goodbody felt the burden of his grief like a thick pall over the room, and he shifted uncomfortably. That drew Hobson's notice, and he turned.

"More tea, Reverend?"

"Yes." Goodbody cleared his throat, feeling out of place and unwanted. "Yes, please." He held out his empty cup and wished he'd thought to ask for the milk to be poured in first. He liked it much better that way, but he had no intention of making a fuss over something so trivial.

"Not pensioned off yet, Hobson, old man?" Trentham asked, and Goodbody gave the barrister a shocked glance at his rudeness. Hobson, however, seemed to take it in stride. His voice was as smooth and calm as ever.

"Not at all."

"You're long past your prime." Trentham held out his empty cup, but Hobson didn't glance in his direction.

"I shall bring fresh tea cakes in a moment, Reverend," Hobson said politely and strode from the parlor.

Trentham muttered something under his breath and poured his own tea, then sat back and began to relate a stipulation in the late earl's will. Reverend Goodbody listened with growing alarm.

He took a hasty sip of his tea and gazed over the brim of the Limoges china cup at the London barrister. The china clattered softly as he set his cup back in the fragile saucer and cleared his throat.

"You're telling me, Mr. Trentham, that according to the late earl's will, Lord Chance is completely dependent on his next of kin—in this case his uncle—until he reaches his majority?"

"That's correct. Of course, there should be no problem with that. Funds are plentiful, and I am to keep a good eye on the expenses incurred by Lord Perry."

Goodbody felt another stirring of disquiet. All the locals knew of the quarrel between Lord Perry and his brother Charles over the former's gambling habits. Why on earth had Lord Wolverton left his son and heir in the care of a man addicted to throwing away money? It didn't make sense, and it certainly didn't sound like the Lord Wolverton whom he had met and admired.

Oliver Trentham smiled, a faint wisp of a smile that did not go unnoticed. "I take it, good Vicar, that you disagree with the late earl's decision."

Embarrassed, Goodbody cleared his throat. "Ah, I would not dare to presume—"

"But of course you would. Most provincials do not

understand the intricacies and complications of the legal system and, therefore, are not qualified to make such decisions. Lord Wolverton, unfortunately, did not have time to make a new will after the death of his eldest son and heir in Paris. So the decision fell upon the courts to place someone who is a family member in charge of his estates until Lord Chance is of age. Naturally, I recommended Wolverton's closest relation, his half-brother Perry. It seemed the wisest course of action, considering the circumstances. If Lord Perry is in charge—"

"Lord Perry can steal much more efficiently and quickly than a stranger," an angry youthful voice interrupted.

Both men turned to view the wrathful figure standing in the doorway and vibrating with emotion.

"Obviously you didn't hear me come in," Chance observed in the same caustic tone Goodbody had heard Lord Wolverton use on more than one occasion. "Enjoying my tea, Trentham?"

Goodbody saw Trentham eye the boy through narrowed eyes when he stalked toward them. Chance was tall for his age, as his father had been as a youth, and had the same quick sparsity of movement. None of his actions was wasted and seemed fueled by a burning intensity. The new earl of Wolverton would be a formidable adversary if he were of age, which he was not. Trentham favored him with a toothy smile.

"I am enjoying your tea immensely, Wolverton, and . . ."

"Don't call me that."

Trentham lifted an iron-gray brow. "But since your father's funeral, you are the earl. You are earl of Wolverton now, or Lord Wolverton, whichever you prefer."

Goodbody was watching Chance's face, and his heart

gave a wrench at the deep furrows of pain in a previously unlined countenance. He decided to intervene.

"My son," he said gently, "as painful as it may be, you must accept what has happened."

"I have accepted it." Chance shot him a quick glance. "But that does not mean that I have to accept Lord Perry or this so-called barrister who preys on the weak and unfortunate like a ravenous barracuda."

Trentham jerked, and the fragile china cup quivered dangerously in his white-fingered grip. "You may have cause to retract that statement one day, my lord."

"I doubt it. You've proven to be nothing else since I have known you."

Goodbody quailed at the relentless hatred in the boy, a hatred so intense and adult that it was frightening. How could a mere youth be filled with such anger and animosity? And convey it with such ease? He watched, fascinated, as Chance gazed down on Trentham with ferocity.

Seeming unperturbed by that fierce glare, Trentham calmly set down his teacup and made a steeple of his hands, blunt-tipped fingers end to end under his clean-shaven chin.

"I suggest," Trentham said mildly, "that you curb your impetuous tongue, young Lancaster. It would not do to make too many enemies at so young an age."

"One should never be too young to recognize a viper —or vipers—in their midst, Trentham." Black eyes gazed steadily at the barrister. "I may be lacking in years, but not intelligence."

"I never thought otherwise."

"Then we understand one another."

Slowly, "Yes, Lord Chance, perhaps we do."

Pale eyes met dark ones, and a look that the good vicar did not understand at all passed between the two. It was as if two tigers had taken each other's measure and established the battle lines. Goodbody shifted uncomfortably in his deep, cushioned chair and cleared his throat again, the tension so thick it was like a fog in the elegant room with its thick rugs and cheerily crackling fire in the grate.

Goodbody crossed his legs and uncrossed them, then rattled his teacup and saucer again and tried for a neutral topic of conversation.

"When are you due back at Eton, my lord?"

An innocent question, so trivial as to be almost ridiculous, but it eased the tension, as he'd hoped. Chance gave him a fraction of polite attention.

"I have a month's excused absence, Reverend." Chance's gaze shifted to rest on the clergyman for an instant before darting back to the barrister.

"You are not expected to stay any longer, Trentham. Hobson will see you out."

The haughty dismissal brought a cynical smile to the barrister's lips.

"As you wish, my lord. I will return with your uncle and the necessary papers within a fortnight." Trentham rose, bowed politely at Goodbody, and crossed the room with as much dignity as possible.

"Bastard," Chance said loudly, and smiled when Trentham's stride faltered. The barrister paused, straightened his shoulders, then continued out the door. The parlor door slammed shut with a loud click. Chance turned back to the vicar.

"I say," Goodbody couldn't help commenting, "is it wise to make an enemy of Trentham? He could do you much harm."

Chance's gaze narrowed, surveying him and making him feel very much like a hapless insect impaled on a hatpin and placed in a collection. His dark, stormy eyes raked the vicar as if trying to decide whether friend or foe, before thawing slightly.

"He will do me a lot of harm anyway, Vicar," the boy finally replied, and once more Goodbody was struck by his mature words and tone.

"But why should he? He was your father's trusted barrister. Shouldn't he be your friend?"

After a moment's hesitation, Chance stalked across the thick carpet to the marble-fronted grate and stared into the flames as if searching for an answer among the leaping orange and crimson tongues. His hands were shoved deep into the pockets of his frock coat. His shoulders slumped briefly, then straightened again.

"No, he's not my friend."

The words had a peculiar vulnerability to them, a trace of childlike helplessness that immediately struck at the vicar's heart. Yet the tense set of the boy's shoulders and the rigid thrust of his jaw made Goodbody think better of offering any solace.

"Well—if there's anything I can do for you, my lord, please send a servant with a note and I will come at once."

Chance turned to nod coolly, his liquid eyes almost level with Goodbody's.

"I won't forget your concern," the young earl said, his voice once more a peculiar mixture of alto and baritone. "A Lancaster always repays his debts."

With that ominous warning hanging in the air, Fenster Goodbody left the sprawling graystone hall of Whiteash Manor. It wasn't until later, when he thought back to the exact tone Chance had used, that he was able to justify the following events.

Chapter 2

A cold wind blew harshly across the winter-bare moors, sweeping dry leaves and the smell of wood smoke with it. Chance paused, reining in the green broke chestnut he was riding. Smoke. No one was supposed to be lighting fires on Wolverton estates. *Poachers* was his first thought. Those lazy gamekeepers would pay for allowing this outrage, by God. He drummed his booted heels into the chestnut's sides and it sprang forward with a snort.

Hoofbeats thundered over the furrowed fields as Chance rode toward the origin of the smoke. He could barely see a thin wisp that curled skyward. As he drew nearer he heard the sound of voices raised in laughter and song, and it raked across his tautly stretched nerves like the stinging stroke of a whip.

Not just poachers, after all—*gypsies*. Gypsies, by God, camping on Wolverton lands, poaching his game.

The rage that always seemed to simmer just beneath his surface these days erupted into action. Chance spurred his mount through the trees in a crashing of branches and thick underbrush. He saw the clearing just ahead of him, and urged the horse faster. A whirlwind of dry leaves geysered upward when the snorting stallion was reined in abruptly; Chance glimpsed startled faces as the chestnut half-reared in a frenzy of thrashing hooves.

He brought the animal down with a firm hand and looked around him.

"Damn you," he snarled, "get off my land at once. I do not tolerate trespassers. . . ."

Someone snatched at his boot, and Chance lashed out with his riding crop, sending the man stumbling backward and cursing in a language he didn't recognize. Clusters of frowning gypsies glared at him from the tight circle of garishly painted wagons, looking sullen and ominous. They stared at him without speaking, and Chance leaned forward to calm his trembling mount with a gentle hand on the chestnut's lathered neck.

"Did you hear me?" he barked when no one spoke or moved. "I demand that you leave at once."

"We heard you," a thickly accented voice replied at last, rumbling across the small clearing like the roar of a lion. "We could not help it. You scream like the peacock, young master."

Laughter greeted his words, and Chance flushed. He swung his mount around. The chestnut danced nervously, eyes rolling and nostrils flaring at the unfamiliar sounds and smells. Chance's knees tightened, and it took several moments to impress his will over that of his agitated mount, until the chestnut finally stood quiet but alert. Chance lifted his head to gaze at the tall gypsy leaning against the thick trunk of a towering oak.

Apparently willing to recognize good horsemanship as well as good horseflesh, the gypsy said, "You ride well."

Chance lifted his brow, countering, "Are you a qualified judge of that?"

"Of course." Muscular arms spread wide and a mocking grin slanted the gypsy's full, mobile mouth. "I am Romany," he said as if that explained everything.

"And I," Chance said, "am a Lancaster."

The gypsy laughed. "You are an Englishman." His words were weighted with contempt, provoking the same response as if he'd thrown down the gauntlet.

Chance stiffened. "Care to make a wager on who's the better horseman—*gypsy?*"

The calculated insult produced the result he'd hoped for. The gypsies, or Romanies as they preferred being called, were notoriously proud. They traveled through England and Europe in their small bands with their brightly painted wagons, working at small jobs when they could and stealing their necessities when they couldn't. Chance knew they had been hounded across half of Europe, yet had retained their fierce pride. That pride would demand that the gypsy answer Chance's challenge, and he did.

He spat on the ground, his mouth curled into a sneer. "What are your stakes, Englishman?"

"If I win, you will leave my lands now, paying me two pence a head for the last night's lodging. If I lose, you will enjoy last night free."

"And tonight? It is close to dark already."

Chance recognized the gypsy's bartering attempt. "Tonight also, then, though I feel awkward taking advantage of such a gullible soul."

"You will soon regret your foolishness, Englishman."

The tall gypsy strode away, returning a few minutes later with a long-legged mare. She appeared more gangly than well-formed, and though her winter coat was well brushed and shining, it did not have the same gleam as the chestnut's. The gypsy swung effortlessly atop the mare's back and gazed at Chance.

"Name the course, Englishman."

"Down the high road to the bridge just before the village, then left and over the rise to the edge of the Welshman's property where the stone fence rises too high to jump, then back down the lower road to the millstream and back here. Agreed?"

"Agreed."

Comrades crowded around the gypsy, chattering in their strange tongue and obviously wishing him well, while Chance remained slightly apart and aloof, watching cynically. He was startled from his observations by the touch of a hand upon his boot, and glanced down.

A girl stood next to his horse, staring up at him with the bluest eyes he'd ever seen. A wild tangle of dark, red-streaked hair fell onto her forehead; dirt smudged her cheeks and nose, and her wide, mobile mouth curved in a sweetly charming smile.

"Here," she said, and held up a length of crimson ribbon. "Wear this as a favor. It will bring you luck against Nicolo."

Chance didn't move to take it. "I don't need luck to beat a gypsy."

Instead of being insulted, the girl laughed. It was a light, tinkly sound like the chime of silver bells in the wind.

"Maybe *you* don't, but your horse does. Rayna is the fastest horse in the land. Take the ribbon. I give it to you willingly."

To his surprise, Chance found himself reaching out for the ribbon. The girl looked close to his age, though it was difficult to tell with all the dirt on her face. She was skinny, her flat chest barely showing any signs of becoming a woman, and angular hips only slightly swelled the bright blue skirt she wore. Her bare toes curled into the dirt and damp leaves of the ground despite the icy chill in the air. Her smooth skin was a peachy gold instead of the dark mahogany of the rest of her people.

"Do you like what you see?" she asked impudently, and he realized that he'd been staring.

He shrugged. "Yes. Though you are the most disheveled girl I've seen in some time, you're also one of the prettiest."

With that, he tucked the ribbon into his pocket and nudged his stallion forward, leaving the gypsy girl staring after him. A glimpse of the smile on her face told him that his comment had pleased her.

The horses pranced and chomped at their bits, eager to be off but held by restraining hands. Someone held up a bright swatch of cloth to indicate that the competitors should be ready. It fluttered in the cold breeze, then was dropped.

As the scarlet bit of material fluttered to the ground the horses burst into action, surging forward neck to neck. Chestnut and bay streaked across the hard winter ground and up the far slope to the high road.

Chance leaned over his mount's neck as they clattered from the softer ground onto the hard-packed dirt road. Fierce exultation replaced his usual cold rage. He needed this outlet for the anger and pain that had been his constant companions of late, and he welcomed the cold bite of the wind in his face and the rhythmic motion of the horse beneath him.

He intended to win this race. Not far behind him, the rasping breath of the gypsy mare wove into the thunder of hooves against the ground, and he nodded in satisfaction. This would be too easy.

They raced for the bridge and across it, the horses turning and stretching out, manes and tails streaming out like banners. Trees, bushes, and small leaning huts whizzed past in a blur as they rode over the stubble of fallow fields. The wind stung his cheeks and made his eyes blur with tears. When he dragged an arm over his face to wipe them away, he was chagrined to realize that he held only a slight lead against the scruffy gypsy horse.

He leaned over the neck, urging his mount faster. Then the chestnut stumbled, and he pulled up to keep from being thrown into the field. He muttered a curse as his lead shortened and the gypsy pony pulled ahead.

Somehow, that scruffy mare possessed more speed than style, and it was suddenly apparent that she would beat his high-bred stallion with very little effort. Chance mentally cursed again. Losing was something he did badly, but it looked as if he would certainly lose this race. He quickly assessed his choices.

The high stone fence encompassing the Welshman's property loomed just ahead. He knew where the stones had tumbled to leave a gap low enough to jump. If he jumped it, he could cut across and save enough time to win the race. But he would also be cheating.

No. I'll win fairly or not at all, by God. . . .

He leaned over the horse's neck, urging him faster, and in moments, had almost caught up to the fleet gypsy pony. The gypsy glanced backward, his grinning face a dark blur against the pale background of leaveless trees and sullen gray skies. *Damn him.* He should have outdistanced that miserable nag long before this.

Still swearing, Chance redoubled his efforts, urging the stallion forward while trying to save the last of his strength for the finish. They were whistling down the lower road now, clods of dirt flying from beneath the hooves, with only the birds as spectators. Just ahead was the millstream, gurgling quietly through a marshy stretch of land. For the first time Chance lifted his riding crop. It slashed down in a whirring arc to land neatly on the chestnut's rump.

Snorting, the stallion leaped ahead with renewed energy. Chance was acutely aware of the wind whipping at him, of the rhythmic pumping of the horse's muscles stretching and striding, of the smell of gorse and damp earth, of the thunder of hoofbeats that sounded like his own beating heart. For several moments it looked as if he had the winning edge, then slowly the gypsy's mare began to pull ahead of the stallion, her velvety nose inching past until she was head and neck ahead.

The contours of the ground changed slightly as the racing horses sped forward, from hard-packed to soft and marshy, so that it slowed their pace. Now it was a struggle to run with the clinging mud sucking at flying hooves, taxing already straining muscles. They were close now, within mere inches of one another, so that Chance could hear the gypsy's harsh breathing as well as the wheezes of the mare.

He lifted his crop again to give the stallion a much needed spur forward. In the process the leather bat accidentally struck the gypsy's mare.

The mare panicked. A high-pitched scream tore into the air, and she began to buck wildly. Her startled rider sailed through the air to land in the middle of the shallow millstream with a loud splash. Chance saw this with astonishment, and circled back to return to the unharmed but furiously raging gypsy.

"You did that on purpose," Nicolo snarled through a muddy shower of water. He struggled to rise, eyes darting to the mare cantering from their view.

Chance reined in on the millbank, unable to hide his amusement at the sight before him. Nicolo's hair was plastered to his head like a black cap, and his clothes hung in dripping tangles.

"No," Chance finally said, "I didn't do it on purpose, but I can't help appreciating the picture you make." He nudged his horse into the stream and leaned down to offer his hand. "Come up behind me and we'll catch your horse."

Nicolo grasped Chance's hand firmly, then gave it a

sharp tug. Unbalanced, Chance tumbled from his saddle into the shockingly cold water. He heard the gypsy shout with laughter as he landed on hands and knees in the shallows.

Choking and gasping at the chill, Chance staggered to his feet, hands clenched into tight fists. "Damn you—"

"Ah, now we will catch my mare," Nicolo cut in, the slash of his brows lifting arrogantly.

Chance's eyes were level with the gypsy's, and he was aware of Nicolo's amused expression. Several heartbeats thudded past before Chance relaxed.

"Now we will catch your mare," he agreed, and reached out for his horse's dangling reins.

Disbelief showed on the faces of those watching when the two drenched horsemen rode into camp.

"Well?" one of the gypsies asked, "who won the race?"

"Neither one of us," Nicolo said at the same moment as Chance replied, "Nicolo did."

They exchanged glances and shrugged, falling silent.

"Eh?" an old woman demanded, coming forward to stand with both hands on her ample hips. "Which is it?"

Chance and Nicolo started to speak at the same time again, then paused.

"Actually," Nicolo finally said, "I was winning when a small . . . uh . . . accident occurred, Lucia."

"Accident?"

"Yes, the stick flew from his hands and struck my mare. You all know how skittish Rayna is, and she bolted, leaving me sitting in the middle of a stream."

"You are *both* wet," someone in the crowd pointed out.

"But of course." Nicolo's brows rose. "You did not expect me to swim alone, did you?"

Laughter greeted that remark. Chance looked around at the uncertain expressions, and made a swift decision. He caught Nicolo's right hand and held it up in a gesture of triumph.

"To the winner of the race." A volley of ragged cheers rose, and when the noise began to fade, Chance added, "And for all—a feast should be given, using the fat plunder I saw when I rode in."

Silence greeted his last words, and Chance's brow lifted. "What? No appetites? Or is it that you're wary of my knowing whose game you've been poaching?"

The woman Nicolo had called Lucia took a step forward. "You are an arrogant rooster, young sir. Say what you mean."

"I already have. I'm hungry, and I do not care where you got the main course."

For a moment no one spoke, then Lucia smiled slightly in a motion that made her leathery face crinkle around the eyes and mouth. "As I said—you are most arrogant. But never let it be said that a Romany had to be asked twice to share his good fortune."

She clapped her hands, and people began to scurry in all directions. Nicolo grinned and slapped Chance on his back, sending him staggering a few steps.

"You said just the right thing, my young friend," Nicolo commented with a wink.

Chance narrowly avoided another hearty slap on the back by stepping to the side. "What was that?"

"*Feast.* Lucia almost laughed. She likes to eat."

He didn't doubt that. Her ample frame was evidence of a fondness for food. Purloined chickens and poached game were soon cooking at Lucia's directions, while the women began to scrape vegetables into various pots.

When the men gathered around the fire with earthenware jugs, Nicolo motioned for Chance to join them. He hesitated. He'd seen the jugs being hefted and knew what was in them. But to refuse could be an insult.

He reached out and took a heavy jug, lifting it as he'd seen the others do. Potent liquor burned a fiery path down his throat and made his eyes water, but he took several hearty swigs before lowering the jug and wiping his mouth with his sleeve. Each person in turn silently lifted his own jug. Only Nicolo gave him a nod of approval.

Fiddles played, an old hand organ was brought out and wound up, and several guitars strummed a lively melody in accompaniment to the thump and jangle of tambourines. The music was loud and unfamiliar, nothing like the country reels he was used to hearing or the stately minuet that his dance masters preferred.

Chance stood to one side, not really a part of the celebration, but somehow unable to leave. There was a gaiety and vibrancy in these people that he found intriguing. It had been a long time since he'd heard laughter that was genuine and not at someone else's expense. Had he ever laughed as naturally? If so, he couldn't remember it. Laughter was something in short supply at Whiteash Manor, and had been since before his parents' deaths.

His throat tightened, and he levered himself away from the gnarled oak trunk where he'd been leaning. Nicolo was only a few feet away, pounding enthusiastically on a tambourine and making a general nuisance of himself.

"Where is the girl I saw earlier?" Chance asked, and Nicolo's hand paused in midair over the stretched skin of the tambourine.

"Girl? What girl?"

Nicolo's eyes were slightly narrowed, focusing on him

with growing suspicion, and Chance wished he hadn't asked. But he had, and he wouldn't back down.

"The one with big blue eyes."

Light sparked Nicolo's eyes. "Ah—you must mean Rhianna."

Rhianna. An unusual name for an unusual girl.

"Yes. Rhianna. Where is she?"

Nicolo shrugged and waved an expansive arm. "Here somewhere. In one of the wagons, perhaps." He squinted at Chance. "Why do you seek her out?"

"I have something of hers that I should return."

"Ah." Nicolo's gaze was narrow and speculative, but he finally nodded. "Very well. There is a wagon by itself at the far edge of the circle. Look there for her."

Rhianna opened the door a small crack when he knocked, and looked slightly surprised at seeing him. Chance thought belatedly of his damp, mud-spattered garments. He held out the wet ribbon, and watched it flutter slightly in the wind.

"It did not help me beat Nicolo."

She took the ribbon. A smile curved the lovely bow of her mouth upward. "Ah, but perhaps it helped you lose gracefully."

For the first time in several months, Chance felt a wave of anticipation, and wondered why. There was nothing he could see in this scrap of a girl that would give him any reason to anticipate her company, yet he did.

"Come and sit by the fire with me, Rhianna."

Her delicate brow rose. "I do not take orders from those I do not know."

"Orders? It was an invitation."

"It sounded more like an order, young sir."

He shrugged. "It was not meant to."

Rhianna leaned against the doorjamb. A dark skein of hair fell over one shoulder in a gleaming fat curl, and he fought the temptation to touch it. She was so pretty, much prettier than any of the girls he knew, and free of pretense and that strict sense of propriety that made females so infinitely boring to him.

He reached out and took her hand in his. "Come walk with me."

She pulled away. "See? Another order. Do you not know how to ask for what you want?"

"I thought I did." He felt a wave of impatience. "Do not play with words. You're different from all the others. Don't disappoint me now."

Her chin lifted, and Chance knew he had made a major error in judgment when she gave him a cold stare.

"If you mean that you think I'm a poor silly gypsy lass who will follow you into the woods for a game of touch and tickle, you're right—I'm different from all the others you must know."

"But that's not—"

"Go back and play great lord among the men, sir. I do not need to hear anything else from you." She stepped back, and the door began to swing shut.

Chance caught it with one hand. "Rhianna, wait. That's not at all what I meant. I just . . . I just wanted to be with you and enjoy your company."

The blue of her eyes had darkened, and she regarded him solemnly for a long moment. It had suddenly become vital that she not think badly of him, and Chance cleared his throat.

"Please—come and walk with me. We can sit by the fire with the others if you like."

She hesitated. He saw the indecision in her eyes, and then she nodded slowly.

"Very well. I will sit by the fire with you. But do not presume to order me about again."

Chance had never met a girl quite like this Rhianna

before. She behaved as if she were royalty. Royalty in bare feet and disheveled hair—it was disconcerting. And more intriguing than he'd thought it would be.

The others made room for them in the circle around the fire, and the smell of roasting meat mingled with the tantalizing fragrance of baking bread. As Rhianna laughed with one of the other girls sitting nearby, he watched in rapt fascination. Her movements were so graceful, and she had the unconscious carriage of a lady. How had this girl come from a people who spent their time in flight from authorities over half of Europe? There was a lively intelligence as well as mischief in her soft blue eyes; he noted how her thick lashes swept out as she teased him with sidelong glances.

She offered him a wood bowl filled with meat and bread. "It is not often we invite others to join us. Eat, if you are hungry, young lordling."

He took the bowl, frowning. "Don't call me that."

"Don't call you what?"

"Lordling."

"Isn't that what you are?"

"No." He set the bowl on the ground, aware of her curious gaze and wishing suddenly he was one of the boys from the village. The gulf between him and this gypsy girl was unbridgeable.

"You are a lord." Rhianna's voice lowered. "I heard Enrico say that you are the young earl everyone says is as wild and fierce as a wolf. Are you?"

He was startled. He'd heard of the rumors, of course; people seemed to make it their good Christian duty to see that he was informed about his lamentable shortcomings. He just hadn't known he was supposed to be fierce.

"Is that what they say about me?"

"Yes. Don't you know?"

"What else do they say?"

Rhianna shifted to sit closer, and he caught a faint whiff of a light, flowery fragrance. "They say, my lord, that you will not live to see your majority, that you will meet a bad end before then."

"Ah. And do they also say that it will be of my own doing, or am I supposed to be done in by my charming uncle?"

Now Rhianna seemed startled. "I don't know what you mean by that—"

"Of course you do. Everyone in Wiltshire has an opinion about it one way or the other." His hand closed around her wrist, holding her when she would have pulled away, his voice harsher than he meant for it to be. "Which do you think it will be, lovely Rhianna? Will I be done in by my uncle so that he inherits—or will I kill the bastard before he can kill me?"

Fright shadowed her eyes for a moment, and he took a deep breath and let her go. "Forgive me."

"I never meant . . ." She swallowed hard, rubbing at her wrist, "I never meant to upset you. It was a jest, my lord."

"Chance. Don't call me *my lord* like that."

"Like what?" She shook back a tangle of dark hair from her eyes, gazing at him with a mixture of caution and curiosity.

"Like . . . like I'm my father." He turned to stare into the fire, feeling the familiar thrust of pain that came whenever he thought of his parents, of the life he'd once had and the life he had now. He sucked in a deep breath, and wood smoke stung his throat and lungs, so that his voice came out in a thick rasp. "I'm not my father."

Rhianna put a hand on his arm, and he turned to look at her. There was no pity in her eyes, which he would have hated, but somehow, a glimmer of understanding shone in the deep blue depths and eased him. Her voice was so soft he had to lean closer to hear.

"My mother died last year. I miss her. People say I'm like her, but I'm not. She was . . . she was beautiful, and always happy and gay, while I am none of those things. I am not my mother, though I wish I were. I wish . . . oh God, I wish she were still here."

Tears welled in her eyes but did not spill onto her cheeks, and Chance felt compelled to put his hand over hers. He couldn't reply; there was nothing to say, and he knew that well enough. No mere words would soothe the pain she felt, or the rage he felt. Nothing but time, Hobson always told him, nothing but time would ease the pain.

They sat there in silent understanding, while around them gay music swirled into the air and sparks from the fire rose skyward. A full moon silvered the earth, hanging heavy and bright above the trees, making black lace of empty branches, and for the first time in months, Chance felt a sense of kinship with another human being.

It was, he thought, more his salvation than any of the words Reverend Goodbody had offered him.

Chapter 3

A weak noon sun glinted in her eyes as Rhianna balanced on her toes, peeping over the thick hedge that shielded the men from her gaze. A wave of impatience made her stomp one foot, and she winced at the twinge of a sharp twig against her bare instep.

"One should not be as curious as the cat," a soft voice murmured behind her, and Rhianna turned with a startled gasp at the sound. Her heartbeat slowed to a normal pace when she recognized Marisa, and she folded her arms over her chest.

"You frightened me."

"Better I than Enrico. Or Lucia."

Rhianna suppressed a shudder. That was true. Harsh recriminations would accompany any discovery either of those made if they caught her peeping.

"I was only watching them for a while."

Marisa stepped into a patch of sunlight lacing through the trees. Her face was lined—and worried, despite the reproof in her tone. "You know it is not allowed. There are things that do not concern you."

"Such as gaming? I have watched many a time, and—"

"That is not what I meant, and you know it. You watch the young earl. It has been noticed by many how you sat close to him last night, and I have been told that he wore your favor in the race."

Rhianna's chin lifted, and she felt the heat of a flush burn her cheeks. "So? It was only a ribbon. And he was alone with no one to cheer for him. I felt sorry."

"I am not a fool." Marisa stepped closer. "Neither is Enrico or Lucia. Do not set your sights upon that young man, my child. He is not Romany."

"Neither am I," Rhianna replied. "Only my mother was a Rom."

Marisa sighed and looked away, her face sad. "Yes, and that is part of the reason our band is no longer allowed to join other Romany. You would not be the first girl left behind when a man has what he wants. Your mother was proof of that, and I am surprised that you do not remember. . . ."

Unwilling to allow her to see how her words stung, Rhianna looked away, back toward the circle of men tossing dice near the fire. Chance was among them, looking more bored than interested as he leaned against a fallen log and watched. He made her think of a sulky angel, beautiful but wicked. When he'd looked at her, there had been a gleam of sardonic knowledge in his dark eyes that had piqued her curiosity. She wished she could talk more with him, despite her aunt's foreboding.

"He seems so sad."

She didn't realize she'd spoken aloud until Marisa said sharply, "Do not trust appearances, child. You know better."

Rhianna stiffened. "This is different."

Marisa exclaimed softly, then asked, "What has he said to you? Promised you?"

"Nothing. He has made no promises. He only asked me to sit with him, and we talked of our dead parents."

For a moment Marisa was silent, and Rhianna could almost hear her sympathy. It was Marisa who had sat with her night after night after her mother's death, Marisa who had held her close and comforted her with soft words and love. Yes, Marisa would understand.

"Rhianna—" Marisa stepped close and put a wool shawl around her shoulders and tied it in the front. "Rhianna, I know your heart is still sad, and I sense that the young earl has the same sort of sadness. But you must not let pity for him make you foolish."

"Pity?" Rhianna shook her head. "No, 'tis not pity I feel for him. I knew when I first saw him that he has felt the same as I. We are kindred souls, Marisa."

Marisa put an arm around Rhianna's shoulders and pulled her close, guiding her gently along. "If you felt only empathy, you could not be hurt."

"I don't understand—"

"I know. But there is a vast difference in the way a woman feels and the way men feel about certain things. Do you not recall that your father abandoned your mother when she became pregnant with you? Cynara was foolish and paid a high price. Don't forget it for a moment. You are not ignorant, Rhianna. I have taught you the things you need to know."

"You have taught me many things." Rhianna lapsed into silence as they walked back to the wagon they shared. It had once been home to her mother also, but now only she and Marisa occupied it. The small wagon still seemed empty without Cynara's grace and beauty to enliven the drab interior.

Cynara, wildly beautiful, tempestuous—her lively presence was sorely missed in the camp, despite her being the cause of their estrangement. Because she had fallen in love with a man not of the Rom, their family was cast out to roam alone. Cynara had not looked at another man in all of Rhianna's thirteen years. Nor did she speak of Rhianna's father. She didn't even know his name. He was a mystery to her, a puzzle that she would probably never solve. Once she'd overheard Marisa saying bitterly that Cynara was wasting away of a broken heart for a man who did not care, but she didn't really believe that. What man would willingly leave such a woman?

Rhianna perched on the edge of the bunk, wishing once again that her mother were still with her, to explain the things she didn't understand, to comfort her with amusing stories.

Marisa seemed to know how she felt, for she began to talk about her youngest sister, reliving Cynara's youth in a way guaranteed to make Rhianna smile.

". . . and then she threw the fish at that old parson and told him to multiply as the Christ had done," Marisa said with relish, laughing. "Of course, he could not, but he knew what she was saying. He allowed her to fish on the Sabbath with no more of his blistering condemnations."

Rhianna laughed. "My mother was very smart. And beautiful. I wish I was like her."

"But child—you are. You look enough like Cynara as a child to be her twin."

"No. My mother had hair as dark as the raven's wing, and golden skin like the finest silk. My hair has red in it, and my skin is much too pale—"

Marisa laughed, and Rhianna glared at her when she said, "You are such a foolish little chick. You see not what others see. But perhaps that is good now. Never fear, my sweet flower. You will bloom one day into the rarest of blossoms. I foresee this."

Rhianna scooted to the edge of her bunk. "What else do you see for me, Marisa? Tell me. You never do, though you tell others what you see for them. I want to know. Oh, please don't refuse."

After a brief hesitation, Marisa said slowly, "I do not tell you because I do not want you to know."

"Why? Is my future that grim?" Rhianna's throat grew tight, and a pang of apprehension made her voice quiver. "You know something—and you won't tell me."

"Rhianna, child. . . ."

"Tell me. Tell me what my future holds, Marisa. You have the gift of sight, and I demand that you warn me."

Marisa stood up, her bright skirt swirling around her ankles as she turned abruptly. For the first time, Rhianna noted the threads of gray in her dark hair and saw the lines in her familiar, dear face. Her heart contracted. She should not insist, but she'd wanted to know for so long, and since her mother's death, the future frightened her.

"Tell me, Marisa."

"I cannot. It has been forbidden."

"Forbidden? By who?"

Marisa waved an arm, and her bracelets jangled loudly. "You must know."

"Enrico. And Manuel. But they have nothing to do with me. Why would they care? Manuel is ill, too ill to even lead us anymore, and Enrico is weak. Nicolo should be the leader of our group, and I am not the first to say it. Why would you listen to them?"

"Because I must. Because—" Marisa turned to face her. "Because your mother wished it so."

"My mother? But she would want me to know. I feel it. I know that she would not want me to be unhappy."

"Knowledge is not always the same thing as happiness, child. Surely you know that."

"No. I don't." She thrust her chin out. "If I could see the future, I would tell. I would have power then and could change my life as well as everyone else's."

"No, no, that would be wrong, child! The gifts you are given are precious and should never be misused. Seeing what may come can be a deliverance or a destruction.

One must be wise enough to choose the right path and decide how to use the knowledge for the good of all."

Rhianna leaned forward, determination making her heart beat faster. "Then tell me, Marisa. Tell me what you see for me in the future. Let me make my own decision."

"You have the power to see for yourself if you will just listen to what your heart and head tell you." Marisa's voice dropped. "Try it. Empty your mind of all distractions that cloud it. Float as if in a dream begun in wine, forget that you have a body holding you earthbound, and think of nothing. . . ."

Rhianna closed her eyes. Nothing came. She clenched her hands into tight fists and tried to think of nothing, but images and sounds from outside kept intruding. At last she gave a sigh and opened her eyes.

"I cannot."

"Perhaps you are just not ready." Marisa sighed softly. "It comes at different times for some. Your time will come, but you have to want it. Right now, you just want me to tell you what I see."

"Yes." Eager, Rhianna said again, "Yes. Tell me."

Marisa's brown eyes were troubled, and she moved to sit at the small table, taking Rhianna's hands between hers.

"I should not, but . . ." She closed her eyes for an instant, and her voice lowered to a husky rasp that made the hair on the back of Rhianna's neck tingle. "There is much that will happen to you soon, but you must be strong. I see great changes coming . . . strong winds that will blow you far, far from here . . . tragedy and pain, but hope not long after. . . . There is a shimmer around you . . . snow? No, a white light—deep and full. An evil moon. . . ."

Her voice lowered even more, so that Rhianna had to lean close to hear, and she shivered when Marisa's eyes flew open and she whispered hoarsely, "Beware the tears of the moon. No—a chain of moon tears, for they will betray you."

"What . . . do you mean?" Rhianna shook her head in confusion, and Marisa blinked as if just waking.

"I don't know. Things just come to me. When the time comes, you will know." She released Rhianna's hands and rose from the table, voice gentle. "You are on the threshold of life now. Many things will happen to you soon, but I cannot always be near to advise you."

"But where—?"

"It will be told to you when you are ready. Do not ask me questions now that I cannot answer." Marisa put her hand on Rhianna's shoulder, fingers digging into her skin, but she scarcely noticed. There was pain in her aunt's eyes, and knowledge. Something was about to happen, something that would change her life, and she knew it.

"Marisa, I cannot think of being without you. . . ."

"Life is not always as we wish it. There are questions that are soon to be answered for you, though you may not like or understand what you hear. Know that I love you. I will always love you, no matter how far apart we may be. I wish—"

A knock at the door stopped her words, and her hand fell away. For a moment, Rhianna was tempted to ask her to ignore the visitor, but then Marisa was opening the door and she saw the young earl standing outside. She rose from the bunk and went to stand behind Marisa.

Sunlight made his dark hair gleam as richly as a raven's glossy wing, and the moody curve of his mouth was set in a determined line. Despite his somewhat sulky arrogance, Rhianna could not help the leap of pleasure she felt at seeing him.

"I would like to see Rhianna," he was saying, and

Marisa reluctantly moved aside, surprising Rhianna. She had not expected her aunt to so docilely acquiesce, though she suspected it must be because of Chance's arrogant air of authority. She stepped forward and paused uncertainly.

"Come walk with me," he said imperatively, then paused to look at her from beneath the thick bristle of his lashes. "Please."

Rhianna felt foolishly pleased by his obvious effort to appease her. She hesitated, then reached for the shawl Marisa had warmed her with earlier. There would be time later to continue their talk.

"Be careful," her aunt said softly, and Rhianna turned.

"There is no danger. We have the earl's permission to be on these lands."

"I was not speaking of that." Marisa's callused hand cupped her chin for a moment. Dark brown eyes searched her face, and then her aunt stepped back. "Remember who you are, child."

"What did she mean by that?" Chance asked when they had walked away from the wagon.

Rhianna shrugged uncertainly. "I don't know. My mother used to tell me that I was descended from kings, but I know that the Romanies all like to believe they are descended from royalty."

Chance stopped and turned to gaze down at her with a faint smile erasing his sulky expression. "I had the thought when I first saw you that you were a princess. Are you?"

Stepping back, she made a deep curtsy, sweeping her skirt out in a mocking gesture. "The princess of pretense. And you, my lord? Are you a prince?"

"No, I'm an earl."

His solemn reply made Rhianna frown. "You are so literal. Don't you know how to pretend?"

"No."

There was so much sincerity in that one short reply that she knew it was the truth. "Then how did you play as a child?"

"I have never been a child. It was not allowed. I had to learn, to be educated, so that one day I would be able to take my proper station in life."

"And now you have."

"No." There was a world of bitterness in his voice. "No, I have not yet taken my proper station. And if my uncle has his way, I never will." His fists clenched, and Rhianna was struck again by the ferocity that vibrated just beneath his surface. "By God, I will not allow him to beat me. . . ."

"I know you won't," she said softly and put a hand on his arm. His muscles were taut and quivering, and after a moment, he relaxed slightly and drew in a deep breath.

"Let's not think of that now. Come and sit under a tree with me, Rhianna. Tell me of your travels."

Time flew past swiftly. As it grew cooler and the sun began to set, the sunny spot beneath a spreading yew became dark and cool. Bright scarlet berries dotted the ground, and Rhianna scooped up a handful.

Chance propped on his elbow to look at her, a stalk of winter grass tucked into a corner of his mouth. Shadows hid one side of his face, and the half-light gave him a rakish, sardonic appearance.

Impulsively, she tossed the berries at him, laughing at his expression of indignant astonishment. "Don't be a sobersides," she said, teasing. "Try smiling on occasion."

With a low growl, he flung himself at her, barely catching the hem of her bright patterned skirt when she tried to escape. Squealing with delight, Rhianna pelted him with whatever missiles were within reach—dead leaves, yew berries, and a tuft of dried grass. Debris showered over him, sticking in his hair, clogging his eye-lashes, and littering his riding jacket.

"You look like a hedgehog," she said on a snort of laughter. "All prickly and . . . fuzzy . . . oh, stop!"

Chance straddled her, easily holding her down, a knee on each side of her squirming body. He grinned, his words slightly breathless. "Are you ticklish, Rhianna? Here? Yes? And how about . . . here?"

His fingers dug into her ribs, and the ticklish spot between her neck and shoulder, then found the tender area behind her knees. She shouted with laughter as she tried to fend off his hands, but he seemed to be every-where at once, wiry muscle and determination, and she soon collapsed into helpless giggles. After a moment he stopped, and rested his palms on his thighs, still grinning down at her.

Breathless, she stared up at him, grinning back. He didn't seem so strange and formidable now, but was a boy like any other.

"I wish you could stay with us," she said impulsively, then wished she hadn't. His grin faded, and he looked away from her toward the distant slopes that hid his home from view.

"I can't."

His tone was flat, emotionless, all laughter gone from his eyes and voice. Rhianna fell silent, and wondered why his uncle was wicked enough to produce the emo-tions she saw flicker briefly on his face.

"You can stay for a little while, can't you?" she per-sisted.

He shrugged. "I suppose I can return when I please."

"Won't someone miss you?"

"No. Only my servant Hobson, perhaps, but no one else." He sat back and raked a hand through his hair in a careless motion. His mouth twisted into the mocking grimace that made him look older and bitter.

"I find that difficult to believe."

"It's true." He brushed angrily at the leaves and dried grass on his coat. "I'm the devil earl, the changeling child, remember? It's probably said that the gypsies stole my parents' real son and replaced him with me. That's what is often said, you know, to frighten village children into behaving—*The gypsies will steal you.*"

"I know."

Rhianna gazed at him for a long moment. Beneath the bitterness and sarcasm lay a great deal of pain, and she wished that she could ease it for him somehow. On impulse, she rose to her knees and kissed him on the cheek.

Chance immediately caught her shoulder before she could pull back, and turned her face toward him with his other hand. His mouth found hers and covered it, shocking her.

His lips were warm and gentle, but it was like no kiss she had ever given or received before. Wide-eyed, she let him kiss her without responding. When he drew back, he gazed at her searchingly; the glitter in his wicked eyes faded.

"You're not ready."

She took a deep breath, surprised to find that he had shaken her. "No. Not for what you want, I think."

A faint smile lifted the corners of his mouth. "I knew that. I suppose I just couldn't resist trying. Are you angry with me?"

"No. Curious, however. What did you expect from me?"

He shrugged. "I'm not certain."

Nothing was said for several minutes, and with the

setting sun, it was chilly and shadowed. A cold wind blew in a mournful wail. Rhianna rose in a quick motion.

A surge of restless energy compelled her to fling aside her shawl and move to the tempo of a silent melody. With her eyes half-closed, she lifted her arms above her head and began snapping her fingers. Remembered music thrummed in her head, and she twisted her body and stamped her feet against the ground, her bracelets jangling a metallic tune. She could feel the swish and sway of her skirts against her bare legs, the damp earth beneath her feet, and the brisk bite of the wind against her skin.

But she focused on the driving urgency inside her that compelled her to dance, to release emotion in the beat and step of rhythm. She danced as she did before the fire at times, wildly, then slowly, swaying like a reed in the wind. For a time, she forgot where she was, forgot Chance and her surroundings as she lost herself in silent sounds. Nothing else mattered, nothing but the dance.

When, finally, she paused, breathless and damp with perspiration, she saw Chance watching her. He was silent, his dark eyes unreadable in the deep shadows. She felt a bit foolish and wondered what he thought of her mad, impromptu dance.

"We should go back," she said and bent to retrieve her shawl so that she did not have to see him laugh at her.

"Yes."

Rhianna straightened, and Chance reached out and took the shawl from her. He pulled it around her shoulders and looped the ends into a loose knot in front. His eyes briefly met hers, and a faint smile touched the corners of his mouth. Then he took her hand in his, tucking it into the crook of his arm as if she were a great lady.

"I'll walk you back to your aunt's wagon," he said, and there was no hint of laughter or cynical amusement in his tone. Instead, there was a gentleness and respect in his touch that surprised and pleased her.

No, he could never be the vicious young man some people claimed he was, she decided.

It was late the following afternoon before Chance went back to Whiteash Manor. He reined in his mount on the crest of a slope overlooking the grounds, reluctant to return. It was an unfamiliar emotion to feel about Whiteash. He'd always loved it, eagerly awaited the opportunity to return every time he left for any length of time.

Evening mists drifted like gauzy streamers among tall, expertly clipped yews and hedges. In summer, honeysuckle and wild roses would fill the air with fragrance. He could remember playing with sticks and hoops in the garden as a young child, laughing with his brothers, teasing his sisters. Of all of them, it seemed odd that he was the only survivor. He and Anthony alone had reached puberty, and there were tiny markers in the family plot to give silent testimony of each loss.

Whiteash, stately gray stone with eight wings and more than three hundred rooms, tall towers, and thousands of glass panes that reflected summer sun with all the radiance of the palace at Versailles. Elegance and luxury, fine furniture and exquisite paintings—all belonging to the new earl of Wolverton—yet not his. Not yet.

Perhaps—not ever.

Lord Perry would still be there, damn him, drinking the late earl's fine wines and brandy, entertaining his London cronies with his good fortune—and his nephew's inheritance.

Rage burned anew, and Chance clenched his jaws, as

he'd begun doing shortly after his uncle's arrival three weeks before. Damn the bloody swine, he'd arrived with an air of insouciance that was infuriating, considering that until his brother's death he'd been hiding from the Bow Street runners sent after him for debts. Perry hadn't hesitated to make his presence felt in the sprawling manor house, much to the dismay of the servants who had been sacked immediately.

Of the long-time retainers, only Hobson remained, and it was a mystery to Chance why he was not gone as well. The new servants were a surly lot and made him think of the seedy characters he'd glimpsed in the stews of London.

So much had changed, but thankfully, the gracious country house showed no changes. *Yet,* Chance amended when he swung down from his horse and gave the chestnut into the hands of the new groom.

"Cool him off well and be certain he receives an extra ration of oats, Barton."

The groom silently took the reins, his gaze hostile. He waited until Chance was almost out of earshot before saying in a low mutter, "Aye, yer bloody lordship."

Chance swung around, tapping his riding crop against his leg. "If you have something to say, Barton, say it loud enough for me to hear."

He saw the groom's startled glance before he looked away. "I ain't got nothin' else to say. *My lord,"* he added sullenly, and Chance fought the temptation to use his riding crop on him. Insolent bastard.

"Very good. Remember that in the future. And Barton —if I should think that my horse is not being treated well, I can promise you more trouble than you would like. While my uncle may have hired you, it is my money that pays you. Do you understand me?"

"Perfectly, my lord."

This time, there was a touch of respect in his tone, and Chance swung back around. Damn Perry for the infernal blackguard he was. If he could think of a way, he'd get rid of him in an instant.

Dusk trailed purple shadows between the gray stones of the manor house and the towering evergreens in the west garden, but the lamps had not been lit on the stone path. One more example of the inefficiency of the new servants Perry had brought in from London.

Chance was fuming when he slammed the door behind him, and it echoed loudly through the quiet, still house.

"Ah, so the prodigal has returned to honor us with his presence," a silky voice said from the shadows of the gloomy marble entrance hall, and Chance turned.

"You make yourself damned comfortable in my home, Lord Perry. Why don't you go back to London?"

Perry stepped from the shadows into the light of a lamp. His once handsome face had settled into lines of dissipation. "Is that any way to greet your doting uncle?"

"I'd rather greet you with a saber, but since I have no desire to spend the rest of my days rotting in prison, I suppose I'll have to wait for you to drink yourself to death on my father's brandy."

"Tsk tsk, what an insufferable whelp you are, m'boy."

Chance stepped closer. "I can be even more insufferable when pushed too far, *Uncle.*"

"Can you? Is that a threat, perchance?"

"Call it a warning."

"I shan't call it anything at all. You bay at the moon like a mad dog, when there is very little you can do."

"I have my barristers working on that." Chance glared at him when Perry gave a bark of laughter.

"Oh, do you mean the barristers on London's West Side that I had to dismiss? They won't be helping you without recompense, my lad, make no mistake about that. And I do not feel inclined to authorize any such expenditures."

"Damn you—"

Lord Perry's hand shot out, and his fist closed in the front of Chance's shirt, catching him by surprise when he lifted him from his feet. Perry was stronger than he looked.

"Where have you been, nephew?"

He hated the spurt of fear that made his stomach knot and his throat tighten, but there was something in his uncle's steady gaze that set his teeth on edge and made him wary.

"Why? You've never cared before."

"I still don't. But I have guests coming this evening, and I need the key to the storerooms. That fool Hobson says you have it."

"More guests? The last set only departed a few days ago. Haven't you lost all my money yet at whist or faro? It would be much more convenient for you to be gaming in London instead of here. Feel free to return."

Perry's grip tightened. "Enough chatter. Where is the key to the storerooms?" When Chance didn't respond, he gave him a rough shake.

Without pausing to think, Chance lifted the riding crop he still carried and slashed it across Perry's face. He gained his release at once and stepped back out of reach.

"You'll ruin me if I let you. I won't. You've already allowed your *guests* to make off with silver that has been in the Lancaster family for generations, and I won't let you rob me blind and do nothing."

"You have no choice." Perry wiped the back of his hand across the raw, bleeding cut on his cheek. "If you do not give me what I want, you'll be locked away until you do. And don't think I can't do it. I can. Who'll stop me—Hobson? I don't think that old man can help himself, much less protect you." Perry stepped closer, his pale eyes glittering in the feeble light of the hall lamp. "Do what I tell you, lad, and you may even live long enough to collect your inheritance."

"If there's any left by then."

"Give me the key. Or Hobson goes tonight. I mean it. By the time either of you can challenge me before a magistrate, that old man will have starved to death and you know it."

Perry held out his hand, and Chance fought waves of helpless fury. He'd wondered at Perry's generosity in not dismissing Hobson. Now he knew why—he was to be held as hostage against Chance's good behavior.

"I'll get it," he said finally. He tried not to notice his uncle's gloating smile when he had the key, but stood stiffly silent until he'd gone, leaving Chance alone in his bedchamber.

He was suddenly sick of the house he'd always loved and longed for fresh air and easy laughter. Not the kind of laughter his uncle and his guests enjoyed, with the dark innuendoes and stifling atmosphere. No, he'd glimpsed enough of that in the three weeks Perry had been in residence.

Gaming with high stakes seemed to be the entertainment of choice, after which the shrill laughter of women Chance had only seen from distances could be heard in his mother's elegant parlors. It made him sick, and nothing eased the rising anger inside him.

Nothing, but the memory of soft feminine laughter and bright blue eyes. Rhianna. If he closed his eyes, he could see her dancing silently on the moors, bare feet skimming over dead grass and her slender body twisting to a melody only she could hear. She was a free spirit, lovely and mercurial. Yes. He would go to see her again, and for a time, would forget everything else.

Chance stared at the charred embers of a fire. He could see deep ruts in the soft ground, made by heavy wagon wheels, but there was little other sign that gypsies had made their camp on Wolverton estates.

For several minutes, he sat his mount and just stared at the emptiness, feeling desolate inside. He hadn't realized until now just how much he'd looked forward to seeing Rhianna again. Even Nicolo.

He lifted his head and stared into the distance. Where could they have gone? He should have come back sooner, but the past three days had been spent guarding what he could of his inheritance. Perry's gaming would deplete his funds within a year if he did not find some way to stop him.

And now even Rhianna was gone. He'd thought about her, thought about what he would say when he saw her again, and how blue her eyes were, and the way her hair gleamed in the sun as if dark fire.

Now she was gone, and he would probably never see her again. He wanted to howl his pain and anger aloud.

But the past weeks had taught him an important lesson—nothing was forever. Even pain.

Chance reined the chestnut around and rode back to Whiteash Manor.

Book Two

England, 1798

Chapter 4

Rhianna perched on the edge of a garden bench and gazed at the stone fences that stitched rolling fields and wooded thickets. A soft breeze blew, tugging at the satin ribbons of her bonnet with brisk persistence. Impulsively, she untied them and pulled off the leghorn straw bonnet.

Serenity House, a stately name for a lovely estate. She hadn't been back to the English countryside in eight years and didn't realize how much she'd missed it. Flowers had begun to blossom, and the grass was a bright, untarnished green between the paving stones of the garden. Sunlight was warm on her face, and she closed her eyes and relished its heat.

"England's nothing like Greece, is it, Poppet?"

Rhianna opened her eyes. "There's nothing like an English garden, either. I'm glad we left London and came back to the country."

Sir Griffyn Llewellyn chuckled. "True. I suppose I should not belittle my beloved town, but the constant rain and fog of London does make a man want to seek sunshine and fresh air."

"London was pleasant enough, and I was glad to be back in England. Eight years is a long time to dwell beneath a foreign sky. We should have returned to England long ago."

There was a brief pause, then Llewellyn stepped

around the bench to gaze down at his only child. "Have you still not forgiven me, 'Anna?"

She shrugged. "There's nothing to forgive."

"Perhaps not to my mind, but I know you've never quite understood why I took you away."

Rhianna smiled slightly. "I understand your reasons, if not your methods."

Llewellyn sighed and motioned for her to move her skirts so that he could sit beside her on the stone bench. "I know I was high-handed, 'Anna, but I was desperate. It had taken me so long to find you, and I was half out of my wits after arguing with that cunning thief who called himself king of the Romany."

"Enrico always knew how to drive a hard bargain."

"I daresay." He sounded disgruntled. "I felt as if I was buying a child instead of claiming my daughter."

She plucked idly at the curved feathers on the crown of her hat, frowning slightly. "What would you have done if he had refused to accept your offer?"

"Employed the aid of the magistrates, as I told him I would. What would you have had me do? You are, after all, my daughter."

Rhianna looked up at him. "Tell me again why you finally decided to look for me." She never tired of hearing the story, of trying to understand it.

Her father's blue eyes met hers. "You know I always searched for your mother. I was a younger son when we met, wild and impetuous, and she was the most beautiful, bewitching woman I'd ever seen. We fell in love, but did not think of the future beyond being together." He paused to clear his throat. "My family did not accept her. And she did not accept them. When she married me, her family disowned her. I was not one of them, and they turned their backs on her. She felt out of place and unwanted, and I can't blame her. My poor Cynara was withering away here, deprived of the freedom she loved. I know she loved me, but when my father and older brother suddenly died and I inherited the title, the thought of being Lady Llewellyn overwhelmed her. She fled. In the confusion of untangling the estates and arranging the funerals, I could not find her. I learned later that as her family had been rejected by the other Romany, they had taken her back. But I never stopped loving her."

"Would you have brought her back if you'd found her?"

Sir Griffyn David Llewellyn, fifth baronet, descended from ancient Welsh kings, stared at his daughter for a long moment. She had never asked this question. Then he said simply, "Yes. I could not have done anything else, whether I'd known about you or not. I always loved her. She was—" He paused and looked out over the garden toward the woods where the gypsies had camped so long ago. "Cynara was," he continued softly, and Rhianna had the feeling that he'd forgotten she was there as he talked, "the most beautiful, *alive* creature I had ever met. No other woman could compete with her. There was a unique quality about her that eclipsed every woman I'd ever met. And still does."

Rhianna's throat tightened, and she fought the rising press of tears. Coming back to England had opened painful memories for both of them, it seemed.

"She never wanted anyone else," she said after a moment. Her father's gaze shifted to her. "I used to wonder why she refused men who came to offer for her, men who would have given her anything she wanted. Of course, as a child I had romantic visions of my mysterious father arriving one day to take us away with him."

"I would have. I tried to find her, but old Manuel hated me and took the entire band away from England. It was only when he was dying that he honored Cynara's last request to allow you to choose which life you wanted."

"I wasn't given that choice."

"No," Llewellyn admitted, "you were not. I knew you would be too young and frightened to want to leave the life you'd known for one you didn't. But have I been such a bad father?"

Rhianna shook her head. "No. No, Papa, you haven't." She put her hand on his arm, and saw his facial muscles relax into an expression of relief. A wave of affection for him washed over her. He tried so hard, and though there were times, like now, when she resented the way he had maneuvered her life, his motive had been love. Remembering that was usually enough to ease the worst of her resentment.

"So now we're back in Wiltshire. What pressing problems made it so urgent for us to leave London, Papa? There's more to it than you've told me, isn't there."

The baronet rose, pulling Rhianna to her feet. Sunlight made his gray hair shine softly and picked out the remnants of copper threading through it.

"As you know, that French madman Napoleon has overrun most of Europe, making our travels too dangerous. The Corsican seems to be everywhere. Except London, thank God. At least that was still the same. But you are right—I have very personal reasons for returning to Wiltshire instead of remaining in London any longer. As you are of marriageable age, I have arranged for you to meet the nephew of one of my dearest friends. There is to be a ball tomorrow night at Huntington Manor, and we are to attend. Ah ah—I know what you're about to say. I see that rebellious gleam in your eyes." He smiled ruefully. "Just meet him. If you do not like him, I shan't press you to marry him, child."

"Marriage?" Rhianna shook her head, reluctant to even consider it. She'd not met anyone who interested her. Most of the eligible suitors had bored her almost to tears. She supposed that anyone who had enjoyed the comparative freedom she had enjoyed as a child would naturally feel stifled by the strict conventions of society.

"I don't care to be married," she said firmly. "And besides—you haven't been well lately. How is your head?"

"A dull ache, nothing serious." He pursed his lips and sighed. "I don't plan to pop off anytime soon, but it is inevitable that I shall not always be here, 'Anna. I should like to see you married and happy, with a man to care for you."

"Then don't leg-shackle me to a dull twit who hunts fox all day and plays whist all night."

"Your language is atrocious. Did Mr. Bellingham teach you to talk thusly?"

She made a face. "I paid attention to those young bucks on Rotten Row, who seem to take great pride in doing exactly the sort of thing I find tedious."

"'Anna . . . just meet him. That's all I ask of you. I think you will like Viscount Roxbury. He's only recently come into the title and is said to be one of the best catches in England."

"Then what would he want with a baronet's daughter?"

Llewellyn looked pained. "A baronet may not be an earl, but my family fought with the Welsh and English kings, and our lineage is just as good as Roxbury's."

"Oh Papa, I did not mean to insult you."

Her father managed a smile. "I'm not insulted. I just want you to be aware of the fact that your lineage is as good or better than anyone's you'll happen to meet at the ball. Remember that."

Rhianna did not mention the snubs she'd overheard in London, the speculation that she was a bastard, a gypsy slut's child by an eccentric Welsh baronet. Even the marriage lines that her father could produce had not mattered to most, but she would not hurt him by pointing out the flaw in his logic.

No, she would go to the ball, as her father wanted. And she would do her best to be polite and pretend to enjoy it, when what she would really like was to miss the ball and ride her favorite horse over the moors. Riding was the only time she felt free.

"I'll wear the new blue silk dress you bought me," she said, and saw her father smile delightedly.

"Splendid. You'll capture the heart of every man there."

Lights glittered from tall, mullioned windows and along the curving drive of the sprawling mansion. Gleaming black landaus emblazoned with family crests waited in line to disgorge passengers at the curved flight of stairs leading up to the front doors. Uniformed footmen in brilliant livery and white-powdered wigs handed ladies from their vehicles to the paving stones.

When their carriage pulled to a halt and the baronet's footman leaped down to open the door, Rhianna gathered her silk skirts in a gloved hand and allowed him to help her to the ground. She stifled a sigh as she ascended the flight of stairs to the front door. She particularly hated these affairs. Too much strong perfume spiced the air and made her nauseous, and the brittle laughter and gay chatter made her ears ring.

Her father leaned forward, squeezing her arm in a comforting gesture. "You're the most beautiful woman here, my child," he whispered. She managed a faint smile as she nervously smoothed her skirts.

She heard their names announced and then everything became a blur as she murmured greetings and tried to recall the proper names and titles of those she was being introduced to as well as those she'd met before.

The women sparkled like jewels, light flashing from brilliant tiaras and family gems that had been brought out for the occasion. Their full skirts were trimmed with gilt and braid and feathers. Rhianna felt very plain in her simple blue silk. She should have worn something more extravagant—more jewels, perhaps, than the simple pearl necklace around her throat and the gold and pearl earrings—or put her hair up in a more ornate style. But no, she preferred comfort to fashion. It was a bone of contention between her and her father as well as her devoted maid, Serena.

Despite the chill of the evening, the press of the crowd and the hundreds of lit tapers made the rooms stuffy and uncomfortable. Rhianna gazed longingly at a set of French doors that opened onto a wide veranda. There had been no sign yet of Lord Roxbury, and her father had decided to search him out, leaving Rhianna in the company of a Lady Shively.

"I'll be back quickly," he murmured and smiled absently at the widowed Lady Shively, who was trying in vain to flirt with him. Rhianna wanted to laugh, but pretended to cough instead, earning a glare from the lady.

"I hope you aren't ill," Lady Shively said with an expression of distaste.

"Not very," Rhianna replied blithely. "The physician said I am almost well. Why, I have not had the flux for two days now, and—was it something I said, my lady?"

Horrified, Lady Shively made her excuses, backed rapidly away, and left Rhianna standing alone in the crowd.

Serves her right for being so condescending, she thought with a pleased smile.

Rhianna made her way determinedly toward the open French doors. It was a relief to step out into the night air. Chinese lanterns lit up the veranda, swaying pools of light that showered over stone urns filled with flowers. Lilacs spiced the air with a sweet fragrance, shadowing a walkway below the veranda.

Rhianna leaned against the veranda wall, looking below into the garden. She heard a woman laugh, and her companion shushed her. Curious, she leaned over the balustrade to see the couple below. Their voices carried on the night air.

"Don't let him hear you, Felicia. I don't want to have to meet him."

"Frightened, my lord?" the woman named Felicia teased. "I have heard that the devil earl is deadly with a sword, and has not yet met his match with pistols."

The man scowled, and Rhianna could hear the anger in his tone when he replied, "No, I am not frightened. I just have no desire to behave as an ill-bred mongrel at a social function."

"Are you saying the earl is an ill-bred mongrel then?" Felicia tapped the gentleman playfully with her folded fan. " 'Tis not his breeding that is at fault, I understand, but his behavior. After all, he did murder his uncle!"

"That was never proven, Felicia."

"Defending him? My, how noble you are, when everyone knows he did it. He was found with the body, and blood was on his hands. Not that I blame him. Lord Montagu was a gamester and a rake, and would have ruined him within the year if he'd not been killed. Still, I find it interesting that the magistrates allowed him to go free. Being an earl has some compensation, wouldn't you say?"

"The magistrates allowed him to go free because he was not proven to be guilty. And he was only a boy at the time."

Who was this devil earl rumored to be a murderer?

"Nonetheless," Felicia was saying gaily, her laughter tinged with that brightness that comes from drinking too much champagne, "the devil earl dares to show his face wherever he pleases, not caring what people say about him. That takes a certain *savoir faire,* I think, don't you?"

"It takes a damnable bit of recklessness is what I think," her companion muttered, and Rhianna noted the way he kept glancing around as if nervous of being overheard. "I say, Felicia, do stop talking about it. Between Wolverton and that bloody highwayman roaming the roads, I am beginning to think the peaceful meadows of Wiltshire have been cursed."

Wolverton. Rhianna paused, trying to remember why that name startled her. Then she recalled a youthful, angry face and an arrogance that disguised grief and unhappiness. Of course. Chance. The young earl who had lost the race against Nicolo so long ago—it seemed if he had not fared well in the years since.

A sudden memory jogged her, of an intense voice filled with bitterness and anger, the words drawled mockingly.

"Which do you think it will be, lovely Rhianna? Will I be done in by my uncle so that he inherits—or will I kill the bastard before he can kill me?"

She shivered. Perhaps there was something to Felicia's assumption that the earl of Wolverton had killed his uncle after all.

Chapter 5

"Good evening, my lord."

Chance turned, and lifted an eyebrow. "I see you have not yet locked up the young ladies to protect them from me, Keswick. How remiss of you."

George Harland Gladwin, Viscount Keswick, had the grace to flush. "You know I never meant that remark in the context it was repeated, Wolverton. It's just that you have a remarkable effect on certain sensitive young ladies, and it can become quite distressing."

Chance lifted his glass in a mocking gesture. "Can it? I always find it entertaining."

Keswick, short and stocky with a kind face, sighed. "If I didn't know you to be a decent sort, I might believe this poppycock you allow people to think. Why don't you deny any of the rumors?"

"What? And deprive the good citizens of Wiltshire their savoring of every delicious detail? Not by any means, Keswick. I could not be so cruel."

Shaking his head, Keswick said, "Who are you hunting tonight, Wolverton?"

"Must I be hunting?"

"Yes. Either a woman or one of your other luckless preys could be the only thing to draw you out to a country ball, and I know it."

"Ah Keswick, you wrong me. You sent me an invitation, did you not?"

"Yes, but you never accept unless you feel it will benefit you. What is the benefit tonight?"

Chance glanced around the crowded room. The noise of music and laughter was almost overpowering. Across the room, he saw Lord Heffington conversing with a man he did not know.

"Who is that talking to Heffington?" he murmured.

Keswick groaned. "Don't try to convince me that you don't have a personal interest in knowing, and I shudder to think what it might be. Another bill in Parliament?"

"I don't sit in Parliament, as you well know." He sipped at his champagne. "Who is he?"

"Viscount Roxbury. Recently inherited the title on his mother's side. A rather disagreeable fellow, but in great demand at gaming tables."

"Do tell. I seem to recall his name being used rather frequently in certain places."

"No doubt. Back off now, Wolf, and show some restraint. Since you rarely attend these affairs, I shall deem it my duty to introduce you to those fortunate few who have yet to make your cynical acquaintance. Come and greet your nearest neighbor. You may remember him, though he left England when you were just a boy. He has recently returned from years abroad."

"How fascinating. I'd much rather drink your champagne—brandy, if you will offer it—and salivate over the delectable lovelies gathered here." Chance let his gaze drift over the crowd, ignoring the curious glances and whispers. "They remind me of a room filled with pigeons —witless and constantly cooing."

"You're damned rude, Wolf," Keswick said with a trace of irritation. "Why do you bother coming if you hate these things so?"

"It gives the locals something else to talk about. And it amuses me to make them nervous."

"Sometimes I must agree with the general perception that named you the devil earl. Come along, and I shall bore you with a round of introductions. And don't show too much interest in the baronet's beautiful daughter, either. 'Anna is not at all suitable for what you'd have in mind."

"Then I won't waste my time meeting her," Chance drawled before taking pity on Keswick's pained expression and allowing him to lead the way across the crowded room.

He wondered why he *had* come. It wasn't just to annoy the other guests. There was always the possibility that he would learn something important, overhear a useful scrap of conversation. But was it worth the hours of maintaining an indifference that he didn't feel? He wasn't at all certain of that.

A hand on his arm stopped him, and he half-turned, not surprised to see Lady Wimberley gazing up at him. Her lovely face was composed and serene, but he recognized the glitter in her large gray eyes.

"You have not called on me lately, Wolverton," she said in a low voice.

"No. I have been rather busy. How is your charming husband, by the way? I understand that he has given up his actress in favor of a squire's wife. I believe the actress had begun to bore him, don't you? Ah well. This must give you much more free time to spend with your head groom."

"Don't be so offensive. I know what game you're playing." She smiled, but it didn't reach her eyes and he could see the fury glittering there instead. "I've been expecting you to visit me, Chance."

"Thalia, do not bore me with strident demands or an inquisition. I do not react favorably to either."

"You do not react well to anything but exactly what

you want." Her mouth thinned into a taut line, and he was aware of the curious glances in their direction. "If we were not in such a public place—" she began, and he cut her off.

"You would hear much more than you want to hear from me. Keswick is waiting."

He turned and left her standing in the doorway, glaring after him furiously. Lady Wimberley had been a distraction, and a pleasant one until she'd begun to make demands of his time and affections. He would send her a necklace as a parting gift and be done with it.

Keswick beckoned to him, lifting an eyebrow and saying in a low tone, "You should really stick to cyprians, you know. I don't think another duel with an angry husband will do you any good."

"It will do the angry husband even less good."

"You can't go through life disposing of men you've cuckolded, for chrissake."

"I don't cuckold them. They do it to themselves."

A troubled expression creased Keswick's face, and Chance felt a pang of regret that he was causing him distress. Of everyone he knew, only Keswick had stood by him while vicious rumors circulated. They'd been boyhood chums, even attended Eton together until fate had stepped in and wrenched Chance's life apart. After his uncle's death, Keswick's father had been appointed his guardian until he reached his majority. Chance joggled Keswick gently and grinned.

"Cheer up, Georgie. I will be a model guest this evening just for you."

Keswick smiled faintly. "Perhaps one of these days I will understand you, Wolf."

"God, I hope not. The notion terrifies me."

Keswick laughed, and Chance resigned himself to being introduced to his neighbor when they stopped beside an older man of medium height and graying red hair.

"This is Sir Griffyn Llewellyn," Keswick said. "His property adjoins yours on the east side."

Sir Griffyn turned with an easy smile. "I met you a long time ago, though you were a small lad then and probably don't recall it. You were out riding with your father, and I had just been unseated by a fiery new stallion. The earl was kind enough to offer me your mount to return home."

"Ah, I do recall that. I was quite angry at the time, I remember. It was a new horse, and I didn't want to see anyone else ride him."

"If I recall correctly, you informed me of that fact in a most decided fashion."

Chance smiled. "And got a thorough caning for my rudeness when we returned home, I assure you."

Llewellyn laughed, then turned toward a young woman who had been dancing with a man Chance recognized as the Viscount Roxbury. Roxbury came to an abrupt halt when he was introduced to Chance.

"Wolverton?" the viscount drawled, "I've heard of you. How surprising to see you here."

"Is it? I'm still allowed in some homes, you know."

"Not many, I understand."

"Roxbury," Llewellyn interrupted, "I was just renewing my acquaintance with Lord Wolverton. I admired his father a great deal."

The implication was obvious, even to Roxbury, and he nodded stiffly before turning to the girl. He bowed, lifting her hand to his lips. Chance saw her frown slightly.

"Until later, Miss Llewellyn. I shall count the hours." Roxbury nodded to the baronet, then strode away. Chance watched him, fighting down the impulse to respond to the cut.

"The earl is our neighbor," Llewellyn was saying to the young woman when Chance's attention returned to him. "I knew him when he was a child. My daughter 'Anna, my lord."

Chance barely glanced at her, more concerned at the moment with Roxbury. Then her face struck a chord of memory and he transferred his attention back to the girl. She was gazing at him expectantly.

"I am pleased to make your acquaintance, Miss Llewellyn," he said finally and was aware of a flare of disappointment in her eyes. There was something vaguely familiar about her, and he tried to recall what he'd heard about Sir Griffyn Llewellyn. So much had been said, and he largely disregarded any rumors or gossip that did not directly affect him, yet he knew there was something he was supposed to recall. The memory teased him, lingering just out of reach.

He stared at her more closely. She was tall for a woman, and slender. Her gown had none of the vulgar display that many of the other women wore, but was simple in style and elegant in fashion. Of course, a woman as lovely as 'Anna Llewellyn could dress in a flour sack and be exquisite.

Her hair was dark, with rich hues of red in the shining mass that curled around her heart-shaped face and fell to her waist in the back. It was a popular hairstyle but somehow, on this particular young woman, it was exotic. There was a vibrancy to her, lurking just beneath her composed surface. He wanted to reach out and take her hand, just to touch her.

Strangest of all, he felt he should know her. But as far as he knew, he had never even seen the baronet's daughter before.

"Would you care to dance, Miss Llewellyn?" he asked impulsively, aware of Keswick's stare. He rarely danced at these functions, declaring it a waste of time and only an unnecessary preamble to what should come later.

To his surprise, she nodded. He took her arm and led her onto the floor. There was a warmth and vibrancy that he could feel even through the silk sleeves of her gown, and he resisted the urge to let his hand move down to settle in the small of her back.

She flicked him a curious upward glance through lashes that were long and lush, her eyes a startling blue that made him think of a summer sky. Her mouth, however, made him think of much more physical pleasures, of soft whispers and heated sheets, the luxurious sensation of a woman's hand sliding over his body as he leisurely kissed her mouth. It occurred to him with a start of surprise that he would very much enjoy seducing 'Anna Llewellyn. He frowned darkly.

Sets had been formed for a country dance, and he fought a wave of impatience when the steps took him away from her so that he could not engage her in conversation. Then he chided himself for being foolish. He did not deflower innocent young women, and it was quite apparent that 'Anna Llewellyn was just that. As he would not offer an honorable proposal, and he intended to ignore the inclination to seduce her, he was wasting his time. Keswick was right.

As soon as the dance ended, he returned her to her father with a polite comment, then escaped as quickly as possible. He found Keswick near the musician's box.

"I'm leaving, George."

Keswick turned. "I am glad to see you again. Don't let the gossip keep you away from Huntington."

"It's been too many years to allow that. I ignore it."

"That must be deuced hard to do."

"Only at times." Chance glanced around him, suddenly stifled by the chatter, music, and laughter. "I'll come to see you soon, George."

"I'll expect you."

Once outside, Chance drew in a deep breath of fresh air. A full moon had risen high in the sky, silvering the ground. It was getting late, and he had work to do. The thought was exhilarating, and he smiled grimly as he contemplated the night ahead.

Rhianna stared after him. He didn't remember her. She shouldn't be surprised. He'd left her behind without a thought so long ago, never bothering to seek her out again. Marisa had been right in warning her away from him, as it was obvious he could put her from his mind quite easily. It had been a long time since she'd thought of the young earl who had captured her imagination and empathy that long-ago day. The events that had followed his visit had eclipsed his memory for a while, and by the time she'd been able to think of anything other than the way her life had so radically changed, Chance had been only a vague, pleasant memory.

Now, she'd met him again, and she wondered how she had ever managed to put him from her mind. The intense boy had grown into a vital man, his presence so forceful no one could ignore him. She'd heard the rumors earlier, and understood them when she'd seen his tall, lithe frame lounging impatiently beside her father.

Chance Lancaster, tenth earl of Wolverton, was not a man one could ignore. Hate, perhaps, or fear, but never ignore. Even Roxbury had muttered an oath beneath his breath upon meeting him, and she'd felt his tension.

Roxbury. She frowned. He was—puzzling. He was handsome enough, she supposed, in a foppish sort of way, but she'd never been fond of men who paid so much attention to their toilette. The intricate neck cloths and tight pantaloons men wore conveyed a certain elegant flair that she found attractive on some gentlemen. On others, she was reminded of peacocks.

Chance, she'd noted, flaunted convention. He had appeared at the ball in tight breeches and calf-length boots of soft leather instead of the *de rigueur* knee breeches and silk hose and buckled pumps the other men were wearing. His neck cloth had been carelessly tied, his frock coat and silk vest impeccable but austere.

He was a man who needed no adornment to be impressive. Just his tall, powerful frame was enough to draw the eye, and the feminine glances in his direction were filled with admiration as well as speculation. Chance tied his dark hair back with a plain ribbon, and his side whiskers were cut short. His square jaw was the same as it had been as a youth's—stubborn and arrogant. And his eyes—oh, those devil-angel eyes, with ridiculously long lashes that could hide the wicked gleam in depths black as sin and filled with mockery. Yes, he was definitely a man who drew attention, and she couldn't help but notice that he completely disregarded the female sighs and glances.

Even hers.

She smiled slightly. It had not escaped her notice that he had apparently decided she was not a candidate for brisk and casual bedding, either. Her swift return to her father's side had given evidence of that. She didn't know whether to be insulted or intrigued.

"More punch, m'dear?" her father asked.

"Yes. It's quite hot in here, don't you think?"

A faint smile tugged at the corners of her father's mouth. "Are you hinting that we should depart, 'Anna?"

"Well, it *is* getting rather late, and I promised Monsieur Fournier that I would meet him early tomorrow."

"Fournier would understand if you were to be late."

Rhianna tucked her hand into the crook of his arm. "But I would really like to get an early start."

He gave her hand an affectionate pat. "I understand, though why you insist upon being scandalous enough to take fencing lessons is beyond me. If it becomes well known, you may never find a suitable husband."

"Now Papa, we made a bargain . . ."

Llewellyn groaned. "Yes, I remember. I shall not take umbrage at your fencing if you will continue your singing lessons and needlepoint."

"I often think you have the best part of the bargain, though I do enjoy matching skills with Monsieur Fournier."

"No doubt. He is one of the foremost fencers in the country." He sighed. "Very well. Let us depart so that you are fresh in the morning. I do not wish to hear Fournier's nasal-toned complaints."

Rhianna smiled. There were times she thought her father really didn't mind her fencing at all. He seemed to take a sort of pleasure in her accomplishments.

"I say," Lord Keswick admonished when they told him they were leaving, "do be careful when traveling tonight. There is a full moon."

Rhianna stared at him. "What on earth can that matter?"

"Do you mean you haven't heard? Oh—I forgot that you have only been back in the country for a few weeks." Keswick glanced at the baronet and lowered his voice. "Highwaymen. Or p'raps I should say, one particular highwayman, has the entire county in an uproar."

"You don't say," the baronet exclaimed. "I take it that he preys in this vicinity."

"Indeed. He particularly likes the well-traveled road to Bath. But only on the night of a full moon. One never knows which full moon, because he ofttimes lets several months go by before riding again. The locals call him the Moon Rider, and claim he can vanish into thin air."

"A highwayman?" Rhianna smiled. "I should think the sheriff would quickly apprehend him if his habits are that well-known, my lord."

"Ah, but therein lies the rub, Miss Llewellyn. None of the authorities have been able to get close enough to him to describe him, much less capture him. Only his victims have been unfortunate enough to see him closely."

She shivered. "Victims? I take it he is a murderer, then."

"Not usually. If a man is foolish enough to resist, the Moon Rider dispatches him quickly enough. His swordsmanship is unequaled. Once, he fought three young bucks at the same time and came out the victor."

"Did he? How impressive. I assume that he steals their valuables, then just disappears like the mist."

Lord Keswick stared at her in mild reproach. "You think I jest."

"Well, it does seem that gossip often grows larger with each telling. Why, for instance, does he only ride on the night of a full moon? It seems rather silly to me and very theatrical."

"P'raps, but that is the truth. The Moon Rider flaunts the conventional security of dark clothes and horse as well. He clads himself in pure white and rides a white stallion."

"Oh, poppycock," Rhianna couldn't help saying. "He would be as easily seen at night as a bonfire!"

"You'd think so, wouldn't you?" A faint smile curved Lord Keswick's mouth, and Rhianna saw that she'd offended him.

"I don't mean to impugn your honesty, my lord, but it does seem rather far-fetched, you must admit."

"If I didn't know better, perhaps I would think so." He made a small bow over her hand, then straightened. "I wish you Godspeed and a safe journey home."

His words of warning lingered in her mind despite her skepticism, and Rhianna barely listened to her father's reproaches as their carriage rocked along the rutted road toward Serenity House.

"I know you were reared to be forthright to the point of rudeness," he was saying with a heavy sigh, "but really, I would think after all these years you would recall the lessons of those expensive tutors I hired. It was very ill-bred and unmannerly to contradict your host, 'Anna."

"If he had said that goblins inhabit St. James's would you not have argued the point, Papa?"

"But that is quite different. And argument is not always the best tactic. Diversion works wonders."

Rhianna smiled reluctantly. "Perhaps I should have mentioned goblins in the church, then, as a distraction."

"It couldn't have been much worse than what you did say."

Silence fell, and in the pale light of the coach lamps, Rhianna saw the disgruntled expression on her father's face. She almost felt sorry for him, though she'd warned him years before that she would not be the tractable, demure daughter that he'd envisioned when he found her. She'd been brought up with the freedom of people who enjoyed life as they found it. When she recalled Sir Griffyn's horror the first time she had stripped to thin petticoats and layers of silver bangles and danced barefoot in the moonlight, she wondered if he really remembered Cynara at all.

Her mother could not have completely cast off her own nature. Did her father seek to change Rhianna so that she would not abandon him as her mother had done? She often wondered if that was behind his almost desperate attempts to instill "gentility" in her.

Rhianna was startled from her musings when the coach rocked violently in a rut.

"Whatever is Beakins doing?" she asked crossly. "He has a heavy hand with the horses, Papa. You must speak to him again."

"Beakins is a very competent coachman." Llewellyn knocked on the roof of the coach with his gold-headed cane, however, shouting at Beakins to be more careful.

There was no reply, and the carriage swayed from side to side, picking up speed. Rhianna grasped a leather strap to keep from sliding to the floor. Llewellyn tapped more angrily on the roof with his cane.

The tiny door snapped open, and there was a brief glimpse of a footman's wide-eyed face. He shouted something in a broad Yorkshire dialect that Rhianna didn't understand, and her father swore softly.

"What did he say, Papa?"

"Blast that Keswick, I believe he brought this on us by repeating that bloody tale," Llewellyn said shortly, and began unscrewing the head of his gold cane.

"Whatever do you mean?" Rhianna gave a start when her father drew out a long, thin sword. "What—" She paused, suddenly understanding. "It's the highwayman, isn't it? That is what he said—*The Moon Rider*. Oh Papa, don't be foolish. Put away your sword. That flimsy length cannot withstand much, as you must know."

"It's for defense, not offense."

Llewellyn's terse comment made Rhianna's throat tighten. She clasped the leather strap more firmly, listening to the sounds from outside the coach. Hoofbeats drummed steadily on the rutted road, and the wheels made a loud, whining sound. She wasn't surprised to hear a shot split the air, and even less surprised when the coach slowed to a halt.

Voices were muffled, and a sharp cry of pain made her shudder with apprehension. There was the unmistakable sound of a scuffle, then total, complete silence.

That was the most unnerving of all. She waited, her hair lifting on the back of her neck. The coach lamps flickered over her father's pale, set face, and she wondered if she looked as anxious.

"Stand and deliver," she heard the highwayman say as the coach door was jerked open. Rhianna gasped at the stark white apparition.

Keswick had not exaggerated. The highwayman was swathed in white from head to foot, and she thought at once of the childhood tales of ghosts that had made her shiver with delicious dread.

There was nothing delicious about this apparition.

A silk mask of snow-white was over his face, dark eyes seeming to burn like banked fires beneath the material. Only his mouth was partially visible, and he was repeating the order to stand and deliver. He stepped closer to the coach, his voice rough and impatient.

Llewellyn leaned forward into the light, and the masked highwayman checked his forward movement.

"We have no valuables," her father said boldly. Lantern light glittered along the slender length of the cane sword he held in one hand. "I demand that you go your own way and leave us in peace."

"Don't be a fool," the Moon Rider said harshly. "Put away your weapon, sir."

"I have never yielded to a coward, and only cowards hide behind a mask, you bloody knave." He gave a thrust of his sword. There was a loud clang of metal and the whisk of steel on steel before Llewellyn's sword went flying through the air.

For a moment, Rhianna thought the highwayman intended to run her father through with his drawn sword. Then he lowered it slightly. She studied him, trying to fix his image in her mind so that she could describe him to the sheriff.

A pistol was tucked into the belt he wore around a long coat of white wool. The night wind tugged at a cape billowing behind him. Boots of white leather fit him to the knee, and his snug breeches were streaked with mud. He should have been a laughable figure, but he exuded such fierce menace that Rhianna could find no jest in what she'd earlier thought an amusing hoax.

"Give me one reason why I should not kill you on the spot," the Moon Rider said softly.

Rhianna shivered. "Please sir—" Her voice quivered and she paused to steady it. "Please—my father means no harm. Let us pass."

"One must pay the toll to pass this road tonight, my lovely lady." He stepped closer, and Rhianna was reminded of the restless prowl of a panther she'd once seen. "What have you to pay me?"

Despite her father's angry growl, Rhianna quickly unfastened her pearl necklace and held it out. "This. Take it and go. It's all of worth that I have, little though it is."

The Moon Rider laughed softly. "Ah, you underestimate yourself, my lady fair." He reached out and took the necklace from her gloved hand, then grasped her fingers. When her father moved suddenly, he was checked by the pistol cocked and aimed at him.

"Do not be hasty, my friend," the highwayman mocked. "A blast of ball and powder is much messier than the clean slice of a sword. Rest easy. I do not intend to debauch your daughter." He pulled her slightly closer. "Though she is a very tempting morsel, I must admit."

"You swine," Llewellyn choked out. Rhianna was

alarmed at his high color. She tugged her hand free of the Moon Rider's grasp.

"You have what you wanted, now go and leave us in peace," she said firmly. For a moment, she thought he would grab her again, but he stepped back.

"My thanks for the necklace."

"Take it to hell with you," Llewellyn snarled. Rhianna put a restraining hand on his arm. The Moon Rider only laughed, however, and reached out for his horse.

Rhianna's eyes widened. She hadn't noticed the horse, but now she saw that it was a magnificent Arabian. Sleek and muscled, the pure white beast was as superb an animal as any she'd ever seen and she couldn't help a soft exclamation of admiration.

"Oh! He's beautiful. . . ."

The Moon Rider swung into his saddle and glanced back at her. "I salute your perception, my fair lady."

Rhianna watched, her fear fading as the highwayman swung his horse around and pounded off into the shadows. He was a vivid contrast to the darker shapes of trees and bushes, easily seen until he crested the hill. Then, to her amazement, with the full moon silvering the ground and making it almost shimmer with light, he seemed to vanish. She blinked. It couldn't be. He was a man, not a ghost.

One of the footmen gave a whimper of pure fear. She ignored it as she stared at the crest of the hill, waiting for she didn't know what.

Then she saw him, a faint outline barely visible. He'd paused and was looking back at the coach. Several heartbeats thudded past, then he was gone again, and she couldn't recall later if he'd actually ridden away or somehow just faded into nothing.

Chapter 6

"What a wretched business!" Rhianna turned to look at her father and paused. "Papa, are you feeling unwell?"

Sir Griffyn put a shaky hand to his head, palm over his eyes. "It's m'head. Dammmmm—damnable ache."

He lurched forward slightly, his weight heavy against her, pressing her sideways against the squabs. "Papa!" she cried, horrified. He said something else then, a meaningless slur of words that seemed to distress him. The footman had come to the carriage door, and was staring inside.

"Fenwick—help Sir Llewellyn sit back against the cushions," she said, forcing herself to remain calm. "I fear he has become ill. We must return to the house posthaste."

It seemed to take forever to reach the comfortable house tucked in the midst of sloping lawns and tall trees, but finally they were home. Servants scurried to Sir Griffyn's side, helping him up the stairs and into the house. Rhianna snapped out orders, fear for her father overriding common courtesy or any other consideration.

"Get a stool for his feet. Put more wood on the fire. And bring him warmed brandy, quickly!"

Sir Griffyn's color had gone ashen. He stumbled between the two burly footmen who were helping him walk. His eyes didn't seem to focus, and his words were an unintelligible slur. When he was seated in a deep-cushioned chair near the fire with his feet up, Rhianna knelt anxiously by his side.

"Papa, I have sent for the physician. He shall be here shortly—oh, Papa, please try to be still."

Sir Griffyn's arms flailed in short, spasmodic motions, and his legs jerked uncontrollably. His mouth was slack as he stared wildly around him. Rhianna was frightened. There was something terribly wrong with him, more than just an ordinary illness. She soothed him as best she could. It seemed to take forever for the physician to arrive from the village.

"Apoplexy," Dr. Throgmorton said gravely. "I fear your father has suffered some sort of cataclysm of the brain."

Rhianna stared at him. "Whatever are you talking about?"

"It's not uncommon and quite often fatal. Sir Griffyn must have had a recent shock or distress to cause this calamity."

"Yes. We were accosted by a highwayman only a short time before he fell ill."

Throgmorton sighed heavily. "It has caused a paralysis of the brain, I fear. In some cases, it descends into dementia of a sort. If he lives, he may become unmanageable. I suggest that you look into an asylum, and—"

"No!" The word exploded from her, and she drew in a deep breath at the physician's startled expression. "I will take care of my father. What can be done for him?"

"Truly, child, he is a complete invalid. It would be much better for him—and for you, as you are young and sensitive—if he were to go to an institution that can care for him properly. They have certain therapeutic measures there—"

"I have seen some of the therapeutic measures in asylums such as you speak of, Doctor. My father will not go to one of them."

Rhianna dragged in a deep breath. Once, not understanding the nature of the outing, she had accompanied some young acquaintances in London to Bedlam. The scenes there had horrified her, and were still imprinted on her mind. No, she would not send her father to a place such as Throgmorton suggested. Not as long as she had wit and body to keep him with her.

"Thank you, Doctor, for coming so quickly. Grayson will show you out."

"Miss Llewellyn, I know this is a shock, but you must see that you cannot provide proper care for him."

"Good evening, sir." Rhianna turned away and went back into her father's bedchamber, shutting the door behind her.

Sir Griffyn lay quietly now, obviously in a drugged sleep, his breathing ragged. She sat in the chair at his bedside. For a long time, she didn't move, but sat staring into the shadows.

"Damn piece of work," Chance muttered in disgust as he tossed the pearl necklace to a table. The entire night had been a disaster. First that boring ball—and the short set-to with Thalia that left a sour taste in his mouth—and then he'd had the bloody bad luck to stop the wrong carriage. He'd not recognized Llewellyn's crest. It was very similar to that of Heffington's, and he'd barely glanced at it before making his move.

He peeled off his gloves and threw them carelessly down next to the necklace. Miss Llewellyn had been right. The pearls weren't worth much. He'd toyed with the notion of stealing a kiss from her, more to pique her than anything else, but a glance at Sir Griffyn's outraged face had persuaded him not to alarm that gentleman any further. He liked the baronet, much to his surprise. There had been a sincerity and decency in his conversation that few men showed him. Odd, that after eight years abroad and only a short stay in the city the baronet should return to his country estates. Local gossip had hinted that bad finances due to recent gambling debts had forced the closing of the country house, but apparently that was incorrect.

Chance moved to the side cabinet and poured brandy into a snifter, swirling it thoughtfully. His mind drifted from Llewellyn to his unfinished business. Heffington had been at the ball. He'd been talking with Roxbury, which led to some interesting speculation. It had not been a casual conversation; he'd seen Heffington grow quite red in the face at one point. Of course, Roxbury did seem to be an unmitigated ass, but there were too many of those for Heffington to become so agitated.

It would have been deuced lucky to discover a link between Heffington and Roxbury, and God knew, he needed a stroke of good fortune. He downed a swallow of brandy, then bent to the task of removing boots and spurs. Mud smeared the thick carpet, and he thought of Hobson's dismay on seeing it. The loyal retainer was almost blind, but not too blind to spot mud on his precious carpets. Chance smiled faintly.

In moments, white breeches and plain white shirt lay atop the discarded boots. He added cape and gloves to the pile. After shrugging into his robe, he moved to the bell pull. Hobson would be expecting his ring, waiting up like an old mother hen to see his charge safely home.

It took longer and longer for the old man to make his way up the stairs, but each time Chance suggested allowing him to retire in comfort to a cozy house of his choosing, he became affronted.

"I came here as a lad, and I shall retire when they lay me out, my lord," Hobson was fond of saying. Chance didn't have the heart to tell him that his efficiency as a servant was more burden than help. He'd rather see Hobson enjoying his last years in idle comfort, but it was apparent that they did not see eye to eye on that subject.

"Was your evening successful, my lord?" Hobson inquired when he entered the room. He began to gather up the soiled garments from the table where Chance had placed them so he wouldn't have to bend. They would be returned spotless and mended, seen to by the old man himself so that none could question.

"No. Only minimally." Chance frowned slightly. The pearl necklace lay atop the table, a silent reproach. He should have left her the necklace—said something theatrically gallant about not casting pearls before swine, he supposed, but he hadn't been in the mood. The irritation of discovering Llewellyn instead of Heffington had been bad enough, but then the baronet's daughter had given him such a scathing glance of contempt that he'd not been able to resist. Only the slight quaver of her voice when he'd threatened to hurt her father had hinted at her vulnerability.

Hobson saw the necklace and lifted it, turning to gaze at Chance. "A pretty enough bauble."

He shrugged. "Only a fraction as lovely as the lady who wore it, however."

"Shall I put it with the others?"

"No. This one—I have other plans for." He held out his hand, and Hobson coiled the necklace in his palm.

"Indeed."

No censure attended his comment, but Chance knew that the old man still disapproved of what he was doing.

Not that he blamed him. A highwayman's life was usually short and rarely profitable. But he was not looking for wealth in jewels and stolen coins. The wealth he sought came most often in the form of hidden papers and confessions blurted out at the point of a sword in moonlit hours.

"Shall I bring you a tray, my lord?"

Chance looked up from the necklace in his palm and shook his head. His fingers closed around the pearls, and he had the idiotic thought that they were still warm from being around 'Anna Llewellyn's lovely throat.

"I'm not hungry, thank you. It's late, and you should be in bed."

"After I clean the mud from the carpet, I shall seek my bed, never fear. I dare not leave it for Mrs. Timmons to find in the morning. She will lament loudly."

"I'll take care of it. I'm tired, and wish to retire without the nauseating scent of cleaning fluid in my nose, thank you."

Hobson's gray brows rose dramatically, and he gave a sniff of disapproval. "A gentleman of your position must not demean himself with such things."

"Then I'll allow Mrs. Timmons to berate me for bringing in mud. Go."

A faint smile curled the edges of Hobson's mouth, and he bowed stiffly. "As you say, my lord. I should like to witness that scene."

Chance's smiling gaze met his, and he silently watched Hobson leave the room. He would never admit it aloud, but he depended on the old man much more than he should. It was a holdover from his youth, he suspected, when there had been no one to care about a surly boy but the old man. Yes, Hobson had stood by him more even than Keswick, and he would never forget it.

Stepping over the clumps of black mud on the carpet,

Chance put the pearl necklace into a small box and tucked it into a drawer. He would see that it was returned to Miss Llewellyn. Not for her sake, but for Sir Griffyn's. He had not yet descended to the level of stealing from men he liked, by God, dissolute wretch though he might be.

There was little he would not stoop to if it was a cause he wished to espouse, but he did have his standards. He sipped his brandy, and it occurred to him that he might like to meet the feisty 'Anna again. She had exhibited most unusual behavior this evening. Most young women swooned prettily, either in real or pretended horror when accosted by a highwayman.

'Anna Llewellyn had not. She had been brusque and angry, afraid only when she thought her father threatened. He was tired of country mice and sluttish ladies, and the thought of verbal fencing and amorous sparring with a worthwhile feminine adversary was intriguing. Yes, he would definitely like to see more of her.

Rhianna gazed blankly at the barrister. "What do you mean, sir?"

Mr. Blemmons, having ridden the eighty miles from London with his thick packets of files, could not meet her gaze. "Just what I said, Miss Llewellyn. There are no funds available."

"No—I don't understand. Though I've never been privy to my father's business affairs, I do know that he's enjoyed substantial success in several endeavors. Do you mean to tell me that there has been a reversal in those enterprises?"

"A severe reversal. Two of his ships were lost at sea several months ago, taken by French corsairs in the name of Napoleon, actually. It was a most grievous loss. Then the investments he'd made last year at the Exchange were dreadfully reduced. Ruined, actually." He hesitated, then gave a polite cough before adding, "Due to the rather high extent of his recent gambling losses, I'm afraid that the baronet lost his remaining money at whist and faro. His gambling debts have now been bought by a single unnamed investor. I am most sorry to burden you with this at this time, Miss Llewellyn, but you must be informed as to the reason that I cannot honor your request for further withdrawals from your father's account at Bailey and Bailey."

"Gambling debts! Has Papa been gambling?"

"Yes, I'm afraid so. And losing, unfortunately. When he was faced with so many financial reversals, Sir Griffyn attempted to replenish his dwindling assets by gambling. But he has ended up giving out so many vowels that if they were all paid, you would not have a shilling left."

Rhianna stood up, agitation making her voice sharp. "Unbelievable." He winced, and she sighed heavily. "I don't mean you, of course, Mr. Blemmons. I meant this impossible situation. What am I to do?"

Mr. Blemmons hesitated, then leaned slightly forward. "At this time, Miss Llewellyn, my suggestion is to liquidate all assets. The house in London, for instance, and its furnishings. I believe Sir Griffyn has quite a few valuable paintings that will bring in tidy sums. There are the horses, of course, and p'raps you can sell the country estate as well."

"Sell Serenity House?" Rhianna gazed at the parlor, and thought suddenly of her mother briefly inhabiting these very rooms. She'd never considered herself attached to material possessions very much, and had watched with fond indulgence her father's avid collecting of art objects and other beautiful things over the years. Yet now, at the notion she would be forced to give up the country estate as well as all the other possessions her father so loved, she rebelled.

"No," she said firmly. "Everything else may go, but not here. Not Serenity House." She met the barrister's startled gaze. "My father loves it here. And—and my mother once lived here with him." She stood up, her skirts rustling. "Make the necessary arrangements for everything else, Mr. Blemmons. I shall do what must be done."

"I understand, Miss Llewellyn." He hesitated, rising in a slow motion to pause thoughtfully. "You may eventually be forced to relinquish Serenity House as well, you know," he said in an apologetic tone. "Unless you make some wise investments or come into an inheritance or"— he coughed politely—"an advantageous marriage. Your creditors will soon demand complete payment."

"How soon?"

He seemed startled once again by her abrupt question. "Well, ah, I—perhaps six months."

"Six months. I see. I shall do what I can. Please bring me any reasonable offers, sir. I will sell my jewelry in order to pay my father's medical bills. Wait a moment, and I will fetch the box for you."

Mr. Blemmons bowed silently, and Rhianna brushed past him. She could have pulled the bell cord to summon a maid, but felt a driving need to be alone for a moment. The effort to remain composed in the face of devastating news and blind panic was almost more than she could bear. How could she keep her chin up and her calm intact when she was terrified?

Oh Marisa, where are you when I need you? I need your strength, your gift of foresight to tell me what to do. . . .

Rhianna lifted her skirts and mounted the gracefully curving flight of stairs to the second floor, her steps more steady than she felt. Outwardly, she knew she looked calm if a bit grave, but inwardly, her horror was rapidly turning to black despair. She had to keep Serenity House for her father. She had to find a way to pay for his physician, and the constant nurse he required. His condition had deteriorated rapidly, and his brief periods of consciousness were accompanied by a wild waving of arms and unintelligible speech.

Once in her bedchamber, Rhianna closed the door behind her, grateful Serena was out of the room. She closed her eyes for a moment, yielding to the clutching desperation that filled her. What could she do? She had no skills, no way to earn the necessary funds to retain so much as one corner of a stable, much less the house and grounds of the estate.

Oh, how could Papa be so foolish as to overextend himself like this?

It was commonplace, she knew, for noblemen to borrow against family estates, against the income of farms and livestock and investments. Yet, she'd never considered that her father would do the same. Or that he would be foolish enough to gamble away what little was left of his fortune.

She thought with sudden longing of the days when she'd not cared for more than a full stomach and a warm place by the fire. And perhaps a joyous dance under the moonlight, with her silver bangles making a rhythmic, happy sound. The simple life of a gypsy had its own rewards, its uncomplicated pleasures, and there were times she missed it keenly.

Rhianna opened her eyes. Gray shafts of light streamed through the tall windows across the room, making tiny squares of light on the carpet. She crossed to her ornate cherry secretary and removed a key from the drawer, then moved to the armoire and took out her jewelry box. The key made a soft clicking sound in the lock, and she flipped back the lid.

None of the jewels meant very much to her in a sentimental way, though most were gifts from her father. She lifted a sparkling emerald necklace, the stones catching fire from the dull light and gleaming in her hand. They were quite lovely, she supposed, and hoped they would bring a great deal in the market. Of course, she fully realized that she would receive far less than their actual value if it was learned that the baronet's pockets were to let. The world was full of vultures much like the highwayman who had taken her pearls.

Another horror. Almost as bad, had been the interview with the sheriff. Hamlin was a rather dull-witted man who was pedantic and prone to irritating repitition of the obvious. He had asked her to describe the stolen necklace so many times that she could have screamed. It wasn't that important. Not nearly as important as her father's descent into oblivion.

Rhianna snapped shut the lid to the box. The Moon Rider had stolen her necklace that night, but stolen much more than that from her father. He'd stolen Sir Griffyn's health.

A frown tucked her brows over her eyes. Marisa's warning from so long ago came to mind suddenly—was this the evil moon she'd been warned about? *Moon Rider.* She shivered.

It occurred to her to wonder if the Moon Rider earned very much at his dishonest trade. He must, or he would not continue risking life and limb in that way.

If only women could dare as much, riding the high roads and demanding money, wearing a disguise. . . . Her heart lurched in sudden excitement. She was as accomplished a rider as any man, and even Monsieur Fournier said she was much too expert with an épée to be female. And after all, she'd learned the finesse of stealing in her early years, hadn't she? Oh, it was insane, but she knew she could do it, and the Moon Rider would get the blame. She owed the damn thief that much, for hurting her father as he had.

Yes, she would soon avenge her father's stolen health, as well as keep him in comfort. And she would do it with the Moon Rider's own tools.

She smiled, feeling the first surge of hope she'd felt since her father's collapse.

Chapter 7

"I'm sorry to inform you, my lord, that Sir Griffyn is indisposed."

"Indisposed. Very well. I'll see Miss Llewellyn then." Chance frowned impatiently when the servant hesitated. "I take it that *she* is not indisposed as well?"

The footman flushed. "No, my lord. I shall see if she is receiving."

Annoyed, and wondering if he'd been wrong about Sir Griffyn's kinder feelings toward him, Chance paced the parlor with long, impatient strides while he waited. It hadn't escaped his notice that he'd been relegated to the small parlor, one normally used for tradesmen and employees. His lip curled slightly. It wasn't as if he weren't accustomed to being refused admittance in certain homes, but he'd had the distinct impression that Sir Griffyn liked him. Not that he'd come just to visit with the baronet. No, the memory of 'Anna Llewellyn's exotically lovely face glaring at him from the dim recesses of a carriage was what had brought him out on a bright spring day. He wanted to see if the little cat still had claws enough to interest him.

A rustle in the hall snared his attention, and Chance turned slowly, his brow lifting at the whispered words he could hear quite easily.

"*Wolverton?* Here?"

"Yes, miss. To see your father."

"Heavens, Fenwick, why didn't you tell me who it was before—never mind. He is in the main parlor, I presume?"

A faintly subdued Fenwick murmured, "No, miss. The small parlor."

"The small—"

"I didn't recognize him, miss, until it was too late. I just didn't think."

"Thank God he's not the king. I suppose I'd find *him* in the kitchen," she snapped quite irritably, and Chance grinned.

Yes, this kitten definitely had claws.

He walked to the far window and stood looking out, his back to the door so that she would have to speak first. He heard the soft clearing of the throat, then Fenwick said, "Miss Llewellyn will see you, my lord."

Chance turned, and his amusement deepened. It was obvious that she had been gardening. Smears of dirt streaked her gown, and tiny clods of mud trailed on the floor behind her. A straw bonnet perched atop her head, and he knew enough about fashion to know that it was a utilitarian bonnet.

He ignored her obvious discomfiture and strode to her and took her hand in his, bowing deeply from the waist. "Miss Llewellyn, I am quite pleased to find you at home. I trust I am not intruding at an inconvenient time?"

"Well, actually, my lord, I was in the garden."

"Ah, an excellent choice on such a lovely day." He let her pull her hand free of his, taking the opportunity to study her as she turned to the hovering footman.

Daylight revealed the strength of character that had not been as easily apparent in the glow of lamps and stifling press of revelers at Huntington. There was intelligence in her soft blue eyes, and a hint of stubbornness in her rounded chin. High cheekbones added to her exotic appearance. The simple gown she wore clung to curves that tempted him to explore.

"Fenwick," she said, "see that tea is brought, if you please. I think we will be more comfortable in the main parlor, where there is an excellent view of the garden."

"As you say, miss."

Fenwick escaped, his dignity intact, and Miss Llewellyn turned back toward Chance. "I'm certain the maid is through dusting in the parlor now, my lord, if you will be kind enough to join me there."

Neatly done, he thought, and bowed slightly. "Please be so kind as to lead the way, Miss Llewellyn. I apologize for not having sent my card first. Here in the country, it is easy to grow lax in adhering to society's rules."

"Which is one reason to be here, I would think."

She paused just inside the parlor door, and he could see the swift glance she gave the room before leading him in. It was apparent no maid had recently cleaned, though he didn't give a fig for her fiction or the light coating of dust atop a japanned side table. He rather liked the fact that she'd thought her footman's feelings important enough to cover up his error.

"Do you prefer country to town life, then, Miss Llewellyn?"

"Infinitely." She paused, obviously nonplussed for some reason, her eyes shadowed. "It does not appear that Papa and I will be returning to London for some time, as I am certain you must be aware."

"No. I was not. The Season begins soon, and I did not know if I would still find you in residence this late."

She frowned, and her gaze shifted to his face. "You jest, my lord."

"Jest? No. I naturally assumed that a lovely young woman would not miss a London Season for any reason."

He saw her stiffen, and had scant opportunity to wonder why before she said shortly, "I find your conversation ill-advised and insupportable. Have you no respect, my lord?"

"Have I shown you a lack of respect, Miss Llewellyn?" He saw her expression shift toward anger, but was mystified as to the reason for it.

"Not myself, perhaps, but certainly my father. It is cruel of you to suggest I would leave him, and I do not appreciate your assumption that I would abandon him in his time of need." Anger darkened her blue eyes to cobalt, fierce beneath the curved shadow of her long lashes. It occurred to Chance that he was missing a key point.

"Miss Llewellyn, how is your father in need? If there are circumstances of which I am unaware, explain them."

His curt command seemed to take her back, and she drew in a deep breath. "You must have heard of his illness."

"I have not. Tell me."

She turned away abruptly as Fenwick entered with a tea tray. It rattled noisily, and Chance fought the urge to take it from him before he spilled the contents to the carpet. He remained silent until the footman had poured tea and departed at a nod from his mistress.

"Tea, my lord?"

He took the cup she offered. "When did Sir Griffyn become ill?"

"Three weeks ago. It came upon him suddenly." She took a sip of tea and looked away, past him to the doors opening to the garden. "Dr. Throgmorton is of the opinion he may not recover, but I think differently."

"A fever?"

"No. Not of the kind you mean, though the physician did say it is some kind of brain fever. Papa is bereft of his usual senses, I'm afraid. He does not appear to notice me, and when he is awake, he cannot speak. He stares . . . stares at the ceiling most of the time."

Chance set down his untouched tea and went to her. "I did not know, Miss Llewellyn. No one told me. I apologize for what must have seemed quite callous remarks," he said sincerely. "I like Sir Griffyn very much. Is there anything I can do for him?"

She shook her head, and burnished curls of hair strayed over her cheek. He resisted the temptation to push them away and let his hand linger on that soft skin.

"No. There is nothing anyone can do for him at this time. The vicar was here to pray for him, and says that it is God's will that this happened." Her mouth set in a taut line. "It was all I could do not to send him away. I cannot believe that any God would deliberately strike down a man in his prime and leave him only a shell of what he once was!"

Her shoulders trembled, and there was a quiver in her voice. Chance thought suddenly of the well-meaning words of Reverend Goodbody when his parents had died. They had only added to his grief instead of easing it.

"God has nothing to do with it. It's blind misfortune that is to blame, Miss Llewellyn."

Bitterly, she said, "Yes, and the heartless malice of a highwayman."

He froze. "Highwayman?"

She shook back the hair from her face, anger mixing with anguish in her eyes as she looked up at him. "Yes. The Moon Rider. He stopped our coach and robbed us. Dr. Throgmorton said that was what brought on the seizure that left Papa as he is now."

His words came out in a rasp. "How could that be?"

"I have no idea, though I have recently begun reading

up on all the medical volumes I can find that relate to the apoplexy such as Papa suffered."

"And have you discovered the cure for his affliction?"

She moved away from him toward the open doors, and a light breeze lifted the edges of her mantelet. Spring in the English countryside still had a tendency toward coolness, and the small silk cape was designed to keep a lady warm.

She turned around. "No. I have not discovered a cure. All I can do for now is tend him the best I can."

Chance hesitated. He wanted to help her, wanted to do something to make up for the fact that he'd been responsible for the baronet's affliction. For the first time in years, words failed him.

He glanced around, suddenly understanding the situation much better. Dust in the parlors could only mean that the staff had been drastically reduced, and the fact that she had been doing the gardening, he interpreted as necessity. Hence, the bumbling footman trying to perform a butler's tasks.

"If you would allow," he said finally, "perhaps I could lend some of my staff to lighten your load . . ."

The offer obviously offended her. She grew taut and pulled away from him, eyes flashing.

"We are not charity cases, my lord. My father and I do not require any of your castoff servants, thank you. We will manage quite well without donations of pity or pence."

Recognizing the stiff pride in her, he did not take offense at her heated refusal. He would have rejected any offer, too, no matter how well meaning. Pity could be a crippling emotion when bestowed on those capable of managing on their own.

"I understand—" he began, and she cut in.

"Yes. You, of all people, should understand about unwanted pity."

Her words startled him. They were familiar for a young woman he'd met only once before, and said as if she knew he would understand. He frowned slightly.

"If I overstepped my bounds, I apologize. However, I want you to feel free to call on me in any matter which you feel I might be helpful. I have a great deal of respect for Sir Griffyn. I would never want to think he felt he could not count on my aid if he needed it."

This offer was met with silence at first, then she nodded gravely. "Thank you, my lord. That is most kind of you. More tea?"

She retreated into the role of hostess, remote and decidedly cool. Chance stayed just long enough to finish his cup of tea, then took his departure with a few stilted phrases unlike those that usually came to him so easily. He knew his role as arrogant earl quite well.

It was the role of malefactor that sat on him so uneasily. He should be used to it. Since Lord Perry's death six years before, he'd been named everything from murderer to wastrel. The names rarely bothered him anymore; yet, to have 'Anna Llewellyn consider him responsible for her father's illness weighed heavily on a conscience he'd thought long dead.

It didn't matter that she blamed the Moon Rider instead of Lord Wolverton. They were one and the same, and he knew it even if she didn't.

Rhianna stared out at the garden long after Wolverton's departure. He still didn't know her. Obviously, their meeting that long-ago day had meant very little to him. She was foolish and naive to think he would remember a gypsy girl. And to care that he didn't.

She drew in a shaky breath. She'd not been able to curb the shiver of expectation in her when he'd looked at her from beneath his ridiculous wealth of lashes. She'd been very aware of him, of his startling good looks, of the perfection of his tailored green riding jacket and tight buff breeches and gleaming top boots. Oh yes, he was magnificent, and he knew it. He wore it with the careless arrogance of an aristocrat, of a man born to wealth and position, and contemptuous of those beneath him.

Yet she remembered the angry boy in wet clothes, with the pain in his eyes and voice, seeking acceptance and affection where he could find it.

Restless, she stepped outside into the garden and took a deep breath. Blossoms brightened the stone tiles with fluffy tufts of red, pink, and white, mixing with blue spires. It was lovely and fragrant in the soft sunshine, and she closed her eyes.

Why had he come? At first, she'd thought he'd come to see about her father, but he'd not even known about the baronet's illness. Probably just a social call, though she'd been given to understand that the earl of Wolverton rarely paid social calls. He was said to be utterly ruthless in business dealings—arrogant and rude to the point of cruelty at times. Many rumors had circulated about him after his departure from the Huntington ball, and she had heard the scraps of gossip with dismay.

Chance—she preferred thinking of him by that name —was coupled with several different high-born ladies, if the gossip were to be believed, the latest being a Lady Thalia Wimberley. It was whispered that Lady Wimberley had set her cap for him despite a husband that was very much alive.

And then there were the other rumors, linking him with forbidden duels and angry husbands, jilted ladies and anxious mamas of hopeful young ladies. It seemed that not even his reputation kept him from being desired as an object of matrimony to some, and Rhianna couldn't help a wry smile. A title and wealth made up for a multitude of sins, apparently.

No wonder Chance had become so impossible.

Yet she couldn't stop thinking of the boy he'd been, hurt and trying not to show it, his arrogance his only weapon against those who tried to take advantage. Had he killed his uncle? The man she saw now was certainly capable of doing such a thing, but the boy?

She didn't know. She honestly didn't know if Chance had been capable of killing him. It was faintly startling to realize that the truth was not that important to her. She still saw his pain and grief, despite his efforts to hide it. That sarcastic veneer and cold arrogance were only thin masquerades.

If her own life weren't in such turmoil, she might remind him of that gypsy girl he'd met so long ago and see if she couldn't break through his facade. But she had her own problems, her own heartaches, and time was too short to waste on what was probably a lost cause. No, she would follow her daring plans and work through this crisis in her own way.

She stood up, smoothing her soiled skirts, her mind already shifting to the almost completed plans. The next full moon was only nine days away. Everything was ready. The high road from Wiltshire to London saw a lot of traffic, including the mail coaches now in use. Yes, if she was careful and did not lose her nerve, she would be able to take care of her father quite well.

All that was necessary now was a full moon and a cloudless sky.

Book Three

Chapter 8

"How very kind of you to come," Rhianna said politely.

Viscount Nelson Roxbury smiled.

"I could do no less once I heard the dreadful news of Sir Griffyn's ill health. It grieves me to think how fine a man he was."

"Still is," Rhianna said tartly. "He's not dead, just ill."

"Of course, of course. I did not mean to intimate that he would not survive this attack, though it is rare."

Rhianna glared at him. "Thank you for your concern." A warm breeze filtered through the open doors of the parlor, bringing in the sweet scent of spring blossoms.

His brow lifted. "Of course I'm concerned. This madman roaming the highroads must be caught and hanged before he does even more damage. Look at what happened to your father. It's not safe in England anymore, and I find that disgraceful."

"Yes, it is getting almost as dangerous as France, is it not?"

Pale blue eyes narrowed at her for an instant, and she wondered why she'd felt the need to prick him. "Yes," he said curtly, "it is. Did the highwayman threaten you as well as your father, by the way?"

"No, only my pearl necklace. Not that it was worth very much. No matter. It won't bring him much more than a pound or two."

"I remember the necklace. It had a diamond clasp in the shape of a cherub, did it not? It looked more valuable than a pound or two."

Rhianna shrugged. "Only sentimental value, I'm afraid."

"How distressing for the villain, but at least you were not harmed."

"No, only my father."

"So true."

Roxbury slanted her a speculative glance that made her wonder about his true motive for coming to see her. He began to roam the parlor restlessly, making small talk that meant nothing. On edge, she forced herself to reply with courtesy.

Occasionally, he accompanied his conversation with a quick glance and smile, but it was shallow, making her think of a trick of light and mirrors. Her patience ended abruptly.

"Is there something wrong, sir?"

Roxbury shrugged negligently and leaned back against a small table, affecting a casual pose.

"Nothing more than usual, I suppose. Why do you ask?"

"No reason, except that you're pacing like a wild animal in my parlor."

"Am I? Sorry." Roxbury's smile was faintly apologetic, his eyes shifting from her to the doors at the far end of the room. Porter, a new servant, paused in dusting a small hall table, then moved silently past. Rhianna heard the far door in the entrance hall close behind him before the viscount turned back to her.

"Rumor has it," he said softly, "that you and the earl of Wolverton are more than just neighbors."

Rhianna could not have been more surprised if he'd

said that he could fly. Staring, she blurted out, "Preposterous! Who on earth could have said such a thing?"

"Lady Wimberley, for one." His bland smile told her nothing. "She is a former mistress of the earl's, and until recently, quite in favor. Now, I believe that she has been cast off and is quite miffed about it." He shrugged. "She believes that you have replaced her, apparently."

"I assure you that nothing could be further from the truth." Stiff with anger, Rhianna could not keep it from showing in her tone. "If you wish to listen to idle gossip, feel free, but do not annoy me with such tripe."

"My, my, you are quite the outraged *femme, n'est-ce pas?* Does this mean that there is an element of truth in the Lady Wimberley's suspicions?"

With a supreme effort, Rhianna kept her voice calm. "I have no intention of discussing this further. Shall I have Fenwick bring round your phaeton?"

Roxbury laughed. "Your feathers are most charming when they are ruffled, dear 'Anna. I have offended you. I am most sorry, but I admit to a bit of jealousy when I heard that you were . . . um . . . attracted to Wolverton. He's not the type of man to appreciate properly your finer points."

"I see. If you don't mind, it's getting rather late in the afternoon and I still have a great deal to do."

"I sense a dismissal." Roxbury's blue eyes gleamed with laughter.

"Let me make it plain—I would like for you to go."

He caught her hand, holding it when she would have pulled away. Though Roxbury was a handsome man, there was none of the attraction she'd felt for Chance. Even his efforts to charm and placate were more annoying than effective. She pulled her hand from his and stepped back. He spread his arms wide and gave her an appealing smile.

"Don't be so cruel to me, my fair lady. I've been swept away by your charm and beauty, can't you tell?"

"Truthfully, the only thing I can tell is that you are after something. I don't know what. I'm not at all certain that I care."

His brow lifted; a shaft of sunlight gleamed in his fair hair and made it look soft and silky. "You're extremely blunt, aren't you? I suppose that suits. Actually, I came to warn you, and I haven't the vaguest notion how to go about it. Your forthrightness has made it much easier."

"Warn me? About what?"

"Sir Griffyn has enemies. For his safety, it would be best if he were to be taken to a secure place far from here. I think—"

"Enemies? What on earth are you talking about? My father may not have been the best businessman in the world, but he's never willingly hurt a living soul. Who would wish to harm him?"

Roxbury gave her a long, searching look before saying slowly, "I don't know. Oh, I realize that sounds absolutely ridiculous, but it's true. I only know that rumors have been about saying the baronet has incurred the wrath of the wrong people. I beg your pardon if you think me impertinent. I'll show myself out."

Rhianna didn't speak as Roxbury gave her a formal bow from the waist, then turned to leave. When he reached the door, however, she said, "Wait."

He turned, and she took in a deep breath. "I did not mean to insult you. Perhaps you are trying to help, but repeating idle gossip is not the best approach."

Making a face, Roxbury nodded. "I agree. I've never had the gift of easy conversation, I fear. Do forgive me."

"You are forgiven, of course. Now, please tell me what you have heard that may affect my father."

"Not much really. Just a few hints here and there,

snippets of rumor that claim the baronet incurred the displeasure of a few men in high places by gaming with funds he did not have. Were you aware that your father is in debt due to high losses?"

"Of course, but not to the extent you refer." Rhianna chewed on her lower lip for a moment, considering what she should say. It was true that Sir Griffyn had gambled in an effort to recoup business losses, but surely he had better sense than to enrage men who could do him much harm.

" 'Anna—Miss Llewellyn—I am sorry to have offended you. If you will take tea with me, I promise not to utter another word about unpleasant subjects."

She managed a faint smile. "I'll have Fenwick bring us a tray. With the understanding that you will inform me as soon as possible should you discover anyone who might wish my father harm."

"But of course. I could do no less for such a lovely lady."

For the rest of his visit, Roxbury made an obvious effort to be polite and charming, but she still had the inescapable feeling that he'd left much unsaid.

Of late, rumors about the viscount had been disturbing to say the least. He was said to have dueled with an earl's son and turned too early, thus causing the young man's death. Because of conflicting stories, Roxbury had not been charged with any crime, and the distraught family had little choice but to bury their son and resentments.

Whispers about Roxbury's excesses could be merely envy, or have only a shadow of truth in them, yet Rhianna was still uneasy in his presence.

•   •   •

The steady *clip-clop* of hooves on the hard-packed road sounded loud in the early evening quiet. Faint light from a quarter moon glinted dully through the trees. A screen of leaves was all that separated Chance from the curved road that led to London. He leaned forward to rest his dark-gloved hand on the neck of his mount, waiting until the approaching rider was almost directly in front of where he hid in the thick roadside hedge. With a grim smile of satisfaction, he recognized his quarry, and reached up to adjust the black mask he wore.

In a burst of motion, he nudged his horse forward at the same instant he pulled a pistol from his waistband, giving the familiar order to "Stand and deliver" as he cut off the rider's flight. Curses filled the soft evening air, mixing with the startled whinny of his victim's horse.

"Damn you," Roxbury snarled as he tried to calm his mount. It took him a moment before he could look up at his assailant, and Chance met his glare with a faint smile.

"Good evening, sir. Be so kind as to toss me your sword and pistol before I relieve you of your valuables."

"Devil take you. I will not."

Chance laughed softly, leveling his pistol at the third button on Roxbury's silk vest. "Then be prepared to die."

He saw Roxbury stiffen, and uncertainty flickered on his outraged countenance. Then, slowly, he unbuckled his light sword and let it fall to the ground.

"Your pistol as well," Chance reminded.

"Do you see a pistol on me?" Roxbury lifted both hands palms outward, his reins clutched in his left hand. "I do not carry a pistol."

"Ah, but I think you do. No self-respecting gentleman such as you would do otherwise."

"What would a bloody ruffian such as you know about gentlemen, pray tell?"

"Tsk tsk, you wound me. I rub elbows with the elite

on a few occasions, sir. And you, I might add, are not one of them. Now—your pistol, or I shall burn a hole in your silk vest with a well-placed ball."

More curses filled the air, but Roxbury slowly complied by reaching into the pocket of his coat and bringing out his pistol. It hit the ground with a dull thud.

"Satisfied?"

"P'raps. Did I detect the faint rustle of paper in your pocket, sir? I'd like to see what you carry."

Roxbury's face darkened, the faint light of dusk making his pale eyes glisten. " 'Tis nothing that would concern you. If you want my money, take it."

"Your generosity is astounding. I intend to take your money. And, I will have everything in your pocket as well."

Chance nudged his mount forward, until he was right beside Roxbury. He saw the lines of impotent fury etched into the viscount's face, and knew the reason.

"You bloody bastard," Roxbury ground out, fists clenching on his leather reins as he glared at Chance. "I'll see you drawn and quartered for this!"

Reaching out, Chance plucked a packet of papers from Roxbury's coat pocket, then reached inside his silk vest to remove a small pouch that clinked softly.

"Not much money, sir. How disappointing. How do you expect me to live on such poor pickings?"

"If you would stick to robbing mail coaches or some of those vulgar Cits on the stage, you'd do better. Take my money, but leave me my papers."

"Valiant try, but I do not like to go home so empty handed. Are these your bank vouchers, p'raps?"

"No, you fool, those papers mean nothing to anyone but myself."

Roxbury darted a hand out for the packet, but Chance was too quick for him. He jerked back and held it just out of reach, jabbing the pistol forward until the barrel grazed the viscount's chest.

"Ah ah—nothing precipitate. You endanger yourself needlessly for a few worthless papers. If they are of so little value, why bother with them?"

Beads of sweat dotted Roxbury's brow. "I told you— they are of little value to anyone but me."

"Dismount," Chance ordered curtly. He thumbed back the hammer on his pistol with an ominous click, and the viscount muttered an oath as he dismounted.

"My appreciation to you, sir," Chance said as he leaned out to snare Roxbury's dangling reins. "Your horse will be waiting for you a mile or two down the road. Do have a nice stroll in the moonlight, old chap."

Roxbury's curses followed him until he was out of earshot, mixing with French epithets that raised Chance's brow. Inventive fellow. And if he was not mistaken, enterprising as well. A cursory glance at Roxbury's papers had shown him nothing of obvious value, but he would send them to his London contact anyway. If they were in code, it would be broken sooner or later.

And if the viscount were innocent, then at least he had managed to discomfit him for a short time. He didn't like Roxbury; it occurred to him to wonder why the viscount was coming from the direction of the baronet's house. Had he been to visit 'Anna Llewellyn? It was rumored all over London that he sought an heiress to bolster his fading family fortune, but there would be no dowry with the baronet's daughter. Could there be some other kind of connection?

Chance frowned. He would not have thought so, but if he'd learned nothing else in his life, he'd learned never to put much stock in appearances. And he'd learned that most women would do anything for financial security.

• • • •

Dusk had settled softly, purple mists lying over vales and gentle hills. There was a sense of expectancy in the night air, soft and in a way, sensuous.

Rhianna laughed at her imaginings. She was letting the tension make her soft headed. Her mount shifted position, hooves striking against a dead limb half-buried beneath dry, rotting leaves and decay made damp with dew. The muscles of her throat grew tight as she idly stroked the gleaming white neck of her horse.

What if someone recognized that this beast was nothing like the magnificent steed of the Moon Rider's? She prayed that her victims would be so distraught they would see only the lethal length of steel rapier and gleam of her pistol instead of a hundred betraying details.

Her costume was quite similar to the Moon Rider's, with its white silk mask and plain linen shirt, the fitted white breeches and even white leather boots. Her cloak was of snow white lamb's wool, concealing and hooded. She counted on it to help hide the fact that this highwayman was a woman. In the chaos of the moment, the only words she need utter were, "Stand and deliver." She practiced saying them in a deep growl over and over, and hoped she would be able to manage the deception well enough. Only the most discerning eye would mark the difference between her and the real highwayman. And as long as the Moon Rider was not standing beside her as evidence, she was safe.

She hoped.

Time passed slowly, and the moon rose higher in the sky until it no longer seemed to just hang on the edge of the moors. Silvery light bathed the ground, giving an eerie glow to mundane surroundings. Rhianna heard the vague rustlings of night creatures, and the muffled call of a hunting owl as it spotted a victim. A frightened squeal ended abruptly, and she visualized the demise of some tiny creature.

A shudder trickled down her spine. Desperation had goaded her into this lunacy. Yet the alternative was to watch her father placed into one of those asylums where the patients were strapped onto hard cots and left to writhe, alone in their internal upheaval. Not as long as she had breath in her body would she allow that to happen.

At best, Sir Griffyn would soon recover. At worst, she would be forced to sell Serenity House and retire with him to a small cottage, eking out a living as best she could. No one had offered a more viable solution.

Except, of course, the barrister who had suggested that she wed quickly. That was an intolerable notion. She could not envision giving up all rights in the hope that the man she wed would be honorable enough to support her father. And in truth, since losing all assets, her marriage choices were slim indeed. Few would wed a dowerless girl rumored to be the illegitimate daughter of a gypsy and an eccentric baronet.

Only Viscount Roxbury had shown any interest, but his infrequent visits made her acutely uncomfortable. She could not help the feeling that there was more behind his interest than she knew.

A faint rattle broke into her musings. Rhianna sat up straight in the saddle. As the rattle grew into the unmistakable rumble of carriage wheels, she drew her sword with a rasping sound. Though fairly familiar with pistols, she preferred the sword, being more certain of it. Pistols were too unpredictable. One never knew if the firing pan were too damp to give spark to the powder, or if the blasted thing would misfire. Pistols were useful only for their unnerving noise and the threat of them, as far as she was concerned. *Barking irons* was an apt slang term for them indeed.

With one hand, she drew up the white neck cloth to disguise the lower portion of her face and muffle her voice, while her other steadied her mount. She waited, muscles taut and quivering with anticipation, until she saw the glow of the coach's side lamps. Then she spurred her mount forward, crashing through the low hedges to a patch of bright moonlight in the road just ahead of the lumbering coach.

Her pistol fired a warning. She heard the shrill scream of the horses and the hoarse oaths of the coachmen and driver. She drew back the second hammer, leveling the clumsy pistol at the driver as he sawed the reins of the frantic horses to keep them from bolting. Finally, he had them under control.

"W'at the 'ell!" the driver snarled, and Rhianna heard the strangled gasp of one of the guards.

"The Moon Rider!"

"Shoot him!" the driver roared furiously, but both the guards seemed frozen by superstitious fear. They stared with bulging eyes at the figure in white.

"By God," the driver growled, " 'is lordship will 'ave yer bloody hides fer this."

But Rhianna noted that he was looking nervous as well, and that he made no attempt to use his whip or weapon on her either. She took a deep breath for courage, and nudged her mount closer.

"Stand and deliver!" she ordered, her voice as gruff as she could make it.

A frightened scream came from inside the coach, and for an instant she sympathized with the occupants. Then the door swung open, and she adjusted position to face a possible threat. It was an elderly gentleman, a painful reminder of Sir Griffyn's abrupt descent into ill health, but she sternly ignored the prick of her conscience.

"Your money, my lord," she snapped curtly. He swore at her. Her drawn sword glittered in the bright press of moonlight as she pointed it at him, keeping the pistol trained on the terrified guards as a warning. Runnels of light sparked from the lethal blade of her sword. After a moment's hesitation, the gentleman withdrew a heavy pouch and flung it to the ground.

"You'll be hanged for this before long," he said in a bitterly furious tone. "Do you think the king's guards aren't aware of your activities?"

"Yet they don't seem to be near," she couldn't resist saying. "How unfortunate."

At her terse orders, the other gentleman in the coach tossed out his money pouch as well. Gallantly, she refused the woman's offer of her jewelry. Then she gave the order for them to ride on and be quick about it, or she would give them more to regret than lost money.

The coach lumbered away. She watched it roll around the next curve before she dismounted to retrieve the money pouches on the ground. She'd barely remounted before a loud crack sounded, and a ball whistled past her head so closely it singed the wool of her cape.

Fear gripped her. She swung her mount around into the woods where she'd hidden earlier. Another shot sounded. Apparently, some distance had given the guards courage and they were in hot pursuit of her now. Rhianna spurred the white horse into a dead run. She knew she was easily visible as long as she was in the dark. She headed for the clearing at the crest of the next hill, praying that what had worked for the Moon Rider, would work for her.

It must have.

As she crested the hill in the blaze of full moon, she

looked behind her. Her pursuers had paused, seeming to falter. Had she blended in with the bright light to give the illusion that she'd vanished?

A faint, terrified cry confirmed it, and she couldn't help a laugh. It echoed down the slope to the misted valley below, peals of triumphant laughter that heralded another successful coup d'état for the villain known as the Moon Rider.

It had been almost too easy, Rhianna thought.

"What in the bloody hell is that nonsense?" Chance gave Hobson a scowl that didn't perturb the servant in the least. "You know very well I didn't ride there last night."

"Ah, but Lord Albritton was held up by a highwayman he swears was the Moon Rider. Says one of his footmen mounted on a post horse managed to wound him, but he still got away. Vanished into the light as always, Albritton claims. Seems that Lord Mutton Stew was with him, and he corroborates the story."

"Mullengrew," Chance corrected with a half-smile. "Damn peculiar, don't you think, Hobson?"

"That someone would use your disguise to his own advantage, my lord? Not so very peculiar. I'm astonished that no one has thought of it before now. Most are quite terrified of you, you know. The Moon Rider is said to be a bit mystical, rather like a pixie or goblin. There are those who even claim the Moon Rider is the devil in disguise."

Chance gave an irritable grunt. "The hell with what those twits say. I'd like to know just who has the bloody nerve to impersonate me." He pushed away from the wall where he'd been leaning. "I think I shall find out, Hobson. And when I do, I can assure you that this fellow will wish he had not been so presumptuous."

Hobson looked gravely at him. "I daresay."

"Lay out my garments, please. I feel the need of some fresh air."

"Fresh air?" Hobson looked startled. " 'Tis not a full moon. Shall I lay out your black cape and mask, my lord?"

"No, I do not intend to ride tonight. I intend to pay a visit to a certain Lord Heffington and one of his cronies."

"Ah. Roxbury, I presume?"

"You presume correctly. It has come to my attention that Lord Roxbury has been promoting vicious gossip about me, and I think it's time to use that as an excuse to confront him. He'll either back it up or back down, and either way, he won't like the ultimate consequences."

Hobson smiled faintly. "Knowing his reputation as a bit hasty with hot words and slow with honorable action, I somehow think he will not have a very pleasant encounter, my lord."

"I don't intend that he shall. Nor do I intend that my impostor shall have a pleasant evening when I confront him, either."

Leaves shivered at the gentle touch of a breeze. Plump, glistening drops of dew slid from a broad oak leaf to fall on the nape of Rhianna's neck. She shivered, and drew up the collar of the cape draped carelessly over her shoulders. A month had passed since her last foray into this mad scheme, and the purloined purses were near empty.

It was long past dark, and the road was empty of travelers. The high road curved and wound from Salisbury to the chalky downs of the rolling plains. Ancient stones stood several miles away, silent and forbidding, casting long shadows in the bright prick of moonlight.

A mysterious place, close enough to cast a superstitious fear over the locals, far enough away to give her the courage to wait in the shadows of the Bath Road for unwary travelers. The fashionable lure of the Bath waters had lost none of its appeal for Londoners despite the risk of highwaymen along the road.

Her hands tightened on the reins of her restive mount when she heard the distant rumble of coach wheels. With a shaky hand, she drew her silk mask over her face and adjusted the folds of the cape to hide the lower half. A lack of masculine features might be noticed, and she dared not risk being challenged again. This time, the footmen might be braver than those of Lord Albritton.

The pistol felt heavy in her hand, and the second pistol tucked into the waistband of her breeches nudged sharply against her stomach. She was taking no chances on being apprehended. With any luck, she would find a wealthy Cit in the carriage barreling down the road toward her.

An erratic flicker of coach lamps made her breath come quickly, and her heartbeat escalated as the coach drew closer. When she could make out the shapes of the driver and footmen atop the swaying vehicle, she spurred her mount into a forward leap.

Again, there was the startled oaths of the driver and the shrill protests of the horses when she fired her pistol into the air. Wheels wobbled in deep ruts as the carriage thundered past instead of stopping. It was a narrow escape, and only her quick reaction kept her from being run over by the vehicle. The loud popping of a whip cracked, punctuating the headlong flight.

For a moment, Rhianna hesitated as she soothed her trembling mount. She'd expected her sudden appearance and pistol to bring the coach to a halt, and had not considered what she would do otherwise. Now, she made a swift decision. Before the footmen and driver could collect their wits enough to retaliate, she must force the coach to a halt.

Her heels dug into her mount's sides and she gave hot pursuit. No answering shot had been fired from muskets, and she gambled on the hope that the footmen were too frightened to return fire. Superstition and the Moon Rider's fierce reputation had worked before; surely it would work now.

Rhianna leaned into the wind as her horse flew down the road, gaining steadily on the heavy carriage. She could see the lamps bobbing like fireflies in the moonlight, could even make out the terrified faces pressed against the coach windows. The world narrowed to the deafening rumble of coach wheels and the thunder of hooves on rutted ground.

It took only a few moments to outrun the coach. She reached out to grasp the leaders of the nearest horse. The whip popped much too close to her, and she ignored it desperately as she tugged sharply at the horse's headgear. The coach was in danger of being overturned at the next curve, and she gauged the chances of her escape should that happen.

Apparently, the driver also saw the danger. He cursed in frustration as he slowed the animals. She immediately released the leaders and brought up her pistol. It gleamed with unmistakable menace in the bright glow of moonlight as she leveled the weapon at the driver and the footman next to him. Only two of them. Surely, she could manage this.

"Stand and deliver," she rasped, her voice hoarse from harsh breaths and the danger of the moment.

An insolent glare was her only reply. She thumbed

back the hammer of her pistol. It sounded loud in the sudden silence. The silk mask drawn over her head muffled the driver's angry reply. Her in-drawn breaths sucked the scratchy wool cape over her mouth, stifling her words.

"Stand and deliver, or die. My pistol is primed and aimed, and you will have little chance if you are foolish enough to attempt shooting me."

It was a bold alternative to give two armed men atop a coach. She tried to still the quiver of her muscles when neither of them moved for a moment. Then one of them gave a croaking noise, and slowly lifted his arms into the air in surrender.

There was no time to feel relief before she heard an alien sound behind her, the thud of hoofbeats and the snorting rasp of a horse. She tensed at this new danger. Her legs tightened around her horse, and she prepared to meet a challenge.

Instead, she heard a faintly amused drawl. "Relinquish your weapons at once. Do hurry, chaps. My associate grows impatient."

Rhianna couldn't move, couldn't imagine what new twist had occurred. Her heart was in her throat, and her chest was tight with fear and apprehension. She dared a quick glance over her shoulder. What she saw made her mouth dry and her hands shake.

The Moon Rider leaned lazily from his saddle, a sardonic smile curling the lips barely visible beneath his silk mask. He was holding something out to her.

"Do take it, my friend. I think it will hold whatever you may find inside the coach."

She looked down at the limp velvet bag he held out. Without further thought, she took it from him, then moved her horse to the now open door of the carriage.

What choice did she have? With the combined threat of highwayman and hostile victims, she had little chance of flight. She would be cut down before getting five yards from the coach.

Her white gloved hand shook slightly as she held out the bag to the emerging passengers. A corpulent Cit in gaudy garments shakily denounced this outrage and promised just retribution, while his womenfolk moaned and wailed loudly as they stripped ears and throats and fingers of a bounty of jewels.

"Two of ye, by God, and fit for the devil hisself!" the Cit was shouting furiously. "The sheriff will hear of this before the night is out, I promise you that much. . . ."

"Perhaps not," the Moon Rider said with an amused laugh. "Unless you find the notion of walking ten miles to Salisbury in the dark attractive."

Rhianna didn't have to turn around to know what he was about. She heard the driver's curses as the harnesses were cut and the matched bays freed. The horses pounded away over the moors in a thunder of hooves.

With the velvet sack filled, Rhianna drew back to wait at the side of the road, uncertain what her next move should be. The thought of facing the Moon Rider was unnerving, but not as unnerving as the risk of being handed over to the infuriated Cit and a magistrate. She hoped there was such a thing as honor among thieves.

All too soon, the Moon Rider approached her, the white horse's hooves a soft clatter on the road. She tensed as he reined in next to her, but her eyes lifted to meet his gaze. She saw the dark glitter of his eyes in the soft moonlight. She had remembered those eyes beneath the silk, seen them in her dreams, nightmare visions that had jerked her awake several nights in a row. Now she knew why.

Anger burned beneath that silk, coupled with a menace she had never before encountered. She drew in a deep breath to speak, but his low drawl stopped her.

"I am considered a fair marksman, my friend, and my pistol is at the ready. Don't be foolish enough to resist."

There was little choice but to go where he led. She had the alarming thought that she might never get away.

Chapter 9

"Keep to the path, my brave friend," Chance cautioned when his prisoner strayed too far to the open field on the left. "We have not yet discussed how you wish to divide the spoils of our little robbery."

Chance rode closer. Damn the impertinence of the young pup. He knew the white-swathed figure had to be young, for he'd heard the quavery voice and discerned the immature muscle beneath the concealing cape. Had he actually thought he could interfere with impunity?

The impostor made a sudden move as if to ride into the open.

Chance's snarl of warning gave him pause. "I wouldn't advise it, you bloody little fool."

Moonlight shimmered in shifting patches through the full summer leaves, dancing on the ground and over the masked face that turned toward him.

"You would shoot me then?" came the husky question.

Chance let a bark of laughter be the only reply, and saw that his meaning was understood.

Wisely, the masquerader did not attempt further flight or speech, but rode stiff and silent along the narrowing path. Chance spoke only to give directions at a fork in the path, riding deeper into the woods. He knew of a hut not far ahead that had been abandoned some years before. There would be privacy enough to do what must be done.

At the bottom of a small hollow next to the gentle curve of a stream, the hut tilted precariously under a huge oak. Some of the thatched roof had fallen in, but most still lay in bundles over the wooden framework. Moonlight picked out the gaping door and empty black holes of the windows. He heard his companion mutter what sounded like an oath.

"Don't you like my choice of hostelry, sir?" he mocked. "I assure you, we will have ample privacy."

Chance swung down from his horse, stripping away his gloves as he took several steps forward. "What? No glib excuses to offer? Your silence disappoints me, sir."

The slight hiss of breath told him that he was closer to infuriating his protagonist than he was to frightening him. More the better. He was itching to have sword in hand, to teach this usurper his proper place and be done with it.

"Get down from your horse, sir. Your cowardice is ill-timed."

Still the figure remained atop his horse, staring down at Chance with taut attention. There was something curious about the way he watched him so silently, as if the least word would precipitate disaster.

Chance took another step forward, unable to keep the anger from his voice. "Look, you bloody pup, you had damn well better dismount and face me on your feet. If you think for one moment that I intend to allow you to get away with impersonating me—and doing a bloody bad job of it at that—then you will find yourself much mistaken. Now *get down* before I cut you to ribbons in your saddle."

His sword was a whisper of steel as he drew it and waited, and finally the figure stirred himself enough to dismount. He was much shorter than Chance had assumed, and slighter of frame. A mere youth, a stripling with no meat, only mettle. It was time this brazen boy learned that he'd best not attempt matters beyond his capabilities.

The answering whisk of a sword being drawn brought a smile to Chance's mouth. The youth's lips parted in a quick exhalation. Apparently, the boy knew enough about the man he faced to be apprehensive.

"En garde," Chance said softly. The other sword flashed up into position. Moonlight glittered along the slender blade, a sword more for fencing than fighting. A gentleman's weapon, pathetic against a highwayman's expert saber.

The first feints and parries were mere preludes to what would follow, a testing of the opponent's reflexes and skill. Chance saw at once that although this youth was quick and agile he had no strength to withstand a prolonged encounter. And so he set about protracting the play, drawing the boy out with a series of moves calculated to overextend his limits.

The clearing rang with the clash of swords and the shuffle of feet over dead leaves and dry twigs. The labored breaths from the boy gave evidence of failing endurance. A faint smile curled Chance's mouth. So this unlicked cub thought he could hold his own as the Moon Rider?

They closed briefly, bodies tense with effort. The youth's eyes flickered up at him with a mixture of hatred and rage. The rage he understood; the hatred startled him. He broke the clasp by shoving the boy away, then swiftly lowered the point of his saber to press against his chest in warning.

"When I tire of fencing with you," he said softly, "I am quite capable of running you through."

"Then do it and be damned."

The hoarse challenge gave Chance pause. Courage was not lacking after all, it seemed, though he had to wonder about the boy's lack of good sense.

Nonplussed, and more than a little irritated at the foolish arrogance, he took a step back and slashed the tip of his saber across the loose folds of linen shirt. It parted easily and soundlessly, the material sliding down in a snowy fall. A thin crimson scratch welled to stain the shirt, and he heard the hiss of pain quickly stifled.

"First blood will satisfy me," Chance said coldly, "though I find myself curious as to what manner of boy is fool enough to attempt such a farce. Take off your mask."

The boy stepped back, holding up the edges of his shirt to cover the bloody scratch, chin lifted defiantly. "I will not. If you want to know my identity, you must learn it by force or kill me."

"You offer me a great temptation." Chance hesitated. The boy's chest was rising in heavy gulps for air, and he seemed unsteady. Anger faded into concern. After all, he'd been a wild and unruly youth himself. And no great harm had been done, save to his reputation. The Moon Rider would never have bungled a holdup as this boy had, nor would he have had to chase down a bloody coach like an eager hound.

After a moment, he lowered his sword point to the ground and leaned on the ornately carved basket hilt. "Don't ever be fool enough to chase after a coach like that. It's too easy to be a target when you make a fool of yourself by baying after your prey like an ancient hound." He saw the youth stiffen with outrage and laughed.

"It's the truth. Tell me, boy, what did you hope to gain by this masquerade? A few baubles? Glory?"

"Money."

"Money. You've a damn foolish way of going about it. I could have killed you twice over, and if not for luck, that cow-handed driver would have run you over on the road. You're fortunate you weren't shot again. Didn't that set-to with Albritton teach you anything?"

The chin lifted higher, stubborn and defensive. "I got away, didn't I?"

"Barely. And probably had damn little to show for it. Did it occur to you that I had a very good notion of where you would be tonight?" He saw the lips part in chagrin. "I didn't think so. If I can figure it out, it won't be too long before the sheriff could do the same. Never strike in the same place twice running and don't be foolish enough to leave yourself no escape."

"Your advice is quite comforting. Does this mean that you desire to take me on as a partner?"

"No, it means that if you ever embark on a career of your own of this nature, you'd bloody well better make sure you spend more time in thought and planning than in the execution of your robbery. Hanging has a dampening effect on most highwaymen."

"No doubt. I shall remember that when I attend yours."

"Cocky little bastard, aren't you." Chance let his gaze rove from the youth's masked face to the slashed front of his shirt, then halted. He must be mistaken. Disbelief shot through him, then his hand flashed out to grasp the startled boy by the shirtfront.

"Stop that!" A hand flailed at him in panic, and the decidedly high tone only cemented his burgeoning suspicion.

He ignored the desperate attempt to dislodge his hand from the ruffled shirt front, and backed his victim up to the nearest broad tree trunk. It took very little effort to pin the wildly waving arms behind and do a cursory exploration with his free hand.

Chance used his body weight to advantage, and let his hand slide beneath the material of the shirt to rest on an unmistakable swell. He could feel the hard little button of a nipple against his palm while his fingers cupped the satiny texture of a decidedly female breast. The soft skin was slightly slick with blood, and he muttered an angry curse.

"Bloody hell. Why didn't you tell me you're a woman? And where did you learn to use a sword so well?"

"Would my being female make that much difference to a highwayman like you? I think not."

He fought the temptation to give her a rough shake. He let his weight hold her squirming body against the trunk until she finally realized that he would not let her go and grew still. His voice was harsh. "Who are you?"

"That is of no consequence. What are your intentions?"

That gave him pause. His gaze narrowed on the face half-hidden by the mask, lingering on her mouth. Behind the silk, eyes that looked to be a dark blue studied him with wary intensity. The thin silk fluttered against her face in a slight ripple. His hand still cupped her breast, and he gave in to the impulse to see her reaction to his touch.

He looked into her eyes and slowly rotated his palm in a gentle, circular motion. She didn't move, but he heard her quickly in-drawn breath. The hard little nipple burned into his palm, and after a moment, he shifted his fingers to tease it to a rigid peak. He glanced down to watch his hand move, mesmerized by the muted sheen of skin like satin and the coral tip of her breast. Silently, he pulled her shirt away until she stood bare-breasted and proud, an exquisite statue of flesh and blood instead of marble.

Her beauty took his breath away. His physical reaction was immediate and masculine, the response of any male to a lovely female. Yet it was startling and faintly disconcerting to find himself so lacking in self-control.

His hand fell away and he took a step back, but she did not make a move to cover herself. She leaned against the tree, hands still behind her, bare breasts gleaming softly in the glow of moonlight, rising and falling with each breath she took. Was it an invitation? A silent enticement for him to continue?

God, he wanted to. Now he saw what he'd been too angry to see before, the slender shape of feminine legs in men's breeches, the shapely turn of a calf in a fitted knee-high boot, the small waist and gentle swell of womanly hips—oh, yes, he wanted to continue. His body ached with the wanting, pressed against his breeches in an unmistakable urgency of need and desire. He wondered if she saw it and if she felt the same as he did.

His gaze lifted, dragged from tempting curves up to the masked face. Her lips were parted, small pink tongue flicking out to wet them in a nervous gesture. She didn't move, didn't resist when he reached out to touch her again, one finger sliding over the firm cushion of her breast, then lightly circling the taut nipple in a teasing caress. Unable to restrain himself, he bent to touch that coral tip with his tongue, and heard her soft gasp of shock. She shuddered but didn't protest when he took the sweet temptation into his mouth and suckled gently.

Not even when he moved to her other breast, washing a path from one to the other with his tongue, did she move. She stood as if rooted, the only sign of life the heat of her skin and the faint, fine trembling of her muscles. The thin line of crimson on her skin from the point of his sword made him feel as if he'd desecrated something sacred. He silently, gently, wiped away the blood with the hem of her shirt until only a faint trace remained.

Her silent acquiescence added to the feeling of unreality, to the dreamlike stillness of her slender body. Chance was afraid to move quickly, for fear of shattering the dream. The shimmer of moonlight and faint scent of wild roses and honeysuckle only heightened the sense of being in a dream.

Had he dreamed this before? This silent seduction, this golden-skinned temptress, felt strangely familiar. There was an odd sensation of having met before, of having stood in the moonlight with this young woman and touched the stars.

Chance lowered his hands, breathing quickly, his body taut with need even while he questioned his own sanity. His mask felt suddenly too confining and hot over his face, as if made of heavy wool instead of thin, cool silk.

For a long moment they stood inches apart, both breathing raggedly, staring at one another as if hypnotized. Then she broke the spell, her words cool and deflating.

"Are you through?"

A dash of cold water in his face would hardly have had more effect. He tensed, and from somewhere, he heard his own voice sound much cooler than he felt.

"For now."

"Am I free to leave?"

He forced a mocking smile, remembering with effort the hard-learned lesson that females could abandon passion at a moment's notice.

"That depends, fair lady, on what you feel free to do once you leave."

She still had made no effort to cover herself, but stood

stiff and proud against the tree trunk, eyes studying him from behind her mask.

"Are there certain requirements?"

"Naturally. You didn't suppose that I would allow you to hunt in my territory, did you? No one does that, least of all a puling chit in men's breeches who has the audacity to aspire to the role of highwayman."

"I see." She paused for a moment. "Then you do not care if I expand my efforts in other territories? Is that what you are saying?"

"It most certainly is not." He reached for his sword, snatching it from the ground and wiping the blade clean with short, savage motions before sheathing it. "I have no intention of allowing you to parade about masquerading as me. You're a reckless embarrassment as a highwayman."

"And if I choose to continue?"

He stared at her in amazement. Unwillingly, his eyes briefly shifted to her bare breasts before he jerked them away again, back to her defiantly lifted chin and stubborn, irritating little mouth.

"I'll stop you, of course."

"And pray, how will you do that, sir? Put a notice in the papers, perhaps, that the genuine Moon Rider will appear on Marlborough Downs the night of the next full moon, and that any other similarly clad highwayman is an impostor? I should like to see that." She pushed away from the tree. He heard the fierce tremor in her voice as she took a step closer to him, the daring, impudent little vixen. "Or perhaps you will kill me instead. That should end it."

"Yes," he heard himself say savagely, "it should. And I might be persuaded to do just that if you insist upon being fool enough to provoke me."

There was a flicker of disquiet in her eyes, and in the

slight falter of her step. "Have you descended to that level then, sir? To kill a rival even though it is a woman?"

Angry now and furious that she would try to take refuge behind her womanhood, he startled a gasp from her by grabbing her wrist and jerking her close. The warm press of her bare skin against his shirt was a reminder of the sweetness he'd tasted so briefly, and for a moment he just glared down at her without speaking.

Then, slowly and distinctly, he said, "If you persist in this idiocy, I will not hesitate to see you bound and delivered to the high sheriff in Salisbury. What happens to you after that will be none of my concern."

It was a very real, convincing threat, and they both knew it. While neither of them was at all certain that he would actually kill her, both knew he would have little compunction in allowing the magistrates to handle her.

After a moment's taut silence, she said softly, "I take your point, sir."

He released her wrist with a shove, and she staggered back a step. Damn her, he was still hard and aching, and if one of them didn't leave quickly, he'd ignore all common sense and give in to the urge to push her to the ground and take her. He wanted her, wanted her more than he could recall ever wanting any woman, and he was damned if he knew why.

Saucy little baggage, he hadn't even seen her face. He was still tempted to yank away her mask and didn't know why he was reluctant. She could be covered with smallpox scars and have a squint for all he knew.

But somehow, he knew that she wouldn't be. He knew in a visceral, instinctive recess, that her face would live up to the alluring promise of her body.

And that thought goaded him much longer than he'd ever deemed possible.

Chapter 10

"Are you unwell, Miss 'Anna?"

She turned blindly, groping for sense behind her maid's words. It came slowly, and she flushed when she realized that Serena was staring at her oddly.

"No. Well—yes. A touch unwell, I think. Just . . . just a headache."

"A headache?"

Serena looked alarmed, and Rhianna thought instantly of her father's painful headaches in the days before the onset of his illness.

"Not that kind of headache. Just the kind that comes in cycles."

Understanding dawned on Serena's face. "I can make you some tea, miss."

"Tea would be nice, thank you." She paused, then added softly, "But enjoy your own tea first. You look rather peaked, and I know the past months have been hard for you."

"Oh, I don't mind it. 'Tis much better than not having a post at all, is what I told me mum when she asked about my wages. At least I have food and a roof over my head, and when things are better, well, I'll be able to help out my family again."

Serena's uncomplaining loyalty made Rhianna's throat tighten with emotion. The few servants left, Serena and

Fenwick and Porter, asked for nothing beyond being allowed to serve. They took care of the baronet with love and devotion, and pulled together to ease Rhianna's worries.

"Thank you," she said softly.

Serena smiled. As if bestowing a gift upon her mistress, the girl leaned forward and said, "I heard a bit o' news about your handsome earl, miss."

"He's not my earl. . . ."

"Oh, I didn't mean no disrespect, Miss 'Anna. Since he has visited you, I only thought you might want to know what they're saying about him now."

Though she knew she shouldn't encourage gossip, Rhianna couldn't resist hearing what was being said about Chance.

"I hope Lord Wolverton is doing well," she said noncommittally.

Serena grinned. " 'Twould seem so. Riever from over at Whiteash Manor told Fenwick—they're cousins, you see—that the earl paid a visit on Lord Heffington. Seems that Lord Roxbury was there, and he's been makin' all kinds of talk about his lordship the earl. Anyway, 'tis said there was a terrific row, with Viscount Roxbury kickin' up a dust about Lord Wolverton cutting off his credit at one of the London gaming hells. Words were exchanged, and before you could say Tom Scat, that nasty viscount attacked the earl with a rapier. Well, it took three footmen and a groom to pry the earl offa Roxbury, and he didn't even bother to draw a weapon on the viscount. Said Roxbury wasn't worth bloodying good steel."

Appalled, Rhianna couldn't speak for a moment. Then she said, "Wolverton could have been killed. He should not have gone there unarmed."

"Oh, he was armed, miss. He just didn't use his sword on the viscount. That's what made Roxbury so blazing mad. All of Wiltshire has been talkin' about it, and sayin' as how the earl always has been dangerous, ever since he was a boy. I mean, to insult Roxbury as he did, reminds people of how his uncle died—"

"Serena." Rhianna put up a hand. "Enough. I've too much on my mind already."

Contrite, Serena nodded understanding. "I s'pose you do, miss. Is it the recent talk of the Moon Rider that has you so upset?"

"The Moon Rider?" Rhianna managed a shrug. "What talk is there now?"

"You mean you haven't heard?" Serena stepped close, her voice lowering as if afraid of being overheard. " 'Tis said that he no longer rides alone, you know. He's been said to have taken a mate." She gave a theatrical shudder. " 'Twill be like the devil takin' a partner, don't you think?"

"I'm certain I don't think about it at all, and if you have any sense, you won't pay attention to gossip either. A mate—more than likely, he's stooped to stealing from other thieves as well."

When Serena twisted her hands in front of her, Rhianna wished she hadn't been so short with her.

"Forgive me, Serena. It's just that I've so much on my mind lately."

"You rest, miss. You worry too much. Things will be better. You'll see."

If only that were true. After Serena left, Rhianna turned back to stare out at the garden. Chance, risking his life and what was left of his reputation with Roxbury —had he learned nothing since he was a boy? He was still impetuous, still wild and reckless.

A faint smile curved her mouth. People changed, she supposed. Who would have ever thought she would be bold enough to pose as a highwayman? She shuddered suddenly. The Moon Rider's warning still echoed in her mind, soft menace underlying his promise.

I will not hesitate to see you bound and delivered to the high sheriff in Salisbury. What happens to you after that will be none of my concern.

She shivered. He would do it, she was certain of that. Yet how could she earn enough funds to support their small household in any other way?

Ideas chased through her mind like birds on the wing, always being rejected by cold common sense. There was no other way to earn the necessary money to pay Sir Griffyn's medical bills or to buy food. The few coins she had left would barely stretch through the next week, and they were much too close to the six months Mr. Blemmons had mentioned.

Rhianna moved to the small chair in front of the window and sat down, her hands twisting in her lap. All the household furniture that could be spared had been sold. Empty rooms had been closed off, paintings taken down from walls, and carpets rolled up and sold as well. The silver was gone, as was the gold plate with the Llewellyn family crest engraved on each piece. The only horse left in the stable was the white horse she'd ridden on her last foray as the Moon Rider.

A feeling of helplessness swamped her, and she fought the urge to bury her face in her hands. Damn that arrogant highwayman. He'd caused this, with his heartless actions, but she was forced to deal with it. She and her family had to bear the consequences, and she hated him for it.

Heat rushed into her cheeks as she recalled the last time she'd seen him, how he'd touched her with his hands and mouth as she'd stood frozen by fear and indecision. There had been a heavy, pounding pulse inside her when he'd caressed her, ignited by the intimacy of the moment and the unfamiliar, shocking touch of his hands and mouth. Mixed with the sear of shock, had been a strange excitement, a restless yearning that she hadn't expected and not known how to deal with. So she'd remained still, churning inside with the heat of her reaction, stunned by the rising sense of urgency that he had provoked.

There were moments it still sent her into turmoil, the memories of his touch, the wicked glitter in his dark eyes that had seemed to mock her reaction. He'd seemed to know how he made her feel, how she would remember it later and writhe with a frustrated yearning she didn't understand and didn't want to acknowledge.

How could she feel that way about a man she'd never really met? A man whose face she'd never seen? It left her unsettled, and with a rising sense of confusion that would probably greatly amuse the Moon Rider if he knew it.

Damn him. Yes, damn him to hell and back.

Rhianna stood up, hands curling into her skirts in tight fists. He thought she would just retreat into a hole and not dare emerge again, be too frightened to confront him in his own territory. Well, he was the cause of her father's illness, by God, and if fortune was with her, the Moon Rider had a surprise in store for him. She would throw down a challenge, and this time, she would not allow him to chase her away so easily. No, this time, she would leave him wondering what had happened.

"Bloody hell!" Chance paced the floor of his chamber, snarling at the unperturbed Hobson, who calmly went about scraping mud clods off the carpet. "The little bitch got away this time, and there wasn't a damn thing I could do about it."

Hobson carefully scraped the last clod of mud from the patterned carpet into a flat metal scoop and stood up. "What would you have done if you'd caught her, my lord?"

Chance paused, staring at him. "Unmasked her and delivered her to the nearest magistrate," he said at last.

Hobson's brow lifted.

"Oh? And how would you have explained your involvement? I am quite certain a bold piece such as this young lady seems to be would not go quietly and without certain accusations of her own."

Speechless, Chance took a moment to answer. "I presume I would have found someone else to do it for me, then. After all, being an earl does have some advantages."

"Ah, and being the earl of Wolverton, a man with a *spotless* reputation, should scotch any temptation to listen to the young lady's words."

"Damn it to bloody hell, your sarcasm is not helpful." Chance took a deep breath, glaring at the still unperturbed Hobson. "Very well," he said after a moment, "perhaps her accusations would be heard. But believed? Who would believe some village whore's assertions over mine in a matter such as that?"

"I was under the impression you did not know her identity."

"I don't."

"Then how can you be certain she is a village whore, my lord? Was her speech vulgar? Cockney, perhaps? Did she appear to be a slattern?"

No. Her voice had been soft and cultured, and there had been no hint of a slattern about her. Her skin had been too soft, her carriage too graceful and assured.

He should have unmasked her. Why hadn't he? It would have been simple enough to just reach out and untie the ribbons that held on her hood and mask, pull them away to reveal her identity. Yet he hadn't. He'd not wanted to know who she was, and he couldn't fathom the reason why. Perhaps because it would have destroyed the illusion, but that was a damn foolish reason.

As foolish as allowing her to escape with only a warning, apparently.

"Devil take the wench," he muttered.

Hobson again lifted his brow in that maddening way he had.

"I take it that means she is a slattern, my lord?"

He sucked in a sharp breath. "Not in the sense you mean, perhaps. But she definitely has the soul of a demi-monde, Hobson, mark my words."

"Then offer her the security of your protection, and she will cease to be a problem and danger, my lord. It has worked since the first man came up with that arrangement, and I see no reason for it not to work with a young woman who obviously desires money to the point of risking life and limb for it."

Chance stared at him a long moment, then gave a bark of laughter. "I should have requested your advice two months ago, Hobson. If I had, it would have saved me from feeling like a bloody ass on the moors last night, watching her pluck the very pigeons I was pursuing."

"Heffington, I presume?"

"You presume correctly. Either he has become an expert gamester—which is highly unlikely—or he has fattened his purse with some very suspicious funds lately. I lean toward the theory that he has recently parted with some highly sensitive documents of great value to Napoleon."

"Quite. A despicable sort of man, in my opinion."

"Yet Heffington is accepted in all the best houses, and is a member of the Carlton House set."

Hobson ignored the bitter sarcasm. "So is your friend Brummel."

"Yes, but he deserves acceptance. Heffington does not." Chance frowned for a moment. Then he looked up with a sardonic smile. "By God, I believe I have an idea, Hobson. You're an absolute genius."

"Quite so, my lord."

Fitful clouds scudded across the face of the full moon, filtering the light. It was a warm night, though the wind was rising and promised rain. Rhianna waited impatiently, adjusting and readjusting her silk mask and her cape. The road from Salisbury to London was as well traveled as the Bath Road, and she was hidden in the bushes where it divided to continue to Bath. An excellent choice, in her opinion, and not one that would invite detection.

A satisfied smile curved her mouth. With the money she had taken the past two months, she'd managed to stave off the seizing of Serenity House. Papa was showing a marked improvement, and she'd even been able to pay reduced wages to her faithful servants. Yes, if she could only take two or three coaches this evening, she should be able to stop for a while.

Once she'd hit upon a strategy, she'd avoided the Moon Rider's interference. She chose roads he did not, and made her moves on the night just before or just after the full moon. The slight difference in pattern had apparently been successful; only once had she come close to being taken by him, and that time she'd managed to evade him by just a few minutes. It had been much too narrow an escape for comfort, but she'd laughed at the thought of his chagrin.

Her mount whickered softly, ears pricking forward.

Rhianna leaned over his neck. "Do you hear a coach coming, Beau?" she whispered softly, heartbeat quickening as it always did just before a coach rumbled into view. She patted his sleek neck, then sat up.

She had an instant's premonition before she heard the husky, "You are much too easy to find, my lady."

Rhianna froze. Her heart seemed to leap into her throat at the soft, menacing words, and she knew without turning who was behind her. Still, she turned slowly to see the pale rider outlined against the dark shadows of trees and bushes.

The darker shape of a drawn pistol was unmistakable, and it was pointed directly at her. His magnificent stallion snorted softly, pawing at the earth.

"Well," Rhianna managed to say coolly, "have you come to take lessons, sir?"

"Not exactly." There was a short pause. "I have come to teach you a lesson, my sweet."

Dark promise was inherent in the words, a malicious whisper in the night, filled with the stuff of nightmare and dread. Rhianna shuddered.

She made no protest when he reached out for her reins. Within a few moments, he had secured her hands in front of her, and was leading her horse down a wooded path that was unfamiliar to her. This entire area was foreign to her, except for the possible escape routes she had investigated ahead of time. She'd followed the Moon Rider's advice to the letter, save for his warning about risking his ire.

The shivers that rippled down her spine had nothing to do with the cool wind whisking over her half-covered face. Rhianna had the brief, hopeless wish that she had listened to him.

•   •   •

It was late when they arrived at their destination. She wasn't surprised to see the same hut where he'd taken her before. The open door creaked softly in the rising wind, a rhythmic, eerie sound that lifted the hairs on the nape of her neck. She slumped wearily in the saddle as he led the horses under a rough structure, apparently a stable of sorts.

Evidently, he intended to delay her delivery to the magistrates until daylight. Probably because he wanted to avoid capture himself. She wasn't naive enough to think he intended personally to deliver her and knew that he must have confederates who would manage that end of it.

What would they do to a woman? She suddenly recalled the public hanging in London of a woman arrested for stealing bread. There had been no mercy shown her, but hoots and shouts of laughter as she'd danced frantically at the end of the gibbet.

No, mercy could not be expected. Not for a highwayman—or woman—who had tweaked the noses of constables for so long. She had to be strong, had to keep from giving in to stark fear, and she had to *think*. There must be a way out of this, there must. She had too many people who depended on her, and she couldn't let them down.

Rhianna offered no protest when he pulled her roughly from her horse and propelled her toward the unwelcoming hut. Beyond a few curt directions, he'd said little on the ride and seemed in no mood now for casual conversation. When she stumbled, he yanked her upright again, his hands guiding her toward the sagging door.

His touch reminded her of how he'd touched her once before, light caresses that had unsettled her beyond belief, gentle explorations that had awakened unfamiliar and frightening sensations in her. Was he too remembering that?

A glance at his face gave her no hint. He'd wanted her before—she'd seen it in the way he held her and touched her, known it for what it was. After all, she had been reared in the freedom of a gypsy camp where sexual matters had been a matter-of-fact part of life.

What had been so shocking about her previous encounter with the Moon Rider had been her reaction to him. Never had a man dared to touch her so intimately, and never had she been so acutely aware of her inexperience.

Perhaps the time had come to use her femininity as well as her wit to her advantage. The stakes were certainly high enough—her life and freedom.

And it wasn't so difficult, she thought when the Moon Rider put a bold hand on her, to barter one for the other.

Chapter 11

Thunder rumbled in the distance, a rolling sound that promised a fierce storm. It was a suitable accompaniment to Chance's mood. While he was a fair hand at intimidating and terrorizing any number of males of various stations in life, the thought of what he seriously contemplated wreaking on a female was faintly abhorrent.

The girl's eyes were dark behind the mask, but he could see the fear in them plain enough, fear and some other emotion he couldn't identify. It made him edgy and hardly improved his mood. She watched him silently when he untied her hands and shoved her to the hard comfort of a three-legged stool, not taking her wary gaze from him as he moved to the stone hearth and knelt beside it.

A neat stack of logs waited in the fireplace, ready for someone to light them. He dug into a coat pocket for the packet that held an ethereal match. He broke the small glass tube and held the spurt of flame to the dry tinder beneath the logs. It caught after a few seconds, flaring quickly and shedding a patch of light in the hut.

Still crouched in front of the hearth, Chance shifted to stare at his prisoner. Her jaw was taut, mouth thinned into a straight line that gave no evidence of surrender. He smiled grimly and saw her uneasy glance toward the open door.

"Ah no, little pigeon, do not even think of flying my cozy coop. Give me a few minutes, and it will be quite homey enough, I think."

"Not as homey as my own parlor," she shot back, and he eyed her closely for a moment. There was something familiar about her voice when she wasn't trying to disguise it, and the odd sense that he'd met her before returned. He stood up and crossed to where she perched atop the stool.

She didn't lift her head to look up at him when he towered over her, but kept her gaze fixed on some distant spot on the floor. His palm cupped her chin and lifted her face. Her eyes widened.

"Perhaps it is time we removed your disguise," he said softly.

She made a strangled sound. "No!" Her hand closed around his wrist with surprising strength. "You obviously have a reason for wanting your identity secret, sir, and I beg of you to grant me the same courtesy."

"Did you grant me the courtesy of heeding my request that you stop impersonating me?"

"You did not request it, you demanded it." She drew in a shaky little breath, then blurted out, "I could not stop, for I knew of no other way to get the money I need. Surely you can understand that."

"No, I cannot understand why anyone would not heed my reasonable demand to stop masquerading as me in my own territory. It goes beyond belief that you were foolish enough to continue."

Her fingers tightened imperceptibly, and he saw her bite her lower lip before she murmured, "I was wrong."

Amused by how much it obviously cost her to admit that, he waited a moment before saying, "Yes. And see what it has gotten you."

Her head tilted back so that she was looking up at him. "Just what has it gotten me?"

"Apprehended." He drew her up slowly, ignoring the slight pressure of her effort to hold him at arm's length. A flicker of sympathy kept him from pressing his point home with the action he'd intended, and he contented himself with resting a hand on her shoulder.

She was shivering; he could feel the fine trembling in her muscles, the tremors that told him her brave facade was much thinner than she would have liked. His hand shifted from her shoulder back to her chin, cupping it lightly. He held her in the firm vise of thumb and fingers, enjoying the rich feel of her skin.

This time, however, he had no intention of allowing himself to be lured into blatant desire. This time, he had a firm purpose in mind that would gain an inevitable victory. A woman in her position would have little choice but to accept his proposition.

Lazily, watching her through half-lowered lashes, he began to flick open the buttons of her shirt. One by one, he undid them, aware of her sudden stillness and tension. She did not speak, but remained stiff and silent as she had the last time.

When he had the blouse undone to her waist, he shoved it from her shoulders down her arms to the elbows. Then he went as still as she, gazing at her bared body with heated interest. He'd not forgotten how lovely she was, how high and proud her breasts or tawny skin, or coral-tipped nipples that seemed to beg for the touch of a man's hand. That particular memory had haunted him more nights than he cared to recall at the moment.

He drew in a deep breath and let his hands fall to his sides, watching her. She did not look at him, but stood in quiet repose. Had she done this so many times that it had no affect on her? Probably, though she had somehow kept that elusive quality of innocence that so intrigued him.

Slowly, deliberately, he reached out to caress her again, with an insolent familiarity calculated to provoke a reaction. Her head snapped up, eyes darting to his face.

"If you have a proposition to make, sir, do so and be done with it. It's quite chilly in the night air."

Once more, she'd managed to make him feel like a hot, untrained schoolboy, and he resented it. His hand dropped to his side, and he kept his tone cool with an effort.

"As a matter of fact, I do have a proposition to make. I'm certain you're not surprised by that, as you must hear many of them."

She gave no reply, but gazed at him steadily. Firelight played over her, and he resisted the temptation to cover her back up with her shirt. He waited for her to react or to speak, but she didn't, and several moments crawled past while he fought the desire to touch her. Finally, he gave in and looked away from the tempting thrust of her breasts, as he was certain she had intended.

He acknowledged her small victory with a wry smile. "Since you seem so curious, I'll present it to you quickly. I cannot afford to have you running amok on the moors and ruining all my plans. Your masquerade as the Moon Rider is quite—shall we say—inconvenient at this time. I am prepared to offer you an alternative to dancing from the end of a gibbet at the magistrate's whim."

He paused, watching her, and her small chin bobbed once in acknowledgment.

"Very well, my talkative miss, here is my proposition —I will pay you fifty pounds a year, which you will earn by being available at my leisure. Do you understand what I mean by that?"

"I'm not an idiot. Certainly I understand. But I require much more than that."

An unaccountable disappointment stabbed him. He had half-expected her to be outraged, denounce him and toss his indecent proposition back in his face. Yet she stood there calmly bartering for more money.

With his lip curled in disgust, he considered her for a moment. "Do you realize I could just take what I want from you without payment?"

She nodded. "Yes. You could. But you won't. Pride won't let you descend to raping a woman. You much prefer sweet agreement to screaming resistance, I think."

Damn the bloody little bitch's perception. How did she know?

"How much do you require?" he asked curtly.

"A hundred pounds a year, and twenty to be distributed among my three servants."

That brought his brow up. "Servants?" He surveyed her with a skepticism that brought a flush to what he could see of her face. Apparently, she realized that he'd thought her a servant herself. Her voice faltered slightly.

"Yes. And I want . . . an allowance for my . . . my mother. She is in ill-health, and I desire that she be cared for. If you cannot meet my requirements, in all fairness you should release me, for I will have agreed but for the terms."

Chance moved to the fireplace and turned with his back to it, staring at her. The heat warmed his back and legs, but he felt a familiar coldness settle inside. This was much too familiar to him, the dickering for sexual favors with a greedy mistress.

"It would be easier," he said brutally, "to turn you over to the magistrate than it would be to meet your demands."

She shrugged carelessly. "Yes, but then I will tell him

how we met. Surely, those in the coach I stopped will recall that there were two of us."

It occurred to him then, as he stood glaring at her, that her unreasonable demands were meant to be refused. She thought he was a highwayman, with little means of his own to support himself. She didn't know he was an earl, with enough money to support a hundred mistresses if he chose. Her cool bartering was meant to shame him. She obviously preferred the magistrate's justice to being his mistress.

A faint smile curved his mouth, and he saw her eyes narrow warily. "I believe we have a bargain, my sweet. A hundred pounds a year, to be paid quarterly, twenty for your servants, and care for your invalid mother. I have a house in upper Wiltshire that will suit nicely, I think."

Shock widened her eyes, and he knew he'd been right.

Rhianna controlled the impulse to flee with an almost visible effort. Her hands curled into fists at her sides. She felt he had bared much more than her breasts to his mocking gaze. He'd stripped her desperate ploy to the bone.

Perhaps she could stall him, pretend to agree, then make her escape at the first opportunity. Damn the rogue, his erotic mouth was curled in a mocking smile that made her want to lash out at him.

Suddenly she had the distinct, uneasy feeling that she had seen that particular smile before.

Though tempted to ask that he remove his mask, since she had no intention of doing the same, she swallowed the impulse. He moved lazily toward her, his stride graceful, yet powerfully controlled. She took a hesitant step back.

"Should our agreement not be documented in writing?" she asked.

"Documented? Bloody hell, the arrangement is not quite the same thing as a marriage, you know. Though I suppose a wife would be near as expensive to maintain."

"But much harder to get rid of later."

"An excellent point." The mocking smile flashed. "Then it will be done, if you insist."

"When the papers are completed, I will keep my part of the bargain, sir. Until then, I—"

"Oh no." He reached out to grab her, his hand closing on her wrist and pulling her up against his hard body. "I have no intention of waiting. And what will a little time matter to a woman so obviously experienced in arranging such advantageous propositions to her own satisfaction?" He held her against him, ignoring her effort to twist away.

Panic flowered into full bloom, and she dug the heels of her hands into his chest to hold him at bay. But the Moon Rider was not to be held at bay, not to be diverted.

"I do not—"

His mouth came down over hers, smothering her words, hot and fierce and wild. She shuddered under the onslaught, felt his anger and bitterness in the ruthless plundering of her mouth. Her struggles slowed finally, the strength of his embrace allowing her little room to resist. This time, his caresses were rough, hands moving over her breasts with a swift certainty that was frightening.

Then his hand moved lower, thrust between her thighs in a quick motion that wrenched them apart, and she felt him touch her intimately. If not for the snug breeches she wore, he would no doubt have done much more than just touch, and she tried to wrest away from him.

She suddenly went limp and compliant in his arms. He lifted his head and stared down at her, the mask making him seem cruel and inhuman.

"What is this bloody new game you're playing?"

"You want me. You have me. 'Tis your game, sir."

His eyes narrowed, dark and angry against the white silk. Then he released her abruptly, so abruptly she had to catch herself from falling to the dirt floor of the hut. A log in the fire popped and hissed, shadows dancing across the room in eerie patterns that made her think of frenzied demons.

They stared at one another, tension vibrating between them like a struck tuning fork. A rumble of thunder shook the ground and hut, and a crack of lightning briefly turned the night as bright as day.

In that brilliant flash of illumination, Rhianna saw the pain and anger in the Moon Rider's eyes, saw the thick brush of his lashes lower in a sulky glide to hide it from her. She stared at the moody curve of his mouth, the strong line of his jaw, and the ebony strands of hair that had escaped from beneath his mask to tangle on his neck.

And she knew, suddenly, with a certainty that left her reeling, who he was.

Chapter 12

Chance stared at her. He sensed something different in her attitude toward him, something disturbing.

Two strides took him to her, and he jerked her blouse back over her bare breasts with angry, impatient motions.

"Get out of here," he said curtly.

She didn't move, didn't attempt to hold the blouse over her breasts, but stood staring at him with wide, unreadable eyes. It was unnerving and infuriating.

His hand cupped her chin, and he saw her slight wince of pain as he gripped it tightly. "If you want to leave with your skin intact, my sweet, I suggest you follow my advice while I'm still in such a mellow mood."

There was enough menace in that one sentence to send her screaming from the hut into the storm, but she still didn't move. His eyes narrowed hotly. His temper was raw, unpredictable at best, and he wished she would heed his warning before he did something they would both regret.

Then she cleared her throat and said softly, "I intend to keep my bargain, sir. Here. Now."

He watched her in disbelief as she shrugged out of the blouse and let it fall to the floor in a glide like the silent fall of snow. Then her fingers were unfastening the buttons of her breeches. Mesmerized, he watched as she removed boots, stockings, and breeches, the flickering flame of the fire an inadequate light.

Finally she stood in front of him wearing only the silk mask and hood over her head and face. His voice came out in a hoarse croak.

"Take off the mask."

She shook her head. "No. Not yet. Will you allow me that one stipulation?"

For the life of him, he couldn't think of a good reason why he shouldn't. And it didn't matter anyway, because she was coming toward him, her slender body a golden wand in the rosy light, more perfect than any he could recall. If there were imperfections, he didn't see them; certainly not in her slim waist and gently swelling hips, nor the firm length of her thighs and calves. She carried herself with the assurance of a young queen, confident and unself-conscious of her body, as if she had been reared to have no modesty or shame about her physical self.

When she reached him, she began unbuttoning his shirt as she had done hers, then reached up to untie the strings that held his cape around his shoulders. That movement snapped his restraint, and with a low, hungry growl, he swept her up into his arms and strode to the far corner of the hut.

A ladder ascended to a loft filled with hay. He carried her up as if she weighed no more than a sack of feathers. She was warm against his bare chest, her curves soft and enticing. He flung his cape down on the mounds of hay, then lowered her to the fragrant bed.

His body ached for release but he held tight to his restraint. This would be no quick sealing of a bargain, but a leisurely exploration of the senses. He'd thought of her too often not to take his time now.

"Undress me," he murmured, watching as she knelt in

front of him on the hay and reached for the knee-ribbons of his breeches. She untied them, flicking them loose to release his boots, then pulling off his footwear with an ease that suggested practice. She peeled away his stockings, then rose to her knees again to reach up for the buttons of his breeches. The movement made her breasts jiggle slightly, a temptation that he could not resist.

While she tugged at the side buttons, he caressed her soft skin, fingers sliding over the smooth rise of breasts to the darker peak. When he rolled the nipple between his thumb and forefinger, she drew in a sharp breath and glanced up at him. Her hands shook slightly as she finished undoing his buttons, then she moved backward and away.

It took him only a moment to strip away his last article of clothing, and he was faintly surprised to note that she had averted her eyes.

He dropped to his knees beside her, straw crackling a faint protest beneath his weight. It occurred to him that he didn't even know her name. He kissed her gently on her chin, then found the pulse in her throat and kissed it before asking, "What do they call you?"

She seemed startled by the question and took a moment to answer. "Cynthia," she finally said, her voice soft in the shadows. "It's Greek for the moon goddess."

He smiled. A country courtesan who knew Greek. The wonders of the world never ceased, but at the moment, he didn't care to debate the wisdom of forming a tryst with a woman who knew such things.

The eroticism of making love to a naked woman in a silk mask and hood overshadowed the surprise that she knew Greek, and he focused on kissing a path from her tempting mouth to the delightful curve of her breast. He lingered there, teasing the nipple into a tight bud with tongue and lips, until he heard her soft moans and trembling sighs. Then he moved to the other breast, lavishing the same attention until she moved restlessly beneath him, her hands moving lightly over his bare back and shoulders.

Her movements were awkward, almost inexperienced, and he shifted position. He kissed her again, coaxing her lips apart to allow his tongue inside, almost groaning when she opened for him. Warm honey and heated velvet, arousing and painful and breathtaking.

"Sweet Cynthia," he muttered hotly, kissing the corners of her mouth, her chin beneath the silk, the soft sweep of her jaw. He stretched out beside her and put a leg over her thighs. The wool cape scratched against his skin, and the sharp crackle of bruised straw snapped a protest. "Open for me," he cajoled, sliding his hand down over her small belly to the juncture of her thighs. She'd clenched them against him, and he could feel the slight quiver of her muscles. His fingers tangled in the burnished nest of curls, the red-gold veil that hid her most intimate parts from him. He stroked his thumb over her, inching lower in a steady, rhythmic glide until she made a strangled sound in the back of her throat.

Her voice quivered slightly. "Are you sure . . . this is what you . . . want?"

The question confounded him. He nuzzled her neck, and gave in to the certainty that he would have to soothe and coax her into doing what they both wanted. He knew she was ready, had felt her betraying dampness, but surrendered to the driving need of a female to be reassured.

"I need you," he said and had the fervent thought that he'd never uttered a truer statement. He was about to explode with frustration and pent-up tension.

He kissed her gently until she began to relax again, until her thighs parted enough to allow his entire hand the task of stroking her. She quivered, small tremors that made her body shudder, and he found that delicious. He glanced up at her, saw her eyes focused on him with an almost bewildered light in them and found that equally delicious. No one had ever taken the time to arouse her, it seemed, and he took great pleasure in bringing her to a gasping release that obviously shocked her.

Small cries like the mews of a kitten drifted into the close air of the loft, and she clutched at him with wild, almost frantic movements. He held her until she quieted, then began again the slow rise of tension with heated kisses and intimate caresses.

This time, when her hips moved restlessly on the wool cape, he moved between her thighs, his body fitting to hers in a smooth glide that made her stiffen. He leaned to kiss her parted lips again, ignoring the faint sound of protest she made when he pressed forward. He ached to feel her close around him, to feel the tight glove of her body sheathe his with damp heat.

Satin resistance met his efforts, and he groaned with a mixture of impatience and anticipation. She was much tighter than he'd thought she'd be, and he drew back a bit before thrusting forward in a single, determined assault. He felt her body shudder, felt an inner barrier briefly bar his progress before yielding, and was shocked. His head jerked back, and he stared down at her.

The silk mask was damp beneath the eyes, and her bottom lip had teeth marks in its smooth swell.

"Is this some kind of trick?" he demanded harshly, half-expecting an angry father to come storming through the door of the hut and demand to see his ruined daughter wed.

Her voice was faint. "No trick. A bargain kept, sir."

For an instant he stared down at her, uncertainly. It

was too late to turn back. Slowly, to keep from hurting her, he began to move in a steady rhythm that gradually increased. Her soft gasps melded into urgent cries, and he forgot about her lost virginity and his carelessness, and everything but the driving need to find the release that this one woman promised him. For some reason, he felt that his salvation lay only in her arms, and he didn't care to explore that emotion any more than was necessary.

Thunder rumbled loudly again, shaking the foundations of the hut, and his hoarse groan of release was lost in the roar of the storm outside. The storm inside was even more fierce, more shattering than anything Mother Nature could produce.

Drained, Chance relaxed gradually, the tension leaving his taut muscles. He held her close to him as the rain began to fall, filtering through the random thatching of the roof to mist his heated skin.

The thatched roof dripped steadily, rain pattering in a light drizzle around them. Occasionally, a drop spattered on her arm or leg, or Chance's back. She held him in a loose clasp of her arms, listening to the steady thud of his heart against her cheek.

So this was what it was all about, this consuming need to be one with a man, to fill the aching void inside with his body. She'd known the particulars, of course, but not how she would feel when she gave herself to a man.

That decision had been abrupt and irreversible, the moment she had realized that the Moon Rider was the same man as the earl of Wolverton. It had struck her suddenly that she was in love with him—had always been in love with him, though the years had kept them apart.

She should have known him at once. Chance, that angry, hurt boy, still fought a private battle against the world. He allowed no one in, took no risks—or prisoners. A faint smile curved her mouth.

She was probably a fool, but even the angry knowledge that he'd caused her father's illness had not mattered. She knew him well enough to sense that he would never have wished her father harm. She recalled his look of shock when she'd told him how she blamed the Moon Rider.

What had seemed disaster only a short time before, had now changed into something else. She wasn't certain yet what she would do when he discovered her identity, as he surely would, but would deal with that when necessary.

The storm had lessened, the thunder now a distant echo of its former fury. She ran a hand over the smooth skin of Chance's back, testing the contours with the pads of her fingers, marveling at the blend of bone and muscle into such pleasing symmetry. Finally he lifted his head, dark eyes pinning her with a steady gaze.

"You should have told me."

His abrupt statement made her smile. "Told you what?"

"Don't pretend you don't know what I'm talking about. I want to know why you didn't."

She shifted a bit on the bed of hay and wool to see him better, tilting her head to an angle. When she smiled and traced the erotic outline of his mouth with a fingertip, he grabbed her hand, squeezing it.

"We made a deal," he reminded her harshly.

His abrupt reminder shattered her contentment. She gave him a mocking smile.

"Yes, we did. Are you displeased with me already?"

"That's not what I'm talking about." He pulled away

from her and sat up, drawing up one knee and draping his arm over it. The silk mask was twisted, and strands of his dark hair tumbled free over his shoulders.

"I can't be manipulated," he said flatly. "Remember that if you have any grand ideas."

Allowing a faint smile to curve her mouth, Rhianna said lightly, "I shall most certainly remember that you cannot be manipulated."

Her hand moved to stroke his thigh in a bold caress, and she felt his shudder when her fingers grazed him. He glanced down to where her hand rested, jet lashes lowering over his eyes. She felt his muscles tighten beneath her palm. When she followed his gaze, she saw bright smears glistening dully on the white wool cape.

"It can be cleaned if you soak the stains in vinegar," she began, and his head jerked up. He gave her a hot, angry glance that silenced her, then rose to his feet in a swift motion like that of an irritated cat.

"I suppose I'm not surprised that it means no more to you than it does," he said sharply.

When she made no reply he gave an impatient exclamation and began jerking on his breeches.

Rhianna watched silently, admiring his lean-muscled arrogance even as she deplored it. He was an earl masquerading as a highwayman. She wondered why. Was he that bored with an indolent life? Had gaming hells and fast horses and faster women begun to lose his interest?

Perhaps that was the reason behind his desire to make her his mistress. A highwaywoman for a highwayman.

It was faintly amusing that he was more disturbed than she was over the loss of her virginity. She had no intention of telling him how little it meant to her that it was lost and how much that he had been the one to take it. She knew, with a sudden, swift certainty unlike anything she'd ever felt before, that their destinies were irrevocably entwined.

What had just happened had been meant to happen. She recalled Marisa's worried eyes and fretful questions so long ago. Her aunt had known then, had foreseen what would happen.

Had Marisa feared her falling in love with the earl? Or were there other reasons her aunt had warned her away from him? Her gaze shifted back to him, and she felt the painful lurch in her chest that she'd felt the day she'd thought she would not see him again.

Wicked, deceitful, arrogant man, as larcenous as any East End pickpocket, as beautiful as any angel. Yes, she must have fallen in love with him when she was thirteen, and only Marisa had seen it.

And he didn't even remember her, didn't recall the gypsy girl in bare feet and bangles.

She propped her head in her palm, wishing she could remove the silk mask and take down the coils of her hair, wishing she could remove Chance's mask and see his face. Not that he would have allowed her to see behind the mask he showed the world; she'd seen that mask at the Huntington ball, seen his casual arrogance and cynical wit, the cool, speculative gaze he gave women that divided them into the available and unavailable category. As he'd done her. Oh, she had been quite aware of what he'd done and been half-angry, half-amused by his insulting insolence.

Was the boy she'd met still inside the man? Waiting, perhaps, to be set free?

There had still been a glimmer of hope in the boy, a small light that had not yet been extinguished by anger and sorrow. If there was even a spark left, she wanted to find it. Perhaps together, they could illuminate the world.

Chapter 13

Chance's mood was far from improved. A single glance at the girl reposing on the bloody wool cape like a contented cat was enough to make his belly knot, however. There was a feline awareness in the steady gaze she gave him, and the hint of a smile touched the curve of lips that had haunted him more nights than he could count.

He scowled, and that didn't seem to perturb her in the least. Somehow, he had lost that useful edge of intimidation as an effective weapon, and he didn't have the vaguest notion how it had happened. Did she think because he'd made her his mistress that he would be sweetly compliant to her wishes?

If so, he would soon show her differently.

Deep shadows shrouded the corners of the hut where the firelight didn't reach, gradually growing longer as the fire burned down. He moved to the ladder, bare feet skimming the half-rotted rungs as he descended. A rung snapped with a loud crack and he plummeted the last few feet to the hard dirt floor of the hut. A splinter stabbed the sole of his foot as he swore violently through his clenched teeth. He glanced up at the loft. If he heard so much as even a hint of muffled laughter, he would not be responsible for his actions.

All remained quiet, however. He stalked in a limp across the floor to the dying fire. No more wood was evident on the empty stone hearth; nothing but the three-legged stool looked even remotely flammable. The thought of going out into the rainy night was less appealing than doing without a fire, and he turned back toward the loft.

"You could use what's left of the ladder," a choked voice suggested from the loft, and the glance he slanted upward was sufficiently dangerous to silence it.

He snatched up the stool and took two steps, flinging it into the fire with a feeling of satisfaction. Flames licked the wooden legs and curled around the seat, sizzling and hissing as resin bubbled to the surface and began to ooze from the soft wood.

No sound came from the loft. There was only the growing beat of the flames and the faint patter of rain against the walls. He stood for a moment, watching the fire, letting it warm his bare chest and feet while he considered his next move. An uneasy feeling pricked along his spine.

Events had not quite moved as he'd planned. He'd planned to seduce her, make her his mistress, then remove her to a far-off cottage in upper Wiltshire, thus removing her from his territory for the present.

What bothered him most, was the inescapable fact that she had precipitated the final seduction, and beyond sharp bargaining, not resisted for a moment the notion of becoming his mistress. So why did that disturb him? After all, he was getting what he wanted. Wasn't he?

Yes, even more than he'd wanted. He'd never had a virgin before, never wanted one. "Too deuced expensive and not at all worth the trouble," he'd always said.

Yet, inexplicably, he'd found both those assertions contradicted in this one small female with long legs and a courtesan's mouth. It was unsettling. He wondered suddenly what she looked like beneath that silk mask.

Abruptly, he decided to investigate.

She watched him warily, eyes shadowed by the silk, the wool cape drawn around her body when he appeared in the loft again. Wood creaked, and chaff hazed the air as he moved over the straw toward her.

"Remove your mask," he said, settling himself cross-legged on the straw.

She stared at him.

"If you expect me to keep my part of the bargain, you had best keep yours." Her chin lifted, pugnacious and defiant. "Part of the bargain was that I leave it on."

"Devil take it, do you think I intend to support a woman whose face I've never seen?"

"It was *your* idiotic suggestion, not mine. If you'd like to retract your offer, I'll give it serious consideration."

Chance stared at her, anger finally overriding amazement. "I'm sure you would—with a healthy fee for services rendered, I imagine."

His sardonic snarl made her stiffen. "No," she said quietly, "I gave myself to you freely."

For some reason, her soft words shamed him. He'd expected anger, or even more bargaining, but not that quiet denial. He looked away, chagrined and uncomfortable.

Honor would not allow him to forcibly remove the mask, but frustration made him grit his teeth.

He rose swiftly to his feet.

"Keep the bloody mask," he said roughly. "Anyone who asks me about it will have to choose between the ravages of leprosy or the pox as a reason for your wearing it."

"Who will ask about it out here?"

He stared at her. "Did you think I intended to keep you in this hut?"

"Well—no, but I assumed . . . that is, I suppose you intend to send for me each time you want me."

"Oh, aye, and sit twiddling my thumbs while I wait for you to arrive. Don't be so bloody naive. Who do you think the house in upper Wiltshire will be for, may I ask?"

Silence greeted his question and was followed by a halting, "My poor invalid mother?"

"Not unless she's twenty years old and has an extremely talented tongue, my sweet. I'm not a philanthropist. If I spend my coin, I expect full payment."

A fist full of white wool cape quivered slightly. She said with injured dignity, "I've no doubt of that. I'm afraid I was swept away by your generosity and did not think the details through. Do forgive me for being carried away by the moment and forgetting that this is only a business arrangement."

His eyes narrowed slightly. There was an edge to her tone that he didn't like, a glint in her eyes that pricked his suspicions.

His hand flashed out to grab her wrist, holding it when she would have pulled away. "Don't think you can dance away from here without me, my sweet. I've no intention of allowing you to get away." He smiled lazily, drawing the tip of his finger over her silk-clad cheek, toying with the edges of the mask while she watched, motionless, eyes wide. "I think I've grown fond of sharp-tongued vipers curled in my bed. Or at least, this sharp-tongued viper."

Her only reply was a soft, choked sound of dismay.

Finally. He'd succeeded in conquering that vicious tongue of hers. It had taken long enough.

Slowly, he pushed her back into the cushion of straw and pulled the cape from around her body, caressing her with leisurely strokes that made her shiver. To his surprise, the urgency was back, hot and wild and pulsing through him in a clamoring demand for ease. Just touching her, gazing at her slender curves while his hands moved darkly over her golden skin, had him aroused.

His gaze lifted to her face, to the silk-clad mystery that was denied him, and he held her eyes with his while he touched and teased, saw her lips part and her breath come more raggedly, until he knew she felt the same sense of driving urgency he felt.

Holding back was difficult when he wanted to give in to lust, to the powerful need to take her without preliminaries, and he remembered why he'd always claimed virgins were not worth the trouble. Yet it would be a sin not to go slowly with a woman like this, a masked siren with rain and the sheen of perspiration misting her naked body.

Chance forgot his anger at her, his frustration, and his suspicion, and turned his attention to hearing her throaty cries against his ear. He kissed and stroked and caressed until she was twisting restlessly under him, reaching up for him and dragging him down to meet her, and then they were both unbuttoning the few fastened buttons of his breeches and he was inside her, her gasp feathering over his masked cheek in a hot rush of pleasure.

It was sweet agony and painful pleasure, a contradictory emotion that got lost somewhere in the rush of more sensory reactions. He lost himself in her, in the soft comfort of her body and the sweetness of her mouth, the fervent way she clung to him, rising to meet him, moving with him to the brink and over.

And in that consuming spiral, echoing in the heated haze that shuddered through him, he thought he heard her say his name. Then he surrendered to the lethargy that waited to claim him and relaxed in her embrace.

•   •   •

She held him for a long time, while his breath slowed to an even, steady rhythm and her own heart stopped its wild thundering.

There was no other way around it, she thought, letting one hand drift over his bare back. She had to leave before he woke. If she didn't, she'd never manage to escape, and it wouldn't be long before he knew who she was.

For herself, she didn't care. But for her father—he would be mortified to have his daughter become the mistress of the earl of Wolverton. While he might like Chance, allowing the earl to ruin his daughter would never be tolerated.

If, indeed, Sir Griffyn ever recovered from his illness enough to worry about such things. *Oh, Papa. . . .*

Rhianna stilled the knife thrust of pain that came each time she thought of her once vital father. Would he ever be as he'd once been? She hadn't realized how much she cared about him until his illness. The first resentment at the way he'd snatched her away from the life she'd always known had long since faded, but underlying her growing affection for him had been a wary reserve.

In the light of his illness, that reserve had vanished as if never there. He needed her, and she—much to her surprise—needed him. Doing the most simple tasks of feeding and dressing him gave her the feeling that she was able to help in some small way with his recovery.

What would he think if he knew about this? About the astonishing fact that she had impulsively given herself to Wolverton?

He would never understand. She knew it. Though he liked Chance, had made many comments deploring the vicious gossip about him, he was protective enough of his daughter to want more for her. A faint smile touched her lips. An earl was a high enough aspiration for most, assuredly, but not under circumstances such as these. One aspired to marriage with an earl, not a tryst in an abandoned hut.

Well, she had never been the docile, demure daughter that Sir Griffyn had envisioned, and she certainly could not change her nature now. There was more of Cynara in her than she'd ever considered, and for the first time, she began to understand her mother's decision to leave everything she'd known for love. Had Cynara felt this way? This wild, hot yearning that exploded so suddenly inside her she had thrown caution to the wind?

Yes, she knew she had. Marisa was right. She was more like her mother than she'd suspected. She had given her body to Chance Lancaster, but more important —she had given her heart. She could only pray that he would cherish it one day.

Her hand shifted to the curved muscle of his shoulder, and he muttered something hoarse and indistinct in his sleep. Ebony strands of hair feathered down his neck and over his shoulder, and she let it slide silkily through her fingers as she studied what she could see of his face. The silk mask hid his expression, the straight line of his nose and shape of cheekbones, but she knew every angle and plane of his face. It was imprinted in her memory, superimposed over the image of him as a boy.

She blinked, eyes stinging from lack of sleep and strain. There was a dull ache between her thighs. Chance had one leg thrown over her thighs as if to hold her there, then he shifted slightly, weight easing. She reached to pull the edges of the wool cape over them. The storm muttered in a low rumble outside, thunder a distant growl. Rain was a soft, musical patter against the walls. Her eyelids drifted shut despite her efforts to remain awake.

When she opened her eyes again, she was horrified to

see that the fire had died down to sullen red embers, and it was near daylight. She had to get away from Chance. . . .

Easing out from under his weight was not as difficult as she'd thought it would be. He slept heavily, the silk mask twisted and rumpled. Gray light shadowed the loft so that she could only make out light and dark, and she made a swift decision.

Naked and shivering, she climbed carefully down the half-rotted ladder to the tumbled pile of her hastily cast-off clothing. Her hands shook so with urgency and apprehension that she could barely get into the snug breeches and shirt, much less the boots. The knee-high boots went under her arm, and she snatched up her cape and stepped out the door of the hut into the damp air.

One of the horses nickered softly, and she quickly put a hand over its nose to silence it. Thank God he'd not unsaddled them, but left them to chew hay beneath the crude shelter.

"Hush, Beau," she murmured as she led him out. He nudged her, and the rattle of bit chains sounded loud in the quiet gloom.

It wasn't until she was mounted and out of the clearing around the hut that she glanced back, and saw no sign of life. It was quiet, with only faint wisps of smoke rising from a hole in the thatched roof.

That worried her, yet she dared not turn back. She was a fool, she knew, to fret over his welfare when he planned to use her for his own ends, but she couldn't help it.

The next time she encountered the Moon Rider, she intended to be armed with better weapons. If her heart was lost to him, then he would have to prove himself worthy of it.

Book Four

Chapter 14

Bitter fury had finally given way to cold determination. Chance had ceased blaming himself for sleeping like a trusting fool, and turned his attention back to the cause of his anger.

Cynthia, she'd said she was called, but he doubted it. It had probably been a fiction, just as her silk mask and masquerade were fictions. Well, he would find her, and next time he would not allow her to throw him off-balance with soft resistance and bold surrender.

Next time, there would be no bargain, but a settling of debts.

His hand clenched into a fist, as he leaned against the window frame, staring out at the garden. Damn her. She remained in his mind, an elusive memory that haunted his nights. Perhaps it was her desertion that intrigued him, the apparent refusal of his proposition that made him so determined to find her. If she was really what she seemed, the arrangements would have satisfied her quite well. Yet, he could not escape the feeling that the girl was much more than he'd thought her.

But if she was not so easily explained, then who was she? He'd met women before who enjoyed a passionate tryst in some secret spot away from the prying eyes of husbands, but never one like the girl who impersonated a highwayman. It was obvious she'd had no intention of accepting his proposition, but her reasons eluded him.

Why would a girl give up her virginity, then abandon the man without at least asking for *some*thing? He wished he knew. And he wished even more that he could find her. . . .

"My lord?"

Chance turned toward Hobson, his gaze taking in the old man's slower steps and labored movements. He really should ignore Hobson's refusals and insist that he retire to a cozy cottage somewhere on the estate.

"Yes, Hobson?"

"There is a young lady to see you, my lord."

"Did she give her name?"

"She did not."

His brow lifted. "Any young lady bold enough to visit me must not have her mama with her. Send her away. If I want that kind of company, I shall seek it out myself."

Hobson hesitated, then said, "Perhaps you should see this young lady, my lord."

"Indeed? Why?"

"I'm not at all certain. But I think she must be quite determined to wait for you. She said she would remain in the parlor until your arrival."

Half-annoyed, half-amused, Chance shrugged. "Very well. Allow her to wait. I'll be down at my convenience."

He let the mysterious young lady linger for an hour before going down to the parlor and then wished he had not been quite so rude. 'Anna Llewellyn rose from a damask-covered chair to greet him, her eyes telling him that she knew he'd deliberately kept her waiting.

"Good afternoon, my lord." Her voice was slightly mocking, and she gave him no more than the barest hint of a curtsy in greeting.

He bowed over her offered hand, holding it a bit longer than was necessary. "I apologize for keeping you waiting, Miss Llewellyn. I was unavoidably detained."

"Of course. I shall come straight to the point of my visit so that you are not inconvenienced further. I was recently given to understand that you have tendered an offer to buy a tract of land from my father."

"That is true. Where our land adjoins with yours lies an excellent parcel of meadow perfect for my cattle. I had entertained the hope that Sir Griffyn's solicitors would seriously consider my offer."

"They did acknowledge it." She paused, and Chance saw a flicker of indecision in her blue eyes. He smiled.

"I see. And advised you against having any dealings with a man as unscrupulous as I am said to be, I'll wager. Unless they're complete lack-wits."

She dragged in a deep breath, and a smile hovered at the corners of her mouth. "Well, yes, as a matter of fact, I *was* told that you have taken unjust advantage of certain locals in the past."

"True enough. These certain locals were foolish enough to think me as stupid as they, and I did deem it amusing to see them squirm." Watching her face, he recognized lively intelligence there, as well as shared amusement, and was not surprised when she nodded.

"I thought as much, and so came to a decision. We shall accept your generous offer."

"I'm pleased." He watched her face and knew that she had to be aware he had no need for that meadow. It was the only way he could find to help Sir Griffyn without it being refused as unwanted charity. He cleared his throat. "Would you care for tea, Miss Llewellyn? We can discuss the details, if you like."

This was a matter for solicitors to handle, and he knew it as well as she. There must have been another reason for her personal visit, and he wanted to give her the opportunity to present it.

She nodded and moved with restless grace to the

doors that looked out over the garden while he rang for a
servant. He watched her, struck again by the notion that
he'd met her long before the Huntington ball. There was
a familiar sense of ease in talking with her, as if they had
shared ideas and experiences before.

Yet he'd spoken with her only briefly, and both times
in strained circumstances.

He saw her flick a glance at him, her lashes lowering
over eyes that were blue and searching. Then she turned
away again, staring out the doors with quiet composure.
He studied her profile, the pure line of sculpted cheek
and throat, the soft curve of lips that made him think of
heated kisses and murmured passion. It was unsettling,
and he frowned. He had not thought of bedding another
woman since that stormy night in the abandoned hut, but
there was something about 'Anna Llewellyn that was as
intriguing as the masked mystery who had escaped him.
There was a certain similarity, perhaps, a grace and style
that reminded him of the woman who called herself
Cynthia.

It was faintly appalling that he could desire two
women at opposite ends of the spectrum and even more
appalling that either of them could have such a devastating effect on him. Why did he inevitably think of them
both in the same breath? It was most disconcerting.

"Tell me, Miss Llewellyn," he said abruptly, "do you
ride?"

"Ride, my lord?" She turned to stare at him, the light
behind her leaving her face in shadow.

"Yes, ride. It is a great pastime here in the country, to
ride out over the moors and enjoy temperate days. Not all
young ladies ride, however, which is why I am asking."

"Is this an invitation, my lord?"

"I believe it is. Would you care to ride out over the

estates with me? Only to survey my new meadow, of course."

"I am not at all certain it would be proper without my maid along. With my father being so ill, I must be careful to preserve my reputation, you know."

Again, that slightly mocking inflection, as if she found the notion amusing and not at all necessary. Chance moved toward her, watching her sudden stillness.

"Bring your maid if you like," he said softly. Her eyes widened, gathering light in the dark centers as if a mirror, the pupils expanding to a ludicrous size. He halted in front of her, gazing down at her upturned face. The tilt of her impudent little nose, set of her chin, and the full, sensual curve of lips made him think of soft whispers in the night.

The feeling of *déjà vu* swept over him again, sharp and disconcerting. When she turned abruptly around and took several steps away, he followed her.

"Why do I have this inescapable feeling that we knew one another before?" he asked shortly and saw her hesitate.

"Well, we are neighbors. I assume that we have met on many past occasions and just never gave it much attention."

"But you haven't lived in Wiltshire long. I seem to recall hearing that you were separated from your father until adolescence, and when reunited, he took you abroad for an education. Is that correct?"

She turned to face him, and he saw the slight quiver of her hands. "More or less."

"How much more and how much less?"

A faint smile touched her lips, drawing his attention again. "You are exacting, Lord Wolverton. And curious to the point of rudeness."

"Most assuredly. One learns more information by asking than by waiting for it to be offered." He wanted to turn her to the light again, to study her face. Maddeningly, recognition eluded him.

"Did we meet as children, Miss Llewellyn?"

"Yes, as a matter of fact, we did meet once."

She waited, quiet and expectant. "I do not remember it," he said finally. "I am certain I should recall meeting you, but I don't."

He saw the faint expression of disappointment that flickered briefly across her face, then it was gone and she was murmuring regrets that she could not stay for tea as her father's illness required her absences to be brief.

It wasn't until she was gone that he remembered something, an odd little flash of memory that was puzzling.

Bangles and bare feet. Why would he think of that?

So, he still didn't recall. Rhianna stared out the window of her coach without really seeing the rolling fields and meadows. There had been a heart-stopping moment when she'd thought he connected her with the night in the abandoned hut, then it was gone. Well, now she knew that if she chanced to meet him out somewhere, he would not connect her with that woman. Or with the gypsy girl. It was somehow disappointing instead of relieving.

Had he ever wondered about the gypsy girl who had given him her ribbon as a favor? Probably not. He'd ridden away from their camp without a backward glance and had not come back. No doubt, he'd put her out of his mind as soon as she was out of sight and never thought of her again.

For a day or two, she'd watched for him, certain he would return, certain there had been a special affinity between them that he could not deny. But there had been no sign of him, and then her father had come to claim her and driven all thoughts of the beautiful, angry young earl from her mind for a time.

And now fate had brought them together again. She wished she knew why.

A wry smile twisted her lips. Chance had not been shy about asking her to ride with him. Apparently, the night in the hut with a masked, willing woman was just one more conquest and hardly memorable enough to keep him from seeking another one. She should have known he would view it that way but had been foolish and naive enough to hope he would not be able to forget her.

Ah, foolish indeed. Lord Wolverton was accustomed to casual conquests, and would not think a quick roll on a bed of hay very important.

But it was to her. Oh yes, it was to her. And she had no intention of allowing him to so easily forget it, or to relegate it to the level of a casual fling. No, Chance Lancaster, earl of Wolverton, Viscount Wolcott, and holder of lesser titles, must soon be forced to deal with the consequences of his actions.

A solution eluded her, even after she'd retired to her chambers and sought refuge in silent contemplation. Restless, Rhianna moved to the French doors to stare out into the garden. Weeds had begun to fray the edges of formerly neat beds again, but valiant blossoms poked bright heads up between paving stones and clumps of grass. Dusk shrouded the distant hills and threw long purple shadows. Birds trilled soft songs, and a light breeze stirred the flowers into a slow dance. Lamps had been lit in some of the rooms facing the garden, squares of light shimmering in the dusky air and over the stones, reminding her of diffused firelight and rain.

The night in the rain with Chance was a haunting

memory. She thought of him even when she didn't want to, remembered his touch, the feel of his hand in her hair and on her body. It was maddening, frustrating—and frightening.

Moving more from instinct than plan, Rhianna found herself stepping through the open French doors and into the fragrant garden. A silent melody from times long past echoed in her head, and she began to strip away her clothing until she stood clad in only a chemise and single petticoat. Then, lifting her arms over her head, she removed the pins that held her hair in a neat coil and dropped them slowly to the terrace. They clattered softly, tiny pings of ivory against stone.

The breeze had quickened, and as she began to move to a melody only she could hear, Rhianna forgot everything but the rhythm of the dances that had been her nightly lullabies as a child. Cynara had danced to these same ancient songs, her graceful movements fascinating her tiny daughter. Rhianna's body recalled them instinctively, and she bent and swayed, bare feet skimming the terrace stones in a graceful pattern.

Thin, white muslin fluttered about her bare legs in a light whisper, and the cool breeze flattened the material against her skin. Twisting, turning, eyes closed and long hair whipping about her shoulders and over her back, Rhianna danced as the moon rose in the sky and lit the night. It hung heavily, a huge golden ball that seemed close enough to reach out and touch. She lifted her hands toward it as if to try, panting slightly from her exertions, her body misted with perspiration. Bathed in soft gold light, she closed her eyes for a moment.

"Cynara. . . ."

The voice was a hoarse croak behind her, and Rhianna's arms dropped to her sides and her eyes flew open as she whirled around with a stifled gasp.

Her father stood staring at her from a doorway across the terrace. Serena stood behind him in the shadows, her face paper white and her hands trembling with excitement. Her eyes met Rhianna's.

"He spoke—I heard him."

"Yes," Rhianna managed to say, "he did." Sir Griffyn stared at her, his eyes more alive than she'd seen them since the night of his attack. Rhianna moved toward him, and heard him mutter clearly, "Cynara."

Her throat tightened. It was the first intelligible word she'd heard him manage in months. Most of his speech was a garbled agony of slurred words no one could understand, and his efforts were as frustrating for him as they were for those attempting to understand. Could he at last be getting better? Heart surging with hope, she moved across the paving stones to her father.

His hand lifted clumsily, and his eyes focused on her. "Cynara."

The guttural word was said in an almost desperate tone, and the light in Sir Griffyn's eyes was full of hope. She took his trembling hand between her own and pressed her cheek against it, her words a soft whisper.

"No, Papa. It's 'Anna. Cynara is—gone."

For a moment, there was no sign he'd understood, or even heard her denial. Then, to Rhianna's dismay, a single tear spilled from his eye and slid silently down one cheek. He shook his head slowly, throat working with ragged movements. Then his shoulders slumped and his head bent forward on his chest as he lapsed back into an unintelligible mutter.

"Oh, Papa," she whispered in a choked voice. She held his hand tightly, but he gave no more sign that he knew she was there, and after a moment, she reluctantly let go and stepped back.

Serena's gaze was sympathetic, her soft brown eyes

wet with tears. "He must 'ave thought you were someone else."

"Yes. He thought I was my mother." Rhianna managed a faint smile. "I've been told that I favor her, and in the moonlight, I suppose he mistook me for her."

"But that's a good sign, ain't it? I mean, that he's able to remember things a bit now?"

"I hope so, Serena. I hope so."

Rhianna watched silently as Serena helped Sir Griffyn back into his room, her heart aching. She needed her father now more than ever before. She wished she hadn't taken him for granted these past years and had allowed him to forge a father-daughter bond between them. But she hadn't. She'd been so angry at first, and hurt that she'd been snatched away from everything she knew and loved, that she'd remained distant. Now, she might never have the chance to know him as well as she wanted.

Was there anything more heart-wrenching than lost opportunities? she wondered. She'd lost her father to the befuddled morass of his mind, and if she did not act, she would lose Chance Lancaster as well.

Her chin lifted, and the breeze blew a strand of hair across her face. If she did not seize the opportunity that awaited her, she may never have another one.

"Who brought this?" Chance stared down at the single white glove in his hand, then flicked a glance up at Riever. "And when in the hell was it delivered?"

Having been in service with the earl for five years as steward, Riever was well accustomed to his master's abrupt manner. His face remained a polite mask.

"Yesterday afternoon, while you were out. He did not say who had sent him, my lord. The messenger wore rather scruffy clothing and had all the appearance of a lad from the village."

"Devil take it!"

"Will there be anything else, my lord?"

"No. Yes." Chance crushed the silk glove in his hand. "Find this scruffy messenger and bring him to me at once. I have several questions for him."

"I shall indeed, my lord."

Riever backed from the room and closed the door softly behind him. Chance opened his fingers to stare at his silk glove, missing since that night in the abandoned hut. Of all the effrontery—and it was obvious she wanted him to know she had discovered his identity—this was most guaranteed to infuriate him. As well as make him wary.

Oh, he knew what she was about, that sly little cat. If he continued his relentless search for her, she would expose him as the Moon Rider. This glove was a warning.

His hand closed around it again, crushing the silk. If she thought he would be so easily frightened, she would soon find that she was very much mistaken.

Leaded glass windows divided the sunlight into pristine diamond shapes on the thick carpet. An open door led into a garden bright with flowers and sunshine. It was a rare day of almost perfect weather.

None of which mattered in the least to Chance. He stared out the open French door without seeing the delicate flowers and lacy green willow fronds.

Superimposed over the thick hedges and neat flower beds, he saw a vague face framed with dark red ringlets. Memory teased him. He *knew* that face—if he could only see it more clearly—but from where? How? And why did he have this inescapable feeling that her identity was important?

He shook his head irritably. In the past years, he'd learned the value of instinct, and he knew he must identify that elusive memory.

A discreet cough distracted him, and he turned. His steward said politely, "My lord, I have the information that you requested."

"Put it on my desk, Riever."

"Certainly, my lord. Will there be anything else?"

"Not at the moment. Wait—did you inquire in the village as I asked you?"

Riever nodded. "Yes. Miss Llewellyn is said to still ride out early of a morning, ofttimes taking the village path."

"Very good. Thank you, Riever."

Chance waited until the steward had left the study and closed the door behind him before moving to his desk. A thick sheaf of papers lay neatly in the exact center. Riever was a stickler for such trivial details, a very irritating habit in Chance's opinion. He flipped up the top page.

A boring list of Baronet Llewellyn's antecedents were in several long rows, dating back to the twelfth century when his ancestors had fought against the Normans as well as the Saxons. They had been outlaws, as had most of the Welsh at that time. Only in the sixteenth century had Llewellyns been given the baronetcy, and for unspecified reasons.

Chance frowned. Baronet titles were handed down from father to son, or sometimes daughter, depending on the rules of succession in their case.

"Probably," Chance murmured wryly, "a bastard line much akin to my father's side of the Lancaster family tree." He scanned the remaining pages, and finally found what he sought. Sir Griffyn had been married only once. His discreetly unnamed wife had left him some twenty-one years before and not been seen since, though the baronet had found their teenage daughter back in 1790. Interesting. At the end of the document, Riever had added his own comments. It was a recital of old rumors, listed after a brief apology for the unreliable sources, which Riever also noted were often more accurate than one supposed.

Chance flipped the pages over and moved back to the open doors, perusing them carefully. After a moment, he lifted his head to gaze thoughtfully out the doors, pondering the possibilities.

Early morning mist lay in ghostly shrouds over the quiet hills. Rhianna drew her mount to a halt and reached down to pat the warm, steamy neck. It was a new horse, yet unused to her, but she had plans for the mare.

"Easy now," she murmured when it tossed its head with a gusty snort. The mane whipped back in stinging strands, and she gave the mare another comforting pat.

Morning was the best time for her solitary rides, when the world was still bright and new and fresh. Only the villagers were usually stirring at this time, and she could smile and greet them as friendly, if somewhat distant, peers. Strange, how she still felt more comfortable with the working class instead of the social set her father had wanted her to join.

There were very few of her contemporaries in London who were of interest to her. Most were content to dwell in the gaiety of cotillions, their main aspirations being to be received in Court. The few occasions Rhianna had attempted to converse with some of the young women had been dismal; very few read, even the popular Fanny Burney, whose novel *Camilla* was one of Rhianna's favorites. No, to a girl who had been brought up in the freedom of a gypsy camp, then educated abroad, the simpering of the young Englishwomen she'd met was more than she could bear.

It was no small wonder to her that Chance had found a way to entertain himself rather than endure what surely must be almost as boring a set of acquaintances. At least men had the excitement of horse racing to spice up their lives; the most a young lady of quality could hope for to enliven her days was a turn in the park on a well-behaved mount. Or a dangerous flirtation with a wicked man.

A faint smile curved her mouth. Rhianna yielded to impulse, kicking the mare in the sides with her heels. The mare responded with a startled *whuff,* and bounded forward. Dirt flung up behind her hooves in thick clods, raining a shower of debris and smelling of fresh earth.

Rhianna suppressed a delighted laugh at the startled faces of villagers she passed trudging along the road. She leaned over the mare's neck and turned her from the road to the gradually sloping meadows. Grass grew belly high in places, swishing against the mare's legs and Rhianna's feet with a dry, whispery sound. Wind whipped at her hair, tugged it free of the braids she'd plaited that morning and tossed loose strands in front of her eyes. The ribbons to her straw hat popped and loosened, and the hat flew off.

It didn't matter. Nothing mattered but the sheer joy and exuberance of flight. The thunder of hooves drowned out the music of birds and babble of a brook splashing over flat rocks, but the whistle of the wind in her ears was one of the sweetest sounds she'd heard in some time.

It was like she imagined flying would be, nothing but the press of wind against her and the sensation of skimming over the earth like a bird. It had been much too long since she'd allowed herself the luxury of riding so freely, too long since she'd thought of nothing but the pure pleasure of a fast horse beneath her and the wind in her ears.

Because she was concentrating so fiercely on the rhythm of hooves and muscle, the steady thunder of pounding hooves behind her did not register at first. It wasn't until a blur of motion to her left caught her eye that she realized the rumble had increased.

Immediate reaction was to swerve to her right, heart thudding as she glanced sideways. For an instant, she saw only a smudge of color, then recognized her pursuer. She reined in, holding tightly to her eager horse and barely keeping her balance as it came to a reluctant halt. Then she pushed the hair from her eyes.

"Lord Wolverton. How surprising to find you out so early of a morning."

He reined in beside her.

"Is it? You don't think I lie abed all day, I hope."

"Actually, I don't think about your habits at all."

Chance looked relaxed and amused. She was only too aware of how windblown and rumpled she must look to him. It didn't improve her temper when his brow lifted as he raked her with an assessing gaze.

"No? How crushing. I, on the other hand, have thought about you."

"Even if I were foolish enough to believe that, I would still never admit to thinking about you."

He laughed. "I admire your frankness, Miss Llewellyn. It's one of your best traits, I think."

"I wonder if you'd say that if I told you how much I dislike being chased down on the moors."

"Chased down? Not at all. I was merely attempting to catch up with you. I thought perhaps your horse had taken off unexpectedly."

Rhianna scowled. "Did I seem to be in distress? I assure you that I am quite capable of managing my mount, Lord Wolverton."

"No doubt. But are you as capable of pleasant conversation? We seem to do nothing but trade snide remarks when we converse. Do you think it possible to accomplish anything so mundane as a friendly discourse?"

"Possible, yes. Probable—very unlikely."

"You don't like me, Miss Llewellyn, and I'd like to know why."

For an instant—just a split second of time—she was tempted to deny his observation with the truth, but then common sense took over.

"It's not that I don't like you," she began, "it's just that we disagree on certain subjects."

"For instance, if I remark how light it is out, you will insist that it is dark as night."

She couldn't help a soft laugh. "Only if it is dark as night, of course."

"I can see I'm not going to make any progress with you."

Chance's grin made her breath catch in her throat, and she was reminded of how devastating he could be when he chose. If she wasn't careful, she'd soon find herself giving him those calf-eyed looks she particularly despised seeing young ladies cast at handsome men. Resolutely, she turned her head to gaze over the moors.

"I should be getting home, I suppose. Papa may need me."

"I'll ride with you then."

Rhianna's gaze shot back to him. He leaned casually over the neck of his horse—a magnificent bay—toying with the long strands of black mane. Sunlight caught in his dark hair and his lashes made winged shadows on his cheeks. His eyes were slightly narrowed, his mouth curved in a faint smile as he regarded her silently. Her throat tightened even more, seeming to hold back her refusal. She gave a solemn nod and kicked her mare into a trot.

For several minutes they rode without speaking. Then Chance said softly, "I truly regret what happened to your father, Miss Llewellyn. Sir Griffyn is a fine man who does not deserve such a fate. Has he shown any improvement?"

Emotion choked her, slowing her response, but finally she said, "Yes. Some improvement. Not enough, however. I had hoped—but only time will tell." She slanted Chance a quick glance. "Why would *you* regret what happened to him, may I ask?"

"Any decent man would regret such a dreadful thing happening to a friend and neighbor. I can't be the only acquaintance who has expressed his regrets."

"Well, no. Lord Roxbury offered his condolences as well."

"Roxbury." Chance scowled, his hands tightening on his reins. "That vain peacock regrets few things, I would think."

"I had heard you were enemies."

"Had you? Not enemies, exactly."

"Combatants, perhaps?"

Chance grinned. "On occasion. Roxbury has a bad habit of annoying me and saying things that he is certain will be told to me at the earliest possible moment. Confronted, however, he loses faith in his observations, I've noticed."

"Why do you dislike him so?"

"He makes it so easy."

Rhianna couldn't help a laugh. "Yes, well he can be a bit abrasive, I suppose."

"What happened to your frankness, pray tell? I much

prefer the unvarnished fact. Roxbury is a simpering idiot with vague visions of glory impeding his thought processes. I recommend immediate decapitation."

Still smiling, Rhianna turned in her saddle to look at Chance. He was watching her, dark eyes glittering beneath his lashes, his erotic mouth slanted up on one side. She sighed silently. It was easy to forgive him almost anything—much too easy. She had to guard against her own wayward heart, or she would find herself at his mercy, and that would never do.

"Oh, so that was what you were attempting to accomplish at Lord Heffington's home recently," she said lightly. "I had heard about that."

"Gossip and evil rumor. I merely embarrassed him by proving what a coward he is. He is an excellent example of it, I might add."

Rhianna gazed at him with open amusement. "Don't be so tactful, my lord. Speak frankly. You're among friends."

Chance startled her by reaching out to take her gloved hand in his, fingers curling over hers in a strong grip. "Am I? Among friends, I mean. I'd certainly like to think so."

Unsettled, she pulled her hand from his clasp and tightened her grip on her reins. Her voice came out quavery and soft, and she silently cursed it as she said, "Of . . . of course you are among friends, my lord. We are neighbors, after all."

"Yes. Remember that. If there is anything at all I can do to help you or your father, do not hesitate to let me know. I will do all in my power to assist you."

Her gaze met his. She recognized remorse and pain in his eyes and knew why he had sought her out. It was not to see her, but to make amends for the suffering he had caused her father. She liked him better for it.

"Of course I will. And when Papa gets well, he will know that you were there for him."

Before Chance could speak, she dug her heels into her mare's sides and shouted over her shoulder, "Race you to my gates!"

She caught a glimpse of his startled expression before he grinned, and the thunder of hoofbeats filled the air. They raced for the bridge and across it, the horses turning and stretching out, manes and tails streaming behind like ragged banners. Trees, bushes, and small leaning huts whizzed past in a blur as they rode over moors ripe with tall grass and gorse.

Just ahead was the millstream, gurgling quietly through a marshy stretch of land beyond the stone bridge. Rhianna edged forward, wind whipping tears from her eyes, aware of Chance just behind. The rhythmic stretching and striding of her horse mixed with the sharp fragrance of gorse and damp earth, with the thunder of hoofbeats that sounded like her heartbeat. For a moment, she thought she might beat him, then—slowly —his mount inched forward until the velvety black muzzle was barely ahead.

Lather flecked horses and riders alike, white foam spattering the air and Rhianna's riding skirt. She leaned over her mare's neck, urging her faster, but it was plain that Chance's bay had greater speed. He passed her, not stopping until they were almost abreast of her father's gates. They both reined in, breathless and laughing.

"You are safely home, my lady," he said gallantly, sweeping her a bow from atop his horse that made her laugh.

"What? No crowing about winning the race?" she teased. "I'm surprised."

"You shouldn't be. I *can* be a gentleman when I choose. But you will forgive me if I claim my prize."

He leaned forward and cupped her chin in his gloved palm, brushing his mouth over her parted lips in a whisper-soft kiss that made her heart thud even faster than the race had done. Then he released her, gave her a faint smile, and turned his horse down the road at a brisk canter.

Rhianna stared after him for several minutes, until he was only a tiny speck of color on the horizon.

"Miss Rhianna, there is a gentleman below to see you," Serena announced. Excitement threaded her voice, and her sharp little face looked expectant.

Rhianna couldn't help the sudden leap of her heart, though she shut her book calmly and stood up. "Who is it?"

"Viscount Roxbury."

"Oh." She ignored the sharp stab of disappointment. It would be foolish to think Chance would come, she supposed. He had made no effort to visit or extend another invitation in the past fortnight and had probably forgotten her again. "Did you show Roxbury to the main parlor? I'm not at all certain Papa is up to having visitors."

"Fenwick did. The viscount asked for you, Miss Rhianna, not your father."

"I see." She smoothed her skirts. Her day dress would be nice enough to receive the viscount. "I cannot imagine what he wants with me."

Serena's brown eyes sparkled. "To court you, I'm quite certain. He has that look about him, miss."

"That look?"

"Aye, you know—sort of impatient and all."

"I don't think Roxbury seriously considers me suitable for courting, Serena." She laughed softly. "He needs a large dowry, not mounting debt."

"But he's here."

"Tell him I'll be right down." She put the book on a table and moved to the mirror, not liking to see the viscount but resigned to it.

A quick glance in the mirror was enough to ascertain that her hair was not too mussed or her gown too wrinkled to receive visitors. She had no illusions about her looks, accepting the fact that she was not a fashionable, petite blond with pale skin the color of milk. Her dark complexion and hair was not at all the fashion, a fact that bothered her not one whit.

Her Fall Season in London's society had been brief and uneventful, and thoroughly boring. Though her dance cards had been full, her indifference to male attention had made her a less than exciting pursuit. To Sir Griffyn's dismay, she had preferred museums and galleries to balls and soirees. It had not distressed her at all to be excluded from Almack's at the edict of Mrs. Drummond Burrell, a patroness whom she had insulted by her very indifference to being included. Her only regrets had been Sir Griffyn's dismay and the unkind resurgence of rumors about her birth.

None of which made her a sought-after matrimonial prize in the London market. So why was Viscount Roxbury bothering to visit? He had not been in contact for some time, save for a brief note, written by his steward, she was certain.

"Well," she told her mirrored image mockingly, "there is only one way to discover what he wants now."

She found Roxbury waiting impatiently in the main parlor and was painfully aware of how empty the room must seem to him. Her chin lifted slightly when he turned to greet her with a raised brow that conveyed arrogant contempt.

"So, the rumors are true, Miss Llewellyn."

"And a good morning to you, too, Lord Roxbury," she said so sharply that a faint flush stained his sharp cheekbones.

"Pardon my abruptness," he said after a moment. "I find myself rather disconcerted by the confirmation of rumors as to your straitened circumstances."

"Do you. No more disconcerted than I have been by the daily evidence of my situation, I am sure." There was no point in attempting to hide the facts. "Is that why you came to visit, my lord? To see if the rumors were true? No need to have stirred yourself. A simple note asking for verification would have suffered."

"Your tongue is sharp, Miss Llewellyn." Roxbury had stiffened, hands behind his back, his elegant clothing a vivid reminder of his station. "I was only showing concern."

Yet Rhianna had no intention of deferring to him. He might be titled, but was wantonly void of manners, in her opinion.

"I have little time to waste on empty courtesies, my lord."

His flush deepened, and for a moment she thought he would leave. Then he drew in a deep breath and blew it out again, eyes dark with anger as he stared at her.

"You are a most unusual young woman. Since you are being so frank, I shall be the same. I came to offer for you."

Shock rendered her speechless, and she could not find her tongue for several moments. Roxbury remained motionless, watching her, his hands still clasped behind his back.

"Offer what?" she finally blurted, and saw his brow lift again in that elegant, mocking rise.

"Offer marriage, of course."

"Whatever for?"

A faint smile curled his lips. "Your bluntness continues to be quite disarming. However, I realize that this must be quite a shock for you, so I understand." He moved to the open doors leading to the garden, and leaned against the frame, his gaze raking over her with a thoroughness that made her feel unclothed.

Still reeling with surprise from his announcement, Rhianna struggled to recover her composure. "I have no dowry to recommend me, my lord. If you think to better yourself, I suggest that you make this same offer to the daughter of an untitled banker. A wealthy Cit is always eager to dower his beloved child in a pleasing, profitable manner."

Roxbury pushed away from the door and strode across the room to her, the faint smile on his mouth growing wider when she took an involuntary step back. He caught her hand in his. "If I told you that I am swept away by your charm and beauty, your grace and intelligence, would that further my suit?"

She withdrew her hand from his grasp. "It would not. It would only serve to convince me that you have a facile tongue when it comes to unwarranted, insincere flattery."

"I am devastated."

"State your true purpose in proposing such a scheme, my lord, and you will at least have my respect."

For a moment, something like admiration flickered in his eyes, then it was gone. "Your father is said to be ill or mad," he said bluntly, putting his hands behind his back again. "Most of your assets have either been sold or will be sold soon. All you have left is this estate, am I correct?"

"The gossipmongers have been busy, I see."

"Quite. You do not need to verify my statements. I have made my inquiries and know them to be true."

"I see." Rhianna gazed at him speculatively. "And so you have, out of the goodness of your heart, come to offer for me in order that my father and I will be cared for. How kind of you, my lord. I find myself speechless at the amazing prospect of your devotion and selflessness."

"You mock me, when you should thank me, Miss Llewellyn. I am, after all, a member of the peerage. My family is an old, valued one on both sides."

"With pockets to let, I understand. Why ally yourself with someone in worse financial straits?"

He turned abruptly away, clearly agitated, his voice a low growl. "You know, of course, of the madness across the Channel."

Startled, it took her a moment to say coolly, "Yes, of course I do."

Roxbury swung back around, eyes glittering with hate and rage. "I am a Royalist."

Rhianna stared at him a moment, disconcerted. This was probably well-known information if one was privy to gossip, but unfortunately, few chose to gossip with her. Only Serena gossiped, and her sources were limited.

"A Royalist—but your name and title . . ."

"My mother's. I was born in Rouen. My father was Comte de la Reine, adviser to Louis and his queen." His mouth twisted with bitter mockery. "He was taken up at the Champ de Mars in Paris and guillotined. My mother and I fled to England. Recently, Talleyrand signed a warrant for my arrest, and demanded I surrender to French justice. Naturally, I dare not. But I have become a political hazard, and if I am to be allowed to remain in England, I must marry."

"Why me?"

He shrugged. "Your father and my uncle are close friends, and my uncle feels that the connection would be a safe one. As you are not politically connected, and your father—forgive me—is no longer in a position to be much of a danger to the Crown, you are the logical choice."

"Preposterous. Some fevered mind dreamed up this entire coil and has convinced you of it despite the lack of credibility. I suggest you seek audience with the king."

"Alas, King George is sunk in the midst of one of his fits and is unavailable for rational decision. Prime Minister Pitt may be sympathetic to Royalists, but he is also a grave enemy of my uncle's. I will find no support in that corner. No, unless I marry quickly, I may find myself sent back to France for trial by the Directory."

It sounded too incredible to believe. Rhianna shook her head. "Though I sympathize, I cannot accept your proposal of marriage, my lord. You are half-English. Entreat the House of Lords for assistance."

"In light of my recent duel with the duke of Burridge's son, I do not think that ploy will help me."

He stepped closer, eyes fixed on her. "You must marry me, Miss Llewellyn."

"And if I don't?"

"Then I will call in the debt your father owes me at the gaming tables. This house will be mine, and you, lovely lady, will be living in the streets with your mad father."

Rhianna put a hand to her throat. "You wouldn't."

"Don't tempt me." He stepped closer, thin mouth curling in a cruel smile. "One way or the other, you will be mine."

Chapter 15

Hobson held out a small silver tray bearing a single white square in the center. Chance glanced at the seal as he lifted the letter from the tray.

"An invitation to another ball at Huntington, I suppose. Keswick must stop trying to make me presentable to society."

"Indeed, my lord." Hobson lifted a brow. " 'Twould seem to me that you would welcome the opportunity to regain your rightful place in society."

Chance tapped the sealed envelope against his palm and smiled slightly. "I'm afraid I'm already occupying my *rightful* place, Hobson. I'm known as a murderer as well as a host of other unseemly epithets, remember?"

"None deserved, my lord."

"Don't be too certain of that. Don't you remember my dear uncle Perry?"

"Only too well." Anger sparked the old man's eyes, and for a brief instant, his normally impassive countenance was creased with loathing. "I abhorred him. Yet we both know you are not the ruthless murderer you have been named."

"What makes you so certain of that?" Chance tossed the letter to a marquetry table and rose from his chair to pace the floor in front of the library windows. This was his favorite room now, comforting and serene, with no reminders of the past to haunt him. It had been completely remodeled after his uncle's untimely death, a haven to retreat to when he wished for privacy. Only Hobson was allowed entry at those times.

"I know that you are not capable of cold-blooded murder, my lord," Hobson said calmly, drawing Chance's ironic attention.

He gave a bark of laughter. "The devil I'm not. I am quite capable of murder, Hobson. Don't you recall how Sir Perry died?"

"Quite well." Hobson's calm gaze focused on him, the old, rheumy eyes never wavering. "Some deaths are earned, my lord."

"And your contention is that Sir Perry's death was earned, Hobson?"

"Well earned."

Chance smiled faintly. There was a certain justice, he supposed, in how Sir Perry had died. Still, the knowledge haunted him, no matter how he wished at times to forget it. He managed a careless shrug.

"Perhaps you're right. And perhaps I should accept George's well-meant invitation to some boring country dance, after all."

But when he slit open the envelope and opened the letter, his reaction was one of angry astonishment, not bored amusement.

"Bad news, my lord?" Hobson asked.

'*Irritating* would be a better word. Highly irritating. Dear, gossipy George informs me that Roxbury is affianced to 'Anna Llewellyn, and he will be my new neighbor."

Darkness again, comforting, silent, shrouding the downs with that eerie softness that she'd grown to depend on for secrecy. The horse shifted, hooves sinking into earth gone soft from a recent rain, and a cluster of oak leaves spilled cool drops from a heavy limb to shower over her.

Rain and the vestiges of a full moon were reminders of a night in an abandoned hut, when the storm outside had paled in comparison to the fierce tempest inside. Rhianna tugged her mask more firmly over her face and thrust all thoughts of Chance Lancaster from her mind. She had other things to worry about this night.

A shudder tickled her spine. Nelson Roxbury—she despised him now, detested the proprietary way he treated her, as if they were already betrothed when they weren't. She'd not accepted his proposal, yet had not quite dared to reject him out of hand, either. She balanced on the brink of disaster and had no place to retreat. Only enough funds to buy back the chits her father had signed to Roxbury would save her now, and she was desperate.

Thus she had changed plans and ridden out into the night again.

None would be expecting the Moon Rider on a quarter moon night. Nor would anyone expect a black-clad rider to swoop down on them. Gone was the white silk, and in its place were garments and mask of ebony, a whisper of shadow on a solid black horse. The only trace of moon was a thin sliver of frosty light, feeble and wavering in faint patches over the moors.

With Sir Griffyn's unexpected spark of recovery, had come new hope—and new needs. The money from the sale of the meadow to Chance had been hoarded carefully, but the London physician she had hired for her father was expensive. Much too expensive to continue bleeding their scant funds dry, especially with Roxbury waiting in the wings like a hungry predator.

The night grew, and even the faint glimmer of light melted into only a distant glow that barely illuminated the ground with a shimmer. Finally Rhianna heard the unmistakable sound of coach wheels and breathed a sigh of relief. She had not been wrong, then.

One hand tightened on the hilt of her sword, the other on the pistol she withdrew from her belt. She waited, and when the coach was only a few yards away, kneed the black horse forward.

Skittish, the mare pranced sideways a few steps before leaping the shallow ditch and scrambling up onto the road. It was a new horse, unfamiliar with night sounds and the dark shadows surrounding it. Coach lights swayed, looking like yellow, glowing eyes in the dark.

Rhianna was forced to soothe the mare a moment as it danced erratically in the road, while the coach rolled by in a thunder of wheels and flying hooves. Mud flew up behind the wheels, spattering in the road and making her mount dance even more nervously. She finally calmed her with an effort, then gave chase, angrily recalling Chance's mocking laughter on another night.

It didn't help to know he was right. She would be an easy target for any man from the top of the coach. Position was a distinct advantage in this game, she'd learned. She urged her mount faster, until she was abreast with the lead coach horse, then turned in her saddle to glance back.

It took a moment for the coachman to react to being followed and an instant longer to come to the realization that it was by a highwayman. That instant gave her the time to level her pistol and fire a warning shot just above his head.

A muttered oath burned the air, but he began slowing the horses. Foam flecked the night, white and dripping, eyes wild as the frightened horses were brought to a halt. Rhianna gave the order to "Stand and deliver."

"Like 'ell!"

Dim light played over the coachman's furious face. Rhianna sucked in a deep breath before squeezing the trigger of her pistol. It fired with an ear-splitting blast that made her hand and wrist ache. More curses filled the air as wood splintered close to the coachman's head.

"The next one will be through your heart," she said calmly. As she took careful aim with her second pistol the coachman wavered, then dropped his half-lifted weapon.

"All right, ye bloody bastard, ye can 'ave the money box atop the coach—w' at's left o' it."

"What do you mean by that?"

"I mean, ye bloody cur, tha' we've already been stopped once this night. There ain't much left."

Rhianna hesitated. He was probably lying, but there was always the possibility he was telling the truth.

"I'll take the money box anyway," she said finally.

He snorted. "O'course ye will, ye bloody blighter. D'ye want me to toss it down to ye?"

"No. To the ground will be sufficient."

Still swearing, the driver reached behind him and began tugging at leather straps holding a small trunk atop the coach. From behind the coach, a uniformed guard stepped into the swaying light of a lantern and paused. Rhianna drew in a sharp breath. The guard was clothed in scarlet, and was unmistakably employed by the government.

His shot went wide, missing her, and she took quick advantage. Leveling her pistol at him, she gave the terse order for him to toss aside his weapon. He hesitated, then threw his empty musket to one side, swearing at her.

"You'll hang for certain, laddie. No quarter is given to any bloke who holds up one of his majesty's coaches."

"You shouldn't be out at night if you don't want to be robbed," she managed to say gruffly.

"Trouble with a broken wheel, then another knight of the road, if it's any of your business," the guard growled.

Rhianna looked from him back to the driver. Passengers inside the coach had pressed faces to the windows, but none dared step outside. Few wished to brave a drawn pistol in the dark, especially when there could always be more than one highwayman. Rhianna counted on that fear as part of her strategy, but it still made her uneasy to have both a guard and a coachman glaring at her.

She moved forward, balancing her pistol, her nerves frayed by the delay. The coachman was watching her, his eyes narrowed with anger and menace. He kept staring at her, until her hand began to waver with nervousness.

Rhianna tried to keep her gaze fixed on the money box he was fumbling with atop the coach, but her eyes shifted between the coachman and guard with growing apprehension. The pistol in her hand felt heavier and heavier, and she did her best to keep it trained on both.

"Step back," she ordered in her gruffest voice when the trunk was on the ground. The coachman threw her a surly glance as he obeyed, hands opening and closing with impotent rage.

"There be a rope waitin' fer ye at Tyburn Hill," he growled when she motioned for him to mount the driver's box again, then ordered the guard to do the same.

"No doubt. But not tonight. Now be on your way quickly before this pistol happens to go off."

She waited until the coach jerked forward and rolled out of sight down the road before dismounting with a sigh of relief. The trunk was locked, a huge padlock that hung through a clasp on the front. She stood a foot away and took aim, and the blast of her pistol briefly lit the dark as she shot off the lock. The smell of burnt leather and hot metal stung her nostrils, acrid smoke curling up from the smoldering trunk. Gingerly, she tossed open the lid, then sat back on her heels.

"Ah, the driver lied."

A smile of satisfaction briefly curved her mouth as she dipped a gloved hand inside to lift out a heavy velvet bag. Rhianna smothered her stinging conscience with the justification that the money she stole would help her father much more than it would be missed by the coach line. Still, at times it was hard to rationalize the certain knowledge that she was as much a thief as the other highwaymen who roamed the high roads.

Rhianna tucked the velvet bag into her belt and caught up the reins to her horse, soothing the nervous animal with a few soft words as she put a foot in the stirrup to mount. Snorting, the mare shied away, and she was forced to hop on one foot to keep her balance.

"Easy, Rayna," she murmured, "easy now."

The mare tossed her head, the whites of her eyes bright in the murky gloom of night. Rhianna tangled one hand in the long mane and held on, fighting mounting frustration as the horse danced sideways.

It wasn't until she heard the sharp snap not far behind her that she understood the animal's agitation, and she barely had time to fling herself back and away as a shot rang out in the dark. A blinding flash of orange punctuated the shadows, and she heard a masculine curse as the ball intended for her passed harmlessly over her head. A severed tree branch dropped heavily to the ground in a shower of rain drops and leaves, almost hitting her.

Her first thought was that it was Chance again, but in almost the same instant, she realized that he would not have shot at her without warning. Heart pounding, she threw her body to the ground, groaning silently as her horse took off down the road. Hoofbeats sounded overloud in the sudden, dead quiet, then faded.

There was no easy escape now, and whoever was shooting at her was still there, waiting in the shadows to try again. She heard muffled curses of anger.

Rhianna lay stiff and silent, peering through the dark. She could hear the snap and crack of dead leaves and twigs, and knew that the man was moving through the bushes. He was making little attempt to be silent now, a sign that he was confident of success.

Her hand tightened around the butt of her pistol, useless now without ball and powder. She briefly regretted the ball used to destroy the lock on the trunk, and stuck the empty pistol into her belt. Then she began to move cautiously through the bushes. Leaves and wet earth clung to her gloved hands, and half-hidden tree roots snagged her clothing as she crawled slowly on her hands and knees. Her breath sounded loud in her ears—surely whoever was stalking her could hear the sound of her tortured breathing.

Fingers of hazy light wavered in spotty fragments, and for an instant, she caught a glimpse of movement just ahead and to her left. Instinctively, she threw herself to the right and rolled. There was a heavy thud and a geyser of damp dirt and half-rotted leaves as a weapon struck the spot where she'd just been. She launched herself to her knees.

Fear spurred her into a run. She forgot about her horse and the stolen money and everything but flight and escape. Tree limbs slashed at her face and tore her mask as she fled, and her chest ached with the effort.

The night seemed alive with menace, lurking behind every bush, within every shadow. Her heart raced and her breath came in shallow gasps. For the first time, Rhianna knew true terror at the thought of capture. She ran heedlessly, ignoring the pain of scraped skin and flaying bushes. Several times she stumbled and fell, but managed to struggle to her feet and go on.

Then a low-hanging limb struck her painfully in the chest. She fell and rolled, tumbling like a rag doll down a steep incline. She couldn't help a small scream when she smacked into a rock jutting up from the ground. For a moment she just lay there, winded and aching. The ground was wet, her clothes torn, the sky dark and barely visible through the tangled trees.

Behind her, someone swore again, harsh and angry. As she got to her feet, the sword belted at her side caught on a root, and it took her a moment to free it, swearing frantically under her breath. Freed at last, she hesitated, then cut to her left through an opening in the trees. A patch of light wavered ahead, a small clearing in the woods. On one side was a thick tangle of bushes that would only slow her. On the other side, the steep pitch of a gully made that direction impassable. She had to cross the clearing. She drew in a deep breath and prayed that her pursuer was not close enough to see her, then stepped into the moonlight.

Rhianna was halfway across when there was a crashing noise behind her. She half-turned, hand grabbing at the hilt of her sword.

"Oh no, you don't," a harsh voice snarled as her wrist was caught in a painful grip. A huge figure towered over her, a dark silhouette against hazy moonlight. There was no time to cry out, no time for anything before she was lifted from her feet and shaken like a rag doll.

"Damn you," her captor growled, giving her a savage shake. "Do you realize how close you came to being shot?"

He set her back on her feet and she tried to kick him, but he easily evaded her attempt. Her attempts to wrest free were futile, and she gave a soft cry of frustration when he yanked free her sword and tossed it away.

"Let go of me," she got out breathlessly, but he ignored her. His hands were rough at her waist, obviously searching for her pistols. They were gone, lost in her flight, she supposed, not that empty pistols would have done her much good anyway. Doubling up a fist, she tried to hit him. He easily ducked the blow and snared both her wrists in one powerful hand. His movement pulled her up against his rock-hard chest, and his muttered oaths snapped her head back to glare up at him. Then recognition struck. Chance. And he was not dressed as the Moon Rider.

For a moment, she went still. She should have been relieved that it was the earl instead of the king's guard, but she wasn't. Fury beat hotly through her, and she lashed out with her feet again.

"You bastard! You *shot* at me!" This earned her another harsh shake, hair straggling over her eyes and partially blinding her.

"You little fool," he grated, "that was the guard. If not for me coming up behind him when he circled back to get you, you'd be dead by now."

"Am I supposed to be grateful?" she snapped.

His grip tightened. "Yes. What the bloody hell are you doing out here tonight? If I hadn't met you before, I would never have known it was you in this ridiculous costume. When you bungled it so badly, I knew it had to be the same idiot I last met botching a simple robbery."

"How comforting." She tried to jerk away, but he held her fast, eyes dark and furious. She put a hand against his hard chest, holding him at arm's length. Her mask was askew, and she tried to straighten it with her free hand.

Aware of his sharpened gaze, she blustered, "What are *you* doing out on the road tonight, may I ask?"

"I do have another life, as you well know. I'm not always lurking in the bushes as you seem to be—hey!"

Rhianna took advantage of his momentary distraction to wrench away and escape into the thick tangle of bushes that lined the clearing on one side. Chance was right behind her, muttering oaths as he followed. He caught her only a few yards from the clearing, jerking her around to face him.

Her breath came raggedly and painfully, chest aching as she tried to shake her hair out of her eyes to glare up at him. Her hand shook as she pushed the hair from her face, fingertips grazing bare skin. She froze. Her mask was gone, torn away in her flight. Quickly, she bent her head, but it was too late.

"Look at me." His hard hand grabbed her chin and lifted her face to the faint glow of moonlight, fingers digging into her skin. Then his grip tightened. *"Miss Llewellyn."*

Chapter 16

"What in the bloody hell are you doing out here?" When she merely stared up at him with a mutinous glare, Chance gave her a rough shake.

Sir Griffyn's daughter, the prim and proper 'Anna Llewellyn—masquerading as a highwayman? The very same "highwayman" who had spent a rainy night of passion in a hut with him before slipping away into the dark without so much as a casual farewell! By God, she'd made a fool of him with her talk of being his mistress.

She was gazing at him with a mixture of defiance and anger, eyes beneath the thick fan of her lashes challenging him to act. Damn her. He had suspected that the mysterious girl who had eluded him so neatly wasn't a common serving wench, but somehow, he had never imagined it would be 'Anna Llewellyn. It all made sense now—the familiar way she walked, talked, her gestures, and the fact that he'd been attracted to both 'Anna Llewellyn and the mysterious highway-woman.

He released his grip on her and took a step back, staring down at her pale face and stormy blue eyes. "You should have told me your identity," he said finally. "You should have let me help you."

She shook back the hair from her face. "I think not, Lord Wolverton. I would rather risk scandal and hanging than swallow your or anyone else's pitying charity."

"Would you now. How interesting. I suppose hanging at Tyburn Hill is infinitely more acceptable."

"Yes."

The single word was grated out from between clenched teeth, and Chance found himself feeling a rare spurt of pity that he knew she would hate. He smiled faintly.

"Cheer up, Miss Llewellyn. You could be shot first instead of hanged."

"Or be bored to death by a lecture from the great earl of Wolverton, I daresay."

His brow lifted, and he raked her disheveled appearance with a dispassionate gaze that made her flush. And well she should flush, the baffling little vixen. He recalled only too well that night in the hut, when she had lain beneath him and yielded herself without a qualm. Her motives had escaped him then, and they certainly eluded logic now. He stared at her narrowly.

"You're damn cheeky for a woman with so few options at this moment. Might I suggest that you curb your impetuous tongue?"

"What do you intend to do with me this time?" she shot back, obviously unimpressed by his thinly veiled warning. "If you're planning another romantic night as punishment, you might consider a more comfortable location than a roofless hut in the rain."

Barely repressing the impulse to give her a good shaking, he kept his tone cool and mocking.

"You're absolutely right. Of course, with a woman of your remarkable talents, I'm not certain just what might be appropriate. While barking irons and flashing swords seem to be more your style, I lean toward a less lethal atmosphere myself."

"What? The great Moon Rider is afraid of a little danger? How disillusioning. I fear I have masqueraded as an unmanly fop instead of—"

Chance's hands curled around her upper arms, lifting her from her feet as he yanked her against his chest. Anger roughened his voice. "Your recklessness outdistances your discretion, Miss Llewellyn. Continue pricking me with that sharp tongue of yours, and I may retaliate in a manner you will find most unpleasant."

Though she glared at him, she didn't offer another comment, and he set her back on her feet, keeping one hand on her arm.

"Very well. Now we must decide what shall be done with you. Your death would certainly not help Sir Griffyn, and if you continue your foolhardy pursuits of coaches guarded by the king's men, you will find your head adorning the London gate as a warning one day soon."

When she didn't speak but continued glaring at him, he reached a decision that he wasn't certain was at all convenient for him, but under the circumstances, necessary. Rather grimly, he muttered, "I'll see you home. I should probably set one of my men at your door to keep you from behaving so recklessly again."

Her mouth opened, and he put up a hand. "As I am aware of your financial circumstances, I shall set my steward to work on your father's behalf—"

"I won't take your charity!"

"Not charity—self-preservation. If I don't provide you some kind of financial assistance, you're quite likely to ruin everything for me."

"Oh yes, your moonlight rides into adventure. I suppose you think yourself above the law, Wolverton? The magistrates would love to hear how an earl has descended into outlawry and thievery just to dispel boredom, I'm certain, and I can provide them with enough details to ensure your arrest." Her lips thinned into a mocking smile. "If you dare try to stop me from doing what I must to help my father, I'll see to it that you pay dearly for your interference."

"You have no idea what you're talking about, as usual. I wonder why I ever thought you might have some sense and intelligence. It's obvious my first impression of you that night at the Huntington ball was quite wrong."

"And my impression of you that night was obviously correct. You are a rogue and a rake and as ruthless a man as I have ever seen."

"Then you should be exercising more caution instead of trying to provoke me into violence."

Her head tilted to one side, russet hair tumbling over her shoulder as she studied him with a delicately lifted brow that plainly said she wasn't afraid of him. He wondered if she knew how desirable she looked, standing in the dim light with her hair tumbling loose and her clothing torn and revealing a golden-skinned shoulder. Even with the shapeless blouse she wore, her curves were evident, pressing against the thin material and reminding him how soft her skin was.

"Violence seems to be your first answer to any situation, my lord," she mocked lightly.

Again he fought the urge to give her another shaking. Damn her, she certainly knew how to goad him into reacting like an impetuous schoolboy instead of a man.

"Miss Llewellyn," he began coolly, "you have chosen to place yourself at my mercy with your actions, and I intend to take steps to stop you from inconveniencing me further. If you do not like my methods, you have only yourself to blame."

She tried to pull away from the hand he still had on her wrist, but to no avail. He held tightly, fingers digging into the soft skin.

"If you let go of me," she said finally, "I won't try to run away."

"If I don't let go of you, you can't run away. I like my approach better, thank you. It's much more certain."

She lapsed into sullen silence again, and he pulled her with him toward the top of the incline. The road snaked along the crest, empty and silent in the waning hours of night. He put two fingers to his mouth and blew a shrill whistle, then waited.

Within minutes, he heard the clatter of hooves along the road and his horse came into view, a dark shadow against filtered moonlight.

"How could you have fooled me so completely?" Chance muttered. "I never expected to discover that my irritating impostor was a well-brought up young woman like yourself."

She laughed softly, mockery edging her words. "You have no idea, my lord, about my upbringing. Your power of perception is rather lacking, I must say."

Chance caught up the reins when his horse halted by his side, then turned with a frown. "What the bloody hell do you mean by that?"

Rhianna stared at him for a long moment, then shook her head. "I have a feeling you will discover the answer to that soon enough, my lord."

He held out the stirrup and motioned for her to mount. Ignoring her questioning glance, he mounted behind her and turned the stallion around. Hoofbeats thundered in the night as he broke into a swift pace on the road leading to the nearest village.

Rhianna was sagging with weariness after a short time. She ached all over and couldn't help but wonder what he planned to do with her. Only that sharp spur of apprehension kept her from giving in to exhaustion.

When faint lights glowed just ahead, Chance reined his horse to a halt. "Pull your cloak around you and put up your hood."

"Why should I?" she found the energy to snap at him.

"It's too far to ride home tonight, and I intend to put up at an inn. Unless you wish to have tongues wagging, you'll do what you can to save your reputation, Miss Llewellyn. After all, a baronet's daughter does not usually ride the moors in mask and breeches, and though these are simple village folk, they are not stupid. They have acute powers of observation at the most inconvenient times, I have noticed."

"What makes you think I care a fig for what people say about me? If I did, I would have hidden in my chambers a long time ago, I can tell you that much."

"If you don't care, think of your father. Would he need that worry heaped on him should he recover soon? I think not."

Seething, Rhianna nonetheless recognized the sense in his warning and pulled up the tattered hood to her cloak. Fortunately, it was long enough to conceal the fact that she wore breeches if she kept it closed around her body.

By the time they rode into the cobbled courtyard, there was little indication that they were anything more than two weary travelers. Vines crawled up stone walls, twining about a wall lantern left burning for guests. A sign creaked gently in the wind, proclaiming the inn to be the Bull and Bear.

Chance dismounted and pulled Rhianna with him, holding her when she stumbled with weariness. For an instant, she allowed herself to lean against him. It felt good to have a strong arm around her shoulders, holding her up with little effort, and she briefly closed her eyes. For so long, she had been the strong one, the one to shoulder all the troubles, that it was a relief to feel protected—even if it was only a momentary illusion.

Then Chance was pushing her forward, up the stone steps to the front door, his arm heavy on her shoulders as if to keep her from running. Rhianna stepped away, and instantly his fingers closed around her wrist and pulled her back, his voice low and harsh.

"Don't try it."

Her temper flared. "I wasn't trying to run, you big lummox. Your arm is heavy."

"Not as heavy as it can be if you try to escape me. Remember that."

She stared at him furiously as he banged on the door with a fist to wake the innkeeper, caught between wishing him a hundred miles away and wishing she knew what to say to end the dissension between them. Perhaps he had a right to be angry, but so did she.

A grumbling, sleepy innkeeper finally opened the door, blinking at them in the dim light. " 'Tis late for guests with no baggage," he muttered suspiciously but became much more amenable when Chance put a silver coin in his hand. "Ye must be weary indeed, yer lordship. Bring yer lady inside while I ready a room fer ye."

Only a few coals glowered in the fireplace of the common room, giving off scant light and heat. The innkeeper lit another candle before scurrying off to ready a room.

Rhianna held the edges of her cloak tightly around her body. It wasn't the best inn, but looked fairly clean despite the lingering aroma. The smell of cabbage and sour ale hung in the air, mixing with the acrid bite of stale smoke. To her dismay, her stomach growled audibly. Chance turned to look at her.

"Is that a hint that I'm to part with another coin for your food?"

Her chin lifted. "I wouldn't dream of expecting you to feed me. I'll pay for my own meal, thank you."

"With what?"

Her hand automatically went to her waist, where she'd tucked the velvet bag of coins into her belt. Nothing was there. With a cry of distress, she felt at the sides for the bag, flinging aside the cloak.

Chance crossed to her quickly and jerked the cloak back around her body, holding it with both hands when she tried to pull away. "Your stolen coins are probably lying in the bushes somewhere. Keep this bloody cloak around you, unless you fancy meeting up with a magistrate this evening."

"But I needed that money," she choked out. "I can't have lost it after I went to so much trouble to get it."

"You should have thought of that earlier." His grip tightened when she tried to jerk away. "Just don't be foolish enough to alert the innkeeper that you are anything more than a weary lady. I'll pay for your damn meal."

"It's not the food!" Tears burned her eyes and threatened to fall, and she held them back with an effort. "Papa shows signs of recovering, and I hoped—"

She halted. It didn't matter what she hoped. There was little money for fancy London physicians, not when creditors lurked like sharks waiting for any morsel. Letters demanding payment had been arriving in droves, and several gentlemen had sent notice of unpaid I.O.U.s her father had signed after losing at the gaming tables. It all seemed so hopeless.

A frown tucked Chance's dark brows together. For a moment, she thought she detected a glimmer of sympathy in his eyes. Was it for her father? It was gone so quickly, however, that perhaps she must have imagined it, for he was back to his usual mocking tone.

"It must take a great deal of food to feed a temper like yours, Miss Llewellyn. I wouldn't dream of denying you enough sustenance to fuel it."

"Your kindness is exceeded only by your arrogance," she snapped at him. He infuriated her by laughing.

"Indeed. Then we are a perfect match, for I daresay I have never seen a more arrogant young woman in my entire life."

"I've seen the company you keep, my lord, and find that difficult to believe."

His brow lifted. "Have you been paying attention to my whereabouts then?"

"Unfortunately I can hardly avoid it."

He laughed again, and before Rhianna could give him the set-down he so richly deserved, the innkeeper returned.

"Yer room is ready, my lord. Second door on the right at the top of the stairs. Shall ye be requiring anything else?"

"Yes. Bread, cheese, and meat, if you have it, as well as a bottle of your best wine. My lady is famished."

When the innkeeper returned with a well-laden tray, Chance took it from him and pressed another coin into his hand. "I'll take the tray. Please see to my horse for the night. Your ostler must be abed."

"Aye, the lad is a sluggard and rarely stirs himself to work, my lord. I'll see to your horse." He hesitated. "Just one horse, my lord?"

"Yes. There was an unfortunate incident, which is the reason we are caught out so late. If you hear news of a loose horse, let me know at once."

Nodding understanding, the innkeeper backed toward the door. "I hope it weren't highwaymen that got yer horse, my lord. They're a bad lot, they are, running the roads at night and terrorizing innocent folks."

"No, nothing like that. The silly mare was frightened by a rabbit and bolted."

"Ah, 'tis a wonder yer lady wasn't bad hurt then."

"She's a bit bruised, but nothing hurts more than her pride at being unseated." Chance ignored Rhianna's choked protest, his booted foot against her ankle a reminder that the innkeeper was listening closely. He smiled blandly. "Good evening, sir."

Chance nudged Rhianna toward the stairwell. She stomped up the narrow, dark stairs to the second floor. A door stood open, feeble light throwing a wavering square into the hallway.

The room looked clean, though sparsely furnished. A stone hearth flanked by two wooden chairs dominated one wall. Beneath a shuttered window, a small table held the burning candle, its flame flickering slightly in the draft entering through the shutters. Light danced over the walls and floor, drawing her eye to the bed against a far wall.

A shabby counterpane draped it, and fat pillows propped against a heavy bedframe. The tiny table next to the bed held a cracked washbowl and pitcher, as well as a few limp towels. Her eye was drawn back to the bed. It was large enough for two people. Was she intended to sleep in it with Chance?

The slamming of the door whirled her around. Chance set the tray of food on the table beneath the window and turned to look at her. His dark eyes were unreadable, hidden by shadows and the ledge of his brow as he gazed at her in silence for a long moment. Then he gave a half-shrug.

"Here's your food. I assume you're still hungry."

She didn't move. The night they'd spent in the hut

flashed through her mind, and she felt an odd sort of breathlessness squeeze her chest. She stared at him until his eyes narrowed.

Then his gaze shifted slowly to the bed against the far wall before moving back to her. A faint half-smile curled his lips, deepening the grooves on each side of his mouth.

" 'Tis said," he murmured, "that there are all different kinds of hunger in this world."

"So I hear," she managed to say coolly. "Don't expect me to appease your appetites." His smile changed to a wide grin, mocking and knowing.

"For a well-brought-up young woman, you're quite a surprise, Miss Llewellyn." He shrugged out of his coat and tossed it to a chair, not even glancing at it when it slipped to the floor. She watched silently while he began to unbutton his shirt, the snowy folds of linen draping over his hands like pale shadows. Candlelight played over him, giving his features stark planes and angles, turning the bare skin of his chest to a burnished sheen.

Her throat tightened when he moved to where she stood in the center of the room and lifted a strand of her hair in his fist, letting it slide over his palm. "I remember the last time you surprised me. . . ."

Rhianna's breath caught. He was much too close, too overwhelming in the small confines of the room. He'd never seemed so large before, so overpoweringly male as he did now in this tiny space. She took an involuntary step back and saw amusement dance in his ebony eyes.

"Afraid, Miss Llewellyn? Not you. Not the scourge of the high roads, the daring knight of the road who plunders helpless victims at the point of a sword. Ah no, you would never admit to it if you were, would you?"

"Don't be an ass."

It was all she could get out, those few scathing words

that only made him laugh. He knew he was intimidating her, and she hated the unsettling feeling.

"For some reason," Chance said softly, "I get the distinct impression that I am making you nervous. Why is that?"

"I'm always nervous around a chuckle-headed scapegallow such as you."

Both his brows lifted. "My, you seem to know a bit of London cant, sweet 'Anna."

"Don't call me that."

"Call you what?—sweet?"

"No. 'Anna. Only my father and my close companions are allowed to address me so familiarly."

Chance laughed softly as he stepped close again, cupping her chin in his palm. "If my memory serves me correctly, we have been extremely close companions— 'Anna. Or do you prefer to be called Cynthia?"

She sucked in a sharp breath. "I have forgotten all about that night and would appreciate not being reminded of it."

"I haven't forgotten it for a moment."

His hand dropped away, and her skin tingled where he'd held her. Though she might lie to him, she had not been able to forget how he'd held her that night with the rain and thunder drowned out by their passion. Oh no, she'd not forgotten for a moment, though there were times she wished she could. In light of his mockery, however, she had no intention of allowing him to guess how much it had meant to her. Her chin lifted defiantly.

"It's ill-bred of you to remind me of my greatest mistake," she said. "Though you may possess titles, it is quite apparent that you do not possess the least bit of culture and decorum."

"How astute you are. And did you arrive at this conclusion alone? Or did the rumors circulating Wiltshire and most of England have anything to do with your brilliant deduction?" He grabbed her wrist when she made a strangled sound. "Oh no, don't get timid now, sweet 'Anna. You've begun the insults—pray continue. Tell me what a rogue I am, the devil earl, the Mephistopheles of the country set." His grip tightened. "It doesn't matter. I've heard them all before, how black a villain I am, and those words and titles have long since ceased to distress me. I don't care what people say, so anything you name me has little effect."

"Even murderer?"

She immediately regretted her hasty retort. Chance's eyes flickered with raw pain before shuttering against her. His grip tightened on her wrist, fingers digging into her tender skin.

"Yes," he said flatly, "even murderer."

Rhianna didn't argue. Despite his sneering words and vows of being unaffected, she could see past his facade to the pain beneath. She remembered the boy, the hurt, angry youth who had watched her dance in the purple light of dusk and shared—for a brief instant—his heartfelt emotions with a kindred soul, and she felt ashamed.

"I'm . . . sorry for what I said. I didn't mean it."

"The hell you didn't." His grip didn't lessen. "You meant it, all right. Don't go cowardly on me now, love. Not when you've been such a courageous little idiot."

Rhianna bit back a whimper at his cruel grip and kept her voice steady. "My lord, you're hurting me. Please let me go."

Chance glanced down, but instead of releasing her or easing his grip, he pulled her against him. Rhianna tried to pull away, but he held her too tightly. He tangled his free hand in her hair and tugged slowly, until her face was lifted to his. A tingle shuddered through her, and she stared up at him as if mesmerized, eyes locked with his hot, dark gaze. Her breath came quickly, heartbeat escalating to a rapid thud that she was certain he could hear.

"You may say you despise me," he muttered, "but 'tis evident that your body does not."

His head lowered, mouth closing over lips parted in protest, smothering her indignant denial. The heat of his kiss scorched her, burning away words and resistance. No, she'd not forgotten how he made her feel, how his touch summoned immediate response and breathless anticipation. She shivered.

Chance made a rough sound deep in his throat that sent another shiver down her spine. This was no gentle kiss, no tentative exploration, but a claiming of her will as well as her body. He backed her toward the bed. She didn't resist. She didn't want to resist. Honesty made her admit to herself that this was what she wanted. Had wanted since that night in the hut when she'd discovered who he was. She would take what she could of Chance Lancaster, what little he would allow her to have.

The pleasure tightened, stretching to a taut tension that was almost painful. She met the intrusion of his tongue in her mouth with her own, and heard him groan.

Unable to stop herself, Rhianna lost herself in his kiss, in his hard embrace and the feel, taste, and smell of him.

The taut trembling inside her did not ease with their kisses. Just the memory of Chance's passion that night in the hut, his burning caresses and hoarse whispers, made any reservations fade away into empty mist. She clung to him when he lifted her, mouth still covered by his and her heart racing.

A moss-stuffed mattress cushioned their weight when he lowered her to the bed and braced himself over her. With one hand on each side of her head, Chance gazed down at her, his eyes searching her face for a long moment. She held her breath. There was something so intent in his dark gaze, an ancient knowledge, that she thought for a brief instant he remembered her from their childhood.

That was dispelled when his fingers curled into her hair to hold her head still and he muttered harshly, "Why do I want you. God only knows, for you've led me a merry chase through half of Wiltshire with your foolish scheme."

Rhianna couldn't answer, she could only gaze up at him while he stared down at her in frustration. Then his head bent again and he kissed her, and she could taste the anger but didn't care. The hot need that he always provoked in her eradicated everything else, and she forgot all but him.

Nothing else mattered, not his painful kiss or grip on her hair, only Chance. His weight lowered slightly, and his free hand shifted to curve down her back, pulling her against his chest. He held her that way for a moment, with her breasts pressed against his bare chest, heavy and throbbing for his touch.

Fevered and aching, she felt him explore her curves, his hands shaping her breasts, belly, and thighs, tugging impatiently at her clothes. She slid her hands over his bare skin beneath the open shirt, her palms skimming the ridged muscles to caress the smooth expanse of his back, urging him closer to her. Warm, smooth muscle flexed beneath her hands, inflaming her need to hold him even closer. Oh yes, she remembered only too well how he felt next to her, and the urgency rose higher until she felt as if she would be consumed by it.

Heat and the yearning to hold him even closer, to let her hands memorize every ridge and angle, made her almost desperate. Need spiraled through her like a storm, burning wherever she touched him, turning to a fierce ache that seared along her nerve ends and made her throb for an end to the emptiness.

"Sweet Jesus," Chance muttered at last, his head lifting as he stared down at her. "What is it about you that makes me so crazy?"

She couldn't answer; if she'd known the answer, she could not have given it. Instead, she curved a hand behind his neck and drew him slowly down again, brushing her mouth over his lips in a light caress that made his breath harsh and his reflexes quick.

Chance nipped lightly at her throat, his hand tightening in the thick coil of her hair to hold her head still and back as he explored wherever he wished.

Rhianna washed the bare skin of his chest with her tongue, tasting the salt and heat, reveling in the smell and nearness of him. Then he muttered something she didn't understand and his head lifted again.

There was a glazed look to his eyes as he hung above her on his braced arms, powerful muscles flexing to hold his weight. His mutter was harsh. "This has to stop."

"It will." Her mouth found the curve of his biceps, and against his warm skin she murmured again, "It will."

"Christ."

The word was torn from him, sounding like a groan, and then he was kissing her again, fierce and hot and wild and driving everything from her mind but the need to be as close as she could get to him. She tingled where his hands grazed her skin as he tugged at her remaining clothing, jerking off her trousers with impatient, almost frantic motions. Cool air whispered over her bared skin, giving scant relief to the heat inside.

When Chance's hand spread over the gentle swell of her belly then moved lower, Rhianna arched upward, seeking his touch. He leaned back and shifted position, his knees spreading her thighs apart to allow his hand freer access, never taking his gaze from what he was doing. Fiery sensations shot through her where he was touching her, igniting the inner heat to a fever pitch that made her move restlessly.

Boldly, she stared up at him, admiring the strong curve of his chest, shoulders, and arms, the way his body was so hard and masculine, so superbly made. Muscles flexed as he moved, his chest rising and falling with ragged motions as he bent forward. With his forearm pressing against one shoulder to hold her, he nipped lightly at the tight bead of her nipple, then drew it into his mouth in rhythmic movements that made her writhe.

"Chance," she managed to say in a gasp as her hands curled into the sheets. She tried to catch her breath, but couldn't. Not with his mouth and hands pushing her ever higher. With every move of his fingers, she edged closer to that elusive shattering that he'd led her to before.

When he moved suddenly, she gave a moan of protest, but he was only shifting to cup her hips in both his hands and pull her closer. Molding her body in his palms, he lifted her slightly, pulling her legs on each side of his.

He was still wearing his trousers, and the material rubbed against her thighs in abrasive caresses as he slid closer. Somehow—had she done it?—his breeches were unbuttoned, and she could feel the heated length of him pushing against her where his hand had been. His head was back, the strong curve of his throat corded with tension, his dark hair loose around his head and shoulders like a shadow. She reached up to touch him, her fingers trailing over the taut muscles of his chest and over the ridges of his belly in a restless motion before moving lower. He groaned softly as her hand found and held him.

" 'Anna," he muttered hoarsely, and her name on his lips sounded like an endearment this time.

Rhianna's hips seemed to move of their own volition, rising toward him yet unable to get close enough, and she made a sound of frustration. He heard it and bent his head, eyes glittering beneath the brush of his lashes and a faint smile on his mouth as he gazed down at her.

"Chance," she whispered fretfully, "please." She knew what she wanted, an end to this aching fire inside her that threatened to flare up in an inferno and consume her.

When she reached out for him again, circling him with her fingers in a bold caress, he caught her wrists and pushed her arms back against the mattress. This brought his body up against hers, a tantalizing scrape of his flesh against the aching focus of need. He was breathing harshly, quick pants for air that seemed painful. His gaze focused on her.

"Be still . . . don't move . . . for a moment."

She smiled, and slowly arched her hips upward, daring him to follow her lead, challenging him to action. His eyes narrowed, and with a low growl, he thrust inside her in a quick, hard motion that sent shock waves through her entire body.

Rhianna welcomed him with a fierceness to match his own, her hands digging into his muscled shoulders to hold on. He drove into her with a ferocity that she welcomed, taking her higher and higher until she thought she could not bear the sweet tension another moment. She couldn't breathe for the searing excitement that coiled like a spring inside her, stretching tighter and tighter until she thought she must explode with it.

Vaguely, she was aware that she was calling his name, her voice a throaty moan in the close air between them. It was a wild, savage mating, a tempestuous storm of passion that swept them to a thundering culmination.

"God . . ." Chance shuddered, his words hoarse

and muffled in her hair and throat. " 'Anna . . .
'Anna. . . ."

Her arms closed around him as she cried out his name
again and felt his body fuse so tightly with hers that she
knew they were one in more than just the flesh. There
was a fusing of spirits as well, a communion of souls that
made the ecstasy that much sweeter.

Hot tears stung her closed eyelids as she held him to
her breast, and felt his strong body slowly relax against
her.

Chapter 17

"Just how well do you know Roxbury?"

Early sunlight glinted in the room, lighting dark corners and gilding prosaic objects with a golden sheen. Chance rolled to one side, and let his gaze linger on the heart-shaped face tilted toward him.

Damn her, she was too distracting with her lips still swollen from his kisses, and her eyes misted with lingering traces of passion. Faint bluish circles like bruised flowers blossomed beneath her eyes, testimony to the fact that they had spent most of the night making love.

And now he had destroyed any tenderness between them with his sharp question. His gaze narrowed on the shadows he glimpsed in her eyes as he waited for an answer. She'd gone still, and her lush lashes lowered to hide her eyes.

"What kind of question is that?"

He smiled, and let his hand drift over the sculpted line of her cheek and throat to the fullness of her breast. The pulse in the hollow of her throat fluttered, and he felt his own body tighten with a surge of desire that surprised and annoyed him. "A simple question, my sweet. And one that begs an answer."

She thrust his hand aside and looked up. Anger sparked her eyes. "A rather inappropriate time to be asking such impudent questions, don't you think?"

"You are evading the question. Perhaps that in itself gives me my answer."

She drew the sheet up and glared at him when he caught it with one hand. "Perhaps I just don't like being questioned as if I were a criminal."

Chance laughed. "But you are a criminal. You're the famous—or should I say *infamous?*—Moon Rider. Think what fun a magistrate would have with that information."

A stricken expression flickered briefly on her face before she looked away, shuttering her eyes again. "I take it that you plan to turn me over to the authorities, then."

"You take it completely wrong, love. I merely pointed out that a magistrate would be most gratified to learn who has been plaguing the high and low roads these past fourteen months."

"You know very well that I've only been riding out for six months."

"Ah, but no one else knows that." Chance let his hand rest on her breast, and noted that she did not push him away. "Now—how well do you know Roxbury?"

"Not very well at all," she replied in a grudging tone. "He holds some chits of my father's."

"Ah. And does he plan to collect?"

Her lashes lifted, and he caught a glimpse of distress in her eyes. "Yes."

"I find that difficult to believe. Roxbury is not a fair hand at gaming, while Sir Griffyn is known to be adept. Are the chits signed by your father?"

"Mr. Blemmons verified the signatures. Papa—made some unwise business decisions in the months before his illness. I can only assume that he did, indeed, lose a great deal of money to Lord Roxbury."

"The devil you say. It seems much more likely that he was cheated. It would be only too easy for Roxbury to sign the chits himself, and your father's condition precludes any argument if Roxbury is a fair hand at forgery."

She gazed up at him with hope dawning in her eyes. "Do you really think that's what happened?"

"It seems likely, but only a thorough investigation would provide any proof." He paused, frowning. "I hazard a guess that your father's debt is behind the premature announcement of your betrothal to Roxbury?"

She hesitated. " 'Tis really none of your business."

"Isn't it? You've invaded my territory, you know my identity, and now you've begun bungling even the most simple hold-up imaginable by attacking a coach guarded by the king's men. Besides—you're encroaching on dangerous grounds that you know nothing about."

Her eyes flashed. "Why should a few pounds here or there matter to you? You're an earl. You have enough money to do what you like. I don't. My father's very life may depend on the few pounds I glean from my midnight raids. And now my freedom has been threatened as well."

She sat up, hair cascading over her shoulders and a loose strand curling around the tip of a bare breast. He resisted the temptation to caress her. Her voice was shaky and thick.

"Have you no soul? Have you truly become the cruel, cold man some name you, my lord?"

"What do you think?"

"I think you're still hiding behind a facade, a wall you've built to keep out the world. You can't have changed so much."

He frowned. "How would you know? Few know how gullible I once was, how absolutely credulous."

She looked away from him, gazing toward the window where the shutters were agape to allow in light and fresh air. The untouched tray still stood on the table beneath the window. Dingy curtains fluttered in a slight breeze, belling out gently.

"I know," she said simply, still not looking at him. "I know how you once were. I was the same, believing in a sane and orderly universe. Time has changed my perceptions, but not my ideals. I refuse to believe that it can have changed you so much, despite the evidence in front of me."

He snorted rudely. "What can you know of what I once was? P'raps I was born this way, a bad seed, a rogue babe in the cradle, fed on dragon's milk and tiger's blood."

Rising from the bed, he stretched lazily and saw her turn to watch. It was most intriguing the way she watched him, with no shame or modesty or crudity but a natural curiosity that was both comforting and stimulating at the same time. A faint smile curved the soft line of her mouth.

"Your erratic kindnesses contradict you, my lord. I have heard of your occasional charities, made in the name of your servant, of course, but made nonetheless. You cannot expect *every*one to believe in your total savagery when you commit an intermittent kindness."

"Bloody hell," he commented without rancor. "I've been found out. I'm actually Father Christmas instead of Satan Incarnate. How inconvenient for the masses. They'll have to ferret out a new villain."

"Make light if you wish, but pray discontinue your masquerade with me."

"Ah." He put one knee on the bed, making the mattress dip and her roll toward him. "Only if you will desist your annoying deception also, my sweet."

"Deception?"

"Aye. You know what I'm talking about." He cupped

her chin in his palm and saw her eyes widen, reflecting light like a mirror.

"What if I had not been there last night? I'll tell you. You'd be dead and your father ruined, though he probably would never know about it."

"Probably not." She knocked his hand away and he let her. "Pray tell me, why do *you* persist in attacking coaches and robbing innocent citizens when it is obvious you do not need the money? For mere sport?"

He had no intention of telling her the truth. Even if he could trust her, the knowledge would endanger her. He shrugged and said, "Yes."

Her lips curled with contempt. "That kind of sport can lead to unfortunate incidents. Such as happened to my father."

That stung. Chance felt a wave of regret and hoped she recognized his sincerity when he said, "That was never meant to happen. I would not have harmed Sir Griffyn for anything, and you can believe that. Your coach was similar to another, and in the dark, I made a mistake."

"A rather costly one, my lord."

He held her gaze with his. "Yes. A very costly one. That is one reason I will not allow you to deny me any longer. I intend to help Sir Griffyn whether you wish it or not."

Her head tilted to one side, eyes dark with emotion. "And do you think that will absolve you of guilt?"

"Absolution is not what I'm looking for. I wish to make his days more comfortable, and if there is hope for him, he shall be helped. You may read anything into my actions that you wish."

For a moment she was silent. "I see," she said finally.

"Now answer my question. How well do you know Roxbury?"

"Do you mean, have I slept with him? Daily. For six years. He was my first lover and I'm mad with passion for him."

Anger made his voice tight. "I know better than that. I was your first lover. Second, I'll grant him, but not the first."

"Ah, I'd forgotten. So you were. Forgive me."

Her bright smile and fluttering of eyelashes infuriated him, and he snarled, "You gave your virginity too lightly to a stranger, it seems."

"Do you think so?" She rose to her knees in the jumble of tangled sheets and coverlet, eyes flashing. "Well, you're wrong. I knew who you were, but I thought you a different man. I see that I was much too credulous. Well, it's too late now to rectify that mistake, but I suppose—"

He snared her arm and jerked her close. "Don't finish that sentence."

"How do you know what I was going to say?"

"I know. I've listened to injured females before, and they all say the same thing. *If you don't want me, there are plenty of men who will,*' and all that rot. Don't make the mistake of playing me like other men, 'Anna. I won't stand for it."

She jerked away, tossing her long hair back behind her shoulders in a silky, graceful motion. The coverlet slipped away, and she made no attempt to retrieve it but knelt there on the mattress in the pale morning light, her bare beauty making him ache for her in spite of his anger. His throat tightened. Scornful blue eyes regarded him for a long moment, lashes making fringed shadows on her angrily flushed cheeks.

"It is not I who am making a mistake, my lord."

Her quiet rebuke silenced him, and he had the uneasy thought that he'd misjudged her. Was there another reason for her taking on his disguise, more than just the money she claimed she needed? Oh, he knew she needed it; he had instructed his barristers to verify the baronet's debts. An inkling of doubt began to surface. Had the real reasons behind his masquerade as a highwayman been discovered? Had someone noticed that important papers turned up missing more often than money or jewelry? Or that the men who carried those secret papers were most often the Moon Rider's victims?

It was said that the most effective way to discover a man's secrets was with a woman's body, yet he was reluctant to believe that of her. Not yet. Not without solid evidence to support the theory.

Releasing the breath he hadn't realized he was holding, Chance said, "Perhaps I am making a mistake, but time will tell that. If you do not intend to wed Roxbury, why do the rumormongers say you're betrothed to him?"

"If that theory is correct, why do they say you're a murderer?" she countered in a mocking, confident drawl.

He smiled. Her eyes widened at his reply: "Because I am."

Rhianna stared unseeing across the moors. She and Chance rode silently, hooves sinking deeply into damp ruts of the road. She rode a rented horse, an ill-tempered beast that resisted any effort at speed; chosen, no doubt, for that very fact.

She slanted a quick glance at Chance's cold profile. He'd barely spoken to her in the past two hours, save to give her terse directions. The closeness she'd shared so briefly with him had been an illusion. Obviously, he would share his body with her, but that was all. She'd been a fool to think they had shared a meeting of souls, an intangible intimacy that only two lovers could possess.

His mocking admission to murder had severed the final bond between them, leaving her shaken and confused. She'd never believed it, never wanted to think him capable of the cold murder of his uncle, yet now it seemed she had no choice but to believe it. Even if his uncle had been a wicked man who deserved to die, she could not condone murder. Had it been self-defense, perhaps? After all, he'd been young and tormented—and she did recall his bitter belief that Lord Perry would kill him first.

Oh, she wished she knew the truth. The first flush of silent shock had melded into disbelieving pain, then questions he refused to answer. Only now, when he was so obviously unconcerned with what she thought, did pain flare into anger. And the anger was so much easier to bear than the aching hurt of the truth, the knowledge that Chance had been nothing more than a mirage all these years. The anguished, vulnerable, boy she'd thought he was no longer existed, had never existed.

"Where are you taking me?" she finally asked when he took a fork in the road leading away from Whiteash Manor. "I thought—"

"You've done too much thinking lately. Let someone do it who is more accustomed to it."

Furious, she lapsed into silence again, until she finally saw his destination.

The iron gates of Viscount Keswick's Huntington estate swung open slowly after Chance identified himself to the gatekeeper. Rhianna's first spurt of dismay turned into anger.

"How dare you!" she snarled softly, jerking on her mount's reins in an effort to turn back. Chance's arm snaked out to grab at them, and the look he gave her was cold.

"Don't make presumptions. George can be trusted. He is not one of the gossipmongers in Wiltshire."

"I refuse to allow you to humiliate me this way."

"You don't have a choice." He yanked the reins away from her, startling her mount into a sudden leap. It took her a moment to calm the animal, and by that time, he'd tightened his grip on her reins.

"You'll find yourself unseated in the drive, my dear, if you're not more careful," he said calmly, ignoring her furious glare.

Rhianna tugged the cloak around her body and sat up straight and stiff in the saddle. She kept her gaze straight ahead, though she could feel his eyes flicking toward her as they cantered up the curved drive.

Flower beds thick with bright blossoms bordered green lawns stretching on each side of the drive. Gardeners and groundsmen obviously kept them well-groomed, and Rhianna recalled how Serenity House had once been as well kept. It did her no good to remember such things now, of course. Flowers were a minor luxury when her father's very health hinged on having enough money for doctors.

When Chance halted their horses in front of wide steps leading up to the main entrance, she took a deep breath. The last time she'd been at Huntington had been the night of the ball, when she'd first seen Chance again after eight years.

The night the Moon Rider had precipitated her father's illness.

Chance was looking at her. She saw him through new eyes now, knowing what she did about him. Was he remembering that night? How his carelessness had hurt a man he claimed to like?

Apparently not, she decided in the next instant when

he informed her that she was not to attempt to prejudice George Gladwin in any way.

"It would only end badly," he added when she remained stiff and silent. "He's an incurable romantic and would try to save you from me, and I would be forced to stop him."

"How was I so wrong about you?" she asked bitterly, and didn't bother to wait for his reply. She shook her head. "You are not the man I thought at all."

"I daresay. Nonetheless, be so good as to follow my advice about George. He's tenderhearted and easily wounded."

"How distressing."

She could feel Chance's narrowed gaze on her and ignored him, even when they were ushered into the main parlor and were greeted by a surprised Viscount Keswick.

"Wolf, old chap," he said warmly, then hesitated when he saw Rhianna standing slightly behind the earl. "I say —is that Miss Llewellyn?"

She stepped forward, chin lifting, well aware of how she must look in the torn cloak and rumpled breeches and shirt.

"Yes, Lord Keswick, it is. I apologize for coming to you in such a tattered state, but—"

"But we were out riding and had an unfortunate accident. Her horse ran away and we were forced to take shelter for the night," Chance put in smoothly. He put an arm around Keswick's shoulders. "Can you put us up for a short time? I fear that we have precipitated some gossip."

"I say. Yes, one can well imagine." Keswick's round face creased in a rueful smile. "Miss Llewellyn, you should know better than to go riding with Wolf. Things always seem to happen around him."

"So I've learned." She managed a smile. "I don't suppose you could find me a change of clothes, could you? I'm at a distinct disadvantage in these things."

"Of course, of course. Some of my youngest sister's garments may fit you. I'll have Therese bring them down from storage. You'll want to clean up, of course."

As he reached for the bell pull, Rhianna said, "I must send a note to my house telling them where I am. My servants worry so, and if Papa's condition should worsen. . . ."

As her voice faltered, Keswick instantly responded. "It shall be done at once, Miss Llewellyn. I shall send Benefield over immediately."

"That would be wonderful." She ignored Chance's quick frown and followed Keswick to a writing table where he drew out clean paper and a sharpened quill and pot of ink. It took her only a moment to scrawl a message to Serena and seal it.

"I'll take it," Chance said, plucking the letter from her hand when she held it out to Keswick. He smiled blandly at her when she opened her mouth to protest. "I'll give Benefield a few shillings to make haste, Miss Llewellyn. It's a long way to ride, and I don't want the poor man to feel put upon."

"How generous, my lord," she said through clenched teeth, eyes narrowing as he tucked the letter into the pocket of his coat. His lips curled in amusement.

"Thank you, Miss Llewellyn."

Fuming, she allowed a maidservant to show her up the wide staircase to a room on the second floor, barely taking note of the elegant furnishings she passed. What was he up to now? He must have some plan, or he would not have brought her here like this and lied so boldly to his friend. Damn him, what could he have in mind?

• • • •

"Wolf, you're up to something."

Chance gave George a mild glance over the rim of his brandy snifter. "Why do you think that?"

"Because I can tell when you aren't being completely truthful." Keswick crossed his legs and frowned as he contemplated a fresh cigar. His gaze finally shifted back to his friend. "What is it? Are you and Miss Llewellyn bound for Gretna Green or some other, less honorable destination?"

"God forbid." Chance gazed at him in amusement. "You must have deplorable taste in literature, Georgie. I have no intentions of eloping with Miss Llewellyn."

"Humph. Hope not. She's betrothed to Roxbury. Be a hell of a broth there, I daresay."

"Would be if she were. She isn't."

George regarded him thoughtfully. "Gossip has it that she is. Fact, Sir Twickenham told me on good authority that he heard it from Roxbury's valet. Betrothed."

"Miss Llewellyn says no, George."

"Does she?" Keswick's brows lifted in pleased surprise. "Good. Can't abide Roxbury most of the time. He's a damned unpleasant fellow."

"So I've discovered."

"Yes. Heard about your set-to with him at Heffington's. You went there deliberately, I'd wager, just to tweak his nose for him."

"You're quite astute at times, Georgie." Chance gave him a grin of genuine amusement. "You should have come along."

"I would have if you'd seen fit to inform me about it. Deuce take it, Wolf, what's got into you lately?"

Chance shrugged. "Why do you think something has 'got into' me?"

"You're behaving damned peculiar. Have been for over a year." Keswick grinned suddenly. "More peculiar than usual, I should clarify."

Stretching his legs out in front of him, Chance leaned back in the chair and laughed. "Don't worry about me, old friend. I've just got a lot on my mind."

"No, it's more than that." Keswick's normally bland expression sharpened. "You've changed. Oh, you've always been reckless, but lately, you seem to have a purpose."

"A purpose?" Chance eyed him closely. "What kind of purpose could I possibly have? Except to get as drunk as possible and bed as many different women as possible?"

"You've never been like that, gossip or not. I know you. Known you much too long to swallow that Banbury tale. No, there's something that's drawn your cork, yet I don't know what it could be. Unless—" His eyes widened. "You ain't gone and fallen in love, have you?"

"Love!" Chance laughed loudly. "Now I *know* you've been reading execrable literature. No, I haven't fallen in love, believe me on that."

George slid a sly glance toward the second floor. "Not even with the ever-so-beautiful Miss Llewellyn? Wouldn't be the first time an earl went over the anvil with a lovely woman of lesser rank."

"Don't try and get me married off, Georgie. I've no intention of marrying yet."

"So you say." Keswick grinned. "Yet you spent the night with her. Sounds to me like she's compromised now."

Chance stared at him. "Don't even say that in jest. If it should get about, it would cause her unnecessary pain and embarrassment. Because I won't marry her, and she'll be ruined. Do you understand?"

For a moment, Keswick just gazed at him, then he

shook his head. "Don't understand you, Wolf, no I don't. But you needn't worry that I'll spill the beans. I wouldn't hurt Miss Llewellyn. She's been through enough lately, what with her father's illness and him being in dun territory so badly."

"What do you know of that? How many debts does Sir Griffyn have out?"

Shrugging, Keswick said, "Don't know. Easy enough to find out, though. Ask any moneylender. Howard and Gibbs would have an excellent notion how much is owed to whom, I imagine."

"I daresay." Chance rose and stretched. "Good of you to let me stay a while, Georgie. The sooner we can concoct a story to keep Miss Llewellyn from being more embarrassed than she already is, the better. Any ideas?"

"No. Wait." Keswick looked up hopefully. "My sister Fran is coming tomorrow for a visit. Couldn't we say that Miss Llewellyn is her guest?"

"Excellent. I knew I could count on you."

"What about her note? Shall I ring for Benefield?"

"No. I'll find him. After I read the note." He ignored Keswick's shocked protest. "It wouldn't do for her to tell the truth when we've come up with a much safer lie, would it?"

"One day, Wolf, your machinations will get you in grave trouble. I predict this with great sorrow."

"No doubt. Meanwhile, I'll do what I can to save the very ungrateful Miss Llewellyn's reputation."

Chapter 18

Rhianna paced restlessly in front of French doors left open to allow in the last warm breezes of August. Dusk lay gently on the ragged gardens of Serenity House, and the first lamps of evening had been lit. Birds rustled in the trees and bushes and murmured drowsy songs. Squares of light slanted across the stone terrace outside her chambers. The air had a silky feel to it, warm and inviting. She blew out a heavy breath and pressed her cheek against the cool glass of a window pane.

The house was quiet, too quiet. Ever since returning from Huntington Hall the week before, she'd not been able to bear solitude. There was too much time to think, too much time to—remember.

Not even visits with her father served to make the hours more bearable. Sir Griffyn's health seemed worse, despite the expensive London physicians hired by the earl. Her lip curled. It seemed that even the earl of Wolverton could not command good health, a fact she had pointed out to Chance with bitter irony the day before.

His brow had quirked upward at her tart comment, but he had not bothered to refute her accusation. He'd merely leaned back against the mantel and murmured that she was expecting a great deal from him. For a moment, she'd been tempted to tell him that as she expected nothing, anything he did was a "great deal," but she hadn't. No, she was too cowardly to risk anything that might help her father, a fact that left her bitterly resenting Chance's involvement. And also his frequent visits. What did he want of her? Why must he remind her of her past foolishness? Just his presence was unsettling, and he seemed to know it.

Fretful, she moved from the French doors to a small, bare marquetry table, and from there to the brocade settee, then back again. An aimless butterfly, flitting from object to object in the room without thought or plan.

It was warm in the house, suffocating, in fact. She stepped out onto the terrace and lifted her loose hair from the back of her neck. Long strands hung heavily over her arms, drifting slightly in a cooler breeze.

Murmurs of voices wafted across the garden to her, and she caught glimpses of Fenwick and Porter as they tended to the evening chores. There were three other servants to help them now, recently arrived from Whiteash Manor at the decree of the earl.

Her arms dropped to her sides, hands curling into fists in her skirts. Damn Chance. He behaved as arbitrarily as he wished and there was little she could do about it. A threat to expose him had been met with amused mockery; he knew that she could not expose him without risking herself, and to do that was to condemn Sir Griffyn to the hell of a public asylum. No, he'd not been especially worried at her empty threat, because he'd recognized it for what it was—a desperate attempt to retain a shred of self-respect.

How could she ever have been so foolish? She'd believed in him, fallen for his charm with a shameful willingness. But she had truly believed that he was a tortured soul, was still the boy who had endured such grief and pain. And now she was suffering the retribution for her rash belief in a man who did not deserve her trust.

Humiliation made her cheeks burn, and the evening breeze seemed suddenly much too warm. She turned to go back inside. Then she heard the faint sounds of music drifting on the air. It was coming from the direction of the stables, light and lively, a charming country song. She grew still, listening, letting the melody seep inside. Music had always had a magical effect on her. It was said to soothe even the most savage of beasts, but for her, it had always been energizing. Instead of lulling her into complacency or peace, a lively tune prompted her to action.

Impulsively, she moved across the stone floor of the terrace to the shadows encroaching along a wall. They swallowed her, soft and welcoming and silent as she began to dance, feet skimming over the cool stones with a light, noiseless touch.

There was solace in dancing, a communion of body and spirit in an expression that needed no words to explain. She was Circe, the enchantress who had captivated an ancient Trojan king and turned his men to swine; then she was Cleopatra, the legendary queen of beauty and charisma, graceful as a willow reed in the wind.

The evening breeze grew cooler; Rhianna heard only the music of tambourines and guitars as she danced, as she lost herself in the rhythm of forgotten melodies. Without knowing quite how, she dimly realized that she was dancing in her petticoat again, her skirt and blouse cast aside, her feet bare.

Yet still she swayed, twisted, turned, feet slapping harder against the stones now; her arms lifted to twine above her head, long hair whipping like silk about her face. Breathless, damp with effort, she paused at last and closed her eyes, tilting back her head with a smile.

"Beautiful," came a soft voice from behind her, and her eyes flew open as she turned with a gasp.

A tall shadow detached itself from the deeper ones

and stepped into a hazy pool of light streaming through a window in a distorted square. Chance, looking like a sardonic angel in tight buff breeches and jackboots, his ebony hair tied back from his face with a black ribbon, raked her with a thoughtful gaze. Her chin lifted.

"Spying again, my lord?"

"Again?" He paused, the light behind him leaving his face in shadow. "I don't recall the last time." He stepped closer, voice deepening. "Or do I?"

Her heart thumped. She stood still, breathing deeply as she waited. His eyes narrowed beneath the ledge of his brow, piercing her with a scrutiny she could feel in her bones.

"It's true, isn't it."

"What is true?"

His voice was rough. "That dance—I've known you before, haven't I? It was a long time ago. . . ."

Silent, she didn't resist when he curled a hand around her wrist and drew her into a hazy patch of lamplight. Nor did she attempt to turn her face. She let the light play over her as she watched his reaction.

Slowly, she tugged free a ribbon from the front of her bodice and held it out to him. It fluttered in the slight breeze, dangling from her fingers as a reminder. Chance blew out a sharp breath. There was a tension in him that she could feel; she knew the exact moment when he was certain he knew.

"The gypsy girl. Rhianna."

It was said with no inflection, no surprise or anger or pleasure. It sounded like a mere acknowledgment of a fact, no more.

"Yes," she said simply.

"Why didn't you tell me? *Christ.* All this time—and you knew who I was, of course."

"Of course. Why should I tell you? I assumed that our first meeting hadn't been important to you."

He released her wrist and stood there, staring down at her in the shadows, thoughts hidden from her. Then he gave a short bark of laughter.

"I should have believed the rumors. I knew there was something about you . . ."

"Would it have made any difference?"

"Yes. No. I don't know." He fell silent for a moment, and the strains of music from the direction of the stables grew faint. " 'Anna—Rhianna. What a bloody fool I've been. You must have enjoyed yourself immensely at my expense."

"Perhaps." No point letting him know how she'd agonized over the situation. His arrogance and conceit was swollen enough.

"It explains a great deal that had me puzzled, I admit." He paused again, eyes reflecting splinters of light in their dark depths. A faint, sardonic smile curled his mouth, irritating her.

"I'm glad that you've been illuminated, my lord. Now, if you don't mind—" She started to brush past him, but he caught her arm again.

"Oh no. Not just yet. For once I'd like some answers before you flee. You always were one to make abrupt departures."

"I don't know what you're talking about."

"Of course you do. Your habit of fleeing without explanation has not lessened with the years. You left without so much as a fare-thee-well the first time I met you."

"How annoying for you, but I seem to recall it quite differently. You rode away from our camp and did not come back."

"Ah, but there you're wrong. I did come back a few

days later, and there was nothing left but embers and cold ruts in the ground."

Suddenly cool in the night air, she crossed her bare arms over her chest. He had come back to look for her. What would have happened if she had been there waiting for him? But what was the use in speculating on the impossible. . . . She tossed the hair from her eyes and lifted an eyebrow.

"So now you've found me again. How heart warming. Shall we celebrate?"

Chance blew out a heavy breath, irritation edging his voice. "Look, I know you're angry at me for interfering in your life. But damn you—you had no compunction in interfering in *my* life." He stepped close, so close she could feel the heat of his body radiating toward her. "Your interference has damn near cost me almost two year's work. Are you aware that the local magistrate has engineered a massive hunt for the wounding of the king's guard? No, I can tell you aren't. Your eyes give you away, m'dear. A successful criminal learns to hide that reaction quickly."

"As you have, I presume?" she managed to snap, though he was right. She hadn't been able to help a spurt of fear at the news. "Does the sheriff have any—suspects?"

"Not yet. But he's not stupid, though not well-versed in the tracking down of elusive highwaymen. It seems that the highwayman who shot the king's guard was described quite thoroughly and in great detail."

Rhianna grimaced. "And I suppose you blame me for your troubles."

"*My* troubles?" He laughed. "No, love. 'Tis not me who was so thoroughly described—it was you."

"Me!"

"Yes, you charming little idiot. You're the one who

halted that coach, and you are the one who shot at the driver and the guard. No one saw me. A fact I point out to you with little hope that you'll follow my future advice on how to stay out of trouble. If you'll remember—"

"Damn you! You think this is funny!"

"No, believe me, I don't." His expression sobered, and he caught her hand when she began to back away. "You're in danger, whether you realize it or not. Your horse was found, and inquiries are being made."

Her heart thudded so hard that it seemed her ribs must be bruised. How could she have been so foolish? So desperate that she ignored common sense? But she had, and now would probably pay a high price. There would be little sympathy for a girl rumored to be the bastard daughter of a gypsy and an eccentric Welsh baronet now thought to be mad.

"Rhianna." Chance's fingers tightened, and she realized he still held her arm. She looked up.

"Yes?"

"Come inside. We'll think of something."

Lamps glowed softly on the table and wall of Rhianna's sitting room. Hazy light caressed the golden curves of her face. She gave him a tentative glance that made Chance's chest tighten. Damn. He really should have known, really should have guessed, but he'd been so used to ignoring his emotions through the years that he hadn't allowed any thoughts of softer times, of lost times, to intrude. And so he hadn't let himself think about that young gypsy girl who had captured his interest and heart so long ago.

"So," he said briskly to hide his turmoil, "now we have to think of a way to keep your head attached to your shoulders until this dies down."

Rhianna stared at him solemnly, silent for once. He

was grateful for that. He pulled the drapes closed over the doors leading to the terrace and turned to look at her. She was standing in a small pool of lamplight, still clad in her thin petticoat and chemise, gauzy wisps of material that did more to enhance than to hide her curves. He looked away with a scowl.

"If you want me to be able to think clearly, you'd best put on a dressing gown, my charming gypsy lass."

She moved across the room to her wardrobe. He shoved one hand into his coat pocket and waited.

"Is this better, my lord?"

He glanced around. She wore a taffeta dressing gown trimmed in fur from neck to ankles.

"Much better. Now, suppose you tell me who knows about your extracurricular activities besides me."

"No one."

"That's highly unlikely. Haven't your absences been noted? What about your riding garb? And where do you sell the jewels you steal?"

Despite his curt questions, she remained calm, her voice steady. "Only Serena would notice my absences, and I have her staying with my father in the evenings. Besides, I go where I wish when I wish, as I have always done."

"Do tell," he said dryly. "And I suppose you wash your own costume."

"I'm quite capable when needs be." She moved across the room and removed a small pouch from a desk drawer. It clinked softly. "This is what remains. Any jewels that I have to sell would not be remarked on, as it is well-known that our circumstances have necessitated the selling of most of our family heirlooms. I am careful not to take unusual pieces that might be recognized. Coin, of course, is easy to spend. Any more questions?"

He sat down in a small chair, crossing his legs so that

his right ankle rested on his left knee. "No, I think that sufficiently answers them. So there is very little that can tie you to the thefts, then."

"So it would seem." She let the slender bag of coins drop to the tabletop with a slight thud. Chance eyed it thoughtfully.

"Burn your disguise. Tonight. Now. It can only endanger you if you keep it."

"What about Rayna?"

Startled, he echoed, "Rayna?"

"My horse. The one the sheriff found."

"Ah. It will take them a few days to locate the owner, long enough for us to have concocted some story." He grinned suddenly. "Rayna is not as fast as her namesake, is she?"

A faint smile curved Rhianna's mouth, though her eyes remained wary and watchful. "No. And I'm not the rider that Nicolo was."

Nicolo. The memories came fast and thick, of that cold winter day so soon after his parents' deaths, the horse-race with Nicolo, and the impish gypsy girl who had intrigued him. And abandoned him.

"Why didn't you tell me, Rhianna? Why didn't you tell me who you were?" he couldn't help asking, though he damned himself for the betrayal.

She shrugged. "I told you. I didn't think it mattered to you. If it mattered to you, you would have remembered —as I remembered."

"*Christ,* it had been so long, and you've changed."

"So have you."

"That's not fair. You knew my name, knew who I was."

He was standing, but didn't remember rising, moving to her and taking her arms. He gave her a little shake.

"What did you expect? That I would take one look at

you and recognize the disheveled gypsy girl instead of the elegantly groomed, poised young woman you are now?"

She stared up at him, eyes a stormy blue. "Perhaps. I certainly thought that after . . . that after what happened between us . . ."

His grip tightened. "I see. You thought that after I made love to a woman wearing a mask, I would remember the thirteen-year-old gypsy girl who barely let me kiss her. I regret I'm not as talented at mind reading as you gypsies seem to be—"

"Stop it!" Her eyes were bright in the dim light. "It didn't really matter to you who I was that night in the hut, did it? You just wanted an easy conquest."

"And I got one."

She recoiled as if he'd slapped her, jerking away from him.

"Rhianna, I didn't mean—"

"How dare you! Do you honestly think you could have taken from me what I freely gave? No, not without killing me first." Her throat worked, silken shudders that hurt him to see, and he lifted a hand palm upward as if to ask forgiveness. Shaking her head, she whispered huskily, "I only gave myself to you because I recognized you, and I saw in your eyes the same pain and rage that I'd seen when you were just a boy. We had a kinship then, you and I, and I thought that p'raps we still had a bond between us, despite all that's happened in our lives. I was mistaken, I see."

The vise around his chest tightened painfully; he had to force out the words.

"No, you're not mistaken. I still feel a bond between us, though I haven't understood it. I never forgot you, though I never let myself think of you." He paused to take a deep breath, not knowing if he could put his feelings into words.

He let his hand fall to his side, balling it into a fist as he turned away. After a moment he asked softly, "Do you remember how angry I was when you first met me? I'd lost my parents, and my uncle was making my life a daily hell. You were the only one who seemed to understand any of what I was going through, the only one who didn't offer empty words that were supposed to make everything better. And then you were gone from my life, as suddenly as you'd come into it. I felt as if I'd been betrayed yet again. I don't expect you to understand, I suppose, but I never let myself think about you for long. It was just another betrayal, another loss, and I had so many already. I wanted to forget you, so I did."

He turned around. She was watching him quietly, unshed tears making her eyes a bright, stormy blue.

"I see," she said after a moment, but it was plain she did not.

"Right-ho." His mouth twisted. "I'll show myself out."

His hand was on the door latch before he heard her say, "Chance—don't go."

He stood with his back to the room, his forehead pressed against the cool wood of the door, and then he felt her hand touch him lightly on the shoulder. He shuddered, an involuntary muscular reaction to the ruthless emotions tearing at him despite his best effort to keep them at bay. She would send him away now. He'd ruined the most precious, fragile thing in his life. But he steeled himself for the inevitable, drawing in a deep breath.

When he turned, she was smiling through the tears flowing freely down her cheeks.

"I love you," she said softly, and he felt something raw and painful shift inside him. He couldn't speak, couldn't say what he knew she wanted to hear.

But then there was no need for words, because she was rising to her toes and putting her arms around his neck, drawing his head down for a kiss. Everything that he wanted to express—his regret over her father, his angry words, the wasted years—he put into his kiss, his mouth moving on her lips with a fierce urgency and need that he hadn't known he could feel. That he had never *wanted* to feel, because it was too dangerous to care that much.

God, he must be crazy, but he knew that this one woman was the only woman for him.

In a desperate attempt to retrieve his balance, he said against her soft lips, "So which woman am I kissing now? Cynthia, 'Anna, or Rhianna?"

She laughed throatily. "Whichever one you prefer."

"All three of them," he said, sweeping her up into his arms and crossing the room with her. He kicked open the door to her bed chamber, then kicked it shut behind him. A single lamp burned on a bedside table, giving off hazy light. He lay her down on the bed, kissing her, kissing her until he felt the hard knot inside him loosen, until he thought of nothing but holding her close.

Rhianna clung to him fiercely, taking his kiss and returning it with matching urgency. She started to say his name but his mouth covered hers again and smothered the words.

"Don't talk," he muttered when he lifted his head. His eyes gleamed darkly in the dim light. "Just love me."

Love him? She could do nothing else. She'd loved him for so long that being able to say it aloud at last had been a sweet relief. Tears still clogged her throat and stung her eyes. Chance dragged a blunt fingertip over her cheek, smearing salty dew across her skin.

"Oh God. Don't cry. I hate tears. Must you?" He

groaned deeply, then gave a sigh of resignation. "It's what I deserve, I suppose, for letting myself—care."

"Chance, do you really—"

He stopped her murmur with another kiss, this one more urgent than the last. She felt his hands at the opening of her dressing gown, flicking open the frogged fastenings that held it closed over her breasts. The edges slid apart in a soft glide, the fur trim tickling the bare skin of her arms.

"All these damn clothes." His mutter was rough, his hands almost as rough as he pushed at the hem of her chemise and tugged at the tapes of her single petticoat. Then he slid his body over her bare curves, his garments harsh against her skin. The buttons of his coat were cold and hard where they pressed into her, and when she made an indistinct sound of protest, he lifted his mouth from hers long enough to shrug out of coat, vest, and shirt.

"Kiss me," he said again, trailing a burning path of kisses from her forehead to her willing lips. "Give me all of you."

Before she could answer or act, he'd captured her mouth with his, his tongue invading her so deeply she felt almost consumed by him. His hands worked at the buttons of his pants as he kissed her, and he managed to free himself swiftly from pants and jackboots. Then his weight rested on her, nestling between her legs, his body burning against her thighs.

She couldn't help a small gasp at the first hard intrusion of him, even as she arched up to accept him. Her heart was pounding fiercely, her lungs working for air.

"Chance," she whispered distractedly, hands cupping his bare shoulders. Light gleamed golden on his skin, made dark shadows on his face. The gauzy bed curtains swayed in a delicate dance above them. "Chance, oh Chance. . . ."

Soft words and soft light, faint whispers in the dark and the night shadows beyond the bed shrouding the rest of the world as if it didn't exist—Chance over her and inside her and holding her and giving her love and life. . . .

He moved in an exquisite glide that swept her up and closer to the heavens, made her forget that anything else existed but him. He was her world; he invaded it, filled her ears with the sound of his ragged breathing, her eyes with the taut, misted curve of his shoulders and angles of his face, filled her body with sweet possession.

Rhianna wanted time to cease, wanted this moment to last forever, to be suspended in the piercing sweetness that she felt now.

Half-sobbing, she pressed her face against his chest, felt his labored breathing and the thunder of his heart like hoofbeats in the wind. Her hands drifted from his shoulders down the curve of his back, fingers skimming over his warm skin in small flutters. Then, boldly, she slid her hands between them and caressed him, heard his response in a ragged groan against her ear.

"Rhianna. . . ."

"Hold me," she whispered. His weight rested on his bent arms, and he shifted to cradle her. That action brought him more fully inside her, and she felt him shudder again. She moved beneath him, hips twisting in a slow glide. Chance held her tightly, his breath feathering over her cheek, his body rocking against her until she felt her tenuous grip on control dissolve into shivering collapse.

Wordless cries filled the air, and she had the distracted thought they were hers but wasn't certain, and she felt the waves of release crash over her, dragging her under before she surfaced, only to go under again. She'd swam in the ocean once, and it was the same weightless feeling as she'd had then, the sensation of being swept along on a tide much too strong to resist. Did she whisper her love again? She wasn't certain of that either.

All that was certain, was that she and Chance were together, and that she would never be alone again. What was in the past, was past. She would believe in him, and no matter what he'd done before, now things would be much different. For both of them. They had each other.

For a long time, she lay staring into the pale shadows, holding his relaxed body in her arms, smiling at the future.

Morning came too quickly. The lamp had long burned down to a faint glimmer, and the ebony shadows of night had turned to a pearly gray that promised sunrise when Rhianna nudged Chance. He stirred slowly, opening one eye as he pulled her closer. Her hair tumbled into her eyes, soft and silky and lit with fire in the faint light. Her mouth was curved in a sleepy smile, her words soft.

"Must you be so energetic so early?"

"Why not?" With a quick motion, he flipped her onto her back and pinned her down, grinning when she protested. "If you don't wish to be . . . ravished . . . my sweet," he said, kissing an enticing portion of her body between the last few words, "then you should . . . wear . . . clothes."

"I *was* wearing clothes."

He kissed the small pulse beneath her left ear. "When? I don't recall that."

"Yesterday."

"Ah. That was before your delightful dance on the

terrace. Did you know that there is the shape of a heart in your ear?"

"Chance! A servant will be here soon to wake me. I'd rather they not find you in my bed."

"Hypocrite."

"Not a hypocrite—a coward. I'm not up to explanations right now."

He kissed the tip of her nose and sat up. "Since when did you feel it necessary to make explanations to servants?"

"Since they seem to take such a personal interest in me and my father. Besides, they've been on reduced wages for so long, I feel as if I owe them something more than mere money."

"All of them?"

"Of course. I couldn't reduce one without reducing all, could I? Surprisingly, none of them have complained. Even the new man, Porter, said that he didn't mind at all, knowing my circumstances."

Chance frowned. "New man? I thought you had cut your staff."

"I did. Porter came to me on recommendation and said he needed the position badly. He said a bed and food was payment enough for now."

"Whose recommendation?"

Rhianna gazed up at him, eyes narrowed with irritation. "Does it really matter?"

"Probably not. I've just got one of those annoying heads for detail, that's all." He laced his fingers through hers and kissed each one of her fingertips before saying, "I hope that my attention to detail will get you out of the mess you've gotten yourself into, my sweet."

"So do I." She took a deep breath. "So do I."

Chance hooked his finger beneath her chin and tilted her face up. Her eyes were wide and blue, shadowed beneath the fringe of her lashes. "I'll do my best. Meanwhile, I have something I'll send over to you." When she made a sound of protest, he kissed her quickly. "Consider it repayment of a debt long owed."

"What debt?" She gave him a puzzled glance, and he grinned.

"You'll see soon enough."

"I hate it when you talk in riddles."

He gave her another quick kiss, then swung his legs over the side of the bed and reached for his clothes. "You'll remember when you see it."

Rhianna settled back into her pillows, making him think of a satisfied cat. "I daresay. I hope it doesn't bite."

"Only a nibble or two." He stepped to the door and opened it a crack, peering out into her sitting room before he emerged. Just before leaving, he glanced back at her with a rueful smile. "I feel like a naughty schoolboy sneaking out of your bed like this."

"You did this as a schoolboy? Tsk, tsk, how precocious of you."

He grinned. "Wasn't it? I earned myself quite a reputation for spending my nights on the lawn, I can tell you."

"No doubt. Believe me, no one here would dare suggest that the wicked earl of Wolverton was anything but pious and pure."

He laughed softly. "Liar. Remember—stay here and don't do anything foolish. If you need me, send a servant and I'll come at once."

"I'll tat lace and read prayers until you say differently," she said with a lift of her brows. He groaned.

"Rhianna, please—just let me handle matters. I'll get you out of this scrape if you let me."

"I'll do my best."

He could only hope that she would.

Chapter 19

"God save us all from fools and politicians." Irritated, Chance crumpled the sheet of paper he held in one hand, then tossed it into the fire. He watched it burn, the edges going from cherry red to black, then dissolving into fiery ashes.

"Trouble, my lord?"

He glanced at Hobson. "Nothing out of the ordinary. Just the dissembling of men who cannot decide which fence they want to straddle, much less which side to choose."

"I see." Hobson carefully arranged a stack of clean neck cloths on a shelf, keeping the starched linen laid out flat so as not to crease. He took pride in caring for his lordship's garments and frequently complained that the valet was too cow-handed to service a gentleman of the first state.

That complaint never failed to amuse Chance, who did not consider himself a gentleman of fashion.

"Where did you send Fisher?" he asked mildly.

Hobson stiffened. "He is attending to the proper cleaning of your coat, my lord. Mrs. Timmons is instructing him on the basics of fine materials."

"Hobson, Fisher is an amiable valet and should be doing the tasks that require his services. You should not concern yourself with matters he can handle."

"Very well, my lord."

Chance sighed. He'd offended him again. The touchy situation required more tact than he could muster.

"Will there be anything else, my lord, before I send Fisher in to you?"

The old man's stiff-necked pride would not allow him to expose his injured feelings, and he stood stiffly in the center of the room.

"I do not require Fisher. I would like for you to give me your opinion on a few matters of importance instead of puttering around with linen."

Hobson's brows lifted, and his eyes lit with interest. "I should be glad to impart whatever speculation I can give, my lord."

Chance lowered his frame into a wing-back chair and motioned for Hobson to do the same. When the old man was seated, hands folded in his lap and his pose alert, Chance said quietly, "There are rumors about that I am a spy for Talleyrand and the French Directory. While it is true that I have intercepted certain documents, as you know, I am, and always have been, a patriot. The rumors can cripple my effectiveness if this gets about."

Hobson's expression was appalled. "Rumors, my lord? But who—how?"

"My opinion is that Heffington and Roxbury started them. Roxbury has had his nose out of joint since our confrontation and would not be above malicious gossip as a way to get back at me." Chance shrugged. "Ordinarily, I would not be bothered by gossip. This, however, strikes a bit too close to the truth to suit me."

"What is it you wish me to do, my lord?"

Chance smiled. Hobson, as always, cut directly to the heart of the matter.

"Hobson, I need for you to ferret about and see what you can discover. My contact has verified my suspicions that Roxbury is carrying vital documents that can harm

England. Heffington is involved, though on a lesser scale, of course. He's much too scatterbrained to be of great value."

"What sort of documents are involved, my lord?"

"Mostly names, I believe." Chance's voice lowered. "A few of the names are of highly placed government officials. These men support Napoleon, and if they succeed in getting the Corsican into England—" He inhaled deeply. "It is well known that Napoleon is more of a threat to our security than the guillotine. He is a threat to every crowned head in Europe."

Hobson frowned. "I agree, my lord. I will certainly see what I can discover."

"Excellent. And one other thing—what do you know about the servants at Serenity House?"

"Servants, my lord?" Hobson looked startled. "Not very much. Except that Riever is said to be a cousin of Fenwick, who was employed there when the baronet returned from abroad."

"I'd like for you to investigate a man by the name of Porter, if you will."

"Porter. By all means. Will there be anything else?"

Chance suppressed a smile. Hobson's chest was puffed out with self-importance. He was suddenly a man with a mission.

"Just one more thing—what have you heard concerning the horse the sheriff found?"

Hobson frowned slightly. "Oddly enough, not much. Sheriff Hamlin is making discreet inquiries. It seems that Hamlin wishes to be quite close-mouthed about what he suspects, but has indicated that the horse he has in his possession may be linked to one of the highwaymen terrorizing Wiltshire." His lips moved into a faint curl. "Certain items were discovered, I believe."

"Bloody hell." Chance rose to pace the floor in short steps. "Do you know what kind of items, Hobson?"

"No, but I will do my best to find out. My third cousin on my mother's side is the sheriff's sister-in-law."

Chance laughed. "Thank God for the intermarrying of Wiltshire residents. Yes, do your best to discover what you can, Hobson."

"Very good, my lord." A pleased smile flickered for an instant on Hobson's normally austere countenance. Chance saw it and hid his own smile. Hobson wouldn't appreciate any hint of indulgence.

"Oh, and Hobson," he added when the old man had reached the door, "please send Riever to me. I have an errand for him."

"Certainly, my lord."

Chance moved to his desk and opened the top drawer, removing the small box he'd placed there months before. He flipped open the lid and took out the strand of pearls that belonged to Rhianna. They gleamed dully, pale globes against his dark hand, looping from his palm to swing gently. A tiny diamond clasp in the shape of a cherub glittered in the light from the window, winking like tiny stars. A pretty enough bauble, though as Rhianna had said, not worth a great deal.

He snapped shut the lid and tied the box with a ribbon. He held it for a moment. Rhianna would remember the pearls and how he had taken them that night. He hoped she had forgiven him for taking them as he had, and for being an indirect cause of her father's illness. It was time the necklace was returned.

Rhianna's foot tapped impatiently against the floor. Early morning sunlight made bright squares on the parlor carpet. "Do you mind coming to the point, sir?"

Viscount Roxbury smiled thinly. "Not at all. I have given you more than ample time to give me an answer. My notes to you have been ignored. Are you avoiding me?"

She hesitated. To answer truthfully would be taking a risk, but to lie was a repellent thought. It was too bad she'd never studied the art of tact more carefully. She cleared her throat.

"It's not that I am not honored by your offer, my lord, but the reason for it is—as any woman could tell you—very difficult to endure. If you were madly in love with me, p'raps I could understand your haste, but to wed you merely to save you from being returned to France lacks the . . . ardor I had always hoped to find in marriage."

"Come, come, lovely 'Anna, is the thought of marriage to me so abhorrent? Besides—I do feel more than just the need to marry for practical reasons." He stepped close and rested a hand on her shoulder. Heavy lashes drifted lower over his pale eyes as he studied her, but she could see only the dark fire of Chance's eyes, and moved away. Roxbury's mouth twisted. "I see. Have you another suitor, perhaps?"

"No." That was true enough. Chance was much more than just a suitor, though marriage had never been mentioned. "I am not ready to think of a lifetime commitment, my lord."

"No? I had heard that you've been riding with Wolverton of late."

She stared at him. "I don't know what you mean."

"Of course you do. I think you should choose your companions more wisely, if you will accept a bit of advice. Meeting Wolverton on the moors leads to all kinds of nasty speculation, you know. As well as risky situations. The devil earl has committed more than one murder, if the stories are to be believed."

"Stories—you mean gossip, don't you?" Anger made her voice shake slightly, and she drew in a quick breath. "None of which was ever proven, I might add."

"Yes, you might add that if it were true. But the earl was found with Lord Perry's body, and he had blood on his hands and clothes. It was well known there was bad feeling between them. Several of Lord Montagu's friends even heard Wolverton make threats on occasion."

"Making threats is not the same thing as murder . . ."

Roxbury laughed. "No, but standing over the body with a dead man's blood still warm on your hands can only be taken as a very strong indication of guilt." He tilted his head to one side. "You are quite defensive about Wolverton. Can the gossip be true about you and him?"

Careful, she warned herself silently. There was no need to alert Roxbury in any way—especially when she had her own doubts about Chance's innocence in his uncle's murder. Still, she would not let what had happened so many years before cast suspicion on him now.

"Of course the gossip isn't true. We're neighbors. He purchased a field from me for some of his cattle. I resent your inference that we are anything more, Lord Roxbury."

"I beg your pardon."

Rhianna pivoted on her heel and stalked toward the parlor door, intending to call a servant and have Roxbury shown out. Before she reached the door, however, there was a discreet knock.

Fenwick stepped into the parlor, his gaze shifting from his mistress to the viscount and back. A worried frown tucked his brows.

"A man to see you, miss," he said, his eyes riveted on Roxbury. "He says he has a package that he must give to you personally."

"A package?" Grateful for the interruption, Rhianna nodded. "Send him in, Fenwick."

When Riever entered the parlor, she wished she'd had the foresight to receive him in another room, but the damage was done. Roxbury laughed softly, and there was a definite tinge of malice to his laughter.

"Wolverton's steward. Ah, the plot thickens," he murmured loud enough for her to hear.

Ignoring him, Rhianna reached out for the small box Riever held, but he did not release it.

The steward hesitated. "Perhaps it would be best if I were to return later, Miss Llewellyn."

Roxbury moved forward, voice smooth. "It seems that I have discovered something rather sordid about you and Wolverton, after all."

Angry, Rhianna turned to him. "I will not tolerate your snide comments, Lord Roxbury."

"Snide? Or truthful?" He smiled. "Take Wolverton's gift, *ma belle*. I will not attempt a peek at what is obviously meant to be hidden between you."

Flustered, Rhianna turned back to Riever, demanded the box, and held out her hand. With obvious reluctance, the steward placed the box in her palm. Her fingers curled around it and she moved to place it upon the mantel.

As she reached up, one of the ribbon loops caught on the tip of her finger. When she disentangled it, the entire ribbon unwound in a satiny slither, and the box fell open, a string of white slipping out. She barely managed to catch it before it fell to the hearth. The lid of the box bounced one way, and the bottom the other. Roxbury bent to retrieve the bottom of the box and held it out, his brow lifted.

He looked pointedly at the pearls spilling from her palm, smooth and shining with a muted luster. The diamond clasp caught the sunlight through the window and reflected it in winking stars.

"A lovely gift," Roxbury commented. "And a most unusual clasp."

"It's not a gift." She slipped the pearls back into the box half with trembling fingers. When Riever held out the lid, she looked up at him. "Tell the earl that I am most grateful for their return, but he needn't have bothered redeeming my necklace from the usurer's for me."

Riever's countenance remained impassive. "I shall certainly give him your message, miss. Is there anything else you would like me to inform his lordship?"

"Only that I will send him payment for his troubles when my steward returns."

"Of course, miss." Riever bowed and left, shutting the door behind him.

Rhianna set the box down on a table and turned. Roxbury met her gaze with a lifted brow. "How neighborly of the earl to return your necklace."

"Yes."

"Do you still deny a connection between you?"

She wished she could tell him to go to the devil and be done with it. But he was too dangerous to antagonize any more than necessary.

"As I told you, we are only neighbors, my lord. He merely wishes to be helpful, knowing my circumstances."

"Nelson. Call me Nelson." Roxbury took her hand despite her effort to avoid him, and held it between his. "I confess that I am relieved to hear that. I am quite attracted to you, you know. I find you refreshingly blunt in a world filled with innuendoes and stale repartee. Though I admit that I need this alliance for practical reasons, I also want you. No—don't pull away. Listen to me for a moment, 'Anna."

"My lord—please."

Roxbury held tight to her hand and slid his other hand behind to curve around her waist. Rhianna stood stiff and still, glaring up at him. When he bent his head and kissed her, she did not respond. She stood woodenly, allowing him to kiss her with as much feeling as she would have given an irritating spaniel licking her ankles.

And Roxbury must have sensed it.

Finally, he lifted his head, eyes narrowed and a hot blue. "I see," he said.

"See what?"

"You aren't being coy at all. I thought you had succumbed to those intriguing little tricks females use to lure a man, but apparently you truly don't care for me."

"Not in the way you seem to wish, no."

There. The truth at last. Relief.

"How distressing." Roxbury stepped back and fished a decorated snuff box from his pocket. It was small and made of gold, etched with ornate designs. He flicked open the top with a graceful twist of his long-fingered hands and took a pinch in a practiced move that grated on Rhianna's nerves. The box gleamed dully in his hand. He smiled. "And how dangerous for you."

"Dangerous?"

"Yes. For your welfare, certainly. Do you think you can go on for long without a protector? Certainly not in the style to which you seem accustomed. All this"—he waved an arm to indicate the house and grounds outside —"will be forfeit if you do not repay your more pressing debts. And of course, there is the expense of your father's care. London physicians are noted for the amount of their bills."

"I detect a threat underlying your concern," she said sharply. "Do you think yourself the man to force me to debtor's prison?"

"I'm quite capable of it."

"Oh, I realize that. And now I realize what a humbug you are, beneath your posturing and pretense to be an aristocrat. You're little more than a masquerade, my lord, a vain and shallow coxcomb. Your visits and attempts to coax me into a romance with you are quite useless."

Roxbury's cold blue eyes glittered with anger. "How pretty a speech. However, you seem to have missed my point. I am not at all concerned with romance or ardor. I am quite concerned with . . . other things. My safety, for one. The money your father owes me, for another."

"Yes—about that money. Did you present the chits to my solicitor, Mr. Blemmons?"

Roxbury's brow lifted in a languid, amused arch. "Of course I did. Didn't Blemmons tell you? You needn't think I haven't gone through the proper channels, *ma belle*. Besides, there are any number of individuals who were present at White's that night, and can verify that your father lost heavily at the tables."

"I find it difficult to believe Papa would lose so much to *you* . . ."

"I'm afraid it doesn't matter whether you believe me or not."

Rhianna saw no hint of concern or dismay on Roxbury's face. He seemed merely sardonically amused, not worried. She drew in another deep breath.

"If the debts are indeed owed you, they will be paid eventually. I—"

"No. Not eventually. Now. If not, I shall take the necessary steps to collect."

Furious, Rhianna lost her tenuous grip on control. "Damn you for a rogue, Roxbury! Take your threats and your face and your . . . your stupid snuff box and get out of my house at once. If I see you here again I'll set the dogs on you. Do I make myself perfectly clear?"

Red with rage, Roxbury said coldly, "Quite clear. You shall soon regret this, I promise you that, you little gypsy slut."

Without pausing to think, Rhianna slapped him. The blow whipped his head to one side, the marks of her palm and fingers leaving angry red weals on his pale cheek. With a growl of fury, he lunged for her, and she stepped neatly aside, reaching for a fireplace poker in the same move. She swung it up and brandished it deftly, as she would have done her sword. It felt good to stand in the graceful pose of a fencer, one arm lifted behind her and the poker held out as if an épée.

"I can use this, make no mistake. I'll skewer you like a boar if you take one more step, so think about what you dare, Roxbury."

Almost incoherent with wrath, Roxbury stepped carefully toward the door, keeping an eye on the sharp end of the poker as he went. "You'll pay for this," he said several times, repeating the litany in French and English phrases that did not bother her one whit.

"No doubt. But you haven't the courage or the means to collect this particular debt, my lord." She jabbed at him with the poker, and he fumbled behind his back for the door latch.

It wasn't until he was out the door and his footsteps had faded into faint echoes, that she thought of the consequences certain to follow. She lowered the poker and buried her face in her palm. What on earth would Chance say?

Hobson lowered his voice to almost a whisper. "I have some vital information for you, my lord."

Chance looked up from the ledgers his steward had given him the day before; the lists of sheep and cattle and marketable crops was no competition for the murmur of excitement in Hobson's voice.

"Tell me, Hobson, before you explode."

"It seems that there is to be an exchange of written lists detailing the names of English men sympathetic to Napoleon." His eyes glittered when Chance made a low exclamation. "Exactly, my lord. These are men in high places, in Parliament and privy to critical information concerning national security."

"Do you know when and where the lists are to be given?"

Hobson nodded, his face creased with suppressed excitement. "The Bull and Bear, out on the north road at midnight. I understand that Lord Heffington is to meet with Roxbury there."

"Heffington." Chance smiled. "Perfect. How did you come by this information, may I ask?"

"The servants, of course. I took the liberty of gaining employment for one of my great-nephews in Lord Heffington's household, and he is a very resourceful lad who knows how to listen at closed doors. He sent me a message not a half hour ago." Hobson gave a little frown. "But you must realize that there is the same risk in our own household, no matter how carefully we may guard against it."

"Which is why I take great pains to leave no written messages unburned, and why you and I converse in my inner study with the doors closed." Chance rose. "You have taken every precaution, I am certain."

"Of course, my lord."

"We need to make plans, then, and—"

A knock at the door interrupted him, and Hobson crossed the room and opened it. After a brief hum of questions, he stood back and allowed Riever into the study. Chance eyed the servant with a lifted brow. Normally unflappable, the young man looked quite perturbed.

Before Chance could question him, a stream of words poured out. When Riever finally paused for breath, Chance nodded.

"You did well, Riever." Chance was already striding toward the door, not waiting for his servant to follow. He took the riding jacket Hobson held out, and asked over his shoulder, "You say Roxbury looked angry?"

"Aye, my lord, he did look a bit put out. I fancied he was attempting to goad Miss Llewellyn into some sort of reaction, though I could be mistaken."

"Probably not." Chance took the stairs down two at a time. Damn Roxbury. If he was trying to coerce Rhianna into marrying him by holding her father's debts over her head, he certainly wouldn't pause at a little intimidation. He should have already taken care of the viscount, but to do so might have alerted him to more important suspicions. *Damn.* If Roxbury had done one thing to harm Rhianna. . . .

He couldn't even finish the thought. It wasn't until he was at Serenity House and ignoring Fenwick's efforts to show him into the front parlor that he allowed himself to contemplate what might have happened. And then he had almost to laugh.

Rhianna looked up from a sheaf of papers scattered over a small table, an expression of mild surprise on her face.

"Chance. What brings you out this afternoon?"

He stopped, feeling faintly foolish and a bit theatrical. "I had the notion that you might need my help," he said dryly and heard Fenwick chuckle behind him. When he turned to look at the servant, the man was shutting the parlor door behind him. He turned back to Rhianna.

"I understand that Roxbury was here."

"Yes. For a short time, though his visit seemed much too long to me." She stood up, catching a loose paper that threatened to fall to the floor before straightening. Her mouth was curved in a smile, her eyes alight with amusement. The low bodice of the blue muslin she wore attracted his attention to the golden skin of her exposed bosom, and he felt himself staring like a schoolboy. When she laughed and said, "Did you think me in danger, perhaps?" he glanced up at her face again.

"The thought did occur to me. I see you're not."

"Not now, anyway. I think the vicious viscount did want to throttle me, but I prevailed."

Chance stared at her narrowly, his voice tight. "Did he attempt to harm you in any way?"

"I never gave him the opportunity." She moved toward him in a graceful glide, the pleated hem of her skirt seeming to flow around her slender ankles. The gown made her look exotic, with her hair down in loose curls around her face like a Greek goddess. His immediate response was purely physical, when he knew he should be thinking of other things. He made a disgruntled sound, and she tilted her head to look up at him.

"Are you upset, Chance?"

"No. Worried for you." That much was true. He worried what would happen if Roxbury guessed how much she meant to him. It would be too easy to use her against him, and he knew it. The knowledge made him irritable.

Rhianna slid her arms around his waist and lay her cheek against his chest. He heard her sigh softly before she murmured, "Don't be too angry with me, but I'm afraid I've made an enemy of him."

"Why would I be angry about that? I considered him an enemy already."

She tilted her head back to gaze up at him and he put his arms around her and held her close. Her body seemed to just melt into his, flowing in soft curves against his belly and thighs with a heat that provoked immediate response. He closed his eyes and pressed his forehead against hers. Enough of this. He had to think, had to plan for the night, not indulge himself with memories and fantasies of Rhianna.

"Why do you two hate each other?" she asked softly, and he drew back to look at her.

"Roxbury represents everything I hate most. He's a liar, a thief, and he has no scruples about doing whatever it takes to get what he wants. He'd hurt you without compunction if it would benefit him."

She frowned. "Granted, he's not the bravest of men. He did turn early in a duel, and it's been said that he's cheated at cards so often he's not allowed at gentlemen's gaming tables. Until today, I never thought he meant me harm."

"Until today?" Chance curled his hands around her upper arms and pushed her to arm's length. "What changed your mind about him today?"

"His superior attitude. The way he seemed to think I would do what he bade me whether I liked it or not. There was no consideration for my feelings or my father's health. He wants to marry me, but I don't think he told me the real reason."

"I think," Chance said slowly, "that it has to do with his mistaken notion that you would lend him respectability."

"Respectability? Me?" She laughed. "Then he has chosen the wrong woman as his wife—considering my birth and lack of *breeding.*"

He recognized the hurt beneath her light tone and pulled her close to him again. Spreading his hand against the back of her head, he stroked her silky hair with gentle motions. He could feel her heart beating; it thudded with the energy of a frightened rabbit. His embrace tightened.

He looked down at her. "It seems that the viscount has been meddling in areas he should not, and I've come into information that will incriminate him."

"Good. He frightens me, with his threats against my father and me." She shuddered. "He intends to put us in debtor's prison if I do not marry him." She looked up at Chance. "What kind of information do you have? Is he planning to overthrow the monarchy? Storm the gates of London?"

"Nothing quite so world shattering. I'm not at liberty to discuss the details, but I can assure you that Roxbury is not the sort of companion you should seek."

"Odd, he said the same thing about you."

Chance scowled. "Devil take him."

Her arms lifted to curl around his neck. "The devil probably doesn't want him. Neither do I, so don't frown so darkly at me. You look positively ferocious when you do." A smile curved her lips. "Since you came to rescue the damsel in distress and the dragon has already been vanquished, can you linger awhile?"

"Temptress."

"Only with you, my lord."

Her mouth brushed over his lips, and for a few minutes he forgot all the reasons he'd rushed to her aid. It wasn't until they were seated on the settee near the fireplace and he'd settled her on his lap with her head nestled under his chin, that he could remember his sense of perspective. He took a deep breath.

"Rhianna, I want you to be extremely careful in the next few days."

"Why?" Her voice was lazy and soft, almost sleepy. She tucked her fingers into his open shirt where she'd worked loose some of the buttons and dragged her fingertips over his bare skin until he kissed her again.

Then he grabbed her hand and held it still, forcing her chin up so that she was looking into his eyes. "Listen, you little minx, stop doing that kind of thing so I can think. I am very serious—can you and your father go away for a while? Go somewhere distant from here?"

She frowned. "Has the sheriff found out—?"

He put his hand over her lips. "Don't say anything. No. Not that I'm aware of, at any rate. It's just that I have some things to do, and I'll feel better if I know you're safe. I can worry about business instead of Roxbury and you."

She sat up suddenly, eyes flashing indignantly. "Do you honestly think I would—"

"No, no, nothing like that. I don't trust Roxbury, that's all."

"Neither do I. But after today, I think I can take care of him easily enough." She gave a soft laugh. "I backed him out of here with a poker, all the way into the front hall. He exhibited no backbone at all."

Chance had to grin at the image her words provoked but still shook his head. "Even a frightened puppy will bite. No, I insist that you leave Wiltshire for a while. I'll send my coach for you and your father in the morning. Take whatever servants you wish to take." He cupped her chin when she started to protest, fingers tightening. "But be discreet. Take only your most loyal, *trusted* servants, like Fenwick."

Her brows dipped over her eyes, and her lashes made long shadows on her cheeks as she absorbed his warning. It was apparent that he was beginning to frighten her, and he wasn't certain that was at all bad. Maybe a little judicious fear would make her more cautious.

"Do you want me out of the way for some definite reason, Chance?"

"Obviously."

"Does this have something to do with the Moon Rider?"

"Perhaps."

She shoved the heels of her hands against his chest and lurched to her feet. "You're being too mysterious. You just want to ride out again, and you don't want to risk me showing up. Isn't there enough adventure in more mundane pastimes? Do you have to play the devil again? Tell me the truth—that's it, isn't it?"

"Not entirely." He stood up, his voice cooler than he felt. "You'll have to trust me, Rhianna."

He thought of what he knew, the information that Hobson had given him earlier about Roxbury. It would be over soon, and then perhaps he could examine his feelings about Rhianna more closely. But now—now he had to focus on the danger at hand.

"Very well," Rhianna was saying, "I'll trust you. But you must also trust me."

"I do."

"Then confide your plans to me."

He blew out an exasperated breath. "Not when it might endanger you unnecessarily."

"Devil take you then."

Hands on hips, she glared up at him with so pugnacious and ferocious an expression that he almost laughed, which would have been a grave tactical error. He managed to keep from laughing, or even smiling.

Jabbing her finger into his chest, Rhianna demanded, "Do you think me incapable? You might need me. If there's trouble, I can help."

"If there's trouble," he said dryly, "you're quite likely

going to be the cause of it. I seem to recall a few narrow escapes of yours."

She stiffened. "If I remember correctly, I held you at bay with my sword for a time one night."

"Not for long and only because I allowed it."

"Oh, of course you'd say that! What man would admit that a woman might be able to match him?"

"Only a man unable to fight back. Rhianna." He took her arm when she whirled away angrily. "Listen to me. It's only my concern for you that makes me reluctant to include you. I don't trust Roxbury. And I don't trust the men he employs. If that angers you, I'm sorry, but you won't change my mind."

"Very well." She met his gaze steadily. "I won't try to change your mind."

He stared at her with growing suspicion. She had capitulated too easily. His eyes narrowed. "You won't do anything foolish?"

"Did I say I would?"

"No, but there are a great many things you've done that you've neglected to mention beforehand."

She slid her arms around his waist, burying her face against his chest. He could feel the warm press of her breath on his skin. Her voice was muffled by the folds of his opened shirt.

"I won't do anything foolish, Chance."

For some reason, he didn't feel in the least bit comforted by her promise.

Chapter 20

"Are you certain you want to go out this late, miss?" Fenwick looked at Rhianna doubtfully.

"Just have the coach brought 'round, please. I won't be gone long, I'm sure."

Fenwick still hesitated. "I don't feel right about you going out alone. Lord Wolverton insisted you not leave here without an escort."

She gave him an impatient glance, but noted the genuine concern in his eyes and sighed. "Very well. I'll take an escort with me." When Fenwick nodded with a smile of relief, she added, "Oh, and send Porter to me, if you will."

"Porter?"

"Yes. I'll take him as my escort."

"Very good, miss."

Porter. Rhianna frowned slightly. She'd been more than a little surprised when the servant had come to her with the startling information that he'd overheard one of the other servants talking about accompanying the earl of Wolverton to The Bull and Bear late this evening. It was supposed to be very secretive, but Porter had thought his mistress should know about it.

"I don't much hold with employees taking advantage of those good enough to employ them in these hard times, miss," he'd said quietly. "And it rather upset me that Denton would leave your service at the earl's beck and call."

"Well, the earl did place him in my employment." She'd paused. "Did you happen to hear why the earl wishes Denton to go with him?"

"Not all of it, miss. Just something about a meeting with the viscount, I believe."

Roxbury. No moonlight raids, as she'd thought, but a confrontation with the viscount that was certain to end badly. Damn Chance, he should have told her about it!

It hadn't taken her long to make her decision to go despite Chance's pains to keep her away. For some reason, she felt the burning need to be there. She didn't stop to question her motives beyond that point, didn't dwell on the possibility that it might really be dangerous. After all, she'd ridden the high roads as the Moon Rider, hadn't she? Been shot at, even crossed swords with a guard or two?

What on earth could happen that she couldn't handle?

The wind promised rain; the sign proclaiming the inn to be The Bull and Bear swung wildly, making a creaking noise. Chance paused beneath it, shuffling his feet in hobnailed boots that were ill-fitting and clumsy. He wore a loose sweater and coarse coat, and a knitted cap covered his hair.

A lantern flickered erratically, casting swaying pools of dim light over stone stoop and ivy-covered walls. When he stepped inside, gusts of smoke and the smell of cooked cabbage assaulted him, along with the faintly sour smell of unwashed bodies. It took a moment for his eyes to adjust, but he finally saw whom he sought in a far corner. Shadows darkened the table where no lamplight reached, but he caught the faint gleam of a pale linen bonnet.

He moved to the table and sat down. His companion kept eyes lowered, hands folded beneath the table. The long vertical brim of the bonnet half-hid the face; only a hint of cheek and jaw could be seen. Chance leaned close.

"Is everything ready?" The bonnet bobbed, and he gave a satisfied grunt of approval. "There will be an extra quid in this for you if all goes well."

"I don't need an extra quid," came the husky, irritated reply. "I'm doing this for king and country, not profit."

Chance shrugged. "Well, you look quite fetching in that bonnet, I must say."

A quick lift of the head and flash of indignant eyes, and Hobson lowered his face again, making a muffled sound of offense. Chance leaned back against the wall behind him. He had to stifle a grin.

Smoke drifted in layers, coming from open fire and kitchen as well as from a few pipe-smokers. It stung his eyes, and he rubbed them with thumb and forefinger. He felt Hobson shift, and heard his mutter of vexation.

"Careful," he murmured, "or the village folk will begin to think we're married, with you grumbling and fussing like an old hen."

Hobson said softly, "Your humor is as ill-advised as your disguise as an itinerant fisherman, my lord."

"No doubt. But we are rather inconspicuous, which is a necessity. I'd like to have this bloody night over with as soon as possible." He glanced toward the door when it opened and let in a gust of fresh air that smelled of rain. "Ah," he said with satisfaction, and Hobson followed his gaze.

Lord Heffington stood just inside the door, brushing rain from his greatcoat and muttering about the weather.

"I believe," Chance observed, "that half of our pair of plotters has arrived at last. I trust that Riever and the others will wait for our signal before acting."

"Quite so, my lord."

Heffington moved to a table in the far corner, where shadows shrouded the occupants.

Time passed, and the common room grew less crowded. Rain spit against the windows. Each time the door opened, the wind snatched at it. Chance crossed his arms on the rough, scarred table and sipped at another pitcher of ale, waiting. Occasionally, Hobson—in his disguise as a goodwife—would offer a shrill comment before lapsing back into his own mug of ale.

More than an hour had passed before Roxbury finally entered the common room and immediately crossed to Heffington. Nerves stretched taut, Chance kept his head down as he watched them. The pair spoke in low tones, heads together across the table. After a few minutes of discussion, Heffington pushed a small packet of papers to Roxbury.

Chance felt a spurt of anger. Roxbury he could almost understand; after all, the man was of French descent. But Heffington was English. Had he no patriotism? Could he so easily betray his country to a man intent on ruling all of Europe?

Realizing that his hands were balled into fists, he slowly relaxed them. No matter. He would get the proof he needed to remove two more threats to England, and let those higher up take care of the rest. It was little enough to do, but sometimes the smallest links could weaken the entire chain of espionage.

Roxbury and Heffington spoke quietly for a few more minutes. The door opened again, cool air whisking into the room and making some of the patrons call out a demand to fill the opening with solid oak. Chance glanced at the doorway, then muttered an oath.

"Look," Hobson whispered, and Chance nodded.

"Bloody hell. What else can go wrong?"

"Do you see who—?"

"I see. What in the blazes is George doing here? And with *her,* for God's sake."

"P'raps he won't notice you."

But that hope was quickly extinguished when Keswick gave a cheery *halloo* and started toward their table.

"I say, Wolf, what the deuce are you doing dressed like a sailor? I almost didn't recognize you. Is this some sort of penance, perhaps?"

Keswick's round face wore an expression of frowning curiosity. The lady with him, however, looked coolly serene.

"How pleasant to see you again, Wolverton," Lady Thalia Wimberley purred. "Is this a masquerade? I'm devastated that I wasn't invited along, but then, you haven't kept in touch lately."

"No." Chance could see Roxbury across the room with Heffington, staring in their direction. He gave up any hope of quietly detaining Roxbury and the vital papers without alerting half the county of his actions. Several options flitted through his mind before he rejected them as too violent and not at all viable. He looked at Lady Wimberley. "What are you doing out on a rainy night like this?"

His glance shifted to Keswick, who lifted his shoulders in a shrug as if to say he didn't know either. Lady Wimberley tucked her hand under Keswick's arm and smiled.

"I coaxed George out with promises of entertainment."

"Actually," Keswick said, "with assurances that I

would find you here, Wolf. And that you needed me. What's going on?"

"Did she?" Chance's brow lifted. "Well, George, perhaps you should direct that question to your charming companion. Maybe she will enlighten you." His eyes narrowed as he raked Thalia with a searching gaze. She looked like a smug cat, and he felt a prickle of alarm.

"But your clothes—hardly suitable for your rank, old boy," George was saying in a puzzled tone. "Is this a new game, perhaps?"

Lady Wimberley laughed softly, and before Chance could stop her, seated herself on his lap. His muscles tightened. He started to push her away, but she caught him by the lapels of his rough coat, a strange smile on her lips that made him pause.

"It is a game of wits," she said gaily. "How intriguing. Let me see . . ." She placed a fingertip on her chin and tilted her head as if to consider. "You're garbed as a fisherman, my lord, so that must mean that you are here to find new sport. Am I correct?"

Lady Wimberley's gaze slid past Chance to the bonneted figure sitting with head lowered to hide the face, and he saw speculation darken her eyes.

"No, Thalia," he said coolly, "I am here to conduct business—which you are interrupting."

"Business? With your lovely companion?" She bent slightly as if to see under the long folds of bonnet hiding Hobson's face. "I have heard much of your new love. Have you taken to donning disguises to escape the latest gossip, my lord? How cowardly. You really should be more open."

When her hand flashed out to tip up the bonnet, Chance caught her wrist, his fingers digging into her skin with a harsh grasp. She gasped in pain. After a moment, he released her arm and shoved her roughly from his lap.

"I suggest that you and George seek your own table. You are not welcome here."

Keswick looked mortified. "So sorry to have intruded, Wolf. See that it's not a good time. Can't think why she insisted. But never mind. Come along, Thalia. Can't you see we're not wanted here?"

Thalia Wimberley glared down at Chance for a moment. He saw the fury in her eyes. He stood up, towering over her, his suspicions rising when she gave him a sly glance.

There was a malicious sparkle in her eyes. "My lord, must you and your charming companion leave so soon?"

"I have a feeling that you are well aware of my reason for leaving as well as my reason for being here, my lady," he observed softly.

"Quite so." She leaned forward, voice lowered so that only he could hear her. "I took your advice, Chance. I found a replacement for you."

He glanced from her toward Roxbury and saw a faint smile curve the viscount's mouth.

"Ah, I see. Not very discriminating of you, Thalia."

"That depends, of course, on what you think I want in a man."

Chance gave her a nasty smile. "Availability must be your main requirement. Which, as you age, comes in shorter and shorter supply, I would think."

She stiffened, gasping with rage. "You bastard! You won't be so smug in a few minutes, I'll wager."

Beyond her, he could see Roxbury standing and looking in their direction. There was something unusual here, and he suspected that Thalia had been sent to delay him. Roxbury would seize the distraction she provided and slip out before he could stop him.

Chance moved instinctively. Whatever else happened, he had to keep Roxbury from getting away with those papers. He moved past Lady Wimberley. She caught at his sleeve, voice rising.

"Lord Wolverton! You must not say those things about my husband!"

Chance saw that several patrons of the inn had turned to listen, and fought a rising wave of fury. He kept his voice low. "Get out of my way, Thalia."

She blocked his progress, eyes glittering with malicious delight. "But my lord," she said in the same high-pitched voice, "If you go to duel my husband, poor Robert will not have any defense against you and you know it. Please say you won't kill him. . . ."

More had turned to stare, and angry mutters grew louder in the crowded room. "Lower your voice," Chance said tightly, but knew she would not obey.

Clutching at his sleeve even while he tried to remove her hand, Lady Wimberley clung to him like a burr in wool, attracting even more attention. His reputation made matters worse, of course, and he could see the distrust and dislike in some of the eyes turned toward him. Chance took her firmly by the arms and shoved her toward Keswick.

"Hold her, George."

Chance heard Hobson mutter something and turned to see Roxbury move toward the door. He started after him. The door to the inn swung open, and Roxbury stepped back. Rain swept in with the wind, dampening the floor and the men standing in the opening.

Flanked by two burly men, Sheriff Hamlin shut the door behind him. Chance glanced toward Roxbury, who was smiling with expectation, not apprehension. Damn. He should have considered that Roxbury might try something like this; he had the chilling sensation of a trap being sprung and took a backward step toward the kitchen.

But when he turned, a man moved from the back of the inn. He held a pistol in one hand and had the unmistakable aura of constabulary about him. Damn Roxbury.

Sheriff Hamlin tugged off his wet hat and slapped it against his thigh, eyeing Chance for a long moment before turning to Roxbury.

"Well, my lord? You sent a message saying it is vital that I join you here. Is this the man?"

"I believe," Roxbury began, "that you need to make an arrest."

Rhianna sat silently; Porter sat opposite her in the coach. Rain beat against the roof and sides, and the vehicle made slow progress on the rutted, muddy roads. She fought a wave of impatience, wondering if she would be in time to keep Chance from challenging Roxbury. She clenched her hands in her lap, rehearsing several eloquent pleas to stop the inevitable confrontation. No risk was worth losing Chance, not even Roxbury's insults to her.

"Are you certain you want to be out on a night like this, milady?" Porter muttered, grabbing at the wall strap when the coach lurched violently into another rut.

She nodded. "Yes. It is a necessity, as you must know since you were the one to tell me about it."

"Aye, but I didn't think you'd be draggin' me along with you."

She eyed him for a moment. Porter had turned out to be most unwilling to accompany her, a fact that was surprising as well as annoying. She'd not wanted to confide in Fenwick, knowing that he disapproved and would probably warn Chance that she intended to try to stop him. Porter had seemed the logical choice.

"Well, I did bring you with me," she said flatly, and

turned to stare out the small, fogged glass of the window. A gust of wind sent rain against the windows, filtering through the cracks to dampen the interior. Porter was probably right. She should have stayed home. It was unlikely that Chance would listen to her, even if she managed by some miracle to arrive in time to keep him and Roxbury from dueling.

She peered out the window as an occasional cottage light came into view, and rebuttoned her gloves. "Cheer up, Porter. We are almost at The Bull and Bear."

Porter made a muffled sound, and she glanced up at him. He was huddled in his greatcoat, a picture of misery in the corner. Despite his surly attitude, she was glad he'd come along. The Moon Rider was not the only highwayman lurking about at nights.

Porter seemed to echo her thoughts, his tone slightly nasty as he said, "We'll be lucky not to be stopped on a night like this, miss. Any bloke would be happy to get his hands on that pearl necklace you're wearin'."

"P'raps I should remove it then," she said coolly, not liking his tone nor his attitude. "It seems to bother you a great deal."

"Aye, lying there around your neck like a string of white moons, it's liable to cause as much trouble for you as it has the earl."

He stopped suddenly, and Rhianna frowned. "What do you mean by that?"

Porter looked away from her, his tone sullen. "Nothing, miss. I spoke out of turn."

"We need to reach The Bull and Bear," she said after a moment.

He nodded. "We're almost there, miss."

• • •

The inn was quiet. Only the faint pop and hiss of logs in the fire could be heard for several shocked moments as those crowded into the common room stopped everything to listen. Chance cocked a brow at the sheriff.

"Are you here in an official capacity, sir?"

Hamlin looked uneasy as he glanced at Roxbury then back to Chance. "Aye," he muttered. "I have some questions I must ask you, my lord."

Chance nodded. "I can well imagine. And I can also guess who suggested you ask them." He glanced at Roxbury.

"My lord," Hamlin said, "I have been given the information that the highwayman's horse we have in our possession is yours. Do you deny it?"

"Of course I deny it. Where did you get such inaccurate information, may I ask?"

Sheriff Hamlin scowled. "I am not at liberty to say."

"No doubt. Perhaps the viscount can enlighten us. I have the inescapable feeling that he is somehow involved in this farce tonight."

Roxbury didn't look at all perturbed, but met Chance's gaze with a faint smile tugging at his mouth. "Don't waste the good sheriff's time with wild improbabilities, Wolverton. It should be plain to any who care to see, that you are well caught."

"Caught? At what?"

After glancing around the crowded common room, Roxbury looked back at Chance with the same maddening smile. "Why, caught at riding the moors on the nights of a full moon, of course. *N'est-ce pas?*"

"No," Chance said coldly, "what you are inferring is not at all the truth. Where is your proof to offer the sheriff, if you claim to know it."

"Aye," Sheriff Hamlin said, stepping forward. "Give

me your proof, Lord Roxbury, and we shall be done with this."

Chance looked from Roxbury to Hamlin and suddenly understood. If he did the logical thing and exposed Roxbury as a spy, it would be viewed as a desperate and ludicrous attempt to cast suspicion elsewhere. Roxbury did not seem at all worried about a public denouement, which could only mean that he did not have the incriminating papers on him. This entire scene was indeed a farce, meant to draw Chance's attention away from the passing of the papers elsewhere. He had allowed his dislike of Roxbury and his attentions to Rhianna to distract him, and this was his retribution.

Bloody hell, he thought without rancor. Those papers were being passed elsewhere tonight, while he was caught here trying to defend himself. And Roxbury knew it. This scene provided the viscount with the perfect alibi against any later accusations. He—or someone else—had planned it most cleverly.

Roxbury smiled. "First, why doesn't Lord Wolverton explain his reasons for being at this inn in such a ridiculous disguise? Does he have something to hide?" Roxbury's smile didn't falter, even when one of the men sitting at a table made a rude noise.

" 'Ere now," someone spoke up, "maybe the earl ain't got to 'ave a reason for bein' about dressed so roughly. Why would 'e need to explain anything to a Frenchie anyway?"

"How about explaining it to me," Sheriff Hamlin said with a scowl. "And don't be so testy, lad. This is none of your affair."

"Maybe not," the man agreed, "but I don't hold with wild accusations made against an Englishman, even if 'e do be the devil earl."

There was a low mutter of agreement in the room, and Lord Roxbury's smile faded.

Chance turned his head to see Hobson gazing at him from across the room. He gave a slight nod of his head in response to Hobson's lifted brow, then turned his attention back to the sheriff and Roxbury. Hobson slipped silently from the common room into the hallway, but was halted by one of the sheriff's constables. After a moment, Hobson was allowed to continue, with the constable at his side.

"Your evidence, my lord?" Chance repeated, fixing the viscount with a steady gaze. "Come on with it. We are all anxious to hear what irrefutable proof you have that will verify I am responsible for the robberies you seem to think I have committed."

"I have an eyewitness who will swear to having seen you in your disguise as the Moon Rider," Roxbury said softly.

"I say!" Keswick exclaimed indignantly. "That simply cannot be!"

"Can't it?" Roxbury turned to Lady Wimberley. "Perhaps the baroness can tell us differently."

Lady Wimberley's malicious smile did nothing to ease Chance's growing suspicions. "Indeed, I can certainly tell you quite a few things, Sheriff Hamlin," she said smoothly. "Lord Wolverton took refuge at my house one night in his guise as the Moon Rider. I vow, I was terrified at the time. If he had not threatened me, I would have told you long before now. It was Lord Roxbury who assured me that you would not let harm come to me or my husband if I told what I knew. . . ."

"Preposterous!" Keswick spluttered. "You've always had a vicious tongue, Lady Wimberley. You merely wish to discredit the earl because he threw you over."

Chance shifted position, and Lady Wimberley gave

him a swift glance of apprehension before turning her attention back to Keswick.

"Lord Wolverton has already discredited himself, as well as you," Lady Wimberley said smoothly. She eased from George's grasp, and he let her go. "You are in this just as deeply, my lord."

Keswick stared at her with an open mouth. "Whatever do you mean?"

"Did you not offer the earl and his—lady—shelter recently?"

"Why yes, but that has nothing to do with—"

"I'll decide what it has to do with this," Hamlin broke in. "Were they in disguise, my lord?"

"Disguise?" Keswick looked bewildered. "No, of course not. Wolf—Lord Wolverton—was dressed simply, but he was not in disguise."

"And Miss Llewellyn?"

Keswick gave Chance an imploring glance, and he shook his head slightly. Poor Keswick. Too honest to lie cleverly, too loyal for his protests to be believed. The perfect witness against him. Oh yes, Roxbury had planned well for this certain conviction.

Chance said kindly, "Tell the truth, George. It really does not matter at this point."

"She was . . . was garbed in breeches."

"Ah." Hamlin smiled with satisfaction. "Breeches. Dark breeches and a shirt, perhaps? Such as the person who shot the king's guard wore?"

"Really, Sheriff. . . ." Keswick looked miserable. "They had been out riding, and Miss Llewellyn's horse bolted. She was unseated."

Hamlin turned to the innkeeper, who was listening avidly. "I believe they stayed here that night, did they not?"

The innkeeper nodded. "Aye, that they did. No baggage. Said as how her horse ran off. Same story they gave to his lordship there."

George shifted from one foot to the other, his open face too honest to hide his sudden discomfort. "Yes, that is true, but that does not mean it is the same horse that was used in a robbery—"

"Sheriff," Roxbury interrupted, "will you do your duty and arrest the earl on suspicion? Or is it only the common man who must suffer the indignity of being questioned?"

"Right you are, Lord Roxbury," Sheriff Hamlin said with a tight smile. "Come along, Lord Wolverton. There are plenty of questions that need to be answered. . . ."

Keswick began a heated protest that drew others in the room into discussion. The noise of excited opinions grew louder. Chance listened with a faint smile, and crossed his arms over his chest as he leaned back against a wall.

He saw the growing chagrin tighten Roxbury's face, and knew that the viscount had not expected any of the villagers to defend the "devil earl." Sheriff Hamlin was shouting and red-faced, and his constables began to grow uneasy.

". . . viscount or earl, a man is subject to the laws of this country," Hamlin was shouting. "If I say the earl goes to jail, go he does!"

Chance straightened. He saw one of the constables turn toward him and knew that he would be taken into custody. He had the brief hope that Hobson would manage to escape or at least alert Riever as to this unexpected reversal of their plans before the constable reached him and began to shackle his wrists.

"Sheriff," he began, but was interrupted by the door to the inn swinging open with a loud bang. A gust of wind and rain swept into the common room. Chance turned, then smothered a curse.

Rhianna stepped into the room, flinging back the rain-damp hood to her cloak. Even her gown beneath the wool cloak was wet, and she shook the skirts free of rain, glancing around the room with growing apprehension until her eyes found Chance. As her servant quietly shut the door, she took several steps forward into the smoky, strained silence.

Her eyes widened when she saw the shackles on his wrists. There was a slight quiver in her voice as she asked, "Chance, what is going on here?"

Roxbury laughed softly, then stepped forward to take her by one arm. "Here is irrefutable proof, Sheriff," he said, holding her tightly when Rhianna attempted to jerk away from him. "These." He pulled aside one fold of her cloak and touched the pearls circling her throat. "Do you not recognize these?"

"Aye, it's a string of pearls," Hamlin snapped in an exasperated tone. "What of it?"

Roxbury smiled. "By amazing coincidence, I believe that Miss Llewellyn reported these stolen by the Moon Rider. Now here they are. Do you not see the unusual clasp?"

Rhianna stood in stiff, shocked silence as Roxbury unfastened the clasp of her pearls and held them up. The pale strand caught the light from a lamp as they swung from the viscount's hand.

Chance started forward, but one of the sheriff's men put out a hand to stop him. He saw the angry confusion in Rhianna's face alter to fear.

"What—? No, you are mistaken. Release my arm, Lord Roxbury."

"After you explain to the sheriff how you came by these pearls, Miss Llewellyn." Roxbury's mouth curled in a faint smile. "Aren't they the same ones you claimed were stolen by the Moon Rider?"

Sheriff Hamlin stepped close to examine the necklace, then gave it back to Roxbury. "Aye, this is the necklace that was described to me. Has the same unusual clasp."

Rhianna succeeded in jerking away from Roxbury, then darted a glance at Chance. He dared not react with everyone watching so closely. She drew in a deep breath and gave a careless shrug. "What of it? Was I supposed to inform the sheriff that I found my own necklace for sale in a private shop and bought it back?"

"So you say." Hamlin's mouth curled into a sneer. "Who had it?"

"Why . . . I don't recall the name of the shop offhand, but I'm certain I have a receipt somewhere." Rhianna glanced at Chance again. He saw the frightened wariness in her eyes.

"I think," Roxbury said smoothly, "that Miss Llewellyn's arrival here was most opportune, sheriff."

"Aye," Hamlin said with a satisfied smile. He swept a gaze around the now quiet common room. "You've all heard the accusations here, and I'll have no saying later that this was not done without proper procedure, lads. And you, Lord Keswick, will be a witness for the prosecution when this case comes to trial."

Keswick gave a slow shake of his head. "I don't know that I am convinced of Wolverton's guilt, Sheriff Hamlin." There was a murmur of agreement in the common room that swelled to a loud buzz when Keswick added, "It still seems to me to be only one man's word against another man's, with a string of improbable circumstances that could be merely coincidence."

"Rubbish," Hamlin said rudely, shouting to be heard over the rumble of voices.

Roxbury beckoned the servant who had accompanied Rhianna to come forward. "Perhaps this man can convince these skeptics, Sheriff. I placed him in Miss Llewellyn's employ when I became suspicious of her close association with the earl. Step up, Porter, and tell us what you have in your possession."

"Certainly, Lord Roxbury." Porter ignored Rhianna's soft exclamation as he said calmly, "I have in my possession certain garments of the lady's that might interest you."

"Garments?" Hamlin looked at Rhianna with grim satisfaction. "Pray, describe them to me."

Roxbury smiled. "These are most unusual garments, sheriff. Pure white, with a long cape and silk mask. . . ."

Chance darted a glance at Rhianna and saw her sudden fright. Damn—she'd not destroyed her costume as he'd told her, and somehow Roxbury had come by it. *Damn, damn, damn.*

Chapter 21

Rain wet the stones in front of The Bull and Bear and seeped under the collar of Rhianna's cloak as she sat quietly atop a horse. Hamlin was mounted beside her, arguing impatiently with Viscount Keswick. She shivered in the damp chill.

"But I insist, Sheriff." Viscount Keswick barred Hamlin's progress, having planted himself in front of the sheriff's horse with the apparent intention of remaining there. He was stubbornly firm despite Hamlin's blustering arguments. He fixed the sheriff with a steady gaze, a reminder of aristocracy at its most arrogant.

Hamlin capitulated. "Very well," he growled, "but you will be the one to wake the magistrate at this hour. Elliot won't like it above half, I'll tell you that much."

"But he will wake for me," Keswick said calmly. "My family is well known to him."

"No doubt." Disgruntled, Hamlin made no effort to hide his irritation. "The earl, however, is being escorted to the town of Avebury to be held until he can be convicted."

"Or cleared."

"Aye," Hamlin sneered, "or cleared."

"No!" Rhianna blurted out, and both men turned to look at her. She leaned forward, desperation making her tense. "Lord Keswick, please do not leave Chance at the mercy of these men."

Keswick looked startled, his round face damp and shiny in the lamplight. He stepped close to her horse and looked up at her. "I assure you that Wolverton will be well cared for, Miss Llewellyn. No one would dare harm an earl, no matter the charges against him. I merely seek to ensure that you will receive the same fair treatment."

"But . . ." She paused, feeling faintly foolish. How could she say that she felt Hamlin was not trustworthy? It was silly and she knew, in light of her own part in this, it would be viewed as a ludicrous attempt to draw attention away from herself.

Keswick gave her a comforting smile. "Here, here, Miss Llewellyn. All that can be done will be done. You must know that I will seek only the best barrister for Wolverton."

Rhianna could not escape the feeling of impending doom that loomed over her. She nodded mutely and looked up to see Hamlin staring at her with narrowed eyes. She shivered again and it had nothing to do with the chill wind and rain.

"As you say, Lord Keswick," she murmured helplessly.

"Come along then." Hamlin gave Keswick a curt nod and spurred his mount forward, dragging Rhianna's horse behind. She had no choice but to follow, clutching at the saddle with her bound hands to keep her balance. Porter rode close behind. It was all she could do to keep from lashing out at him with vile epithets. To think she had believed in him enough to take him into her employ, and this was how she was repaid. . . .

As if reading her mind, Porter murmured, "Not quite what you expected of me, hey?"

She gave him a cold stare. "Not quite."

He laughed softly and tugged at the bill of his hat. "I

daresay. But, one must go where the money pays best, you know."

"If one is dishonest and unscrupulous, I should imagine so." She turned her head and did not allow Porter to provoke her into speech again. Not until she saw the magistrate's half-beamed house looming up in the rainy night did she speak and then it was only a sort of wordless moan.

Jail. She'd heard of the dire consequences of going to prison and did not anticipate any sympathy from the magistrate despite Keswick's assurances. He would not view the gypsy daughter of the baronet in a kind light, she was certain.

Magistrate Elliot seemed more than disgruntled at being pulled from his warm bed on a chill, rainy night. He glared at them over the rim of his spectacles as he motioned them into his study and closed the door. The lamp in his hand distorted his face in varying degrees of light and shadow, and cast shallow threads of light as Elliot grumbled.

"What are you doing here on a night like this, Hamlin? If it's another of your harebrained notions, I won't take it well at all."

Hamlin stiffened, obviously affronted. When Elliot was seated behind his desk, Hamlin cleared his throat. "I daresay you shall think it important when you hear the details, sir."

"So cease your melodramatics and tell them."

Rhianna didn't resist when the sheriff pulled her forward, yanking the hood from her cloak to reveal her face. He held her arm tightly.

"I have arrested this woman as being an accomplice to the Moon Rider."

"Yes," Keswick interrupted, "but he is wrong, sir."

"Who are you?" Elliot peered narrowly at Keswick in the dim light.

"George Harland Gladwin, Viscount Keswick, your honor. You are familiar with my family, I believe."

"Ah yes, so I am." Elliot paused, frown deepening. "Why are you here tonight, my lord?"

"To assist Miss Llewellyn and the earl. I have known the earl for many years, and—"

"The earl? What earl? What does an earl have to do with this drivel about a slip of a girl being the Moon Rider?"

"You misunderstand, sir," Hamlin began, giving Keswick a furious glance. "She is an accomplice to—"

Keswick's voice overrode Hamlin's. "Wolverton, but it is all a mistake—"

Elliot's fist slammed against the desktop. "Enough! It is late, much too late to be bombarded with wild accusations about highwaymen. Or women, as the case may be."

"Your honor," Hamlin said impatiently, "I presented you with detailed information earlier, listing my reasons for the imminent arrest of the earl of Wolverton. Do you not recall?"

"No, I do not recall. Are you certain this information was directed to me, Sheriff?"

"I did give it to your clerk, your honor."

Elliot glared at him. "You know very well that my clerk is lax in passing along such things. You have been instructed to give them directly to me. All right, Hamlin—tell me in extremely short sentences what proof you have, and I will give you my decision."

"Very well, your honor." Hamlin's grip tightened when Rhianna shrank away from him. "Miss Llewellyn's pearls were reported stolen by the Moon Rider. Yet she still has those pearls in her possession. Viscount Roxbury swears to the fact he saw them delivered to her by Wolverton's steward only two days hence. I took them from her not an hour ago."

Elliot frowned. "The pearls that were described in the letters circulated to shop owners a few months ago?"

"Yes, sir. With the unusual clasp."

"I see." Elliot leaned forward, his eyes riveting Rhianna into place. "Let me see these pearls, Mr. Hamlin."

Sheriff Hamlin put a hand into his pocket, then grew still. He swore softly. "Your honor, I'm afraid that I do not have the pearl necklace with me."

"No?" Elliot's brow lifted. "You just told me you had taken the evidence."

"I . . . I did, sir, but it seems that I have left them behind in the possession of Viscount Roxbury."

Keswick edged forward. "Without the evidence, your honor, I do not see how you can hold either Miss Llewellyn or the earl."

Elliot frowned. "I do not see the earl here, my lord. I see only Miss Llewellyn, who is said to still have stolen pearls in her possession."

"Sheriff Hamlin was afraid to allow the earl and Miss Llewellyn private conversation and so sent the earl to Avebury, your honor. I pray that you will effect Wolverton's release immediately as well as Miss Llewellyn's."

"No," Hamlin objected. "I have another witness with me, a servant by the name of Porter who can testify not only to Miss Llewellyn's possession of the pearls, but to a costume he discovered in her home. If you will allow him to speak, your honor—"

Elliot held up a hand and sighed. "It is too late to treat this as if it were already on the docket, sheriff. I am only a magistrate, not an entire court."

"But will you sign the papers of arrest, your honor?" Hamlin demanded. "It is vital that the persons responsible for the wounding of the king's guard be confined, as you well know."

"Yes, I've had any number of scathing missives about this subject from the king's minister." Elliot clasped his hands together atop his desk and regarded Rhianna with a long, searching stare. "I find it difficult to imagine his response if I send him this girl as the culprit. He would most likely remove me from my post."

"My point exactly, your honor," Keswick argued. "What would the king say if this proper young woman and an earl were accused wrongfully? Despite his somewhat tarnished reputation, Lord Wolverton *is* a member of the aristocracy, and King George holds such privilege of birth most dear."

"My lord," Elliot said after a brief moment of heavy silence, "I understand your sentiments. However, there is a question here of settling the accusations. I will not commend Miss Llewellyn to gaol tonight—"

"Sir!" Hamlin exclaimed furiously and was silenced by Elliot's frosty glare.

"—but," the magistrate continued, "I will have her kept under house arrest at her own home until we have the evidence in hand, or it is proven false. Will that satisfy your lordship?"

Keswick nodded. "For the moment. And Wolverton? What of him?"

"Ah yes, the earl." Elliot was silent for a moment. "He is a different matter, I suppose, since Hamlin seems to feel he has sufficient evidence to arrest a member of the aristocracy. Perhaps—just for now, Lord Keswick—the earl should remain in the custody of the Avebury officials."

"Devil take it, this is preposterous!" Keswick snapped. "I hope you can explain your position to the king's minister with sufficient cause, sir."

"So do I." Elliot gazed at Rhianna for so long she felt her knees tremble. He smiled faintly. "So do I, Lord Keswick. Sheriff Hamlin, send three of your constables along with Miss Llewellyn, and post them at her door. Miss Llewellyn, you are not to leave your home until given permission, or you shall be in violation of my edict and considered an escaped felon. Do I make myself clear?"

She hardly recognized her quivery voice. "Yes, your honor. You are quite clear."

"Good. Now leave, so I may seek my bed. My gout has flared up most inconveniently. Good evening."

Darkness shrouded him. Chance blinked slowly, trying to adjust to the absence of light. It was so silent that he could almost hear his heart beat, and there was a musty odor permeating the air. He moved again and flinched.

His head hurt. Blood pounded in his ears. The last thing he remembered was struggling with Hamlin's men, and that was hazy. There had been three of them, and he'd had the satisfaction of putting one of them on the floor before a blow had sent him staggering. Another blow to the head had exploded light behind his eyes, and the next thing he knew, he was waking to this utter darkness.

He tried to move and wasn't surprised to find that his arms were bound behind him. Even his legs were bound at the ankles. His eyes closed again. How had he been fool enough to let this happen?

Rhianna had been taken, probably arrested. She would be hanged if he could not help her. Leaning back, he tried to make sense of the darkness, blinking as his eyes slowly adjusted to the differences in shadow. Instead of stones beneath him, he felt the rough scratch of wood. He could see no bars, hear no murmurs of guards or other prisoners. It occurred to him that he was not in a prison cell as he'd first thought. But if not—where?

Chance shifted position, and his foot struck something solid. It gave a bit under his boot, and he shoved at it again. It felt as if it might be a man, but no one protested at his kicking them, so he wasn't certain.

Twisting, he managed to squirm onto his side despite his throbbing head, until he was close enough to run a hand over the mysterious object. It was rough and coarse, and he realized that it was a bag of grain. More bags towered up and over him in bulky stacks. A granary? He went still again. Over the beat of his heart and the blood in his ears, he could discern the faint trickle of water. A mill. He had been taken to a mill.

He let his head rest against the sack of grain. If he had not been taken to a gaol, then he was in a much worse situation than he'd first thought. Images returned to haunt him, images of Roxbury's smug expression and the sheriff's satisfied smile. *Hamlin.* It would not be the first time an official had been lured from his duty by promises of wealth. And Hamlin had always destested him.

Chance closed his eyes. The fact that he'd been taken to a desolate spot was ominous enough. He could well imagine the rest of the plans for him. Damn. This could be any mill, anywhere in Wiltshire. He tried to think, but his head ached so abominably, he could only remember the locations of two mills, one of them on Wolverton estates.

Bloody hell. First, he had to gather his strength, then he would set about finding a way to escape. Wherever he was, it had to be reasonably close by. They wouldn't have had the time to take him far.

Escape echoed in his head over and over, and he had a vision of Rhianna standing there in the meeting room of The Bull and Bear, fear and defiance in her lovely eyes.

Damn her impetuous nature, if she'd only stayed home, she would not be in danger now. Why hadn't she listened?

Chance stared into the darkness, thinking of Rhianna. He felt an almost overwhelming sense of despair. She was in danger, and he couldn't help her. It was agonizing.

Oddly, he wished that he could cry. He didn't recall the last time he'd wept; maybe he never had. And he probably never would. One had to be able to actually *feel* to cry, he'd heard. And he was accustomed to stuffing his emotions safely away into some deep inner pocket and forgetting them.

As he had Rhianna.

Easy, really, to put unpleasant memories safely away into a box. Package them neatly and forget to remember things that hurt. And he was a master at it, an expert at feeling nothing.

Rhianna had been part of that terrible time so long ago, the only bright spot in days of darkness, but she'd been there so briefly that he hadn't been able to allow himself to think of her. And so after years of not thinking of her, years of restless yearning for something that had no name, he'd stumbled across her again. And not known it.

He laughed, a hollow sound in the black shadows that enveloped him. How could he not have recognized her? Instead, he'd found himself inexplicably attracted to whom he thought were two different women, when both of them were the one he'd lost so long ago. He should have known immediately who she was; there should have been some grand and dramatic denouement when he'd announced his discovery of her identity. Yet the discovery that 'Anna was Rhianna, had been anticlimactic and flat, leaving him feeling deflated.

He'd been blind, so blind. If he let himself, he could see her staring up at him at Keswick's boring country ball, see her wide blue eyes filled with expectation. And he'd not known, not seen beyond the obvious, not recognized her. She must have been devastated by his ignorance.

Now, he might never have the opportunity to tell her that he loved her. *Love.* He knew so little of it. How could he be certain that what he felt for Rhianna was love? He rested his head on his drawn-up knees and drew in a deep breath.

Perhaps, because for the first time in his memory, he knew that if he lost her, he would be lost as well. He was willing to risk everything for her, willing to risk peace and sanity and life and limb, just to keep her near him. But would she know, though he hadn't said it? Would she somehow see into his soul and know that he'd never forgotten her despite years of numbness? He hoped so. Odd, after so many years of reckless indifference to whether he lived or died, now he had a reason to live and it was likely that he would die before the night ended.

The fates must be laughing at him, as they had always done.

A snippet of verse came to him suddenly, learned when he was a boy. *It lies not in our power to love or hate. For will in us is overruled by fate.*

He'd thought of it often at one time. As true today, he supposed, as it had ever been. Why had he thought he could win? Life wasn't that fair. Hadn't he discovered that years and years ago? And yet he'd gone on hoping— dumb bastard that he was—the hope lying deep inside him where he'd never thought to look. There was no other explanation for going on living when all reason bade one to surrender to the inevitable.

Until now. Until he'd found a single, shining reason to wake up each morning.

Chance jerked to his knees, clumsily, rage rapidly replacing his former apathy and resignation. No, by God, Roxbury would not beat him, would not destroy Rhianna. . . .

Chapter 22

Rhianna stared numbly at Hobson. He didn't look at her, but his gaze kept straying around the parlor as if he were unable to bear the news he'd brought. Rain and night still shrouded the windows with gloom, and the lamps shed fitful light in the parlor.

"What do you mean, Hobson?"

"Exactly what I said, Miss Llewellyn." He gave her a miserable glance, then looked down at his feet again. "I have failed. That dreadful constable clung to me so closely that I thought I'd never get away from him. By the time I managed, Lord Wolverton had disappeared."

Rhianna collapsed into a chair, knees too weak to support her any longer. "I thought he'd been taken to Avebury to be held there."

"Aye, so we were told. But it seems that he never made it that far, and Hamlin claims ignorance of his whereabouts. I fear that the sheriff may be in league with Viscount Roxbury in some way."

"In league—? But how can that be?"

Hobson sighed. "Hamlin has always hated the aristocracy, that much is well known. P'raps he saw in Roxbury's offer a means of avenging himself against insults, real or imagined, that he has suffered through the years. At any rate, that is not important." He leaned forward, fixing her with a steady stare. "What is important, is finding the earl. You must help me."

"I?" She stared up at him. "But I am under house arrest, as you must know. They even sent Lord Keswick away."

"I am well aware of that. It took a great deal of effort just to secure a few moments' private conversation with you. Thank heavens I have relatives who still remember their duty to their elders." His voice lowered. "Will you help?"

"Gladly, but how can I?"

"Riever and the others are searching, but you are needed to provide a distraction not only for the sheriff but for Roxbury. Time is of the essence, Miss Llewellyn. We must not waste it."

She stood up, the prospect of action dissipating the sense of helplessness that had crippled her since being arrested. "Only tell me what to do, and I will give it my best."

Hobson smiled slightly. "I knew you would. Tell me, is your maid Serena a loyal girl?"

Rhianna smiled. "Quite loyal."

"And she is just your size, it seems, though her hair is a bit darker. Surely, a shawl could disguise that?"

"I see what you are suggesting." She stepped to the door, and when one of the constables blocked the doorway, asked to see her maid. The man glanced at Hobson as if to ascertain the fact that he was still there and had not caused any problems, then nodded. When he'd gone, Rhianna turned back to Hobson. "But how are we to get away?"

"Ah, leave the details to me. As I mentioned, several of my relatives are scattered about. Wiltshire is home to a host of my nieces and nephews, some of whom are employed in official capacities. . . ."

Within an hour, Rhianna and Hobson were racing away from Serenity House in a closed carriage. Serena now wore her mistress's clothes, while Rhianna wore her maid's. The maid had eagerly agreed to help, as Rhianna had hoped. Now, Serena remained in Rhianna's darkened bedchamber, disguised as Rhianna.

It had gone well, though there had been a few nervous moments when one of the constables had attempted to flirt with the girl he thought was the maid. Fenwick's timely intervention had rescued her from discovery, and he had been instrumental in sneaking Rhianna from the house to the far end of the garden. Once she stepped through the garden gate into the road, Hobson was there with a carriage.

Rhianna had looked away from the still form of the constable lying on the ground, and climbed into the carriage. "You did not—?"

"Kill him?" Hobson shut the door and sat back. "No. By the time he wakes, however, he'll have a nasty headache. It was necessary, you understand."

She drew in a shaky breath. "Yes, I understand. But there are other things that are still very unclear."

The carriage increased its speed. She turned to look at him, the dim interior light leaving half Hobson's face in shadow. "Hobson, please tell me the truth. I know there is much more behind Roxbury's accusations than there appears to be on the surface. I have the inescapable feeling that I am only a small part of this affair."

"Quite so, miss." Hobson squared his shoulders and seemed to school his emotions. He stared down at his gloved hands for several minutes before turning back to her. "You must understand that what I am about to tell you is not the entire story, but all I can reveal at this time."

"Of course."

"Very good." He blew out a heavy breath. "Roxbury is involved in shady dealings that could affect national security. His lordship has been attempting to circumvent him for some time. Last night he hoped to deliver the *coup de grace* to a disreputable plan, but instead he walked into a trap. Roxbury must have discovered that Lord Chance knew about his clandestine activities."

Rhianna shuddered. She had the sinking feeling that she was to blame, that Roxbury had divined Chance's involvement because of her.

"It's my fault," she said.

Hobson shook his head. "No. The earl knew well the risks he was taking. Your appearance at the inn may have involved you, but it did not change what would have happened anyway." His voice grew grim. "I discovered that much when I witnessed Roxbury's confederates out on the north road. They met—just as the viscount said they would—and the information was exchanged."

"Then all this was for nothing."

"Oh no. Riever took the earl's men with him. They were magnificent. The vital information is now safely in proper hands."

"Thank God. Chance will be so glad."

"He will be if we can find him before—"

As he jerked to a halt, Rhianna couldn't help a soft cry of dismay. Hobson gave her a reassuring smile, and she managed a tremulous response.

"I'm honored that you trust me this much." She put a hand over the fist he had clenched on his knee. "You know that I care very deeply for the earl, don't you."

He nodded, smiling faintly. "I saw it coming long before he did. He's a stubborn one, that boy."

Rhianna recalled Chance's words so long before, when he'd been a boy and said that only Hobson would care if he never went home. The old servant truly loved him; it was obvious.

She said with a small catch in her voice, "Tell me about him, Hobson. I know so little, really."

"Tell you about him?" he repeated slowly. " 'Tis difficult to say, miss. He had such a hard time of it when he was a lad, and had to mature before he was ready. Oh, I suppose he had good times, before Lord Charles and his mother died. There were five children, you know."

"Five?"

Hobson nodded. "Aye. Three boys and two girls. All but Chance and Anthony died young. Anthony was the heir. He lived to be almost twenty, but had some foolish notion about going to Paris. It was the time of the revolution, and there was a massacre in Paris." He grimaced. "Lord Anthony was caught up in it, and his being an English citizen did not aid him in the least. He was . . . was killed, as were so many aristocrats. His poor parents grieved. I do believe grief weakened them, so that when the head groom brought back a fever from Hampstead Hall, they had no resistance to it. They died quickly. Lord Chance was still at Eton, having just been sent back after burying his brother, and so escaped the fever that swept through Whiteash Manor. It decimated the servants mostly. I was very fortunate to have escaped it myself."

Rhianna didn't speak when he lapsed into thoughtful silence, but waited for him to continue. The coach rumbled slowly over rutted roads thick with mud. After a few moments Hobson glanced at her, a faint smile on his lips.

"Excuse me. I seem to have a tendency to lose myself in memories. As I was saying, I escaped the fever, as did Lord Chance. But it left him orphaned, with a title and vast fortune. A barrister came down from London with the news that his lordship had been appointed a guardian until he came into his majority."

"His uncle."

"Aye. Lord Perry Montagu, as big a wastrel and malcontent as anyone could ever hope to meet." His lip curled in utter contempt, and she was surprised at the glitter of hatred in his eyes after all these years. "Montagu seemed determined to go through Chance's inheritance before the boy could reach his majority, and that ravenous barrister who suggested him as guardian was little better. Whiteash became a haven for the dissolute characters Montagu had associated with in London. Gamesters, loose women, thieves, and cutthroats frequented the elegant halls until I was near despair. Lord Chance—" He paused, then added more quietly, "Lord Chance had little stomach for it, but Montagu held a trump card, so to speak."

"A trump card?"

He nodded grimly. "Myself. Montagu threatened to do me harm if Chance did not voluntarily give him the keys to the storerooms. I was all that the boy had left, and Montagu knew it." He cleared his throat. "At any rate, matters came to an end one stormy spring night."

"The night Lord Perry was killed." Rhianna wasn't certain she wanted to hear the rest, but said softly, "I can understand why Chance would be moved to kill his uncle."

"Aye, so can I."

The coach lurched to one side, and Hobson regained his balance with effort. Rhianna braced herself with an arm against the luxurious velvet squabs of the earl's coach.

"How did it happen?" she asked when it seemed as if the old man was lost in memories again. Hobson gave her a quick glance.

"I probably shouldn't tell, but if anyone should know the truth, it's you."

"The truth?" Her heart seemed to lodge in her throat, and her stomach lurched. She thought of the rumors, of the taut expression on Chance's face when she had mentioned his uncle's murder. And—inwardly cringing—she thought of the time she had called him a murderer. She drew in a deep breath and asked, "What—is the truth?"

A troubled frown creased Hobson's face. "Montagu had been drunk for four days. Drank the last of the Madeira in the cellar, and I'd once thought it impossible for the supply to be consumed in my lifetime. But Montagu drank it as if it were well water. Gave it to his friends, spilled it and—but that is irrelevant. At any rate, he was in an ugly mood. Called me down to the front parlor. He'd managed to catch one of the best carpets on fire. A huge hole had burned through, and it was still smoldering. I used what was left in his glass to throw on it. In retrospect, it was a foolish thing to do. I could have made the fire worse, but fortunately, the dregs did not flare up into flames. But Montagu was furious that I had wasted the last bit of his Madeira. He began to rage, and struck me with his fist."

Voice quavering, Hobson continued huskily, "It was at that moment that Lord Chance came in. He was young and strong and not drunk, and he began to shove Montagu about the room, yelling at him that he'd had enough. He told him to get out before he killed him. That made Montagu laugh. He stood there in the center of the room and laughed like a crazy man." He paused and looked at Rhianna. "Montagu was quite strong, you see, and fancied himself a bit of a pugilist. Been a few rounds with Mendoza, I believe."

"The famous pugilist?"

"He wasn't so famous then, I'll warrant. Anyway, they quarreled, and Montagu lunged at Chance. A fight ensued. It was extremely violent. They raged back and forth, and I just knew that at any moment, Montagu would overpower the boy." His voice quivered again with suppressed emotion. "Blood covered both of them. Montagu had cuts on his face, and Lord Chance looked as if he'd been run over by a coach. Clothes torn, both of them panting like enraged bulls—I knew they were like to kill one another. Then Montagu snatched up the empty bottle of Madeira and brought it down on Lord Chance's head. It shattered the bottle, save for a long, sharp piece that was the neck. His lordship went down, unconscious."

"Do you mean Chance?"

Hobson nodded. "Aye. I thought he was dead. I could see no sign of life, and he was so bloody . . . so bloody. It was all over him, you see, on his face and hands—Montagu swayed back and forth over him, shouting for him to get up or he'd skewer him with the broken bottle. He . . . he lunged, and to this day I don't quite recall how it happened, but all of a sudden I was there. I took the bottle from him, and he grabbed for it. He . . . I think he slipped on the blood, or perhaps tripped on the hole burned into the carpet, but he fell against me. Then he had the queerest expression on his face, as if I had said something very awkward, and I felt this tug on my arm. I looked down—he'd fallen against the end of the broken bottle, you see, and it had pierced his chest. He fell back after a moment, very slowly, as if it were a dream. I just watched. Oh, the things that went through my mind in those few seconds . . . I saw the sheriff coming after me, my arrest and hanging—and I didn't care. Do you know why? Because he was dying. He would no longer torment Lord Chance, and I was glad—fiercely glad. Montagu lay there, gasping and holding his hand over the bottle sticking up out of his chest. . . . I began to think he would *not* die, that he would tell what had happened, and somehow blame Chance for it."

His voice trailed into silence again. Rhianna stared at him, trying to absorb what he was telling her, knowing that it was a purging of sorts for Hobson to confess his part in the death of Lord Montagu. She put her hand on his trembling arm.

"What happened then, Hobson?"

"I sat there and waited for him to die. I didn't go for help until he quit moving," the old man said simply. "I had to let him die. You see that, don't you?"

A shiver went down her spine, but she nodded slowly. "Yes," she agreed, "you had to. It was the right thing to do."

Hobson sat back against the squabs and nodded. "Yes. I thought so. But when Mrs. Beasley came into the parlor and found me sitting there and Lord Chance crouched over the body, shaking Montagu, she immediately leaped to the assumption that he'd been done in by his lordship. I tried to tell her the truth then, but she was a silly rabbit and ran from the room screaming." He frowned. "I knew she'd gone for the authorities."

"And all this time, Chance has thought he murdered his uncle," Rhianna mused aloud. Hobson made a startled sound.

"No! No, no, you misunderstand. He knew. He knew he had not done it."

"Then why—?"

"Why did he take the blame? He knew no one would hang him for it. I would have been hanged. He was an earl and a boy and had been tormented by his uncle. Sympathy was with him. He made me . . . . made me promise not to tell anyone what had really happened. And so all these years. . . ."

"All these years," she finished softly, "he's carried the burden that you feel is yours to bear."

Tears glittered in Hobson's eyes. "Aye. 'Twas my fault, yet he's borne the guilt for me."

"Because you were there for him when he really needed you, Hobson. You saved him. I remember him saying that only you would miss him if he never returned. You were all he had, and he couldn't lose you, too."

He thought about that for a moment, then nodded. "P'raps you're right, miss."

"I know I am. It was his choice, and he chose wisely."

The coach lurched again, then settled into a faster pace. Hobson glanced out the window. "I hope so. Let us see what can be done to help find Lord Chance."

Chapter 23

Light stabbed the darkness, waking Chance. It hurt his eyes and made him squint. He wasn't at all surprised to hear Roxbury's voice come out of the shadows behind the lantern.

"So, Wolverton, have you had time to think over your folly?"

Chance didn't reply. He waited, flexing his cramped fingers behind his back. He wished his arms were untied so that he could wrap his hands around the viscount's throat. There was the scuffle of boots across the wood floor, and in the distance, the sound of rushing water had grown loud. Roxbury must have left open a door. The fetid, damp smell had grown stronger, mixed now with the stench of rotting wood.

As his eyes adjusted to the spears of light threading over the floor, Chance could see stacks of grain sacks around him. Instead of the grinding noise of grain being ground by the huge gristmill into flour or meal, there was only the splashing hum of falling water.

He blinked. Tiny splinters of light filtered through cracks in the wooden walls. It must be daylight. He'd spent the night in the mill. His arms were almost numb, though he'd done his best to keep the blood flowing by flexing and unflexing his hands. The pain had slowly changed to a paralysis he could not fight. He shifted position, drawing his legs up under him as best he could.

Roxbury moved closer. The lantern swayed in his grip, held high, casting erratic pools of light over the musty room. "You don't look so vigorous now, Wolverton. Have you lost your fight?"

Chance glanced up. He cautiously tested the strength of the ropes around his ankles and found them as snug as before. Bloody hell. By now, his arms were nearly useless, and he wasn't that certain of his legs. He'd sat too long in the damp chill.

A grin gleamed in Roxbury's face, and Chance smothered the almost overpowering urge to wipe it away. He had to remain calm, had to wait and hope.

"Ah well," Roxbury said with a mocking sigh, "I suppose you've decided not to talk to me. How crushing. Was it something I said?"

No, it's what you are, Chance said silently. He hoped his contemptuous silence was effectively conveyed to the viscount. After a moment, Roxbury laughed softly.

"You're so easy to read, Wolverton. You think me a vain, foolish traitor. But, only note who it is who is in bonds and who stands here freely, *n'est-ce pas?* Shall I tell you how easy it was to arrange your downfall?"

"My consent will hardly matter. You will anyway," Chance muttered thickly.

"True. I should like for you to know how stupid you have been through all this." Roxbury set the lantern on the lid of a barrel and seated himself on a stack of grain bags.

Chance squinted against the bright light of the lantern and shoved himself to a sitting position. "I admit that I underestimated you. I never thought you could devise and carry out an elaborate ruse such as the one at The Bull and Bear. However did you manage it?"

Roxbury's mouth tightened at Chance's mocking words, and he snarled, "*Cochon!* Do you think yourself so clever? It is not I who sit bound in a mill waiting for my fate, but you. Nor has your lovely *amour* been so fortunate. She will certainly hang for her part in this."

"So why aren't I in gaol with her? If you are so certain you have the necessary evidence to convict us, why am I sitting in a damp mill instead of in gaol?"

"Because it is you who are the most dangerous to our cause. You know things that are best left unsaid in a room of magistrates." Roxbury smiled slightly. "Accusations made at a climactic moment in an inn are one thing —accusations made to the proper authorities are another thing entirely."

"Which is why I didn't bother at The Bull and Bear. Now I know that it would have been useless anyway, as Hamlin is in your pay. Isn't he?"

"Very good, Wolverton. Your powers of perception improve at last. Too bad you did not see beyond your emotions earlier." Roxbury put his hands on his knees and leaned forward. "It was the woman who was your undoing, you know. If you had not allowed your feelings for her to lead you into unwise reactions, I would not have found the proof I needed to set up our little farce of earlier. But the return of her pearls—a most gallant act on your part—gave me the necessary evidence to present your guilt."

He reached into his pocket and drew out the pearls, holding them up so the light made the small globes gleam. "They are not worth much in monetary terms, but these pearls have condemned you, *mon ami*."

"If you needed evidence to convict me, why go through this elaborate scheme just to kill me in a gristmill?"

"To murder a member of the aristocracy, even a dissolute earl such as yourself, is too perilous a scheme. It would draw much unwanted attention in the wrong corners of this cursed country. No, your demise must be handled with all delicacy. If you are proven to be the Moon Rider in the midst of a public tavern, then later found dead from an attempt at escape, it will be much easier to accept than if you are just found murdered along the roadside. *N'est-ce pas?*"

"And Rhianna's part in all this? Why bother with her?"

"She would create much fuss and, therefore, must be discredited along with you. Then, no one is likely to believe her protests of innocence and cries for justice on the behalf of her dead highwayman lover."

"Quite ingenious in a rather diabolic manner, I suppose. Why involve Keswick?"

Roxbury shrugged and replaced the pearls in his coat pocket. "The viscount's dismay over the damning truth is what convinced those peasants at the inn of your guilt. If he admitted that you and Miss Llewellyn arrived at his house in disguise, it makes the rest much more believable."

"And Lady Wimberley?"

"Ah, she lured George to the inn, and her melodramatic protests were a nice touch, I thought. She also reminded those gathered as to your lurid past." His smile was nasty. "You have not been such a pleasant fellow at times."

That was true enough. Chance eased his aching muscles into a more comfortable position. "What of the papers you were to pass last night, Roxbury? Was that only part of the trick?"

"Ah no. That, as your mysterious contact informed you, was quite true. There was to be an exchange of papers last evening." Roxbury laughed. "Indeed, that part also went quite well."

Chance frowned. "You still have the list with you?"

"The list? Do you mean the paper you saw Heffington

give me while you lurked in the shadows? Of course I do." He withdrew a sheaf of paper from his inner pocket and held it up, still smiling. "This list details Heffington's assets and liabilities for his farm in Kent. It has nothing to do with the list you seek."

"Where is that list?"

"Oh, do you think still of national security? You are a determined man, Wolverton. Perhaps that explains your success until now. If it will make you happy, I shall tell you that the list of names you want is quite safe. It was simple enough to let fall the information that the exchange would be made at the tavern. Unfortunately for you and England, the exchange took place last night on the north road. My confederates should be halfway to France by now."

"What do you gain personally, may I ask? You're not the type of man to be swept away by patriotic fervor."

Roxbury's eyes narrowed. "Money, of course. Influence with my superiors. And a position in the cabinet can be quite lucrative if one knows what to do. Besides, France is my native country. Here, there are too many bourgeoisie to suit me."

"An unpopular opinion in your own beloved country. It could cost you your head."

"It certainly cost my father his." Roxbury took a deep breath. "But with Napoleon in power, some semblance of sanity may be restored to France."

A slight draft made the flames in the lantern dance over the storeroom, and Chance glanced toward the door. Several shadows moved outside. He looked back at the viscount.

"Sanity? With a despot like Napoleon? That is too ridiculous even for someone like you, Roxbury. Napoleon does not want France to be a powerful nation. He wants *Napoleon* to be a powerful man."

"Napoleon and France are indivisble."

Chance gave a hoot of derisive laughter and saw the viscount's hands clench. "No one really believes that, do they, Roxbury? Who has been feeding you that drivel? I wager it's an Englishman who soothes your conscience with such absurd platitudes. . . ."

"Shut up!" Roxbury surged to his feet, glaring down at Chance. "You will soon regret your mockery, Wolverton."

"Will I? Not as much as you will soon regret your rash beliefs, Roxbury."

Turning, Roxbury snapped out an order. The shadows outside the door grew sharper, and Chance saw two burly men enter the mill. He tensed, expecting the worst.

Roxbury reached into his vest pocket and removed a gold-etched snuff box. He flicked it open with a graceful twist of his wrist. He took a delicate pinch of tobacco and inhaled it, then sneezed into a lacy handkerchief.

One of the men paused beside the viscount. "We've just had word from—"

"Silence," Roxbury said sharply. "Step over here and give me the message."

Chance tugged at the ropes on his ankles again, but they did not loosen. He shifted, and could tell from the rising tone of the conversation, that Roxbury was displeased over something. When the viscount returned, Chance looked up with a mocking smile.

"Bad news, Roxbury?"

Roxbury gave a snap of his fingers, and Chance was jerked to his feet. He almost fell; his numbed legs would not hold him up, and one of the men laughed harshly as he caught him by the back of his rough jacket and held him.

"He'll not make it far, guv'nor."

Roxbury said sharply, "Drag him if needs be, but bring him along quickly. And don't call me by vulgar names."

"He's bloody heavy," the man grumbled. "This one ain't no small bloke."

"Then untie his feet and let him walk, but bring him out quickly and put him in the back of the cart. I don't have much time to spare."

It occurred to Chance that Roxbury did not sound as jubilant as he should. In fact, he sounded angry and frustrated. Hadn't matters gone well? For all appearances, they had; after all, safely getting the vital names of cabinet members to his accomplices would be a feat to satisfy him. Roxbury moved aside as one of the men crouched to untie the bonds circling Chance's ankles.

Even untying his feet didn't help; the circulation was slow in returning, and cramps stabbed his muscles with piercing pain. Chance wobbled like a toddler and felt a wave of frustration. Escape was impossible if he didn't regain his strength. He looked up and saw a glitter of amusement in the viscount's pale, sleepy eyes.

He swallowed the urge to curse Roxbury roundly. It would do no good and only please the viscount to have provoked a reaction. Resentment rose in his throat, almost choking him. Surprisingly, he felt a surge of strength return to his legs, along with needle-sharp prickings as the blood flowed more freely. The rough fisherman's boots he wore rubbed over his calves; he stomped his feet against the wood planking of the floor and felt it tremble slightly.

"Bring him," Roxbury said, and Chance was shoved roughly forward.

"We shall wait here for our assistants," Hobson said as the carriage drew to a halt on the crest of a slope. He reached around Rhianna to open the door. "Let us alight."

As the sun rose over the tops of hills outlined in mist and shadow, Rhianna could see sharper silhouettes against the growing light. She blinked and felt a shiver ripple down her spine as she stepped from the carriage.

"That . . . that looks so familiar," she murmured.

Hobson agreed. "Yes, I should think it would. It has been a long time for you, I imagine."

They stood just outside their carriage, waiting. Hobson stood quietly. Rhianna pulled her cloak around her more tightly, shivering again as she studied the hillside.

"Hobson, are those—?"

"Wagons? Yes, Miss Llewellyn. They arrived two days ago, and I believe you know some of the occupants."

She began to move toward the line of wagons, half-stumbling in the wet grass and mud, heedless of her shoes or the wet hem of her gown. A fire burned in the center of the grouped wagons, and she saw a figure moving toward her. Her throat tightened, and she broke into a run, lifting the hem of her gown as she raced over the rutted meadow.

"Marisa!" Was that her voice? Shaky and thick with emotion? She stumbled closer and called again, more strongly, "Marisa. . . ."

Arms opened wide to enfold her. Bracelets clinked softly. "Child," Marisa said with a husky tremor in her voice, and Rhianna gave a soft cry.

With her face buried against her aunt's shoulder, she said in a muffled voice, "I thought never to see you again."

"And I you." The embrace tightened. "And I you. . . ."

Rhianna lifted her face and realized with a faint twinge of surprise that she was crying. Tears wet her face and made damp spots on Marisa's gaily patterned blouse. Not quite believing she was not dreaming, she touched her aunt lightly on the cheek.

"It really is you. After all these years."

Marisa caught her arm, the bracelets she wore jangling. "Yes. I had to see you again. You are even more beautiful than Cynara, and I never thought she would have a rival."

Rhianna smiled through her tears. "Cynara's closest rival was always you, Marisa."

Tears wet her aunt's eyes, making them glisten darkly. Her smile was wobbly, quivering on her lips with suppressed emotion. Then she seemed to collect herself and released Rhianna's arm and straightened.

"Well. So I finally arrive, only to discover that you are in danger. Your Papa was worried."

Rhianna stared at her. "Papa? Have . . . have you been to see him?"

"Of course. I went there first."

"But the constables. . . ."

"Were not there. I left before you arrived."

"Papa is . . . not well."

"That was quite evident. He felt much better after I gave him some of my elixir, though he could use a lot more."

"Elixir?"

Marisa nodded. "The juice of raw onions and garlic. It seems to work best, though not exactly pleasant. I have discovered that I have a gift for healing."

Rhianna gazed at her helplessly for a moment. "But the doctor said—" she began, and Marisa made a rude sound.

"Some doctors cannot see the obvious. Your maid told me the doctor said cataclysm of the brain. I'm not trained in healing, but even I could see that he needs a change of

diet and time to regain what he lost. Blood pudding."
Marisa snorted. "That sort of diet will kill him before
long. I told Sir Griffyn he is too fat and needs diet and
exercise, not a corset and brandy."

"The doctor thought that his illness was brought on by
a sudden shock."

Marisa shook her head. "No. Did he not complain of
headaches before collapsing?" She didn't wait for confirmation, but continued, "I believe there was a weakness
that caused it. Therefore, it is only reasonable that re-
building his strength will recapture most of his loss."

"Marisa. . . ." Rhianna's legs wobbled, and before
she realized it, she was sitting on the wet grass in a rustle
of skirts and cloak.

Marisa knelt beside her. She put a tender hand on her
niece's head. "I have been told of your troubles. The
angry young earl. It is he who worries you."

"Yes." The single word came out in a husky whisper.
"He is . . . in danger—"

"I know." Marisa, still kneeling beside her, closed her
eyes. Even in the misty light, Rhianna could see the same
distant expression come over her that she'd seen so long
ago, when she'd stepped into the realms of the future.
She waited, holding her breath, hoping. Marisa didn't
move or speak for several minutes, but remained in a
crouch, head tilted back and eyes tightly closed. Rhianna
spoke softly.

"Tell me, Marisa. Tell me what you see."

"Darkness. Water. A wheel." Her eyes opened, but
they were not focusing on Rhianna, but on visions only
she could see. "He is alone. And he is angry. I see death.
Blood and flames and grief, the past and present destroyed. . . ."

A shudder ran down her spine. Rhianna lurched to her
feet, fear and desperation filling her. "I must find him."

"No." Marisa clutched at her cloak. "I cannot see who meets death. I am afraid for you."

She tugged the folds of her cloak free. "I cannot just wait idly! I will find him. I must."

"Ah, still the same impetuous child you always were. Listen to me, Rhianna, and do not endanger yourself when I have only just found you again."

She struggled briefly with conflicting emotions and hoped her aunt understood when she said softly, "I will not lose him again. I cannot."

"You will be in danger."

"I don't care. Without him, nothing will matter."

Marisa's mouth twisted with anguish. "I recall your mother saying the same thing . . . ah, how I wish Nicolo were here to stop you."

"Nicolo—" She had a sudden vision of her former friend racing against Chance, both of them young and wild. "Is he here also?"

"He will be back soon. He is the leader now."

"Manuel—?"

"Dead six years ago. Enrico is gone. Nicolo has led our tiny group these past four years." She took Rhianna's hand between hers, eyes searching her face. "Will you wait for him to come back? He will help you."

Hobson said from behind Rhianna, "He is the reason we are here. I asked for his help, but without Miss Llewellyn to plead my cause, I was refused." Rhianna turned. Hobson gazed at her gravely. "You must ask this Nicolo to lend his aid. Wiltshire is too large and our numbers too small. We need men and horses."

"Will he listen to me?" Rhianna turned back to Marisa. "Will Nicolo help us find Chance?"

•   •   •

Rhianna reined in on the rising slope of a hill overlooking the stream that ran between her father's property and Lancaster land. She paused, frowning. A brisk wind blew the hair from her eyes and chilled her cheeks.

"Is this where you think he might be, miss?"

She slid a glance toward Hobson. He sat his mount with surprising agility for his age. "Yes. It is the closest mill to the village. Did you send the message to the earl's men?"

"Yes. I am certain they are now out scouring the moors and villages for him. More are to join forces with us here."

"I hope no one alerts the sheriff."

"As do I." Hobson shifted position in his saddle. "Hamlin lacks imagination and is very single-minded. He would see only that you were somehow involved and not obeying his edict to remain at Serenity House. I have an inescapable feeling that he would hinder our search for the earl."

"Yes, I rather thought so myself." Rhianna gazed out over the gurgling waters of the millstream. Marisa's words rang in her ears. *Darkness. Water. A wheel.* The mill was the obvious conclusion. Was she right? She dragged in a deep breath. "How many mills are there in Wiltshire, Hobson?"

"Several. Only two nearby, however. Your belief that his lordship is being held here is most logical."

She nodded. "I'm certain of it. Marisa is rarely wrong when she has the sight."

"And do you not have the sight also? After all, you're one of them."

Rhianna gave him a startled glance. "No. Well—I don't think so, though at times, I've known things without knowing how."

"P'raps you've not allowed yourself to develop the gift

of sight. I've heard that one must nurture a talent, for it to grow to its fullest extent."

"That's what Marisa once told me, but I've never been very good at it." She looked at him curiously. "It's odd to hear someone who isn't Romany speak of foresight as a gift or talent."

Hobson shrugged. "I believe that I'm capable of accepting things I don't quite understand. I'm not as narrow-minded as some I know."

"Apparently not." Rhianna smiled. Hobson had a depth she had not expected. No wonder Chance loved the old man. He did not revile what he did not understand but had a tolerance that was unusual. "Well," she said after a moment, "shall we wait on the others or go ahead and see if he is down there?"

Hobson glanced at the sword belted at Rhianna's side, his own hand resting on a pistol stuck into the waist of his trousers. Then he looked over the moors, where nothing moved but the wind. Behind him, one of the gypsies riding with them muttered the opinion that they wait on the others to arrive. Hobson looked back at Rhianna.

"P'raps it wouldn't hurt to just see if he is there."

She smiled. "I agree."

But when they reached the mill and slipped quietly into the deserted building, they saw no sign of Chance. It wasn't until Rhianna stepped into the storeroom that she found any evidence that he'd been there at all.

Her foot brushed against a small, soft object on the floor, and she started to step past it. Then she paused, suddenly certain that she had found something. She knelt, fumbled in the gloom for a moment, then curled her fingers around what felt like a thick wool sock. She lifted it, squinting in the darkness broken only by light from the opened door and splinters of light shining through the planked walls. Her breath caught.

"Hobson. Look."

He came to peer at the object she held up. " 'Tis the hat his lordship wore last night," he breathed softly. "You were right. He was here."

Her hand closed around the knit hat in frustration. "But where is he now?"

A dark strip of cloth had been wound around his eyes, blindfolding him. Chance worked the ropes binding his wrists with subtle motions that he hoped were not noticed. The cart dipped into a rut with a jarring movement that tossed him against the side, sending pain radiating through his already cramped muscles. He damned Roxbury and his accomplices impartially and never paused in trying to work the ropes loose from his wrists.

Had they decided to dispose of him in a less public place? It was apparent to him that he would no longer be needed as hostage. Something untoward must have happened to catapult Roxbury into this sort of panic. He wished he knew what it was. He wished he had his hands free and a good sword balanced in his palm.

Bloody hell. He wished he knew where Rhianna was and if she was safe. He could only pray that Hobson would see to her safety. None of this would matter quite so much if he knew that she would be safe.

A faint, grim smile curled his lips. Always before, he'd felt a sort of pitying contempt for men besotted by a woman. Now, somehow, he'd joined their ranks without knowing quite how or when.

And he didn't mind.

He laughed softly and felt one of the men with Roxbury give him a sharp nudge.

"Quiet, ye bleedin' sod, or I'll whack yer head wi' my stick."

Oh, of course he would. And enjoy doing it, probably. It never ceased to amaze him how some men were excited by the prospect of inflicting pain on others. P'raps because he was so accustomed to inflicting pain on himself, he found it ludicrously unnecessary to practice it on others.

Cautiously, Chance lifted his head from the prickly nest of straw that filled the back of the cart. The wheels of the cart strained through mud with a squishy sound; they must be on a road not well traveled. He wished he could see. *Damn.* He had wishes enough to burn, it seemed, yet Roxbury was the man who held all the cards of fate in his grip.

Finally ending his excruciating wait for the inevitable, the cart jerked to a halt. Roxbury said something in a low tone that Chance didn't hear, then he was dragged from the back of the cart and stood on his feet. He heard a familiar voice respond to Roxbury and frowned as he tried to recognize it.

It hit him just before he was forced up the stairs, that the voice had sounded suspiciously like that of Fisher, his amiable valet. But it couldn't be. If it were, then that meant they were at Whiteash Manor.

He felt a rush of warm air and knew they were inside a house by the subtle change of footing beneath him. Their steps echoed loudly. It felt as if he walked on smooth marble, then over a threshold to step on a thick carpet. There was the smell of lemon oil and beeswax, mixing with the pungent aroma of wood smoke. Somewhere a door closed, and he heard the muted murmur of voices. A fire popped and crackled with a cheery sound; he heard the steady ticking of a clock.

Steeling himself when he felt someone brush against

him, Chance spread his legs for balance, expecting to be shoved. Instead, he was grabbed and pushed downward, coming to rest on the seat of a chair. With his hands still bound behind him, he was held there for a moment by a hand on his shoulder.

"Release him," came a soft, silky voice, making the hair on the back of Chance's neck prickle. "And take off the blindfold. How melodramatic you are, Roxbury."

The hand lifted from his shoulder and someone snatched away the cloth covering his eyes. Chance blinked, trying to focus his blurred vision on the figure in front of him. Then he felt as if he'd been kicked in the belly, as if time had suddenly swept backward and he was a frightened boy again, facing his tormentor with more bravado than courage. His throat worked, his lips moving to form a single word filled with utter loathing.

"You!"

Chapter 24

Oliver Trentham smiled at Chance, a slight lifting of the corners of his mouth that provoked memories long buried. "You don't appear glad to see me, my lord."

"Should I be?" Chance's shock faded slowly and was replaced with burning hatred. "I would have thought someone had murdered you in your bed long before now, Trentham."

"Ah no, not at all." The smile remained, cool and as cruel as a cat's that toyed with its prey.

He remembered that smile, recalled it directed at him with smug satisfaction on the rainy, cold day of his parents' burial.

"Would you care for tea, Lord Wolverton?"

"You seem to be misguided. This is my home, not yours, and I don't recall inviting you here."

Trentham gestured, and Chance felt the hatred rise in his throat, almost choking him. Trentham had been part of his torment so long ago, the guiding force behind his uncle's brief reign as guardian. Only the merciful intervention of his father's former barrister and childhood friend had prevented Trentham from wresting what was left of Chance's fortune away from him after Perry's death. The legal struggle had been long and vicious before it had ended with the court's decision to appoint another trustee.

"Must you waste time in reliving old memories?" Roxbury demanded testily. "There is much to do yet."

He paced the floor in front of the fireplace. Firedogs gleamed with a dull brassy sheen. Trentham shrugged casually.

"Do not alarm yourself, Nelson. We have time. Who would look for his lordship here?" He paused, eyes resting on Chance thoughtfully for a moment before he looked back at Roxbury. "Were the servants sent away as I told you?"

"Yes. Fisher took care of that, after receiving the note from Hobson."

"And the men who ride to join the gypsies? They are aware of nothing?"

Roxbury shook his head. "Nothing. They think they ride to rescue their precious lordship here."

"Very good. You are an excellent student, Nelson."

"Then cease all this vacillation and get on with it. I am in danger as long as Wolverton lives."

"Yes, yes, I am aware of that. But do not begrudge an old man his pleasures. I have waited a long time to bring the earl down. I promised him vengeance years ago, and I do not intend to rush my enjoyment of his destruction now."

"Do you truly think my destruction will benefit you, Trentham?" Chance snarled.

"Immensely. Not only will I derive great satisfaction but I will reap financial rewards as well." Trentham laughed softly. "I have been promised Whiteash once you are dead."

Chance began to understand. He looked from Trentham to Roxbury and back. "You brought the viscount to England," he said and saw the barrister's smiling agreement.

"Of course. My first thought was to place him near you

until you inevitably dueled—Roxbury is a master swords-man, you know—but then circumstances dictated a much more satisfying and less risky plan. The convenient arrival of your little gypsy slut—and yes, I had you fol-lowed years ago when you first met her—gave me an-other idea. It pleased me at the time to remove her from your vicinity, hence the gypsy leader's decision to inform her father of her whereabouts, but I've kept up with her. Details are the building blocks of any successful plan, you know."

"So I'm told."

"And you should have paid closer attention. Your ef-fort to intercept documents from Roxbury was laughable. Did you truly think to just demand he hand them over?"

Chance didn't reply, and after a moment, Trentham shrugged. "No matter, Wolverton. I know, of course, that you have been quite successful in intercepting much in-formation in the past. Your disguise as the Moon Rider was extremely baffling at first. When I realized that the annoying highwayman was actually you, I began to make my plans for your demise. But you eluded me every time. One does not just boldly eliminate an earl, no matter how irritating he may be, I'm afraid. It's just not done. I pondered the problem for some time before ar-riving at an obvious conclusion. Then you complicated matters. Suddenly, there were two of you. Until quite recently, I was not able to discern the identity of your companion." He made a steeple of his fingers and rested his clean-shaven chin on the tips. "It was very unwise of you to allow her to assist you."

Trentham shifted position in his chair, carefully ar-ranging a blanket around his legs to keep out the chill. Chance recognized the blanket as one of his mother's.

"I had to stop you," the barrister was saying. Chance stared at Trentham's face, trying to concentrate on anything but the incessant thoughts of murder that circled in his brain. He gazed at the thin lips and slightly overlapping front teeth. A horse's teeth, long and yellow. They bared in a smile.

"Roxbury was brought here to manage that, you know. As was the charming gypsy girl. I had hoped that he might be able to worm his way into Miss Llewellyn's confidence, and through her, get to you. Imagine my surprise when I was informed of her duplicity."

Chance's jaw clenched. "How distressing for you."

"Quite. Just as distressing was the baronet's gambling losses to me via Roxbury. P'raps it would have been much simpler had they remained abroad and perhaps even have spared her life. Now, of course, she must die as well. She could bring up embarrassing facts that would not suit at all."

Rage pounded through him, and Chance looked away from Oliver Trentham's toothy smile. His throat was tight; he surreptitiously worked at the ropes binding his wrists behind him.

"You won't be able to get away with this," Chance said when it seemed as if Trentham expected some sort of reply or outburst. "There are too many men who know enough to stop you."

"Really? Who, may I ask? Excepting the names on the list that, unfortunately, was given into the wrong hands last night"—his glance darted to Roxbury, who made an incoherent sound in his throat—"no one suspects me at all. I'm simply a London barrister, living a quiet life and harming no one."

Sudden hope flared. Chance paused in working at the ropes binding him, jerking his glance back to Trentham. "The list was intercepted?"

"You must know it was." Roxbury swore softly in French and English, his hands curling into fists. He banged his hands on the mantel, making crystal candlesticks dance precariously. "It was your man who was responsible for it."

"Hobson." Chance smiled with satisfaction.

Trentham's lip curled. "Aye, Hobson. He's been allowed to live much too long, but that condition will end shortly."

Chance managed a careless shrug. He flexed his wrists again and felt the ropes loosen a bit more. "I think not."

"Then you're wrong. Unless I'm very much mistaken, my men are even now surrounding your servant and the gypsy slut. How unfortunate that you will not be alive to see them die as well, but one must make certain concessions to duty, I suppose."

A final twist, and the ropes around his wrists were loose enough to free him. Chance remained stiff, arms behind him as if still bound, eyes riveted on Roxbury. His chair creaked, sounding loud in the sudden silence.

Trentham laughed softly. "I do not tolerate failure well, you know, Lord Wolverton. Do not think that you will be able to help them." He glanced at Roxbury. "Isn't that right, Lord Roxbury?"

Roxbury's eyes gleamed with soft excitement in the light of fire and lamps. "Quite right. No failure is ever tolerated."

Chance was looking at Roxbury, waiting for the move of sword or pistol, nerves and muscles taut and ready. He only hoped that he could react in time, could at least stay alive long enough to save Rhianna. He tensed, watching. Yet when the loud report of a pistol sounded, Roxbury still had not reached for his weapon.

Throwing himself from the chair to the floor, Chance rolled instinctively. He glanced toward Roxbury, expecting to see him taking aim, but instead, the viscount wore a curious expression on his face. He looked startled, and vaguely puzzled. His fingers moved slowly to pluck at the front of his vest, and then Chance saw the faint wisps of smoke rising from a charred hole in Roxbury's chest.

"Mon Dieu," the viscount muttered thickly, his eyes still faintly perplexed. He looked up, his gaze focusing on Chance for an instant before turning to Trentham.

Oliver Trentham still sat in his chair, a smoking pistol in a hand just above the blanket's edge. "There, there, Nelson, I couldn't let anyone else harm you. You failed me, of course, and that means death, but I truly regret the necessity."

"You—shot me."

"Absolutely correct. You are as astute as always. Now have the good sense to die before I am forced to shoot you again."

A snarl of incredulous rage twisted Roxbury's face. He lunged toward Trentham; the pistol exploded again with a loud roar. Roxbury staggered, yet still did not fall. He reached the barrister and wrenched the empty weapon away from him, flinging it aside. Trentham cried out; Chance saw the quick flash of a sword being drawn, saw Trentham try to rise from his chair and run before Roxbury slashed at him with the blade.

Grunting, Trentham lurched forward, grabbing at a table as he went down. A lamp teetered dangerously on the table's edge. Roxbury slashed with the sword again.

Blood flew out in a spattering arc, and Chance knew the barrister had been mortally wounded. Light skittered along the sinister edge of the sword in deadly flashes as it was lifted yet again.

Chance rolled to his feet and stood up. Roxbury didn't seem to notice him; his attention was focused on the man writhing on the floor.

"Damn you," he snarled, breathing harshly through his nose and clenched teeth. Trentham gasped for air, a soft, gurgling sound. Roxbury prodded him with a foot. "You'd try to kill me when I've worked for you, risked my life for you, and this is—*damn* you!"

Trentham slid an agonized glance upward. "How—? I shot you . . . twice."

Roxbury slid a hand into his vest pocket. A string of pearls slipped out to tumble to the floor. He ignored them, then held up an object between his forefinger and thumb. It looked like a chunk of ruined metal.

"My snuff box. A gift from you to me. Do you recall that, perhaps, Trentham?"

Reaching upward, Trentham made a sound of distress that ended in a choked cough. Then his eyes rolled back and he collapsed in a heap of bloodied clothes and death. Roxbury stared down at him for a long moment as if mesmerized, then prodded him with his foot again. No response. Opening his fingers, he let the damaged snuff box clatter to the floor to land next to Trentham's body.

By the time he looked up Chance was on his feet, watching him warily. He had no weapon. Roxbury had one, possibly two. For a suspended moment in time, both men just stared at one another across Trentham's body.

Chance saw the instant Roxbury made his decision; he snatched up the overturned chair he'd sat in, holding it in front of him. Roxbury's first slash sliced cleanly through two wood legs before Chance could jerk away. Miraculously, he was unscratched. He glanced around for a weapon, anything that might be useful.

Slowly, backing across the room with the chair held in front of him, Chance saw the grim determination in Roxbury's eyes. The sword flashed again and again, slicing through the wood chair until it splintered into useless pieces. He had only a small length of polished rail in one hand, but held it in front of him as if it were a sword.

With a swift twist of his wrist, Roxbury severed the slender length of wood in two.

"Don't drag this out," the viscount said roughly. "You don't have a prayer."

Chance didn't reply. He bumped against a table, and heard the faint rattle of glass. A quick sideways glance showed him the oil lamp balanced on the edge. When Roxbury lunged with the sword again, Chance hooked the lamp in one hand and flung it with all his strength.

It smashed into Roxbury with a crash, spilling oil and flame. For a shocked instant, the viscount didn't react, then there was a *whoosh* of sound, and he erupted into a pillar of fire. He screamed and dropped his sword. Chance scooped it up, then snatched up a rug to beat out the flames enveloping Roxbury.

But the viscount fled across the room in frenzied flight, igniting small fires along the way. Screams echoed from the walls. Drawn draperies burst into flames when he flung himself at a window. Chance pursued him, yelling at him to be still, to let him help. Roxbury was past listening.

Then the entire room exploded into flame, crackling and roaring with an unearthly sound. It spread in tiny paths, licking greedily over wool carpets, hissing up table legs, devouring brocade. Chance put an arm up to hide his face from the intense heat. Smoke lay in hazy layers. He looked at Roxbury. The screaming had quieted, and the viscount seemed to just blend into the wall of flame that had once been draperies.

A loud, piercing shriek split the air, sounding almost human. Above Chance the wood beams burned brightly in the ceiling, the intense heat cracking the oak. He ran for the door. The brass latch scorched his hand and he swore, then tried it again.

Locked. He turned. The windows were a solid sheet of

orange and yellow flames. The door was his only chance. He put his shoulder against it with a thud, but it did not budge. It was a solid wood door, made of English oak, the sturdiest wood in the world.

Smoke burned his eyes and nose, filled his lungs. It occurred to him with a sort of irrational logic that this was the very room where Perry Montagu had died so long ago. Perhaps there was a certain macabre justice to his dying in the same room.

Rhianna and Hobson saw the smoke at the same time. It rose lazily above the treetops, smudging the horizon with black clouds.

Hobson gave a strangled sound. "Whiteash," he whispered hoarsely. The bandage around his head was stained with spots of blood, and his face was almost as pale as the cloth.

"Are you sure?" a voice inquired, and Rhianna turned to look at Nicolo. The gypsy met her glance with a lifted brow.

"I am only too familiar with the exact location of the manor," Hobson snapped, spurring his horse into a swift pace.

After a brief hesitation, Rhianna and Nicolo followed. She leaned toward the gypsy leader and asked, "Do you think Chance is there?"

He shrugged. "We've not found him elsewhere, and one of the men we captured did say that he was to be taken to meet someone at the manor."

She groaned. "Do you feel up to another fight?"

Nicolo grinned, teeth flashing whitely in his sweat-and-dirt-streaked face. "Always. It gave me much pleasure to cross swords with the men who would have hurt you." He flexed his arm to show the bulge of muscle beneath his shirt. "I have not changed since last seeing you, eh?"

"Only to grow more vain," she retorted, but felt a spurt of relief that Nicolo and the men he'd brought with him to her rescue would now help Chance.

Laughing, Nicolo said, "Bah, you just hate to admit that I am stronger than you. You have changed, however. You are good with a sword. Did your earl teach you that?"

She shook her head, glancing again at the sky darkening with smoke. "No."

For several moments they rode silently. The thunder of hooves on ground still wet from rain was rhythmic. There were eight of them left. The fight with Roxbury's men had been brutal and deadly. Two of the earl's men still lay dead near the mill, while Fenwick was gravely wounded. Marisa was tending him, and said he would live, with her care.

Her throat tightened. It had been terrifying, and for a time, she'd thought the struggle lost. They had come on them so quickly, catching them unaware as they emerged from the mill into daylight, and she could still recall the paralyzing instant of fear at the first shots.

If not for Nicolo's timely arrival with help, they might very well have all been killed. Later, she would thank him properly. Now, terror for Chance left her mind and body numb.

That terror was not lessened when they thundered down the curve of the driveway leading to the manor and saw the towering flames. Rhianna reined to a horrified halt. An entire wing was engulfed with fire, and men and women and even children formed a line to pass buckets from the well. It was a futile effort at best, she thought, and nudged her horse forward.

The animal resisted, eyes wild as the smoke drifted in

thick layers and tiny sparks filled the air like fireflies. A loud explosion sounded, and with a groan, charred bricks began to tumble from the walls to the ground. Glass shattered in a piercing shriek. People screamed and dropped their buckets, running for safety.

Rhianna looked for Hobson, but he was not in sight. Her horse danced frantically, and finally she dismounted and turned it loose. It fled with a frightened whinny, and she saw Nicolo glance at her in surprise. She shrugged.

"I have to find Hobson. He will know who to ask—"

"It's dangerous. Stay here. I will find him." Nicolo reined his horse around, disappearing into the crowd of people.

Smoke billowed up in thick black clouds, burning her eyes and nose. Rhianna glanced around. She had no intention of standing quietly by while others looked for Chance. She would find him.

Chaos surged around her in waves that seemed to grow and recede, as if ocean waves breaking upon the shore. People screamed and shouted orders, and the roar and heat of the fire was almost like a living entity. It blustered and threatened, rising above the stones of Whiteash Manor like a devouring beast.

Rhianna pushed through the crowd, searching, her eyes constantly watching for a tall, broad-shouldered figure among those fighting the fire. He was here. She felt it. She felt his presence as one feels the changing of seasons. He was that much a part of her, that close, that she could feel him with her even when he wasn't.

No one had seen the earl, some answering impatiently when she stopped them to ask, others looking at her as if she were suspicious. The wind seemed to be rising, carrying smoke and tiny specks of ashes on the currents. She coughed and blinked, then bent to dip the edge of her cloak in an abandoned bucket of water. She pressed it over her nose and mouth. Despair began to thicken her throat.

It was a scene from a nightmare, the red flames searing the sky, smoke blackening the air and people shouting and screaming in an incomprehensible beat of noise. She'd never thought of fire being loud before, but there was a pulsing roar of flame that was deafening. Intense heat wafted out in waves.

As the flames consumed everything flammable, the fire began to subside. People moved forward again, and buckets were taken up. Rhianna stared up at the once-gracious house. Chance's home, the inheritance he'd suffered so much to keep would never be the same. It was slowly dying before her eyes, and in a way, she was glad he was not here to see it. It was almost too painful to watch.

She moved to help, passing heavy buckets from person to person in a ceaseless motion until her arms ached.

Nicolo found her in the middle of a line, and came to her on foot, his brow lowered. "Hobson is resting at the gatehouse, overcome by smoke. He'll be all right."

She brushed the hair from her eyes with the back of one hand, and felt the damp smear of soot streak her face. "Have you heard word of the earl?"

He hesitated and glanced away. Rhianna's throat grew tight with suspense. "Have you?" she repeated sharply. He shook his head without looking at her.

It was the man beside her who answered wearily. "Aye. 'Tis said that his lordship was trapped inside and perished in the flames."

Said bluntly, the words seemed to hang in the air without meaning. Nicolo gave a harsh curse. Rhianna stared at him numbly. Then she turned slowly to stare at the smoldering stones and blackened timbers sticking up skeletal fingers. Whiteash Manor was in ruins. Only one wing remained, a miracle of stone detached from the main house and charred by smoke. The setting sun was a hazy red beyond the moors and trees.

"No," she said in a whisper. "That's not true. I'd know if he was dead, and I don't feel it. Do you hear me?"

Nicolo put a hand on her shoulder, but she shrugged it away, angry suddenly. He looked at her. She shook her head again, backing away a step.

Again, the man beside her spoke up. "Someone saw a body in one of the rooms, but it has been too hot yet to look for it. Besides, I think it would be nothing but ashes by now."

"Shut up!" Nicolo growled so fiercely that the man gave a frightened squeak and fled. The gypsy turned to Rhianna.

She met his gaze, and saw sorrow and pity in his eyes. Her heart sank. He thought Chance dead. She began to shake her head from side to side.

"No. No, it's not true." The bucket dropped from her suddenly numb fingers, splashing water over her legs and feet. Then she pushed through the people pressing close and fled blindly. Someone called out to her but she ignored them. She ran without thinking, without seeing. Close-cropped lawns and ash-covered hedges gave way to trees, and when she finally stopped to catch her breath, Rhianna numbly realized that she must have gone farther than she thought.

She sank to her knees on a mossy knoll. Damp leaves cushioned her hands as she leaned forward; the leaves shifted with a faint whisper beneath her palms. The noise from the manor was muffled and far away. Smoke still permeated the air, but it was much fainter here, only a light haze that didn't sting her nose or eyes.

Yet the tears came anyway, flooding her face and wetting the ground. Huge, painful sobs racked her, tearing at her chest, throat, and heart. Her ribs ached with the effort of holding them back; shadowed trees seemed to absorb her grief in dark silence.

When she stopped at last, aching, she bent her head back and stared up at the patches of sky she could see through the leaves overhead. A bird called gently, and there was an answer. She shuddered.

He couldn't be dead. There was a terrible mistake. She knew it. If he was dead, she would have sensed it, just like she'd known when he was in danger. Her hands clenched into fists. She had to try and concentrate, nurture the gift of sight as Marisa had told her to do.

Closing her eyes, she drew in a deep breath of air that held only a trace of smoke, and focused on Chance. She visualized his face, the smudge of his thick eyelashes over eyes as hot and dark as pitch, and the sulky curve of his mouth when he was angry with her. She blocked out all sound around her, all feeling, and focused on all the images of him she could dredge up. She remembered the first time she'd seen him and how sullen he'd looked, like a fallen angel. She'd thought him beautiful even then, and when she'd met him again at Keswick's ball, she'd had to fight her instant attraction to him.

Chance, with his erotically shaped mouth and devilish eyes, and his husky voice that could make her heart beat faster even when he was saying things she didn't want to hear. He was still alive. She knew he was.

She opened her eyes and blinked. Fading sunlight edged a tall shadow standing beneath the trees, outlining it with gold light. It seemed ethereal, other-worldly, a shimmering image that lacked substance. Heart hammering in her chest, she had the thought that she was seeing a ghost. Did she conjure him up with desperation, perhaps?

Slowly, she rose to her feet, her voice a husky whisper. "Chance."

The shadow moved, and the illusion shattered. The voice that answered was husky and hoarse, unfamiliar.

"Rhianna."

"Chance. You're not—"

"Dead?" His lips twisted. Again that painful rasp, as if it hurt to talk. "No. No thanks to Roxbury, the poor fool. He had us locked in my study when the fire started."

A feeling of unreality swept over her. She stared as he stood there looking at her, seeming unwilling to approach. A light breeze ruffled his hair, bringing the smell of smoke with it. She looked past him for a moment, in the direction of the still burning manor.

"Rhianna?"

She turned to look at him. He was holding something out to her, and she saw a flash of white beneath the soot.

"I brought you . . . these. They belong . . . to you."

"My pearls," she murmured. "You brought my pearls. . . ."

"Yes." His arm fell to his side, the pearls slipping from his fingers to fall to the grass.

Rhianna asked softly, "How did you escape, Chance?"

His shoulders lifted in a faint shrug. "Went through a burning window." He held up his hands, and she saw the seared skin on his palms. "It was my only choice."

"Roxbury—?"

"Dead. Along with Trentham."

She shook her head in growing confusion. "I don't know who Trentham is."

"I'll tell you about it later, love." He took a step closer, and she saw how he stumbled. "Do you suppose we could discuss this another time? I've had the devil of a time finding you in all this chaos. I'd like to just hold you." He swayed, weariness etched into his face. "God, I just want to hold you. . . ."

Rhianna couldn't move, could only stare numbly as he sank to his knees on the ground in a slow collapse. He bent his head and put his burned palms on his thighs. His shoulders trembled, and when he lifted his face, she saw the pale tracks of tears on his cheeks. They made silvery marks on his sooty face, like banners of grief held back too long.

Rhianna's throat tightened. She recognized his grief, and thought of the youth who hadn't been able to weep for his dead parents. That had been so long ago, and now here was the man, emotions raw, waiting for her to come to him.

Something broke loose inside, that tautly held sense of disbelief, and she was running to him, feet seeming to skim over the ground without touching it, throwing herself into his arms despite the soot covering him, kissing his face over and over, tears wetting them both.

He held her so tightly that she could barely breathe, and she heard his voice, rusty and thick from the smoke, say, "I love you. God, I thought I'd lost you but here you are. . . ."

His voice broke, and she felt a long shudder go through him. She buried her face in the smoky ruin of his sweater. *He loves me.* She wanted to laugh, to shout her joy to the treetops, but when she opened her lips, only a faint sigh slid between them.

He curled a finger beneath her chin and tilted her face up, brushing away the residue of tears from her cheek with his thumb. "I don't intend to let you from my sight again," he said in the same rough whisper. He bent to touch her lips lightly with his, then lifted his head. "It's too dangerous to let you run loose. Will you marry me so that I can save myself a lot of time and trouble?"

She put her hand on his chest and found her voice. "No other reason?"

His arms tightened, and his heart beat with a strong, steady rhythm beneath her palm.

"Just that I love you. That I'll always love you. And if you say no, I'll wander the moors forever, alone and lost and—"

She stopped his words with her mouth, bringing his head down for a kiss with her hand behind his neck, holding him. A flash of insight suddenly sped through her mind, and she had a vision of herself and Chance together through the years. It was quickly gone, but she'd seen enough to make her smile.

Epilogue

1802

Fenster Goodbody sat outside the tiny stone chapel. A gentle sun shone down on spring flowers, and there was the sense of the earth reawakening from a long winter's sleep. A soft wind blew bright promises over the moors.

"Fenster?"

He half-turned. "Yes, Lavinia. I'm on the front steps."

His wife appeared in the doorway, hair bound up in a neat kerchief and a feather duster in her hand. "The chapel is ready for the christening."

Fenster nodded, pleased. "Another Lancaster. I recall christening Lord Chance so many years ago. . . ."

"Yes, and a perfect hellion he was, too."

The vicar frowned slightly. "He had reason, I believe."

Lavinia Goodbody sat down in a flurry of skirts, her brow furrowed in thought. "I suppose that's true enough. And his life has been cursed until now."

"But now things seem to be going so well for him. His wife adores him, it's plain, and they have a beautiful son." He smiled serenely. "I'm honored to be asked to christen the child."

"But the godparents they chose!" Lavinia snorted. "I mean, Hobson, a servant! And to have a gypsy woman as godmother—well, such things are simply not done."

"But she is the child's great-aunt. And she seems quite

nice, though she wears so many bracelets, I often feel as if I'm constantly hearing bells."

Mouth pursed with disapproval, his wife shook her head slowly. "If you ask me, she and Sir Griffyn are much too friendly since he has recovered. I wouldn't be surprised if—well, I won't say it."

"Please don't. It's unseemly to gossip about those we don't know that well."

Lavinia sighed. "Did you hear that the new manor house is said to be even more magnificent than the old one?"

The vicar slid her a sly glance and said softly, "Did I tell you that we are invited to the house after the christening, Lavinia?"

Her eyes opened wide, mouth dropping open a little. "Is that so? I was never invited to the old manor, you know—oh, my, what shall I wear?"

He patted her hand comfortingly. "You'll find the right gown, I'm certain. It's to be a grand affair. I understand that marble was brought over from Italy for the floors, and new books have been ordered for the library. . . ."

"Jewelry. I shall wear my mother's diamond brooch. It's nice, I think," Lavinia mused aloud, "and I have the diamond earrings to go with it. Yes. That's what I'll wear." She slid her husband a worried glance. "Do you think I should hide them in my petticoat until we arrive at the manor?"

"Whatever for?" he asked in astonishment.

Her eyes widened. "Why, to keep the Moon Rider from stealing my jewelry, of course. They did set this christening for the morning before a full moon, for some reason that probably has to do with gypsy curses or something, and you know that the Moon Rider lurks—"

"Lavinia. There has been no sign of the Moon Rider for almost three years. Why must everyone in Wiltshire continue to insist that he still rides? It is my belief that he has retired to some foreign country—perhaps France now that we have signed a truce with them. Not that I trust Napoleon to keep it, but we shall see. Whatever, the myth of a man being able to disappear into the mist and light should be disregarded as completely false."

She shook her head stubbornly. "No. The Moon Rider is still out there. People swear they've seen him, and his mate as well. Though there are no more moonlight raids they still ride, then fade into the moonlight. Even the new sheriff is said to have seen them. I'm taking no chances with my mother's brooch. I intend to hide it in a secret pocket beneath my petticoat."

Sighing, Goodbody said, "I don't think he ever really existed as people say. I think that the Moon Rider was a fable invented by frightened victims of common robbers."

Lavinia looked up with a faint frown. "Do you now?" She looked toward the gently sloping moors and the road that twisted over them. A faint smile lifted her lips. "No, they ride, Fenster. They ride still. . . ."

Virginia Brown
Writing as Virginia Lynn

Since 1983, when she first began her writing career, *Virginia Brown* has written over thirty romance novels.

Three of her titles have either won or been nominated for the *Romantic Times* Reviewer's Choice awards and she has been honored once again with a nomination for a Career Achievement Award for Love and Laughter. Her last four books were on national bestseller lists.

A native Tennessean, Ms. Brown enjoyed a childhood traveling with her parents as a "military brat," and still likes to see new places and research her novels. Her lifelong dream is to have a retreat in Texas where her dogs, cats, and children can roam happily, and she can find enough wide open spaces to fuel her imagination.

Don't miss these fabulous
Bantam women's fiction titles

On Sale in June

MIDNIGHT WARRIOR
by Iris Johansen
New York Times bestselling author of *The Beloved Scoundrel*
A passionate new tale of danger, adventure, and romance
that sweeps from a Saxon stronghold to a lovers' bower in
the cool, jade green forests of Wales.
❑ *29946-8 $5.99/6.99 in Canada*

BLUE MOON
by Luanne Rice
The moving novel of a family that discovers the everyday
magic of life and the extraordinary power of love.
"Eloquent...A moving and complete tale of the complicated
phenomenon we call family."—*People*
❑ *56818-3 $5.99/6.99 in Canada*

VELVET
by Jane Feather, bestsellin g, award-winning author of *Virtue*
"An author to treasure.."—*Romantic Times*
❑ *56469-2 $5.50/6.99 in Canada*

WITCH DANCE
by Peggy Webb
Dr. Kate Malone brings modern medicine to the Chickasaw
people and finds danger as well as a magnificent Indian chieftain.
❑ *56057-3 $4.99/5.99 in Canada*

Ask for these books at your local bookstore
or use this page to order.

❑ Please send me the books I have checked above. I am enclosing $ _____ (add $2.50
to cover postage and handling). Send check or money order, no cash or C. O. D.'s please.

Name_____

Address_____

City/ State/ Zip _____

Send order to: Bantam Books, Dept. FN141, 2451 S. Wolf Rd., Des Plaines, IL 60018
Allow four to six weeks for delivery.
Prices and availability subject to change without notice.   FN141 6/94

The Very Best in Historical Women's Fiction

Rosanne Bittner

_____ 28599-8 EMBERS OF THE HEART .. $5.99/$6.99 in Canada
_____ 28319-7 MONTANA WOMAN $4.99/5.99
_____ 29033-9 IN THE SHADOW OF THE MOUNTAINS $5.50/6.99
_____ 29014-2 SONG OF THE WOLF $4.99/5.99
_____ 29015-0 THUNDER ON THE PLAINS $5.99/6.99
_____ 29807-0 OUTLAW HEARTS $5.99/6.99

Iris Johansen

_____ 28855-5 THE WIND DANCER $4.95/5.95
_____ 29032-0 STORM WINDS $4.99/5.99
_____ 29244-7 REAP THE WIND $4.99/5.99
_____ 29604-3 THE GOLDEN BARBARIAN $4.99/5.99
_____ 29944-1 THE MAGNIFICENT ROGUE $5.99/6.99
_____ 29968-9 THE TIGER PRINCE $5.50/6.50
_____ 29871-0 LAST BRIDGE HOME $4.50/5.50

Susan Johnson

_____ 29125-4 FORBIDDEN $4.99/5.99
_____ 29312-5 SINFUL $4.99/5.99
_____ 29957-3 BLAZE $5.50/6.50
_____ 29959-X SILVER FLAME $5.50/6.50
_____ 29955-7 OUTLAW $5.50/6.50

Teresa Medeiros

_____ 29407-5 HEATHER AND VELVET $4.99/5.99
_____ 29409-1 ONCE AN ANGEL $5.50/6.50
_____ 29408-3 A WHISPER OF ROSES $5.50/6.50

Patricia Potter

_____ 29070-3 LIGHTNING $4.99/5.99
_____ 29071-1 LAWLESS $4.99/5.99
_____ 29069-X RAINBOW $5.50/6.50
_____ 56199-5 RENEGADE $5.50/6.50
_____ 56225-8 NOTORIOUS $5.50/6.50

Deborah Smith

_____ 28759-1 THE BELOVED WOMAN $4.50/5.50
_____ 29092-4 FOLLOW THE SUN $4.99/5.99
_____ 29107-6 MIRACLE $4.50/5.50
_____ 29690-6 BLUE WILLOW $5.50/6.50

Ask for these titles at your bookstore or use this page to order.

Please send me the books I have checked above. I am enclosing $ _____ (add $2.50 to cover postage and handling). Send check or money order, no cash or C. O. D.'s please.

Mr./ Ms. _____

Address _____

City/ State/ Zip _____

Send order to: Bantam Books, Dept. FN 17, 2451 S. Wolf Road, Des Plaines, IL 60018
Please allow four to six weeks for delivery.
Prices and availability subject to change without notice.